Danica Winters  selling author who their ability to di occasionally a touc she can be found i patience while she tries to hone her skills at various crafts—quilting, pottery and painting are not her areas of expertise. She believes the cup is neither half-full nor half-empty, but it better be filled with wine. Visit her website at danicawinters.net

Ever since **Lisa Childs** read her first romance novel (a Mills & Boon story, of course) at age eleven, all she wanted was to be a romance writer. With over seventy novels published with Mills & Boon, Lisa is living her dream. She is an award-winning, bestselling romance author. She loves to hear from readers, who can contact her on Facebook or through her website, lisachilds.com

Also by Danica Winters

Hidden Truth
In His Sights
Her Assassin For Hire
Protective Operation
Ms Calculation
Mr Serious
Mr Taken
Ms Demeanour
Smoke and Ashes
Dust Up with the Detective

Also by Lisa Childs

His Christmas Assignment
Bodyguard Daddy
Bodyguard's Baby Surprise
Beauty and the Bodyguard
Nanny Bodyguard
Single Mum's Bodyguard
In the Bodyguard's Arms
Colton Christmas Conspiracy
Colton 911: Baby's Bodyguard
Colton's Cinderella Bride

Discover more at millsandboon.co.uk

A LOADED QUESTION

DANICA WINTERS

COLTON 911: UNLIKELY ALIBI

LISA CHILDS

MILLS & BOON

First Published in Great Britain 2021
by Mills & Boon, an imprint of HarperCollins*Publishers*
1 London Bridge Street, London, SE1 9GF

A Loaded Question © 2021 Danica Winters
Colton 911: Unlikely Alibi © 2021 Harlequin Books S.A.

Special thanks and acknowledgement are given to Lisa Childs for her contribution to the *Colton 911: Chicago* series.

ISBN: 978-0-263-28322-8

0121

MIX
Paper from
responsible sources

FSC
www.fsc.org
FSC® C007454

This book is produced from independently certified FSC™ paper to ensure responsible forest management.

For more information visit: www.harpercollins.co.uk/green

Printed and bound in Spain
by CPI, Barcelona

A LOADED QUESTION

DANICA WINTERS

This book is dedicated to all those folks who spend far too many holidays behind a computer, rifle, or going dark. Thanks for making this world a safer place. You are the true heroes.

Thank you to all those who have helped make this book and this series come to life. This has been a fun series to create and see grow and change over time. I hope that these characters and their stories are just as real to you as they are to me.

A special shout-out to my editors and my agent, Jill Marsal. Your constant and unwavering faith in me is humbling and greatly appreciated.

Also, thank you to Jennifer (who keeps me fed with homemade cookies), Kristin, Clare, Melanie, Herb, Penny, Joe, Mike and Troy. These folks are my behind-the-scenes helpers who help me research, write, edit and even beta read these books at (sometimes) very short notice. To say it takes a village is an understatement!

Prologue

Nothing is ever easy... The biggest understatement of the millennia. There was nothing worse than being imperfectly human.

Troy Spade's mission was supposed to be relatively simple, just a protective security detail to take their medium-risk VIP to the border checkpoint, hand their strap hanger off to the next team, and then they were to head back to the tactical operations center. Intense, but normal. If they didn't screw things up, they would be done within a couple of hours, debriefed and back to playing *Halo* on the Xbox.

Tiff glanced over at him, sending him a smile as she drove. He both loved and hated her for the sexy look. This wasn't the time or the place to bring up all the things they meant to one another. And yet, with that sex-laced smile, all he could think about was running his fingers down her soft, perfect skin as they lay in her bed. This morning, when they had woken up, she had given him a similar smile, except thoroughly sated, well loved and blissful. He was hers and she was his. In that single action, she and their love were everything he needed.

She was his happy place, and he could think of

nothing better than spending his days in the constant conflicts that came with war-torn nations and private contracting, and his nights in the peace of her embrace. He had it all.

He took in a breath. Underneath the scent of sand, sweat and gun oil he could still make out the scent of her on him. He loved the way she naturally smelled of woman, and when she wore perfume, it only intensified his need to hold her in his arms once again.

Dammit, Troy. Come back to reality, he thought, checking himself. *This. This right here is why being with her isn't a good idea.*

He couldn't have love. Love was a weakness. Love would compromise their objectivity. Love could lead to only one thing—failure. And failure wasn't an option. In their line of work, failure was death.

A stray piece of hair had slipped out from under her helmet and was threatening to fall into her eyes as she drove. He was tempted to reach over and fix it for her, but that was the last damn thing he could do. He peered into the back seat where their gunners were seated, watching out the windows and looking for any possible threats.

If they even guessed that there was something between him and Tiff, Troy's butt would be on the line, and one, if not both him and Tiff, would be on the next plane back to the States. Then the honeymoon would really be over and he would have to go back to some dead-end job where he struggled to make ends meet.

Not an option.

As the detail team leader, they followed behind the VIP, driving offset as they cruised to the objective. He glanced down at his watch. Ten more minutes, if the roads remained clear, and they would be at the Albanian border. Ten more and they would be headed back. Within the hour they would be safe... *She* would be safe. And maybe, for at least a few hours, he could finally relax. Well, at least relax as much as any person could who was hunkered down in enemy territory, where they stuck out and were about as welcome as a saddle sore.

Oh, the things he would do for money.

The car in front of them wove to the right as they moved to the left in their trademark zigzag pattern. Ahead of them, on the opposite side of the road, a small white car pulled over and stopped. The gunner behind and to his left steadied a bead on the sedan's driver though the car had gotten out of the convoy's path. If random vehicles didn't get out of the way, their convoy would have no qualms in chewing them up and spitting them out.

Just as they were about to pass by the white car, the driver flipped a U-turn, and tires squealing on the hot blacktop, the car charged in the other direction.

Troy turned to Tiffany and opened his mouth, about to issue a warning about the odd behavior, when the up-armored vehicle they were riding in quaked. In slow motion, the black hood of their Suburban launched upward as the violent boom rattled him to his core.

He'd never heard a sound quite like it, the tearing of metal, his friends' screams swirled with his own, and it all mixed with the thrashing of his heart. It meant only one thing...

We're hit.

The world twisted around him as he tried to get his bearings. Their SUV careened through the air, flipping hood over bumper as they took the full impact of the explosively formed penetrator... It had to be an EFP—it was the only thing that could have blown them up like this. Or it could have been an IED. But that wouldn't have hit this hard or done this much damage. Maybe it was an RPG, but again, it wouldn't have screwed them up like this. Definitely an EFP.

The irony didn't escape him that even though they had yet to land, he was arguing with himself about what they had just experienced. Dissociation at its best. Maybe dying wouldn't be so bad after all—at least he wasn't swirling that cognitive drain. An odd sense of peace drifted through him.

Tiffany's cry pulled him back to reality...to the terror that filled him, the smell of burning rubber and the acrid smoke that filled the air, and to the pain radiating up from his legs. He started to move to see if he even had legs; as he did, he spotted the blood. The crimson liquid was spattered across the inside of the snowflake-patterned broken glass of the front windshield.

It was supposed to be bulletproof.

Definitely an EFP.

A droplet of blood slipped over the glass, toward the ground flashing by them.

There was a strangled cry, the sound a soft mew, like that of the breathless.

Tiff.

He looked over. She stared at him with a wide-eyed, terrified look upon her face. Her mouth was open, the strangled sound still twisting from her lips. The steering wheel she had been holding was gone, as was everything below her shoulder. At the center of her chest, impaled in her core, was a long jagged piece of metal that looked like it had once belonged to the engine block.

Following his gaze, she looked down at the shrapnel in her chest and then back up at him. Her wail stopped as the last bits of breath rattled from her body.

The car slammed down, hitting the asphalt with the screech and shudder of metal meeting stone. There was a shatter of glass as it broke away and exploded through the air and hit his face. It felt like the cold, icy graupel that came on a cold winter day, except each impact was followed by the hot ooze of rising blood.

Tiff's gaze met his and she smiled through her pain. The light in her eyes, the spark that drew him like a moth, dimmed, and he watched as her life slipped away.

This was it. He was in hell. Everything he had ever done had caught up to him. Here. Now.

It had to be hell… Only in hell would he be forced to watch the woman he loved die…and not be able to do a damn thing to save her.

Chapter One

Everyone was fighting a battle—whether it be in the Siberian tundra, the Afghanistan deserts or in the territory of the heart. And just like all battles, there could be only one victor…and, regardless of conqueror or conquered, all lost something.

Kate Scot had won many battles, and yet had gone on to lose what she held dear more times than she cared to admit. Most recently, that loss came in the form of her apartment and dog—now both in the hands of her ex-boyfriend. She would really miss that dog; she'd had Max since he was just eight weeks old.

But she didn't hate her ex for kicking her to the curb. Far from it. Given her line of work, it was only a matter of time before he figured out that he was too good for her and it was time to move on to someone else—someone who could dote on and fall over him in ways she never could. Not to mention her inability to completely open up with him.

He had deserved better. And she definitely needed to be alone for a while, and out of the game that was dating.

Dating was for people who had a vacant space in their heart, a space that could be unlocked and given freely—again, something she'd never been capable of doing, or perhaps even willing to do.

She held no doubts that it was the warrior mentality and her training that kept her feelings from ever entering the equation. As a woman in her field, she was constantly falling under the scrutiny of those around her—they pressed her for weakness, both consciously and subconsciously, regularly checking her boundaries and her capabilities. For that reason, above all, she had to be the best of the best within her team.

And it was this thirst for recognition and push to prove herself that had resulted in her receiving the email that now nearly pulsed with its red "immediate attention required" subject line. The sender, Aaron Peahen, was from the Billings office, and though they were from the same state, there was little love between them. Peahen had a penchant for bringing out the worst in her, and from the times they had worked on joint assignments—the last of which had ended with them throwing insults under their breath at one another—she didn't bring the best out in him, either.

He appeared to be so old-school that he operated as if having women in the agency was some kind of nuisance the male agents had to grin and bear in order to make the public happy. He would never, no matter how well respected she was, accept that she was just as valuable a team member as he.

No doubt, he had sent her this case to set her up for failure, or send her on some wild-goose chase.

Just like warm milk, regardless of what Peahen sent her, she doubted it got better with age.

She clicked on the offending flag. As she read the email, she could hear Peahen's deep, rasping smoker's voice like he was standing over her shoulder instead of six hours away across the state.

Agent Scot,
It has come to my attention that you have materials associated with a case I'm currently working. Do you have time for a phone call? Better yet, I would appreciate you just sending me everything pertinent to case #HJ1085-090.

Your prompt response would be appreciated, but I know this can be a problem for you. Regardless, I need this within seventy-two hours, or I will be forced to contact your superiors regarding the matter.
Agent Peahen

Agent Peacock was more like it. He was all show and no teeth.

And there she had thought, for nearly a moment, that she didn't absolutely despise her fellow agent. Wrong. What a jerk. He couldn't treat everyone else this way or he would have been out on his butt and pounding the pavement long ago... Nope, this kind of derision seemed to be aimed straight at her center mass.

Well, he could fire away.

She clicked on her files, opening up the requested information. It was last time-stamped nearly five years ago, and as she scrolled through her file, she could barely recall the information about a bank robbery she had investigated when she had been new to the area.

The investigation hadn't gone anywhere, and within a month of her initial investigation, it was allowed to go to the recesses of her computer files to catch dust.

Until now, and Agent Peacock wanted to take the case under his wing.

Rage bubbled up from her core. No doubt Agent Peacock had some kind of plan to grandstand and show what a great agent he was by playing off some failed case of hers.

She let an audible grumble slip past her lips.

"You okay over there, K?" Agent Hunt asked, looking up from his computer for a brief moment. He was paying only half attention, but she appreciated that he had even seemed to notice that something was amiss.

Before she could even answer, Hunt had turned back to his work on the screen.

That, that right there was one of her favorite things about their team. They all cared about each other, but not enough to pry or ask too many stupid questions. More, they never found the need to do any more talking than absolutely necessary to get the job done. With it came little miscommunication, hurt feelings or stepping on each other's toes.

She pressed back from the desk, her chair rolling over the hard plastic on the floor, making a crushing sound.

"Eating sunflower seeds again?" Agent Hunt asked. "That is a disgusting habit, you know."

Of course, he would be keyed in on her one little quirk. She should have been more careful to keep her mess from hitting the floor.

"We all have something we do to pacify ourselves. Don't get me started about your gum popping." She smiled at him, hoping he would realize she wasn't about to say anything about his tics.

Hunt chuckled as she stood up, grabbed her suit jacket and slipped it over her arms. "Where you going?"

"Out."

In all honesty, she didn't know. The only thing she knew was that she could not continue to sit there and stare at Peahen's email for another second. Sure, she could've just sent him the information he wanted and gotten him out of her hair, but she'd never been the type to give in that easily. If he wanted to be a jerk, two could play that game.

She pulled up the file on her phone, and waiting for it to load, she looked over at Agent Hunt. "You want to go for a ride? Are you working on something?"

Agent Hunt shrugged. "As luck would have it, I'm currently beating level 2421 on *Candy Crush*, so…"

"Then grab your jacket. I may end up needing someone to keep me from throttling Peahen." She chuckled.

"Do I even want to know?" Agent Hunt asked.

She shook her head. "Probably not, but at the very least we can both get out of the office for an hour and take a ride in America's finest fleet car." She laughed as she motioned toward the window where parked out in front of the building was a late-model Crown Victoria she was sure had likely once belonged to someone sent to a retirement home. In fact, she could have sworn that upon getting in the first time she had smelled baby powder, Bengay and menthol Halls.

"With a line like that, how could a boy say no?" He stood up and grabbed his jacket, holding it over his arm rather than putting it on. The simple action made her wonder if he didn't feel the same drive to constantly be on point, like she did.

Yet, if someone saw him and recognized him as an

agent, they would think nothing of his prowess or experience just because he wasn't wearing a jacket. However, if she simply went with her jacket unbuttoned, she would instantly be seen as less authoritative.

She sighed. She had to knock it off. Picking nits would do nothing to stop the infestation of sexism that ran rampant throughout law enforcement. She just needed to buck up, focus on the task at hand and show Agent Peacock who he was dealing with.

Making their way out of the nondescript brick federal building that sat within the heart of the city of Missoula, she stopped and pulled out a stick of gum. She had to kick the sunflower seed habit. That or she would have to step up her running time.

Regardless, as they got into the fleet car, she missed the salty crunch and snap of the sunflower seed shells when she bit down on the kernels. Calories or no, she loved them. Then again, it always seemed like the things she really cared about the most were things that also caused her the most harm.

As she looked in the rearview mirror and put the car in gear, she watched as a black van stopped at the light—directly behind them and blocking their departure.

She didn't like it, the feeling of being trapped in her parking space. It wasn't an emergency by any means, but this lack of foresight when setting this building up for agents like her—people who had places to be—it gnawed at her. If the people in the van wished harm upon her, it would have been easy to follow through. In fact, this was exactly how she would have set it up, by boxing her into her parking spot, then slipping out of the driver's side and silently moving to her window.

A quick double tap of the trigger and the driver and the van could pull away within seconds, likely unnoticed and unseen by the general public, and leaving her and Agent Hunt dead.

But maybe she was warped.

No, there was a major difference between paranoid and protective. This, this oversight, was a matter of safety, not her neurosis.

She would need to get a sit-down with the region's special agent in charge, or SAC, and have them look into the logistics.

Moving to grab her phone and send the agent a text, she heard a crunch of metal and the squeal of brakes from behind her. She jerked, looking up. The van behind her was sitting askew, the back end now resting on the hood of a red Miata. A kid was in the car's driver seat. The poor thing looked terrified as he unbuckled his seat belt and stepped out of his car.

Walking to the front of his car, he put his hands over his mouth and squatted down, then stood back up. He mouthed a series of expletives, and from the look on his face, he was likely already envisioning the tongue-lashing he would receive when he told his parents about the accident.

She didn't envy him, or those days.

"Did you see that? Holy crap," Agent Hunt said from beside her.

"I know." She glanced back in the side mirror, watching without being seen.

The side door of the van wheeled open with a characteristic sound of heavy metal grinding against metal. A man, maybe in his early thirties, with dark hair, brooding eyes and a cleft in his chin, stepped out of the van's side door. Just the sight of him made her gut clench. There was something about him, something that drew her in and yet spoke of danger.

She turned in her seat, hoping to get a better view.

As he stepped onto the street, he looked up at her and their eyes met. For a split second, she thought of looking away, but she checked herself. She wasn't a demure woman, no matter how handsome the man whose gaze met hers.

He gave her a stiff nod.

As he turned, he gave her one more appraising glance and rushed to shut the van's door. He moved with the practiced, smooth movements of someone like her—someone who spent their life in the shadows. As the door shut, she looked into the vehicle. Behind him, lining the walls, was a collection of surveillance systems.

Her breath caught in her throat as she instinctively reached for her sidearm.

Not for the first time, her gut was right—the man was nothing but danger.

Chapter Two

He was a broken man. With every day that slipped by, he found himself sinking further and further into his all-consuming sadness. He had to do something to pull out of this funk before he disappeared into himself and his work, forever.

For the last year, ever since Tiff's death, he had been living day to day only through the habitual motion that came with being a private contractor with STEALTH. In truth, they were his saving grace. Though he had worked for a variety of security companies, if it wasn't for the Martins, he wasn't sure he could have gotten on with another contracting group in the state he was in.

He wasn't doing great—even he could admit it. Thinking about it, he wasn't sure he had said more than a word or two in the last month aside from what he had to say for work. Strangely, the realization didn't bother him. He didn't mind being alone.

It was almost a comfort to know he was the silent harbinger of death. He was like a shadow—no, a ghost—who could come and go around the world, doing his job and never really being noticed. He was completely, inarguably free.

Maybe that made him better than most in their line of

work. With the ability to be anonymous came the talent
to disappear into a crowd. And in being invisible came
a great deal of power. The unseen and unnoticed could
do anything, go anywhere, take anything and slip away
just as unnoticed as they had been when they arrived.

He was a warrior—a Spartan. A man kept at the
edges of society to do the things that most were incapable of doing. His only loyalty was to his brothers and sisters in arms and to those they were sworn
to protect. He was at worst the monster under the bed,
and at best the man who everyone called when there
was no one else to save them. But he would never call
himself a hero.

Antihero, maybe.

Dealer of death. Maybe.

Instrument of powerful women and men. *Definitely.*

And just as with Tiff, he was merely another piece
of a giant puzzle, whose pieces were constantly shifting and swirling until they were destroyed before a real
picture appeared. They were part of the action and reaction, the tug-of-war between factions, governments
and companies with agendas and guidelines he would
never know.

Well, at least usually. This month was far simpler
than most. He had been tasked with attempting to hack
into a machining company that may or may not have
been selling state military secrets to China or another
opposing faction. The company had hired them to spy
on their employees—and make sure they were not, in
fact, selling secrets—and also to check the measures
the company had in place to prevent such actions. Millions of dollars, as well as their current and future contracts, were all on the line.

His investigation and attempts to breach through company security measures could literally make or break the business.

No pressure.

As long as the company had done their legwork and vetted, trained and kept their employees and IT personnel reasonably happy, he doubted he would find anything—or at least anybody who was selling secrets. In cases like these, in which there had been a leak or suspected leak of classified information, the breaches were usually not done maliciously or for monetary gain by the person or people responsible. Nine times out of ten, at least in the cases he had surveilled, an employee had merely said something over the phone, in an email or near their at-home smart device. The captured and recorded conversations then fell into the wrong hands, and the person responsible for the breach was none the wiser that they had just lost millions of dollars' worth of secrets. It was seemingly innocuous moments of ineptitude that often led to the biggest corporate losses.

No matter how many classes he taught to these large companies and their employees, their general lack of understanding of how modern infiltration tactics worked appalled him. No matter how many times he tried to tell people that modern tech was a tremendous risk to their secrets, it was amazing how many CEOs, COOs and CFOs still openly talked, emailed and chatted about their company's secrets. More often than not, they didn't spill major secrets in one sitting. Rather, they told the truth and secrets in small, chewable bits—bits that those listening and transcribing could eventually piece together. A ghost could get just about anything so long as they stayed unknown.

Add in a phone call from someone on the infiltration team's staff, and *bingo*—whoever was eliciting information would likely have more than they could even use.

And though he couldn't help but shake his head at the civilian population's general lack of awareness when it came to safety, he couldn't help but be a little grateful. With everyone turning a blind eye to security weaknesses, he had the opportunity to use it to his advantage. The good guys and the bad guys thought the same way. Once a person understood a bit about the human psyche and the common "it can't happen to me" mentality, it was easy to get almost anything he wanted.

He glanced around at the equipment that surrounded him inside the van. This much equipment may have been a bit overkill, but it was better to have it and not need it than need something and not have it—but that could have been the good old Boy Scout in him.

"How much closer you want me to get before you attempt to break into their system through their Wi-Fi?" Mike asked, looking back at him from the driver's seat as they pulled to a stop at the light. "Did Zoey manage to hack in?"

Troy opened his mouth to tell him no, but as he started to speak, he was stopped by the telltale sound of squealing brakes behind them and the inevitable thud and crunch as he was tossed forward from his seat.

Troy landed on his hands and knees between the two front seats in the van. He jumped into action, did a rapid self-assessment and then cleared Mike for injuries. They would both be fine. He glanced back to the equipment. Nothing looked any the worse for wear.

A thin shaft of daylight shone through the base of the van's back doors, and even from where he sat, he could make out the unmistakable red paint of a car's hood wedged under their bumper.

Son of a... Not today. Not right now.

They had a job to do. And the last thing they needed was some local law-enforcement officer poking around. Though he hoped they would be smart enough not to ask too many questions once they established who he and Mike, and STEALTH—the private contracting company that had given him this assignment—were working for.

Federal and international acronyms, those of the law-enforcement kind, with enough weight to them that they could get out of pretty much any situation.

A minor traffic accident was going to be no big deal. Heck, a smile and a nod and it could all be over and they could all be back on their merry ways.

Or at least he hoped so. But, just like in the past, the minute he assumed anything was going to be simple was the minute he got bit squarely in the rear end.

Mike started to unbuckle, going for the door.

"Wait here. I can handle this," Troy said, moving to the back and stepping out of the side door.

"It's just a kid," Mike said, giving him a wary look.

"Don't worry. I'm not going to kill him," Troy said with a chuckle. Who did Mike think he was? He was a man who sought to eliminate the evil from this world, not add to it.

He stepped out of the van, pushing back his hair from his face as the wind caught it. He hated his hair this long, but ever since coming back stateside, he had wanted to shake things up a bit. It wasn't what most people would call lengthy at a few inches, but to him it was past the point of acceptable.

Assessing the area around him, he glanced at the black car with its backup lights on. Looking at him was a woman. Thick brunette hair, the kind he'd like to run his fingers through, hazel eyes and—from what he could see of her—a pinup figure.

He quickly glanced away.

No. She couldn't notice him, or them or this. *I am a ghost. No one sees me.*

He glanced back at the woman, who was now fully turned around and staring at him and the van. He smoothly shut the door and blocked the view of the equipment inside.

As he looked to her, their eyes locked. In that moment, there was no glancing away, no ignoring the ache in his chest and no way he could go unnoticed.

She had *seen* him.

For the first time in a year, someone besides his team had noticed his existence. It was as if in that moment, with those piercing hazel eyes, she made him *real*.

Chapter Three

Once, while at training at Quantico, Kate had walked into a trap she could have never seen coming, and the mistake had consumed her. It was strange and inexplicable, but the man in the rearview mirror made her feel exactly the same way. She had the same sickening knot in her stomach that told her it wasn't just some random coincidence that he had wrecked right into her life.

What if he was watching her?

She tried to shake the feeling off, but couldn't stop herself from devolving into a hyper state of paranoia.

During their live training sessions at Quantico, they were often required to do open surveillance exercises where they too were being surveilled. It was one of her most and least favorite drills. She loved the art that came with the background work and the setup that came before going after their target, but she hated the fear and anxiety that came with constantly looking over her shoulder.

Seeing that van parked behind them in the street—it made all of her hate and anxiety come crashing back down.

She was never alone.

No matter where she went in the world, or what she

did within the Bureau, someone would always be watching over her. And there was always a trap waiting for her if she took one step off the prescribed path.

Before going to work as a special agent, Kate had prided herself on being a rule follower. She was the kind of woman who was perpetually ten minutes early, never came to a party empty-handed and was always on time with her thank-you notes to hosts and hostesses. If she had been raised in the South instead of on the Oregon coast, she would have been the next debutante princess.

It was what had made it an easy choice for her to head directly to the doors of the FBI as soon as she graduated college summa cum laude from Vassar. The physical and psych testing had been no big deal for her to pass, but when it came to spatial awareness and tactical directives, she had struggled. Being able to memorize license plates forward and backward of every car around her, and then keeping track of people's faces, clothes and assumed beliefs and values… It had all been an incredible struggle.

Looking back, she would have happily done three years of organic chemistry over having to go through another round of surveillance training.

She could have never been a spook.

Agent Hunt cleared his throat beside her, pulling her attention back to the moment at hand. "You okay over there?"

She didn't answer. Instead, she glanced back up at the rearview mirror and watched as the dark-haired man walked around to the end of the van and stopped beside the kid. The boy who had rear-ended him was midmeltdown, tears streaking down his adolescent cheeks, and she didn't have to hear his words to know that he was apologizing profusely.

The man from the van reached up and put his hand on the kid's shoulder, but there was something jerky and forced in the way he moved, as if actually touching another person was causing him some kind of physical discomfort.

The strange realization made her smile. At least she wasn't the only one with war wounds.

"Kate?" Agent Hunt asked.

"Huh?"

"I think it would be a good idea if we headed inside. We don't need to get wrapped up in whatever is going on here," Agent Hunt said with a smile. "I should have guessed that things would go all kinds of wheels up the second we try to take a break. The BuGods have it out for us," he said, using the slang for the Bureau.

She chuckled at his lame attempt at a joke. As flat as it fell, she appreciated the fact that when he must have noticed her discomfort, he had gone out of his way to console her in the only way he could. "No matter what anyone says, Hunt, you are a good dude."

Hunt put his hand to his chest and gave her a look of surprise. "What do you mean? Do people really think I'm *not* a good guy? What the hell, man?"

"Last time I checked, I'm not a man. Not with a set of girls like—" She motioned toward her chest.

"Whoa," he said, stopping her midsentence. "I didn't mean *man* to be pejorative."

She laughed, the sound throaty. "Breaking out the big words, you must have known you screwed up right there."

He put his hands up in surrender. "Two rules that

can't be broken in our world… No one disrespects you, and—"

"Don't leave your service arm in the bathroom. Plain and simple." She finished his sentence, chuckling.

"One freaking time," Hunt scoffed. "I had the flu. I learned my lesson. One you will never let me forget."

She was playing with him, but she could still make out the unmistakable edge of butt-hurt in his tone. "If you would have done that back at the farm, you would have been out on your ass. You and I both know that you are lucky that I was the one to come across it. If it would have been Agent Raft, you would have been looking for another job—sans gun—within the Bu."

"Blah, blah…" he said, waving her off. "I know. I owe you one." He reached down and took hold of the door handle, moving to get out of the car. "On that note, I'm not staying here to take any more of your crap. Man or woman, if I wanted my ass kicked, I would stay home."

"How your girlfriend puts up with you, I will never know," she teased.

He opened the door and stepped out, but not before sticking his head back in so he could get the last word. "That may be a mystery, but why you are still single is as clear as an effing bell." He gave her a wilting smile and slammed the door shut before she could get in the final strike.

Dammit. She had started with a lunge and he'd parried, and his riposte was only fair play. She couldn't let his sharp swordlike words plunge too deep, and yet she could still very much feel their mark.

There was no doubt that she needed to be alone. The last man she had dated had been more than three years ago after they had met on a dating app. It had devolved into sexually explicit text messages that she should have known better than to send, text messages that later had come back to haunt her when her private phone records had been brought into a court case. Her texts had cost her the case, as they called into question her credibility.

She'd never been more hurt or angry in all of her life than she had been in the moment when her then boyfriend had taken the stand and told the world all about her sexual preferences. She couldn't blame him for speaking the truth, he'd been under oath and the defense attorney had been playing sleazeball, but she'd never make the mistake of trusting another human being for as long as she lived—not even Hunt was free from her stalemate.

After a stern talking-to and a reprimand that had cost her a raise and a move up in the ranks, she had found herself working in the FBI's Missoula field office. In all reality, it was a far better result than she had expected at the time. Luckily, her superior officer had taken pity on her and understood that life and love had a way of cutting the best out at the knees.

After what was the most embarrassing moment of her life, she had vowed never to love again.

Love meant weakness. Weakness meant pain. Pain meant failure. And she couldn't fail, dammit.

There was a popping sound outside her car. The sound was distinct, although it was muffled by her windows. There was only one thing that could make that noise—a rifle.

She turned around in her seat only to see the boy who had been standing behind the van drop to the ground. Had he been hit?

Instinctively, she reached to her sidearm, unholstering it as she hurried out of her car. She moved behind her door as she tried to distinguish which direction the gunfire had come from. The dark-haired man dropped down, covering the boy with his own body as two more rounds tore through the air. There was a ping as the rounds struck the metal siding of the van.

What in the hell was going on? Who was shooting? Who were they shooting at?

She looked toward the west, in the direction of the source of the sound. From where she was located, she spotted the shimmer of a distant scope and a black rifle muzzle just inside a window at the top floor of the apartment building two blocks from them. There was a muzzle flash, but she barely heard the rip of the bullet as it tore through the air and struck the front of the van.

Kate tucked in behind the body of her car, out of the line of sight from what she assumed was the shooter.

"Stay down!" the man atop the boy yelled at her.

Like she needed a reminder that she didn't want some person taking potshots at her.

Then again, if the man lying in the middle of the road thought that she needed his help, he mustn't have had a clue who she was.

He wasn't her enemy.

And yet that didn't guarantee he played for the same side, the side of honor.

Good Samaritan or not, he was involved in something that was causing gunfire to rain down upon them. In her entire career, she'd been in only three active shooter scenarios. None of the shooters in those cases had made it out alive.

She grabbed her handset and radioed in to the local

dispatcher. She identified herself, then continued. "We have an active shooter, possible mass shooting in progress on the 200 block of Pine. Shooter is in the Sol building 400 block of Pine, fifth floor. Requesting all available resources."

The dispatcher cleared her request. There was the crackle and fade in the background as the dispatcher went to work sending the information about the shooting out to all the applicable channels.

She would have all the help she needed in less than a few minutes, but a lot could happen while she waited.

Five rounds pinged through the air and struck the van. She braced for potential impact. Moving so she remained under cover, she glanced at the van's windshield. It had the unmistakable spiderwebbed marks where the shooter's rounds had struck just where a driver's head would have been, but none of them had pierced through. Bulletproof glass. An armored van.

There was a sinking feeling in her gut that told her she was dealing with what people in her line of work called the "icemen." She couldn't be one hundred percent sure, but with a military-grade van, intel equipment and two ghosts…it seemed highly likely that she had just come in contact with corporate espionage.

But what in the hell would intellectual spies be doing in the middle of Montana, where on the most exciting days a bear wandered into the center of the city?

What did I walk into?

There was the piercing wail of police sirens.

If they were smart, whoever was behind the attack was going to be long gone before they arrived.

The window in which she had first spotted the shooter now stood empty, as if only moments before there hadn't been a sniper posted inside, bearing down on her.

She sank to her haunches, taking a moment to collect herself. Her hands were shaking and the realization both surprised and disappointed her.

There had been far more terrifying moments at Quantico, live firing drills and mental warfare, and she'd never reacted like this. Why here? Why now?

Had living in this relatively peaceful city—until this very moment, that was—made her lose her edge?

No one could see her like this.

She bit the inside of her cheek, hard. The taste of coppery blood filled her mouth and pulled her back to reality. This was nothing more than another day in the office. This was nothing to get upset over. Emotions were killers.

Focus.

The man she had first seen get out of the van moved off the boy, who appeared to be okay, just shaken. She guessed he'd dropped at the first sound of the gun or been so startled he'd lost his balance. The man raised his SIG Sauer, and pointing in the direction of the shooter, he helped the boy to safety behind the van, then made his way over toward her.

"Are you okay?" he asked.

She slipped her service arm back into the holster, though as she did, she wasn't exactly sure whether to do so was in her best interest or not. The shooter could come at them from another direction at any moment. And yet the foreboding that had been filling her had subsided.

Though she didn't believe in intuition when it came

to her job, there were times when she still adhered to the magic of the feeling.

The dark-haired man extended his hand, an unspoken offer to help her to her feet. She'd always loved a chivalrous man; true gentlemen might have been one of her greatest weaknesses.

Slipping her hand into his, she let him help her up. "I don't see any blood," he said, giving her an appraising, thoughtful glance.

Though she shouldn't have been, she was slightly disappointed in his seeming lack of interest in her ample assets.

She'd always been proud of her décolletage, and yet he was a man who didn't seem to really care.

This iceman was even more cold than the work she presumed he did.

A gentleman who was mysterious, chivalrous and seemingly indifferent to her charms.

Crap.

This kind of wispy, dry ice always had a way of seeping through her armor and straight into her heart. When something that cold met her heart, it would end up only shattered into a million pieces.

Her hand was warm and she realized that she was still holding his as she leaned back against her car. She pulled away.

For the first time in her life, she wished for a firefight. Unlike the man who helped her, snipers presented less danger.

Chapter Four

"I'm Troy," he said, looking at the beautiful woman who had the look of a frightened deer in her eyes.

As soon as his name flew past his lips, the look of fear left her face. "Troy," she said, clipped. "Are you active?"

He tried to control his autonomic response at her overly prying question. He grunted unintelligibly in response, giving her nothing.

Who in the hell was this woman? Using his peripheral vision, in hopes of not giving himself and his inspection away, he looked her over. She was brunette and wearing the dark suit of a professional, but pinned to her lapel was an American flag, and a lanyard was tucked under her shirt, her name badge and tin star hidden from view, but not hidden from those like him who were accustomed to looking for such things.

The FBI really needed to work on their disguises. Or perhaps some of their power lay in the fact that they hid just under the average person's radar. Thanks to his outlier status, and the knowledge that came with it, this lifted veil spoke of her underlying authority. Maybe that was exactly what the Bureau wanted.

He'd always had a sense of antagonism when it came

to the BuCrew and their seeming ambivalence to those they deemed "less than," especially since, in the few times he'd worked with their teams, he had found himself labeled as one within that camp.

She gave him a disarming smile, the practiced smile of someone in control.

His hackles rose slightly, but perhaps it was just residual emotions from the firefight. At least he hoped so; he'd never been the kind of man who had been put off by a woman in control—in fact, he always found it a bit of a turn-on. His girlfriend before Tiff had been a CEO for a small manufacturing firm in San Francisco, and was nothing but power…except in the bedroom. There, she was all his.

He tried to ignore the way the woman's jacket pulled tight as she crossed her arms over her chest. If he had to guess, she was a little like his ex—the perfect combination between self-confidence and power mixed with sensuality and acquiescence. Then again, passion and power could have a beautiful place when it came to bedroom activities as well.

His body stirred to life and he looked away and toward the direction where the shooter had been posted. What jerk thought about tits when Mike was sitting in the van and a teenager was leaning shell-shocked on the vehicle?

Work needed his attention. More accurately, they needed to get the hell out of Dodge before their bosses caught wind of what had happened. Not that they would be the first intel officers to find themselves on the wrong end of a set of handcuffs.

Unlike the Bu woman, he didn't have a readily accessible get-out-of-jail-free card; his took a few more phone calls.

When it came to trouble in the form of violence and women, avoidance was best.

He turned his back to the woman, and she let out a little squeak as he walked to the boy. Mike was with him, double-checking to make sure he was unscathed.

"What? What happened?" the boy stammered, his eyes wide. His pants were wet, a common result of this type of event, and a sense of pity filled Troy.

This was one day that was going to stick with this kid forever. He'd probably wake up sweating in the night. Question his role in the accident and the precursors to the shooting. He would blame himself.

Troy would have to make an effort to check on the kid's welfare for the next few years. An event like this often had two unexpected consequences for a kid: moving forward and using the violence to his benefit, or tarnishing his trust in humanity and imbuing the boy with a sense of fear so great that it would lead to further violence or death. He had to hope that, for the kid's sake, he would find himself coming down with a savior complex.

"It's going to be okay…" He paused, hoping the kid would give him his name.

"John."

Good—he was off to a good start in getting the boy calmed down.

There were footsteps behind him as the FBI woman came over. "John, it's great to meet you. I'm Kate Scot. I'm an agent with the Federal Bureau of Investigation. I'm here to let you know that everything is going to be okay."

She was about as subtle as a fist to the face. And people judged him for his line of work. He sighed, and she sent him a sideways glance.

A police cruiser pulled up and onto the corner, three more in its wake, effectively closing down the intersection and boxing them in, trapping him. He resisted the urge to retreat into the shadows and disappear before there was no longer an option and he was incapacitated; these were the good guys. They were doing their jobs. He didn't have to like it, just accept their actions for what they were—an attempt to keep the general public safe.

Besides, they were good, but he was better. If he wanted out, he'd get out.

No cage was strong enough to keep him.

A string of LEOs rolled out of the car as the men and women flooded out from inside the federal building.

"The shooter disappeared. We need to cordon off an area four blocks wide. Shut everything down," Agent Scot ordered, taking control of the scene as she motioned for the crews to move out.

There was a flurry of motion as the city police officers went into action.

They could do as much as they wanted, but given the limited resources and the size of the city, the chances of getting their hands on the shooter were slim to none. At least, not right away. First, they needed to get their hands on witnesses, anyone who could have possibly seen the shooter coming or going from the building.

The one thing they did have going for them was that Missoula was a city small enough for people to take note of each other. It wasn't like New York, where the population was just a faceless audience in an individual's life.

The man who had initially been in the car with Agent Scot rushed over to her side. "You okay?" the man asked, giving her an evaluating glance, one that made an odd and unwelcome wiggle of possessiveness move through him.

What in the hell was wrong with him?

There was a tap on his shoulder. Mike was standing behind him. "We need to get out of here. There are too many people sniffing around. If we don't get out now, our entire mission is going to be compromised. You know Zoey will have our asses if we aren't careful."

Zoey Martin, their boss at STEALTH, would have their asses regardless of what they did. That woman was hell on wheels, and yet they loved her all the more for her unflappability and take-no-crap attitude.

Mike slipped back into the van and Troy moved to follow. As he opened the door of their van, a hand gripped his wrist from behind. Instinctually, he raised his elbow, readying himself to strike whoever dared to touch him.

"Where do you think you're going?" Agent Scot asked.

He lowered his elbow, gently twisting his wrist to break her grasp, but she held on only tighter. Yielding, he stopped. "I have a job to do."

"You can't leave the scene without someone taking a statement. And what about the kid?" she asked, pointing in the direction of the boy who had started this fiasco.

"Let him go. We will take care of our end of things, accident-wise. He is going to have one hell of a crappy day without adding our repair bill to his list of concerns. Call it a Christmas gift."

She chuckled, but the sound was dark and matched the world around them. "First, Christmas is six months away. Second, you can't think that we are going to let you take this van. It is critical evidence in our investigation. You better get real comfortable while we unscrew this situation."

"I have a job to do. *We* have a job to do," he said, motioning toward Mike, who was sitting back in the driver's seat.

"I don't care if you are the president and are on your way to the Oval Office. Your van and both of you are staying here. The only question is whether it will be thanks to handcuffs or not."

Dammit.

That jumped to handcuffs a hell of a lot faster than he had anticipated. It was too bad that her first reference to handcuffs involved a crime scene instead of a bedroom activity.

"And don't think I don't know exactly who in the hell you are and what you do," she said, her voice barely above a whisper.

His blood ran cold. If she knew who he was, he was as good as dead. Had his identity been compromised? Was that how the shooter had found them?

If people knew him, there would be other killers to follow. He had an enemies list at least as long as his arm, and not half as dignified.

She had to have been playing him. Damn, he hoped so.

"Then who am I?" he asked, hoping she would falter.

"Do you want to play that game, Iceman?"

He tensed, trying to hide the response by slipping out of her grip once and for all. He didn't need her taking his pulse and acting like a human lie detector. Some things he could control, but his heart wasn't one of them.

"I have no idea what you are talking about." His rebuttal sounded feeble and understated even to his own ears.

"You can try to lie to me all you want, but John Q doesn't roll around a small Montana town with a half-a-million-dollar van filled with spy equipment." She paused. "Who do you work for?"

Oh, hell no.

He opened his mouth, but she put her hand up and stopped him midvowel.

"And don't you start the nonsense about 'If I told you, I'd have to kill you.' We both know that is crap, and neither of us has time for that kind of stupidity. So, in an effort for transparency and if we are possibly going to be joining forces, you need to tell me the truth."

His appreciation for her compounded tenfold. In other circumstances, he would have happily worked to get this woman into his bed—handcuffs or no.

Stop.

Though he liked to think of himself as a man who respected women and their boundaries, rare moments like these made him wonder if he needed to work on his self-awareness. Beautiful, filled with spunk and courage, she attracted him. It was really too bad that she wasn't more of a terror. Then at least he could tell himself that she wasn't his type, but as it stood, she was entirely too much like a woman he could have been interested in.

"Answer me, and quit playing games," she pressed.

He had to check his grin. Though he hadn't been trying to keep her on her toes, it appeared he was doing exactly that. And she was reading it as him trying to control the conversation.

She must have been thinking him far smarter than he thought himself.

"If I tell you who I am, I need you to make me a promise."

She raised her brow, giving him a doubtful look. "What?"

His gut roiled. Everything in his life depended on his abilities to stay in the shadows and remain unseen. Though he would never call himself anything remotely close to a hero, he did strive to work for the greater good and be the person who saved lives of people he would never meet and who would never know the sacrifices he made for their safety. If he was outed, his life and the lives of the people whom he strove to help would all be put into danger. And that was to say nothing about his job. Even if he managed to live through the exposure, he would have nothing left—arguably, he would be better off dead.

The Russian proverb came to mind: *Doveryáy, no proveryáy.* Trust, but verify.

Unfortunately, in a situation like this, verification would have to come quickly.

"Do you play politics?" he asked.

She frowned. "That's not a promise."

"Just answer me."

"I avoid them like the plague," she said, looking over her shoulder.

That would have to do, for now. "If I tell you who

I am, and who I work for, I need to trust that you can keep it a secret. I need your protection."

Her mouth opened and closed twice before she seemed to find the words she was struggling to say. "You can trust me."

"My life depends on it." He reinforced his words by reaching down and touching her hand. "Truly."

"I'm yours…your ally." She looked him in the eye. There were dark brown flecks interspersed throughout her hazel eyes.

Though there was no one standing too close, and even those who were close enough to hear were far too busy to be listening, he leaned into her. She smelled like coffee and sunflower oil, but beneath the smell of her office was the jasmine scent of her body wash. "I'm an operator with STEALTH."

She took a big step back from him, but he wasn't sure if it was because of his candor or his proximity.

"You work for the Martins?" she asked, her voice airy and any disbelief she may have had now completely gone.

He nodded.

She ran her hands down over her face, smearing her black eyeliner at the corner of her left eye. He wanted to reach up and clear the smudge for her, but he already felt vulnerable and he didn't need to make things worse.

Agent Scot swallowed hard. "With you here, it's no wonder there was a shoot-out. It's a miracle that anyone was left standing."

Chapter Five

There was trust, and then there was "I am trusting you with my life" trust. Few and far between had ever asked such a thing of her, and rarely in the first five minutes of knowing their name.

Wait—he'd never even told Kate his full name.

She thought about asking him his personal details— she would need them for her investigation—but at the same time, if she pressed him, she wasn't sure he would give her a real answer. She had worked with his kind before, and his kind weren't known for giving their trust even when they were on the same team. Trust was something that had to be earned and then tried before the recipient even knew it was a viable option.

This man was good in all the wrong ways; he was going to be nothing but a pain in her ass. Yet she didn't shirk from the possibility of being nearer to him.

Though there was no doubt that she shouldn't have been drawn to bad boys, there was something primitive in her need to be with them. Thankfully, she'd learned to quell that pull ever since her college boyfriend— Alex, a marine who'd loved to tell her that she needed to lose twenty pounds while he stuffed his face with Cheetos. She could have still punched him in the face.

But she'd heard it said that a person had to really love to really hate.

Her cell phone buzzed from inside her pocket and she pulled it out. Fifteen missed calls and twice that in texts. Even the crew in Salt Lake City had tried to contact her. Word had spread fast about the shooting.

"I want you to know, I had nothing to do with what happened here today," the dark-haired man said. "But whoever pulled that trigger...they had to have known that I was coming. Which means that if I don't get the hell out of here, I'm putting myself and my team at risk. If you need me, you know how to get in touch." He bladed his feet, moving toward the sidewalk.

"You're not going anywhere," she said, sounding more authoritarian than she felt next to the man. "I appreciate what you are saying, but I can't let you go. No matter who you work for. Zoey and I are friends. I can give her a call and get you cleared by your team if you'd like, but I need you. As I see it, you are the reason this all went down, even if you don't think you are. They weren't shooting at me, and they weren't shooting aimlessly at the people on the street. Whoever was behind this, they were going for a kill shot on your driver. They just underestimated their opponents."

His jaw clenched as he seemed to be trying to cover his tells and his body language. The attempt told her more than if he had spoken—he knew she was right. At least he was smart enough not to try to deny her rationale.

"Iceman, how good are you at your job?" she asked.

"Until this morning?"

She chuckled. "You want to go with me while I clear the floors?"

It was dangerous bringing this stranger with her and there were better ways to keep him under her team's thumb, but no one would keep better control of him than her.

His eyes widened. "Seriously?"

"How long have you been in the game?" From the little crow's-feet around his eyes and his fading tan, she guessed he was about thirty and had been in the desert not too long ago.

"Contracting?"

"Let's say all special security operations," she said, hoping to lead him.

"I've been at it long enough to know how to clear a building and get my hands on a shooter."

Of course, that would be his answer. "Then don't let me down and don't leave my ass hanging." She waved for him to follow her as she yelled commands out at her team. "Hunt, you head the scene here. We're going to do a sweep at the shooter's location."

"Roger that," Agent Hunt said, a frown on his face.

She charged down the road, clearing as she worked toward the Sol building. There was a SWAT team posted at the building's doors, and as she approached, the sergeant waved at her to stop until she lifted her badge, flashing it for clearance.

"Did you get a visual on our shooter?" she asked.

The sergeant lowered his assault rifle to his side, the action seeming somehow resigned. "Not yet. However, we found evidence that he may have discarded his clothes in a dumpster behind the building."

Crap.

Their shooter was among them, and smart as hell.

"Did you pull any lookie-loos who spotted the shooter? Saw his face?" she asked.

The sergeant pinched his lips and shook his head. "No one so far. You guys will have more luck."

Yeah, the SWAT crew was more concerned with kicking doors than they were with collecting statements.

"We swept the fifth floor. Dude left his gun. MK12 Model 1."

She nodded. This guy must have been planning on leaving the gun behind all along. Either he was super-confident it held no clues to his identity, or he'd planted false ones on it. Or he was just careless.

There were far better, more expensive sniper guns out there. If she was going to pull the trigger like the man had, she would have used the M110 SASS. Something like that would have run between eight to ten thousand, versus the couple-thousand-dollar model that the shooter had dumped.

Then she was assuming that money was some kind of deciding factor. If their sniper was being funded by a paramilitary, corporation or government, a price point for a leftover gun was probably the last thing on their minds.

She couldn't assume anything yet, but the more details she could piece together, the more she could try to build a profile around their shooter, their identity and their motive.

The iceman stepped around her. "Did they leave any brass?"

The sergeant looked him up and down, feeling him out for a fed. "Who in the hell are you?"

He chuckled. "Call me Troy."

"Well, *Troy*, as a matter of fact, there were at least a

dozen spent casings. What the hell does that matter?" The sergeant spit out his name, making her wonder if they were having some kind of caveman fight over the woman—her—in their presence.

Men.

"Keep your guys on scene," she said, trying to ignore the battling testosterone around her. "Let me know if you find anything else. And make sure to send me pictures of the area in which you found the clothes. My team will be in shortly to collect the evidence."

"10-4," the sergeant said, turning toward his crew.

They made their way inside and she could sense that Troy wanted to take the lead in the way he kept pressing in close from behind her. He was so close; she was almost certain that if she held her breath she could have heard his heart beat.

The building was silent, the kind of quiet that came just after a storm, a quiet that promised that there was more to come, but it was only a matter of time.

SWAT had cleared the building, but the electricity that came with fear and crime still filled the air.

"Take three steps back," she ordered as they reached the bottom of the stairwell. Her voice echoed against the concrete, bouncing until it disappeared into the shadows overhead.

From behind her, she could make out the distinct sound of steel scraping against hard plastic as he pulled his sidearm from its holster. She followed suit, slipping her gun out, though she doubted she would have to pull the trigger. It was better to be safe than wish she had been at the ready.

She moved forward, Troy giving her space. Their footfalls filled the quiet air, the only other sound their breathing as they ascended the staircase. The fifth floor was deadly silent, as if even the building knew what had happened within its core.

It was all office spaces, most completely abandoned and neglected, with dusty boxes in their corners and the windows covered with old newspapers. The door was open to the office space that had held the shooter. There was an old desk in front of the window. Upon it sat the assault rifle, mounted on a tripod and lifted with sandbags.

On the desk were the spent casings.

She put away her weapon, took out her camera and started snapping pictures from a variety of angles, hoping to catch things that she was yet to notice. She'd have plenty of time back in the office to dissect the images, but for now she had to look at the big picture.

From where she stood, she could see people milling around Troy's van. It wasn't a difficult shot to hit the van; in fact, it was the perfect setup.

"I don't think the boy, John, was in on the shooting."

Troy shook his head as she looked back at him. "Nah, the kid was just at the wrong place at the wrong time."

"You want to tell me what led up to the accident?"

"I told you... I didn't have—"

"Anything to do with the shooting," she said, finishing his sentence. "But we both know that you can't deny you were the target. You said it yourself. But that's not what I was asking. I was asking what led up to the accident." She paused, looking at him.

He was staring at the floor as if, somewhere in the dust, he could find the words that she wanted to hear.

"If you want me to protect you, to keep your secret,

then we are going to have to start out with some god-damned truths. Do you understand me?" she pressed.

He looked up at her. "What do you really want to know?"

"Who would want you dead? At least today?"

"It could be any number of people." He sighed. "This shooter, they could have been after me or Mike. It's hard to tell."

"How long have you been working with your driver? He's a contractor too, right?"

"Mike's my brother. I would trust him with my life. And we've been working tight together for the last two years. I'm the one who got him into the game—for better or worse." A certain guilt seemed to tinge his words.

"What's your last name? Are you one of the Martins?"

"No. My name is Troy, Troy Spade."

She gave him the side-eye as she tried to watch him for any deceptive behaviors.

"I'm telling the truth. And, to be honest, it's the first time I've spoken my full, real name since I was hired on at STEALTH."

"Are you operating under an alias?"

He simply nodded. "It's possible that the company I'm investigating is the one behind this," he said, motioning around the room.

"What company is that?" she asked.

"They are called ConFlux. They have a headquarters downtown and—"

"Are associated with military machining," she said, interrupting and finishing his sentence as all the blood drained from her face.

"You know them?"

She nodded, the motion slow and smooth. "Yeah, I'm familiar."

Troy said nothing, just watched her as if he could hear there was more to the story and was simply going to outwait her for the details.

There was no use in holding out.

"ConFlux is owned by my family. My father is the CEO. My mother… She used to run the financials, but retired five years ago."

A quick curse escaped his mouth. Then he remained mute, his entire body tense and his pupils dilated as his fight response appeared to kick in. Nothing could have prepared her for this, for staring down her enemy…an enemy who had just entrusted her with his life.

She thought she had known true silence, but as she stood in that room with the man who had been sent to investigate her family's company, the world around her became deafeningly quiet.

Chapter Six

That was what he got for believing in trust, even if it was only for a millisecond. What the hell had he been thinking in giving the woman his real name without more vetting? Dammit.

Know thine enemy.

Lesson number one. He had known the owner had a daughter and she was local, but in all of his background work, he'd found nothing to indicate that she was working for the FBI. The only thing he had found about the girl, Kate, was some high school track stats and a picture from when she was out with her friends—she'd been around sixteen. The gangly, awkward girl he had seen looked nothing like the stunningly beautiful, confident agent who now stood beside him.

This kind of thing, this right here, was going to get him killed. And screw it, if it was his fault and he died it was one thing…but if Mike got hurt or killed because of the mistake, he was never going to forgive himself.

He had to go into damage control before something happened that he couldn't take back.

"If it makes you feel better, I don't think that your 'rents have anything to do with this shooting. At least, I hope not," he lied through his teeth, trying to cover the tells he knew she was searching him for. "Besides, what would your parents have to hide or cover up?" He could hear himself blabbering; he needed to shut the hell up, so he pinched the inside of his arm with his hand as he moved to holster his weapon.

Though he wasn't sure he had sold his lies well enough, especially with the verbal diarrhea that had escaped his lips, she let out a relieved sigh.

"My parents are good people. They haven't had any kind of trouble—at least, none I know of—since they started the company. You're right. They wouldn't do something like this."

He walked around the room, careful not to disturb the scene. The SWAT team had been right about the weapon, but of course they would be knowledgeable about such things—it was their job. He bent down, looking closer at one of the spent casings, not touching the brass.

Often, the one way shooters made a mistake was when they failed to cover their tracks while loading their weapon. He'd heard of more than a few cases being solved thanks to rogue fingerprints on brass or a hair caught in the magazine. It was the little things that always screwed a person.

"See something?" she asked, moving beside him and looking over his shoulder.

It was good that she wasn't a little thing. She had more power in her stature and presence than most, and damn if it didn't make him ache for her to step just a little bit closer.

He turned to face her, careful to avoid the tension that threatened to erupt between them. With the naked eye, he couldn't see a print, but he wasn't about to mess with possible trace evidence by handling the round. Instead, he moved closer and to the right for a better look. From the outside, it appeared typical and one of a million others like it, and yet there was more to it than most would realize. "This is the NATO 5.56 casing."

She stared at him like he had grown a horn out of the middle of his forehead. "What are you thinking?"

"Just that whoever pulled the trigger knew their craft. This round is consumed en masse by military and police officers alike. As for the general public, it's a known quantity but harder to get."

"You think that our shooter was military or law enforcement?"

He shrugged. "It's a place to start. Though, most of the military guys I work with usually use Federal brand rounds. It's more of a personal preference thing, but whatever…" He slowly stood up, feeling like a complete dork for going down the rabbit hole that was munitions and guns. "Did you get enough pictures?" He motioned toward her phone.

"I think I have gotten everything here." She slipped her camera back into her pocket as she walked toward the window and looked outside.

Her body was silhouetted by the midday light, and he couldn't help but notice the faint line where her panty pulled against her hip beneath her suit trousers. Damn, he would have loved to run his finger right over that spot, to touch her skin, to feel her silky underwear in his hands.

Whoa—where had that come from? He was a professional, on a job, and though he appreciated a good-looking woman as much as the next man, he'd locked down those kinds of strong feelings for a while. *Don't touch, don't be touched, don't get hurt*. That was his new mantra.

Looking away, he walked toward the office's door.

The place had the distinct odor of spent gun powder and sweat. "Whoever our shooter was, they must have been sitting up here for hours waiting for their shot."

"Why do you say that?"

"Take a deep breath," he said. "Smell that? This dude was ripe."

She squinted her eyes, like she was trying to decide whether or not he was messing with her, but then she cracked a smile. "I thought a rat had died in the wall or something. You telling me that's man?"

"Clearly, you haven't spent enough time in a Connex with twenty other dudes," he said with a laugh. "This is nothing. After a while in a container unit, you start considering how many rounds you would be willing to take just so you don't have to lie next to a bunch of dudes after egg MREs."

She laughed out loud. "You did not just go there."

He had to admit that he loved the sound of her laugh. It was clean and bright, coming from a place deep within her that he doubted rarely saw the light of day. He'd give a lot to hear that sound again. "You went with the dead rat. You started this," he said, laughing.

Damn, he could get used to this.

Truth be told, the only person he'd been talking to as of late was Mike and, like living in the Connex, it made him consider going rogue.

"Let's go," she said, walking past him and out into the hall.

She took a deep breath of the nonfetid air. He'd gotten to her, and the conniving part of him kind of loved it. There was something about this kind of nuanced game that stoked his soul, even if there was no chance of anything more than them becoming friends. With her, he would take what he could get.

He felt a vague flicker deep within, as if some ember was being sparked to life, something he'd not sensed in a long time. It caused both pain and joy. He tried not to think of the pain.

Their footfalls sounded on the concrete as they made their way downstairs. They slipped out of the back of the building, and there was the dumpster that the SWAT team had mentioned. Beside it were two tac'd-up SWAT members. They were holding their ARs to their chests like they were their lifelines. He'd always appreciated a locked and loaded Spec Ops team, but it may have been overkill when it came to guarding the trash.

The team leader bobbed his head, acknowledging Kate, but he did little to cover the contempt in his face when he glanced over at Troy. He didn't blame the guy. If he saw some grunt following around on the heels of a good-looking agent, he would have wondered what the hell was up too.

"Anyone see anything?" she asked.

The guy shook his head.

She took out her camera and took pictures of the dumpster. Opening up the lid a bit wider, he could make out desert khaki tactical pants and a gray hoodie. After getting a variety of pictures, she motioned for the SWAT guy. "Have your team bag these up and drop them off at Evidence. I'll have my team take care of them from there."

"10-4," the man said.

She moved away from the team, her face awash with

concentration. He wished he could know what she was thinking. If he was in charge of this investigation, they wouldn't have been standing around; he would have been calling in drones and moving satellites in order to get a pin on their shooter. But then again, this wasn't his investigation and this wasn't a war-torn region of some developing nation. This was America, home of the brave and the situationally unaware.

He regularly forgot how different his view was of the world—that was, until he was back down in the reality of living in a nation where safety had given rise to comfort and comfort had given rise to blindness.

Not that Kate was blind.

He walked behind her like a lost puppy, heading back to the car crash scene, feeling more and more out of place every second he was forced to follow. "If you wanted, I could—" He started to speak, but she stopped him with a touch.

"You don't get to go anywhere." She looked annoyed as she lifted her cell phone to her ear and started speaking to someone on the other end.

"Yeah, anything?" she said.

He wasn't trying to eavesdrop, but she wasn't trying to disguise her conversation, either.

Kate watched him as the person on the other end of the line must have been speaking.

"See what you can pull. No crosshatching on the brass. Normal markings." She continued giving a report of what they had seen. After a few minutes, she clicked off the call and moved to send whomever she had been talking to the pictures she had taken.

He was dying to ask her the specifics of her conversation, but as much as he was curious, he wouldn't—if someone asked him questions like that, the last thing they would get would be any real answers.

"So, tell me more about you," she said, turning back to him. She motioned for him to follow her in the direction from which they had come. "What brings you here, besides my family's company?"

He was really hoping she had forgotten about that admission. Fat chance. She was too smart to let it go, and it was just this kind of thinking that drew him toward her.

"Who were you talking to?" he asked, trying to turn the conversation away from anything that would cause him discomfort or lead him into making any more mistakes.

"That was Agent Hunt. No one has spotted our shooter, so it looks like we are going to be working from the ground up. However, we do have beat cops working the perimeter. They put up roadblocks. Yet I have a feeling that, given the professionalism of our shooter, we have a better chance of finding Waldo."

He glanced around the area. Unlike many metropolitan cities, Missoula was conspicuously devoid of any eyes in the sky. Until now, it was one of the reasons he had enjoyed doing the job he did in this state. He didn't need to worry about his actions being tracked. The lack of tech was probably a major thorn in her side, though, especially if she had ever worked in the tech sectors within the Bureau.

Once again, he was reminded of how little he could gather about her. He'd like to know a lot more, not just for anything related to his job but because she intrigued him. For now, all he could glean from her would have to come from watching and listening, looking for patterns and tells in her person.

Right now, she was standing tall, confident in her abilities and who she was as a person. Maybe she felt that way, maybe she was putting on a show just for him. The truth would come out, eventually.

"If I were you, and I'm not saying you don't know how to do your job, but I would start having my guys tap into all the camera systems within three miles. There are a limited number of choke points in this city. If you look close enough at who is coming and going, I'm sure we can get a visual on this guy."

Her brows rose. "I have my crew working on that, among a few other things."

Raising his hands, palms up, he showed his surrender. "I didn't mean anything—was just trying to give you some helpful suggestions, maybe a starting block or two."

"A good starting block would be to get a key on why someone would want to shoot you and Mike down there," she said, motioning in the direction of his van.

Mike was handcuffed, his hands tight between his back, and he was leaning against the federal building. The man beside him, who Troy recognized as Agent Hunt, was talking on the phone. He was waving his hands around, and the way his face puckered made Troy wonder if the guy was talking to one of the STEALTH crew.

Troy chuckled under his breath. Mike's face was pinched into a tight scowl, and even from a block away, he could read his lips loud and clear. He was an unhappy camper, and he could only guess what Mike had said that had led to him getting a set of silver bracelets. If a bad guy had tried restraining his brother, they would have ended up in a body bag.

"If you want me to tell you anything, we're going to have to be on the same team." He pointed at his brother. "If you don't have your guys let him go, there is no way on this green earth that I'm going to talk to you…with or without handcuffs."

Kate looked over at his brother and then motioned to the agent beside him. "What in the hell are you thinking?" she yelled, jogging slightly to get over to them and through the crowd of officers and bystanders that had started to accumulate in the wake of the shooting. "Folks, this is an active crime scene!"

The people milling around barely seemed to notice the woman yelling in their midst.

There was an older man milling about, talking to someone on his telephone. His eyes were wide and his words were coming fast as he paced, all evidence of stress behavior.

As he watched the man, he was reminded how different he was from the public; he didn't have the same response. He'd gone through far too many rapid stress adaptation drills for something like a little shooting to get under his skin. Everyone was alive and unhurt. What more could people want?

He followed behind Kate as she made her way to Mike. His brother's face was tight and red, and he could only imagine how the conversation would go once they got the hell away from this S-show.

Though it seemed impossible, Mike was a guy who liked sticking deeper to the shadows than him. Mike was a night owl, wanting to do nothing more than watch, listen and document his enemies. When he did pull the trigger, he only had to pull it once. But it had been a long time since Mike had been the one to draw down.

Though, right in this moment, Troy held no doubts that it was exactly what Mike wanted to do.

His brother was maturing as a person; if nothing else, he would have to buy him a beer later and congratulate him on his personal growth.

Mike looked over at him, and as he spotted Kate, he stopped talking and stood up a bit against the building, puffing his chest out.

Maybe he had a little bit more personal growth to go—especially when it came to the fairer, and arguably wiser, sex.

Agent Hunt said something and Mike turned around as the officer reached for the cuffs, but he didn't take his eyes off Kate. An odd wave of possessiveness washed over Troy and he took an almost imperceptible movement closer to the woman. Mike must have seen it because he sent him a sly grin as he approached.

Slipping the cuffs off, Mike turned back around and rubbed his wrists. He glared at Agent Hunt. "I would like to reiterate that putting me in cuffs was more than a little unprofessional, ass—"

"Nope, don't say it," Troy said, cutting his brother off before he spouted something that they would both come to regret. "Kate, this is Mike Spade. He is a fellow contractor..." He sighed. "And this piece of meat is my brother, for better or worse."

She extended her hand, but not without Troy noticing that Mike was staring at her chest region. "Nice to meet you, Mike. You are a fellow contractor?"

Mike gave him a WTF look that made him yearn to flip his brother the bird. *He* wasn't the one who'd had to be rescued from cuffs; Mike had no business to judge.

"It's okay—your brother and I have established that

we are on a trajectory that is going to need some fine-tuning and honesty. If not, your next trajectory will be to jail—no matter how much I like Zoey and the rest of the Martins."

Mike's eyebrows shot up with surprise. "You know the Martins?"

She laughed. "This is far too small of a town for us *not* to know your bosses. We've had a few run-ins with their *friends* in the past."

"If you like Zoey, then you are off to a good start with me." Some of the tension eased from Mike's body. "But I can't say the same about my brother...or his big goddamned mouth."

"Your brother is tighter than a snare drum, so don't jump down his throat too much," Kate said, surprising him.

Why had she risen to his defense?

He glanced over at her, and for a split second, their eyes met. Those hazel eyes... They would be the end of him. Even if they were hedging their bets with one another, he couldn't deny that she was one of the most beautiful women he had ever met. Her long brunette hair had started to gather at the back of her neck where it rubbed against her suit jacket.

Tiff had always hated to wear her hair down. She complained that it got into a rat's nest in the back. For a while Tiffany had tried to wear it loose anytime they weren't training or on assignments, but after six months she had decided that when it came to pleasing him, keeping her tresses free and flowing wasn't worth the effort. He had totally understood. Not long after, she had cut six inches off her hair. She'd never been more beautiful. And then a month later...she was gone.

Yes, he couldn't get involved with another woman—not even the beautiful Kate Scot, despite the instant connection he'd felt with her, the light that had flicked back on deep inside. Sure, they had a lifestyle in common, maybe even a way of thinking and a schedule that was like his own, but they were far too alike for a real relationship. But she had made an effort to keep him happy in her investigation. That had to count for something. Yet he couldn't make the mistake of falling for anyone. When he did, it ended only in heartbreak and death—Tiffany was proof of that.

If he hadn't gotten involved with her, she would have probably worked with a different unit, she wouldn't have gotten into the up-armored vehicle with him, and there were a million other little things that she had done to put herself in the line of fire for him. Love had made them both blind, and worse—blind to the dangerous world that they had chosen.

No matter what he yearned for, he wouldn't put another person he cared about at risk.

Chapter Seven

There were mistakes, and then there were getting-people-killed mistakes. And she had the sinking feeling that Troy Spade was about to become one of those mistakes.

He sat in the interrogation room inside the federal building; he'd been there for the last two hours. Against Agent Hunt's wishes, she had ordered everyone sandwiches and drinks from Doc's and had them delivered while the rest of her teams cleaned up the streets and sent her emails with all the superfluous details she would have to spend the rest of the night poring over.

She glanced up at the video feed and watched as Mike and Troy sat at the interrogation table, finishing up their lunches. Mike was talking animatedly, but she couldn't make out exactly what he was telling his brother.

Though Troy had told her that they were brothers, looking at them on the feed, it was hard to see their likeness. Troy was taller and his hair was darker than that of Mike's, who was shorter and a tad on the heavier side. They both had the V-shaped, muscular torso that came with a military contractor lifestyle, a life that was made or broken on a person's ability to get themselves out of any catastrophic event in which they found themselves—even when they were an iceman.

She had met a few contractors in her years at the Bureau, and a few of her friends had even left the agency in order to go into the private security sector. The money was always one heck of a draw. The feds paid her just enough to keep her, but not a heck of a lot more.

Contractors raked it in. But, for what it was worth, the men she had run into that lived in that world never saved up… Instead, they had made it to burn it and had an attitude of "We're all gonna die soon, so spend it all now."

It wasn't one of her favorite qualities.

It made her wonder what kind of man Troy was, if he was one of the typical contractors who didn't give a single thought to tomorrow as today was still up for grabs.

She walked to the interrogation room and tapped on the door. Mike's deep baritone voice silenced. "You guys done making up in there, or do you want another minute or two?"

"Just giving each other back rubs in here—you are good," Troy said. "But if Mike doesn't watch himself, he's going to get another chewing."

Kate laughed as she walked in and came over to the table. The interrogation room was soft and friendly, designed to put people at ease. There was a couch against the wall; in front of it was a table covered in a variety of magazines, including everything from *Guns & Ammo* to *Tactical Life*. Maybe she needed to talk to someone about getting a little *Cosmo* up in this joint. Not everyone wanted to read about grain weights and the benefits of a new butt plate.

"I hope you don't mind having to wait in here," she started.

"And I hope you know that it is about the last god-damned place we want to be," Mike said, his voice barely more than a growl. "There you were, touting that we should be allies, and you stick us up in this closet."

"But I did feed you," she said, straddling a chair as she sat down across from them. She picked at a piece of a leftover sandwich and popped a bit of the bread into her mouth like it could act as some kind of salve to the animosity that Mike felt toward her. "And if you wanted, we could head out and get a couple beers once my investigation is complete. I'd love to pick your brains a little bit more about what you do and how a girl like me could get into it." She sucked in a breath, just deep enough to make her breasts press against her shirt.

Yeah, she totally wasn't above using her body as a weapon. Especially when it came to two door kickers.

Mike stopped talking while Troy gave her a knowing and deflating smile.

"How did you guys become cybersecurity experts?"

Troy put his hands up, palms facing her. "Look, we aren't what I would call 'cybersecurity experts.' Rather, we are both guys who are just doing what we get paid to do... And it may or may not involve a little bit in the tech world."

"I've heard a hell of a lot of hedging and dismissing titles in my day, but you and I both know that what you just said has to be one of the biggest loads of garbage anyone has ever tried to hand my way," she said, throwing Troy a cut-the-crap look.

He chuckled. "All I meant is that there are players in the CS world who are a hell of a lot better than we are, more experienced and a heck of a lot better at writing code."

"And yet you are paid…and paid well, I would assume…in the private securities world," she argued. "I'm not a stupid woman, and I would appreciate it if you would treat me with just a small amount of respect. Let's start by dropping the bull with each other. I didn't get to where I am in the FBI without being good at something. You didn't get where you are without being good at what you do."

Mike laughed as he looked toward his brother. "Hey, man, you finally found your match. Good luck with this."

Troy smirked at him, and the simple back-and-forth between the two made her like them both just a little bit more. It would have been fun to be a member of their tribe, running operations with them—even if it was in the back of their van.

He glanced over at her. "I'm not being dismissive of our abilities, just honest. We are good, but there are better. We are more specialized than the normal contractors. Mike and I both started out playing in the Sandbox in the fertile crescent area. From there, it was a bunch of hits and misses."

He was hardly the first of his kind who had started his career in the Middle East, nor would he be the last. Many men who came out of a variety of government agencies came home, retired and didn't know what their next steps should be. Some became lobbyists, took positions in governmental offices, and others just couldn't get enough of the fray and went back to work in the private sectors. Mike and Troy were definitely of the latter group.

They were kick-ass-and-take-names types, all in the shadow world of counterintelligence. And she'd be lying if it didn't make Troy look about ten degrees hotter than she already saw him. Dammit, she needed to ignore her weakness for the mysterious hero types.

There was a picture of the St. Andrews Golf Course on the wall above Troy's head, and she forced herself to look at it for a long moment. Anything to not look at him, but make it appear as if she was. He was in the hot seat, but if she wasn't careful in ignoring his odd but magnetic charms, she would find herself there instead. No, thanks.

There was a knock on the door and it cracked open. Her father stuck his head in the entry. "Kate, can I talk to you for a second?"

She couldn't have been more surprised if the Easter Bunny had hopped into the room carrying a basket of grenades.

"Dad?" As soon as she spoke, she realized her misstep in recognizing him in front of the two men she had been trying to dig into. She turned to them. "Excuse me for a moment," she said, standing up.

"Actually, this affects them," her father said, motioning toward the two men. "I'm here to let you know that this questioning needs to come to an end. You are done here."

Though a million comebacks flipped into the front of her mind, she said nothing and instead took her father by the hand and led him out of the room. "What are you doing here, Dad?" she asked as soon as the door clicked shut behind them.

Agent Hunt was standing just down the hallway; he gave her a pinched expression as though he had tried to stop her father from barging into her questioning, but Solomon Scot had proved too formidable an opponent. Though she knew and understood what Agent Hunt had probably had to put up with from her dad, he had screwed up royally in allowing him anywhere near her work.

"Hunt," she said, condemnation flooding her tone.

"I'm sorry," he moaned. "He came armed." He pointed to two men behind him who were carrying the telltale briefcases of well-paid lawyers.

Her spirit slipped, threatening to leave her body at the sight of the two suit-clad men. There was nothing she hated more than a sleazy defense attorney, unless it was two sleazy defense attorneys.

"I see you brought your henchmen. What did your men in there do that would require that level of defense?" she asked, nudging her chin in the direction of the lawyers.

"*They* didn't do anything they weren't paid to do." He put his hand on her shoulder. "If I was really upset, do you think I would have come down here myself? I would have just sent my men. I'm here to talk to you, to let you know that my team is not guilty of any wrongdoing in what transpired today. And if you wish to pursue any sort of legal action, it would be a foolhardy endeavor." He gave her the look, the same look he had given her as a child when the discussion was over.

Well, she wasn't a child anymore. She was almost thirty years old and well outside the realm of requiring her father's permission—especially when it came to her job. Nonetheless, that didn't mean he was wrong in his handling of the situation. If she was in his shoes and her company's name made it into headlines related to a shooting—since Troy and Mike worked for him through STEALTH—she would have brought along a set of lawyers as well.

His company, his reputation and her family's fortune depended on the business prospering.

"I have no intention of arresting your men. So far as I've learned, they are not the guilty party here. They did not pull the trigger, but I'm interested in why they were involved in a shooting. So far, they haven't given me any information."

Her father nearly cracked a smile, but it was so rare she wasn't sure she had actually seen what she thought she had seen flicker over his face. "They are under several NDAs that prohibit what and with whom they can speak. I'm sure you know all about them."

Just because his contractors had signed nondisclosure agreements didn't mean they could get out of this situation without filling in some critical details.

"I don't have a problem working around your NDAs, but I do need to get a positive ID on our shooter and make sure that nothing like this happens in Missoula again." She tried to stare her father down, but he didn't break his gaze. "If you have any idea who was up there, pulling the trigger, then you need to tell me. Right now."

Her father gripped her shoulder a little tighter and gave it a hard squeeze. "The person or group responsible for the shooting will not be caught. Not by you and not by me. You would be smart to just brush this event under the rug." He paused. "Now, I know you need to make a series of public statements and cross your *t*'s and dot your *i*'s, but I would request that you protect my teams and our family's company by keeping our names out of the headlines. Do whatever you need to do, but let's try to bury this as quickly and efficiently as possible."

She had a sickening feeling that her father was right. They wouldn't find this person. Her family's company, from what little she had managed to glean over dinners and overheard phone calls, had been taking military machining contracts for years. Once she'd heard talk of them building parts for a specialized aircraft that reportedly could be virtually "invisible" to their enemies.

She had a fair amount of acumen when it came to understanding some of the tech that was at America's disposal, but when it came to this, she felt out of her depth. And being out of her depth wasn't something she was accustomed to, and she didn't relish the sting it delivered. What she did know, with absolute certainty, was that her family now found themselves enmeshed in something with an odor to it.

Hunt appeared to be busy doing something on his phone and she stepped closer to her father so only he could hear what she said. "I will do what I can. Call it a professional favor. I'll pull my crews back on this, at least a little bit... Appearances." She glanced over her father's shoulder. Hunt seemed oblivious to their conversation, but she knew he was trying to listen in. "This can't happen again."

Her father nodded. "I will take care of things on my side."

It was the closest thing she could have gotten to a tacit admission that her father had a hand in today's events, and she hated it. She didn't like what was going on here, but she wasn't going to create a scene until she knew more.

She should have been dragging his ass into the interrogation room and having another agent working him over for answers, but with her father, that kind of thing never worked. This was hardly the first time he had found his feet in the fire. And even if she tried to get him to talk, all that would happen would be another swift end to any sort of questioning, thanks to his menagerie of lawyers.

"Will you please release them?" her father asked, motioning in the direction of Mike and Troy.

"They were never really being held. They could walk whenever they would have liked," she said, heading back into the interrogation room. Reaching into her pocket, she grabbed a business card and handed it to Troy. "If you need anything, let me know. Or if you think about anything that you can tell me that would stop this from happening again, I'm here."

Her father took the card from Troy's hands and ripped it in half, throwing the bits left of it down on the floor. "He won't be needing that. He has a job to do, a job that doesn't need FBI oversight. If I were you, I would make an effort to get things sorted with the public. And, from what I hear, you have something waiting from Agent Peahen. If I were you, I would jump."

Her chest tightened. How in the hell did her father know anything about what was going on in her inbox, her job? She tried to check any emotions from showing on her features. He couldn't know that he had gotten a reaction; if he did, it would be like blood in the water.

If it had been anyone else standing in front of her and pulling this kind of nonsense, they would have had their ass on the floor and their wrists in shackles. But no, not him, not the patriarch of her family, the man who cared for legacy and politics often to the detriment of the people he said he loved the most.

She could only imagine what he had gotten himself into, but she held no doubts that because of her family she was about to find herself swimming with sharks.

Chapter Eight

Troy sat outside of Kate's house for the second night in a row, staring at the yellow light that burned through the curtains of her front room. Occasionally a shadow would move by the window, teasing him with the flutter of the curtain. Tonight, he had sworn that he had almost seen her, twice.

He had looked into her just enough since the shooting to know she wasn't married, no kids and had graduated from Vassar with honors. Smart woman...driven woman...and perhaps she was the kind of woman who didn't want the tie-downs that came with a family. Or maybe she was the kind who was so myopically focused on her career that such things had never played a major part in her life.

Though he had sat outside of at least a hundred other houses in the dark in the middle of the night and watched over thousands of people, this was the first time he really felt uncomfortable. Yet, with a shooter on the loose, he couldn't ignore the nagging feeling that told him she was in danger, and that she needed him.

Or maybe it was the fact that he found her so goddamned sexy that bothered him the most. Generally, the people he watched were just put into one of two categories: high-or low-value targets. This time, his target didn't quite fit into either of those neat little squares.

He was too emotionally invested in this woman's welfare. There was nothing better than complete, abject dissociation when it came to emotions and specifically any sort of feeling that was registered in or near the heart. Both nights he had mulled over the whys of his being here, but it all came down to one thing—even if he never spoke to her again and she never knew that he was out here and patrolling for danger, that was okay. He would have done his duty. Hopefully nothing would happen, no shooter would show up in the middle of the night or bear down on her when she was leaving her house in the morning as she made her way to the federal building.

Hopefully he was making something out of nothing and she was completely safe. But, until he knew that this thing with the sniper was under control and in no way connected to her, he had to stay vigilant. STEALTH hadn't turned up anything of value yet, but it seemed awfully coincidental that the daughter of the owner of the company they were working for was at the scene of the shooting. In fact, the more he thought about it, the more he wondered if she was the sniper's target. Instead of waiting for Mike and him to drive by a random street, it made more sense the sniper had been staked out to catch action at the Bureau building.

He had to be the hero in the night, the hero that she never knew existed... He was her warrior, her guard, so she didn't have to stand alone.

This was who he had been meant to become. The keeper of the peace. The protector of the innocent. The man in the shadows.

Though he shouldn't have, he found himself smiling at the thought.

There was a flutter of the curtain as she must have breezed by. Things had been quiet in Kate's house for the last twenty minutes and the only other movement had been the flicker of her television. Besides the rustle of her curtains, everything seemed in order. It was nearly the time she normally shut down the downstairs for the night and made her way up to her bedroom. To a fault, her schedule was almost down to the minute. Predictability and patterns could be the downfall of even the best.

He tried to reassure himself that she would be fine, that the shooter probably wasn't coming after her, but with her jumping into the fight as she had—well, she had put herself into a new set of crosshairs: her father's. Who knew what her father would do to keep his secrets—secrets that not even Troy was completely privy to. As far as STEALTH and Zoey were concerned, he was on a need-to-know basis. And, with ConFlux, that meant he was given the basic details and an objective.

He didn't mind working for Kate's father, Solomon Scot, but the man was one step from being a criminal, as far as he could tell. And yet many of the best and most profitable businesses he worked for were just that way. He didn't have qualms with people playing for keeps, particularly in the modern game of business that involved corporate espionage, dirty code, and terrorism at every level—especially in anything that involved health care, banking, insurance, government and military. Though those were the biggest players impacted in the corporate world, they were hardly an exhaustive list.

Cyber attackers loved to go after anything that

showed a vulnerability, often with or without hope of financial gains. But in cases like the one with ConFlux, the company had more on the table and at risk than most in their field—thanks to their engineering, designing and machining.

He looked down at his phone as it vibrated on his wrist with a message. He had an email coming in from Zoey, nothing more than a status check. He needed to call her and let her know he was fine; no doubt she had been watching everything unfold. She'd made it no secret that she wasn't on board with his watching over Kate when his focus was supposed to be elsewhere, but she hadn't stood in his way, either. It probably helped that Zoey knew Kate. They ran in the same circles and played the same political games—more, both knew exactly how much could be at stake if this thing was poorly handled. It would be all their necks on the line if an innocent person, especially someone from the Bureau, turned up dead.

He couldn't stand the thought. Though he was more than aware he couldn't have any sort of feelings for the woman who was central to his being there, he couldn't help some of the fantasies that had moved through his mind. His personal favorite were the thoughts about what she liked in bed. When he'd met her, she'd seemed like the high-and-tight kind of woman, always in control… If he had to bet, she was probably the person in a relationship who was more of a pleaser. Maybe a bit more docile and less commanding, a bit of yin to the yang of her hard exterior.

The thought made his body come to life.

He had to think of anything other than her…the way her suit pants hugged her curvy hips… He could definitely take hold of those hips. Turn her around. Kiss the back of her neck as he pressed against her.

Stop.

He had to stop thinking about her.

This had to be the last night he was out here. No more. This being out here, thinking about her, it was all getting to be too much. Maybe he needed to call one of his brothers and have them take watch for a while. At least until he could get control back over his emotions. This emotions thing—there was a reason it wasn't his style.

Thankfully, Kate hadn't asked him a damn thing about himself, his team or his family before her father arrived on scene and bailed his ass out. Though he was gifted at deflecting questions and at deception during interrogation, he wasn't sure that he could have maneuvered around Kate's questioning. There was something about her. Maybe it was the way she laughed, or the light in her eyes when she smiled, or maybe it was the softness that flecked her words when she talked to him, but there was something that made him want to open up to her.

There was a tap on the passenger's-side window. Kate stood, looking in. He sent her a guilty smile as he rolled down his car's window. How in the hell had she gotten the drop on him? "You know, if you are going to sit out here all night, you are going to need some coffee. Want to come inside?" She nudged her chin in the direction of her house.

"I have been told I'm good at surveillance. Thanks for proving all those people wrong," he said, with a nervous, uncomfortable laugh.

"You did fine. I'm just a little bit better than most

when it comes to watching my six." She leaned into the car. She must have sneaked her ass out of the house and around him without noticing. He looked down the road in both directions. Just like him, she had obviously done more than her fair share of slinking around in the night, finding her way through the shadows.

"How long have you known I was out here?" he asked.

"My neighbor, old Mrs. Evans, called and told me that there was a guy watching my place the night after the shooting. Buddy, you're not in Kansas anymore. Here, the neighborhood watch has a few things to teach the Bu. I really thought you'd get bored and head out. How long are you planning on keeping this up?"

"Just until I know you are safe. Which, apparently, you are, thanks to old Mrs. Evans." He laughed, and his sense of ineptitude slipped away. In all honesty, he had gotten bold in his surveillance. Maybe a little part of him had wanted her to notice him, not that he would ever admit that to her...especially not the part about his sitting out here and letting his mind occasionally wander to a place in which he wondered what color panties she was wearing.

Thank you, nosy neighbor.

"Come on," she said, waving him out of the car as she made her way to the front door. "And if you are going to really watch someone, I would hope you would know that you should change out the model of car you drive once in a while."

He laughed, unbuckling his seat belt. "Oh, I will have to write that one down," he teased. "If you want to know the truth, I'm not getting paid to sit out here. This hunk of junk—" he pointed toward the old sedan

"—is my personal vehicle. She ain't much, but in Missoula she *usually* blends in."

"She, eh?" She quirked her brow as she smiled at him. "Why do I get the feeling that this is the only woman in your life?"

He wasn't quite sure what to make of her tone. There was a nuance to it that had him thinking that she was flirting with him or at the very least checking his relationship status, but he'd never been good enough with the opposite sex to read between those kinds of lines. He had to tread lightly and hope for the best on this one. "We are in a committed relationship."

She laughed, not giving anything away that he could read as she turned and made her way toward her front door. He followed her inside. Her house was typical of suburban Montana. It was a '70s-style two-story with a sunken living room and a bay window centering the wall. There was fresh carpet and new tile floors. The walls were covered in what looked to be a new coat of gray paint, and clean white baseboards adorned the floors. The entire place smelled like air fresheners and paint.

"How long have you been living here?" he asked, closing and locking the door. He glanced over at the pristine white couch in the center of the living room.

A true-crime show played on the television, but she barely seemed to notice.

She sighed as she slipped off her shoes and set them neatly on the floor beside the couch, then sat down. "Come on, now. You found where I live. You don't have to pretend like you didn't dig into exactly who I am and how I got to where I am."

There was a certain edge to her voice that made him

wonder if there was some kind of past there beyond the stuff he already knew, but he wasn't sure he should press too much. The last thing he wanted to do was to make her clam up. He wanted her to be his friend...and who knew, maybe she would even take it easy on him and let him slip into her bed on an occasion or two. If he had to bet, she was probably wearing black panties. Cotton.

She leaned back, her breasts pressing against her shirt. He had seen her do that move once before, making him wonder if it was a concerted effort on her part to make him forget who and where he was and what he was doing.

And damn if it didn't work.

She was so beautiful.

"You get pretty much everything you want, don't you?" he asked, with a disarming laugh.

"What?" She giggled. "Why do you say that?"

"Really?" he asked, raising a brow.

She had to know how gorgeous she was, and he wasn't about to admit out loud that she turned him on. Nope, he was already out on a ledge by being here in her house. Zoey would have had a conniption fit if she knew where he was right now.

"I'm curious—are you going to tell me why you think I always get my way?" she pressed, a demure smile on her lips.

Jeez, she was going to give him a heart attack with that smile. "You didn't tell your father I was here, did you?" he asked, trying to take the pressure off him.

Her smile disappeared. "Why would I do something that stupid?"

It wouldn't have been stupid of her to have let her father know about his surveillance. If anything, it would have been a predictable move. If he was her, he would have been digging around to learn everything he could about Mike and him and their roles inside her father's organization. And yet he had heard her father pull her off the shooter investigation. Did Mr. Scot really wield that much power over his daughter…enough for a few simple words to put a stop to a federal investigation?

If that was true, maybe he was barking up the wrong tree in attempting to get to know her a bit better.

Then again, he wasn't here to seduce her. If something happened between them, it would be only an added benefit. He tried not to look at her as she readjusted herself on the couch. Her smile, her laugh, her body were all driving him crazy.

He grumbled inwardly.

"So, you haven't told anyone that I'm here?" he asked, giving her a soft, inquisitive look that he hoped put her more at ease.

She shook her head. "Do I need to?" She paused. "From what little time we spent together, I didn't pick up on anything that made me think you were a danger to me. A danger to others…now, that is an entirely different thing. But me… I… You seem to have a soft spot. I mean, why else would you spend all that time outside of a girl's house, standing guard?"

"What the hell?" he asked, the words spilling from his lips like cheap wine.

Had he been that obvious?

Ugh. He could kick his own ass. Here he was, thinking he was so coy, maybe even edging on a little bit of Rico Suave, and yet…the slap of reality stung.

"You can try to deny it, but I have made a profession

out of my ability to read people." She giggled. "Besides, it's not just every person I bring in for an interview who turns up at my house a few hours later."

"I wanted to make sure you were home, safe and sound. The shooter had to have gotten a bead on you. They have to know who you are. And even if they're not coming for you, you just never know if there are others out there who want to do you harm."

"I appreciate your concern. But are you watching my whole team? The shooter could have gotten a bead on them too." She smiled up at him and patted the couch beside her. "You don't think I thought about why and what would have brought you out here? To an address I didn't give you and I have worked hard to keep private?"

He took a sudden liking to the cuticle along the side of his thumb, picking away a nonexistent piece of skin.

"You don't have to be embarrassed," she continued. "I'm not upset. I'm impressed you found me. And I'd be lying if I didn't say I was a little flattered. My ex-boyfriend couldn't even bother to text half the time. Once, he was working in Japan for two weeks and I didn't hear a damn thing." She stopped talking and took a breath, making him wonder if she regretted sharing so much about her past. "It's nice to know someone cares enough about my welfare that they would go to such work to find me."

"Zoey pointed me in the right direction," he said, trying to downplay the exact thing he was glad she had noticed.

"So, she knows you are here?" She looked at him.

He nodded. "She wants to keep you safe almost as much as I do. Even if she thinks I'm overdoing it."

"As long as that is why you are really here." She narrowed her eyes. "Or did my father send you to watch me? To make sure I was doing as he ordered?"

He put his hands up in surrender, catching her gaze. "No, I promise you. He doesn't even know I'm here. And if he did…" He looked away, composing himself. "I'm not sure I would have a job when he was done with me."

There was an uncomfortable silence between them. He hadn't meant that her father didn't care about her welfare—far from it, if he had to venture a guess—but he didn't want to head down that conversation path when things had been going so well between them… Flirty, even.

"Uh," she said, searching for the right thing to say… something that wouldn't brush against the tension that was filling the air of the room, he guessed. "Do you want something to drink? Sorry. I don't mean to be a bad host."

He laughed. "You weren't expecting me, so is it still considered hosting if I show up like a stray dog?"

"A stray dog? Is that what we call surveillance now?" She giggled as she walked toward the side bar between the kitchen and the living room. "Do you drink?"

"I haven't in a long time, not because I'm opposed, just too busy to carve time out." He rubbed his hand over the back of his neck. "Not to mention the fact that I don't bounce back from a night out like I used to."

She laughed. "Come on, now. You're not old. What are you, like, thirty-four?" She glanced over at him, no doubt looking for a smattering of gray at the temples or a few stray lines near the corners of his eyes.

"Ouch," he said, looking at himself in the mirror that was on the wall behind the couch. "Do I really look that old?" He ran his hands over the start of scruff that was building up on his chin. There were the starts of a few wrinkles here and there, but nothing that was super noticeable to a person who wasn't looking for them.

She grimaced, her nose doing this cute wrinkling thing that almost made him weak at the knees. "Sorry. I guess I'm not as good as I thought… How old are you?"

He smiled over at her, and there was a little sparkle in her hazel eyes. "I'm thirty-three. I won't be thirty-four for a couple more weeks."

She reached over and playfully cuffed his arm. "Has anyone ever told you that you are a pain in the ass? You made me feel terrible!"

He laughed, feeling a tad bit evil but glad he had made her feel something. "You were close. And, yes, a great number of people have referenced that as one of my many character flaws."

"Oh, one of many, eh?" She raised a brow. "Is there a long list? Wine?"

He nodded and she took out a bottle from the rack and started to open it as he thought of all the things others liked to point out were wrong with him—one of his previous girlfriends had loved to remind him of how he was never there, even when he was in the same room. She wasn't wrong.

"Do you really want to know about me?" he asked, fidgeting with the side pocket on his tactical pants.

She cleared her throat as she uncorked the bottle with a heady pop. It was a welcome sound. "You don't have to tell me anything you don't want to. I was just thinking that you know much more about me than I do about you. I just have to even out our playing field."

"I didn't mean to make things awkward. I'm just

surprised is all," he said, grabbing two glasses hanging from the side bar. He took the bottle from her and poured them each a glass, like he had done it a thousand times in her living room before. "I don't get asked a lot of questions. And I'm normally only around Mike. He's not much of a conversationalist. I guess I've just become a bit of a hermit."

She laughed, putting down the corkscrew and taking one of the glasses he offered her. "A bit of a hermit? Come on, now. You're one step away from living in a cave." She gave him a long sideways gaze that made his chest clench.

"Speaking of awkward and honesty, I've spent more than a night or two in caves around the world. Safest place you can be sometimes." He took a long drink of the wine, and he didn't taste anything other than the pasty flavor that came with being uncomfortably close to a beautiful woman whom he'd had more than a few dirty thoughts about.

Was it going to be one of *those* nights? He had to pull his act together.

"I shouldn't have come out here," he said, putting down his nearly empty glass. "I'll go."

"No." She touched his arm. He should have pulled away, but he remained still. "You don't have to leave. And, as luck has it, I like a little bit of awkward. Just promise me that next time you come to my house, you just knock on the door. You are welcome here." She slipped her fingers down his skin, leaving a fire behind, as she poured him a fresh glass. "As it so happens, I'm not much of a social butterfly, either."

"Do you think two introverts can make a good relationship?" he asked, taking his glass of wine.

"I do." She lifted her glass, sipping. "So, I'm assuming you're not married?"

"Only to my little car out there." He shrugged. "My job has been the kind where I am sent all over the world. I don't know when I'll come back. Doesn't make for great relationships. Phone calls and texts are a far cry from real intimacy. And the distance… It is rough when you both are living your own lives, lives that don't really include each other."

"What do you mean your job *has been* that kind of thing?" she asked, walking over to the couch and sitting down.

She hadn't run away when he'd admitted to his inability to commit, something he was glad to get out in the open. It was a good sign, but he hated to get his hopes up too much. "Recently, my job shifted from military-style operations into more of the corporate surveillance."

"Like what you are doing for my father?"

He joined her on the couch, being careful to give her space. "I don't really work directly for your father. My company is contracted for some *things* for his company, but I work for STEALTH."

"You know that is nothing more than semantics, right?" She moved and her knee brushed against his, making a fire race through him where they had touched. "And you made your position with my father and the effects of his wrath clear. So, why don't we cut the crap. Let's just be open and honest with each other. We are both cut from the same cloth, and as it is, we're going to have to either give all or nothing."

He ran his thumb up and down the stem of his glass, thinking about all the things he wanted to tell her, very few of which had anything to do with his job. "It's not that I don't want to be open. It's just…you have to know, just like you, secrets are my life. There are a million things I could never tell you and you will never be able to tell me."

And how could they build a friendship on that kind of quicksand?

In the end, it came to one decision: trust or get out.

He had already trusted her before. He had given her his job and his identity. For a man like him, who was still dark… If anything, it was stupid of him. And yet he had already made the leap of faith. What were a few more steps? She wasn't just some random person. She had gone through hundreds of hours of background checks and security clearances—possibly even more than him.

But he'd read too many reports and gone to too many classes to just ignore all the warning signs that came before opening up. What he was finding hardest to ignore were the feelings that filled him when he looked into her eyes, feelings that made him want to reveal more than just his professional background, but how the source of the dull ache in his heart seemed to ease when he was near her.

"I respect your need for privacy—you know I do," she said, sounding demure. She cleared her throat, like she was trying to shift the timbre of her voice from questioning to reassuring. "How much did you know about me when you took this job?"

He swallowed another drink, this time slower and more deliberate, letting the strawberry and moss flavors of the wine melt into his tongue. "Honestly, I knew your father had two daughters, but I didn't know much about you. Just the basics. And you can believe he didn't mention that you were working for the Bureau."

"Would it have made a difference if he had?" she asked.

He paused, thinking for a moment. "No. I don't think it would have. Normally, a corporate owner's family plays no role in my investigation unless they work for the company involved."

"I know you probably don't want to tell me, but you know I have to ask…"

He sighed, knowing the question even before it slipped from her lips. Didn't she know he was struggling in his attempt to stay quiet? "You know I can't tell you what I was hired to look into or why. That is between my company and your father and his board. But I can say that I don't think your father is looking for trouble. If anything, quite the opposite." Was that why she'd let him in, been acting so friendly—just to get this info?

She reached over and put her hand on his knee as a softness came over her features. "Thank you."

He stared down at her hand before he put his hand atop hers and gave it a light squeeze. "You're welcome. I can only imagine what you are going through right now, but you are taking all this like a champ. I'm impressed. I know it's hard when you are forced to face drama that surrounds your family, especially when it has the potential to affect your job and your standing in it."

"You're the strong one," she said. "You stood out there, under fire, and instead of running, you moved to cover the innocent."

He felt many things, especially with his hand on

hers, but strength wasn't even close to the top of the list… In fact, all he could think about were his many weaknesses.

"I'm not strong. I'm well trained and it's my job to protect those who can't protect themselves." He pulled his hand from hers, regretting it as soon as her face fell.

Was it possible that she was as confused as he was? He veered from thinking she was interested in him to thinking she was interested only in what he could tell her about his work for her father.

They hadn't known each other long enough or well enough to find themselves in the situation they were in, but there was no denying there was something moving between them—and not the freak-in-the-sheet kind of thing. No, there was a deeper feeling than just mutual attraction. It was more like a deep understanding and respect.

Yeah, she was going to be dangerous to have in his life in any capacity.

He stood up and refilled their glasses, draining his and then filling it again, emptying the bottle. Though drinking wasn't their best option, when he was feeling the way he was toward her, staying sober was entirely too stressful. The last thing he wanted to do was be even more awkward than he already was.

Hopefully she had a thing for goofy dudes, dudes who didn't quite fit into any box and constantly found themselves at least three steps from normal.

"How deep does this thing with my father run? Are there people in the Department of Defense involved in his *stuff*, or is your involvement just a preventative sort of thing?"

He sucked on his teeth for a moment before he finally decided to answer. Maybe it was the slight buzz he was starting to feel or being near her, but he had to give her something she could work with—the more she knew, the more she'd be able to stay safe. "Preventative. Your father is doing what he can to take steps to keep anything from becoming a larger-scale problem."

"So, you're saying that he thinks there is someone in his company who is spying?" she asked, not bothering to beat around the bush.

He liked that she just jumped on his olive branch and tried to make it into a spear. "It's not about what he thinks or doesn't think—it's about what my team and I are able to prove. Zoey's digging deeper into the cyber side of things, but we're trying to find where the strong and weak points are in the organization."

She sent him a pointed smile. "You know, it would have been a lot easier if you had just told me all this from the beginning instead of making me pry it out of you." She took a sip of wine, and as she did, he could have sworn a faint redness took to her cheeks. "If I had to guess, your not wanting to tell me had more to do with the fact that you wanted to see me again than it did with your need for secrecy."

"Come on—you know I have to protect my company's secrets. It can literally come down to life and death." As he spoke, the heady warmth of the wine slipped through him, filling him with reckless bravado. She wanted truth? He'd give it to her. "But I have to say, holding out until you and I have found ourselves here… It definitely was an added benefit. If I was a smarter man, I would have planned this out instead of merely falling ass first into it."

"You mean when I caught you lurking outside?" She

paused for a split second. "And you can be as self-deprecating as you like, but we both know you're not a stupid man. If you were, you'd have had a damn short shelf life in the contracting world. Zoey doesn't allow for anything or anyone but the best."

"Zoey is tough." He gave her a sly grin as he reached over and took her hand. She didn't pull away and instead laced her fingers between his. This was all...so fast, and yet it felt so perfect. "And as for lurking, ouch, that's a little harsh. Don't ya think? I just wanted to make sure you had the highest level of security—call it tactical protection."

She leaned close, her breath caressing the side of his face as she whispered into his ear. "You can call it what you like, but I know why you are doing what you're doing. I know what you're feeling." She pressed her cheek against his.

In that moment, nothing else in the world mattered. There was only her and the way she felt pressed against him and how, with this oh-so-complicated touch, his world expanded.

Chapter Nine

Troy smelled like the inside of his car, an aroma of bar soap, protein bars and his clean-scented cologne. If someone had told Kate that this mixture of scents would be the greatest aphrodisiac she had ever experienced, she would have called them crazy. And yet here she was…her face pressed against his as she worked through all the feelings inside of her and how most were in direct competition with all the things she wanted to do with him and to his body.

Confused, there was only one thing that moved to the front of her mind, one thought, one need, one desire… She had to kiss him. To feel his lips pressed against hers. To hear the sound he made when her tongue skipped over the subtle ridges and valleys of his lips.

She grazed her thumb over the back of his, imagining what it would feel like to have his hands travel down her body as she kissed him. Would he know what she liked? Or was he the kind of lover who needed to be told what to do, to be trained in the art of pleasing her?

Troy seemed like the kind of man who was a bit uncomfortable around women, but that could have been the residual effects of his lonely job. And she wasn't one to judge when it came to sexual acumen. Sure, she'd been with a few men, but that didn't mean she was a sex expert.

She chuckled.

"Something funny?" he asked, leaning back and away from her touch.

The place where their skin had touched started to chill.

Why did I have to laugh?

One stupid thought and the greatest feeling she'd had in months had been stripped away from her. Why did she have to be such an idiot sometimes? Why couldn't she have played this whole thing with suave coolness?

Oh wait—she was a normal woman, that was why.

She sighed.

"You don't want to know what I was thinking," she said with a light chuckle.

If he knew the random thoughts that passed through her mind, he would probably head back out to his car, leaving only dust motes in his wake.

"If it makes you feel better, you and I were probably thinking about the same damn thing," he said, looking her square in the eye.

He had the most seductive green eyes, and gazing into them was like standing in the heart of a Texas prairie in the middle of spring. There were so many different levels of the color, many she could have never imagined to be real.

She reached up and ran her hand over the stubble on his chin, her mind wandering from his words and settling back onto his features…the strong line of his jaw and the near ninety-degree line at its edge. Even his ears were in perfect proportion to the rest of his face… Her gaze drifted downward, toward his chest.

Before she could stop herself, her fingers twisted from his face, grazing over the soft cotton of his T-shirt and stopping just over his heart. It pulsed against her fingers. She put her palm down, feeling the quickening rumble as her hand cupped his perfect round pecs.

He flexed, smiling at her. "Do you like my moobs?" he teased.

She didn't just like them. "Given the right amount of invitation mixed with the correct amount of loosened inhibitions, and you know I would motorboat those things." She laughed, throwing her head back in joy.

He smirked. "Invitation? Hmm… I can't say that I've ever been asked if another person could motorboat my chest." He tapped his finger on his chin as if he was seriously contemplating the idea. "I'm flummoxed."

"Oh, did you just say *flummoxed*?" She laughed harder, her belly starting to ache. "You are cut off from any more wine."

"Don't be such a hater. There is nothing wrong with the word *flummoxed*. My grandfather loved that word."

"The fact that your grandfather loved it should be reason enough for you to leave that one in the past." She giggled, looking up at him from under her eyelashes.

He reached up and took her hand, which was still resting over his heart. "I haven't laughed this hard in a long time," he said. Lifting her hand to his lips, he gave her fingers a soft, tender kiss.

She could have died in that moment and considered her life well lived.

Of course, as if she had called down the wrath of the karma gods, her phone rang. It vibrated on the table in front of the couch just inches from their knees, repeating its angry buzzing like it was a hornet stuck behind a piece of glass.

He let go of her, and her hand drifted to her lap.

"You probably need to answer that," he said, motioning to her phone but seeming to respect her privacy enough not to grab it and hand it over to her.

The simple action, or inaction, made her think about what they would be like if they were a couple. She could almost imagine a Friday night, him going out to take down a company while she dug into crime-scene photos and tried to develop timelines for murders.

"Probably a robocall. Get lots of those."

The phone stopped its hornet dance and she relaxed back into the couch, hoping that they could pick up where they had left off, but not knowing exactly how she should start again.

"So, tell me more about your family. I know you said you have brothers…" she started.

The cute little smirk of his, the one that always seemed to appear when she did something slightly inept, reappeared. "I'm one of six kids. I'm the third in line to the throne, right ahead of Mike."

She was a bit surprised that he hadn't tried to put her off when she'd asked about his private life. "All boys?"

He shook his head. "Nah, five boys and a girl." He shrugged. "My parents were saints and possibly highly confused. I can't imagine raising six kids, not to mention six highly energetic and trouble-seeking children. We were *the worst*."

"I can only imagine. I am one of two girls and we were bad…but six… Ouch."

He chuckled. "Both my parents worked full-time, which meant we were all on our own, for the most part.

AJ, my oldest brother, tried to keep us in line, but most of the time he was the ringleader more than anything else."

"Oh yeah?" she asked, not wanting to stand in his way of opening up to her.

"Christmas was when we seemed to all be at our finest. There was nothing more fun than lining up the glass bulb ornaments and pinging them off with a BB gun." He laughed as he spoke, the words spilling out between chuckles. "I'm telling you, our parents should have quit at one… But my mother was an angel, seriously. She never mentioned a damn thing about all the missing ornaments. And I'm sure, though we tried to clean and hide the evidence after our target practices, she had to have known what we were up to when she had to buy new ornaments each and every year."

She laughed, but it was just as much at him and the joy in his face as it was for the craziness she was sure had taken place within his family. "I bet they got cheaper over time. You're lucky she didn't start buying the unbreakable plastic ones just to mess with you guys."

"If they would have been a thing back then, I'm sure she would have." He was laughing, but there was a whisper of sadness in the sound. "She was a great woman. Both of my parents were."

Kate stopped laughing. "I'm so sorry. How long have they been gone?"

"They've both been gone a couple of years now. They died on Christmas Eve in a car accident." He ran his finger over the glass. "They lived in Renton, near Seattle—where we all grew up. They were coming to Montana to spend the Christmas with me, Mike and Elle.

We were all just starting our jobs with STEALTH. They were hit by a semi on Snoqualmie Pass. Died instantly."

"Holy crap, Troy... I can't even... I'm so, so very sorry." She couldn't even imagine the pain that must have come with that kind of traumatic event. She had thought dealing with her mother's breast cancer had been hard, but thankfully her mother had survived.

She didn't have the corner on the market when it came to hardship and suffering. If anything, his history was hands down more heart wrenching. All of a sudden, she felt entirely too sober, but she was grateful that he was finally giving her a piece of himself. He was starting to make a bit more sense.

But not why he had chosen to go into governmental contracting work. It wasn't a job that most could do. It was a job that was often not regulated, which made it like the Wild West and him a cowboy.

"Why did you choose to become a contractor? Was it because of the loss of your parents?"

"No, that happened after I was already training for STEALTH. I had been working as a contractor for a few other companies before that. I liked the work. I guess I got into the work because I was such a free-flying kid. We all went into contracting. In fact, my siblings and I all work for STEALTH."

That was amazing. One contractor in a family could be hard on the entire dynamic, thanks to the secrets, the going black and the disappearances out into the world for sometimes *years*...but six? Damn.

Maybe it worked better because they all lived in the same world and all worked for the same company. It had to allow them more candor when it came to the work they did. Maybe it was the best way to keep a family together.

"I haven't heard of a whole lot of female contractors. Especially when it comes to working out in the Sandbox. How does your sister like it?"

"She is far tougher than I am."

She nibbled at the corner of her lip. "What about the sexism?" Her thoughts moved to Agent Peahen...and all the work that would be waiting for her in the morning. It still rankled that her father had urged her to work with the man. She knew her dad had a lot of connections, and his reference to Peahen meant the agent had probably complained about her to her father. How petty.

She tried to ignore the gnaw of guilt that fluttered through her as she considered all the things she needed to do, but for once she could take a night for herself. It was terrible, but it had been entirely too long since she'd had a man in her house, not to mention edging in on her feelings.

"My sister doesn't open up to me a lot about the way men treat her, but I know it can't be easy. There aren't many women who get into contracting, for a reason. And as much as I would love to support having women in every role in the different teams, it would be really hard. There are places in the world where they just can't do what I do. They would end up dead."

She bristled. "Are you saying that you don't think women should be contractors?"

He shook his head, hard. "That's not what I'm saying. There are certainly jobs they are better at than men. Women can get into places that I can't. Females are an asset...and a detriment... But the same can be said about men. It's just about using the right people for the right job. And when a higher-up gets it wrong…it can be a real problem. Or if they get a team that doesn't work cohesively together… Yeah, no. It's bad news." There was a strangled sound to his words, a noise between deep anger and heartache, as though he was trying to hold back emotions that threatened to break through his stoic dam and flood into his voice.

There was something there, something that rested right below the surface, but she wasn't sure whether or not she should push him for answers. It was better to have things happen naturally, if they were meant to happen at all.

"I quit the Sandbox a couple of years ago, you know…after an attack. I had broken the rules. It cost me."

"I'm sure you didn't do anything that bad. You seem like such a good man," she said, gripping his hand with hers.

"It wasn't about me being a good man…or a bad man. It was about me making the wrong decisions." He paused and slipped his hand from hers, patting it as he stood up and moved away from her. "I got into a relationship that was ill-advised. I loved her… And it was that love, our relationship, that ended up costing her the ultimate price."

She didn't know what to say. "I'm sorry" seemed too feeble a response to the pain he was so clearly feeling when he spoke about the woman he had loved. So, she said nothing in hopes that it would respect whatever it was that was going on inside of him.

"We were hit with an EFP. She took shrapnel straight to the heart." He leaned against the side bar, putting his arms over his chest. "Her death, without a doubt, was my fault. I will have to live with the guilt of that knowledge for the rest of my life."

The guilt he was feeling was likely not his to bear, but there was nothing she could say that would assuage what he was feeling. Right now, all he needed was to be heard. And, if that was all she could do to make him feel better, she was willing to sit there and be the ear he obviously so desperately needed.

"I know, logically, that I didn't put that EFP out there. I couldn't have known it was there, or that it was coming for us, or that it would have hit the up-armored unit just right…but if I had stopped things before they had gotten serious, she wouldn't have been out there. She probably would have taken a transfer out of the hellhole. She would probably be the one working for STEALTH now, not me."

"So, you have survivor's guilt too?" she asked, her words soft and nonjudgmental.

He ran his hands down over his face. "I don't know why I told you all this. Needless to say, if I ever went to therapy, I'm sure that they would have a field day. I put the *fire* in *dumpster fire.*"

She didn't agree. Not in the slightest. "You are just a man with wounds. It comes with the territory."

"Of being alive." He finished her thought, a thought she wasn't going to say.

"I'm sorry for taking things here," he said with a sigh. "I was rather hoping things between us would go a bit of a different direction… Though, now I'm not so sure that's a good idea—with me being the grim reaper and all."

She chuckled, though she shouldn't have. In moments like this, when darkness loomed heavy, the only thing that could make it all okay was levity. "Does the grim reaper have a sidekick?"

He looked at her, surprise and relief marking his features. "You know, I never thought about that. Maybe his sidekick would be his scythe."

"Not my favorite nickname, but it's still kinda badass, Grim."

"We may be among the strangest friends on the planet," he said, laughing.

He had called them friends… They were steadily moving in the direction she had wanted while still staying safely behind the line of a relationship. They could toe the line, but she would have to play it safe when it came to him.

She had to keep this professional, or at least try to. He was work, or at least he had to appear to be only a part of her work to the outside world. And that was to mention nothing about what her bosses within the Bureau would surmise. If they found out that the target of the shooting was sitting in her living room drinking wine, there would definitely be an internal investigation. Oh, and Peahen would have a field day when he heard about her unprofessionalism—he already had a chip on his shoulder.

"There is nothing I like more than to exist in the world of the strange, the dark horse and the odd ducks. We are the ones who keep the world fresh, away from the habitual monotony that comes with simply surviving. I've always wanted more than that. It's how I found myself doing what I'm doing. I never thought about it in grim terms, but I really do love being the scythe when it comes to cutting down evil."

"I know that feeling," he said, a tenderness that

looked very similar to adoration upon his features. "We really would make one hell of a team."

There was a knock on the door, making her jump.

Who would be knocking on her door this late at night? For a moment, they sat in silence. Troy's hand was on his sidearm, and as she looked to him, he pressed his finger to his lips and silently roll-walked toward the bay window that looked out and onto the front porch.

He slipped behind the curtain, moving so he could make out whoever was standing at the door. As he looked, his hand moved from his weapon and his body relaxed from his action-ready tightness. "It's one of your friends from the Bureau," he said, shrugging as though he wasn't completely sure. "Older guy, maybe midfifties. Looks like he's driving a black Suburban, someone else is in the passenger side, but they are parked right in front of your place. They aren't trying to be covert, that's for damn sure."

Then he wasn't talking about Agent Hunt, who was just moving into his early forties.

Who else from the Bureau would show up on her doorstep in the middle of the night? The phone call... What if it had been Raft, the special agent in charge for her division? Her stomach dropped. She moved to ask Troy to leave the room and stay out of sight, but as she looked to where he had been standing, he was already gone.

He must have known what was at stake for her as well. She'd have to thank him later.

The door opened without a sound. Standing on the doorstep was Agent Peahen. Fury roiled through her. "What in the hell are you doing here? You didn't seriously drive here all the way from Billings, did you?"

Peahen's face puckered, his lips pulled into the closest thing to a sneer without actually being one. Their distaste for one another was mutual. "Thanks for the warm welcome."

"Why are you on my doorstep?" she asked.

Had there been some kind of informational breach in which everyone in the effing world had suddenly been informed of her address? If Peahen had found her, it was time to move again.

"I wouldn't be on your doorstep if I didn't have to be. And yet here I find myself." Peahen grumbled something she couldn't quite make out. "I'm here for the files you promised me. You have access to them, correct? I'm not leaving here until you have forwarded them all to me."

"Why do you care so much about a burglary that happened five years ago?" She tried not to sound as annoyed as she felt. She never had sent him those files, mostly because she'd not wanted to jump when he ordered her to. And because her father had mentioned it as well.

"What do you care? You didn't solve it."

Kate gritted her teeth in an attempt to keep from taking him down with a quick two-finger jab to the throat. "Has there been another burglary, something you think may be tied to the case? Or are you reopening the investigation for another reason?"

He groaned, leaning his head back, as if the mere fact she had questions before she blindly handed her case over was out of line. "Look, I don't have to answer your questions. I'm not here to be interrogated. Now, you can give them to me willingly, or I will go over your head—in fact, you're lucky I haven't already done that."

The fact that he was standing on her doorstep, threatening her with going above her head, was odd. He'd already done this—told her he'd go to her superiors. Why hadn't he by now? Billings was a hell of a drive from Missoula. It certainly wasn't on his way to anything, at least not that she could think of.

"Peahen, I've no problem giving you the files. I have them with me. But before you do anything, I need to know why you need them and what you're actually doing here in Missoula." She gave him a critical look. "And don't give me any of that *I'm not here for an interrogation* nonsense. You can't expect me to just give you files, without asking a few questions. You are not that kind of friend, and you know it."

He snickered. "For someone that is inept at her job, you sure ask a lot of questions. Maybe if you treated your suspects the same way you're treating me, you would break a lot more cases."

Her hands balled into tight fists. No one would think anything of her slugging him if they had been there to hear what he was saying. "You're one to judge, Peahen. The last time I checked, I actually have a higher prosecution rate than you do."

"Fine." Peahen turned to leave. "You are going to regret the fact you're being such a little… Well, so *unprofessional*. And when your dad hears how you treated me, you're going to get it from every side. You deserve whatever consequences come your way. Whether you want to admit it or not, we fight for the same team."

"Stop right there," she said, charging out the door after Peahen. "My father mentioned you the other day and now you're mentioning him. What the hell is going on with you two? Did you have something to do with the shooting in Missoula the other day? Is that why you're here?"

"Not that it's any of your business, but I had a meeting in town. I was just getting back from Salt Lake City and the regional headquarters. It was easier just to come over here and take care of it in person."

She wasn't sure if she believed him or not. Yet there was something to his voice that made her think he was telling the truth. He wasn't displaying any of the typical signs of deception, but that didn't mean anything, considering he knew just as well as she did what those signs were. He could have easily been trying to deceive her.

"And what about your ongoing *friendship* with my father?" she asked.

Peahen sniffed, annoyed. "Your father and I go way back, long before you even joined the agency."

She'd had no idea. In fact, her father had never mentioned a connection with Peahen before this week. Had Peahen been part of the reason that she had been picked up by the agency? The thought petrified her. For her security clearances, there was no doubt in her mind that they had looked into her and all the people connected to her. Peahen had to have been asked about her, and the fact that she was currently an agent meant that he had to have said something to her credit.

The possibility that he had done her a favor without her even knowing it still didn't make up for what a jerk he was every time she had dealt with him over the last five years.

For a moment, she considered asking him into the house, but she glanced over her shoulder in the direction of where Troy had been standing. If Peahen got nosy, or turned down the wrong hall, he very well could end up face-to-face with Troy. She didn't need them in the room together.

"Let me go grab my phone, and I'll send in the files. I want you to promise me that you'll keep me up-to-date with your findings on this case."

"That's fine," Peahen said.

She jogged back up the steps and to the living room. Grabbing her phone, she made her way back outside.

Peahen look slightly less annoyed than he had five minutes ago, but only slightly. He wore the same pinched expression he always did, making her wonder if that was just his face. If he was married, she felt sorry for the woman.

After a few searches through her files, she sent off the email. "It should be in your inbox."

"Great." Peahen's lips quivered into what she assumed was almost a smile. "And, believe it or not, your dad is a good man. You should take it easy on him… and me…once in a while." With that, he turned and strode away, obviously not waiting for her to say anything in return.

A tightness she hadn't realized she'd been experiencing in her chest loosened. She'd never believed anything Peahen had ever told her, but it could have been their acrimonious personalities at fault rather than any particular transgression toward one another. His evaluation of her father, and the fact Peahen had acted in favor of her in the past… Well, it changed things.

And though her father was by no means a perfect man, it was good to know he wasn't evil or corrupt— at least she assumed.

She loved him and her mother, and they had done much to show her love when she was a child.

When she'd been younger, she had been studying the violin. Twice a year for what must have been fifteen years, she had performed in recitals. During high school, she had played with the Missoula Symphony as the youngest first chair. She'd played with them for four years before she had gone to Vassar. Her parents had never missed a single performance, not even when her mother had been diagnosed with breast cancer and had been seeking treatment.

It was strange, but after what had happened the other day, those memories and their support had started to lose their texture, like someone had started to pull at the strings that wove together to make her soul. In essence, it was as if her father's possible complicity in the shooting had made her question everything—even who she was.

And here she was, back in that same confusing reality in which she didn't know who or what was the driving force in her life—and all thanks to a five-minute meeting with a man she had thought was her enemy.

She made her way back inside. After—well, *if*—Troy went home, she would have to dig deeper into the old burglary case. There was something that they were all looking for, and she had a feeling that it went far deeper than she had initially assumed.

The house was silent as she closed the door behind her. "Troy, you can come out now. Thank you for what you did back there. It would have been hard to explain why you are here." She paused, waiting for Troy to answer. There was no response.

Making her way around the house, her heart sank as she realized that Troy was gone.

Chapter Ten

He shouldn't have just left Kate like that last night, but in the moment, he hadn't known what to do. All he had known for sure was that, for her sake, he couldn't be seen in her house or anywhere near her property. After he'd alerted Kate to the BuCar outside her house, he had slipped out the back and around the block. When he'd gotten into his car and driven away, the last thing he had seen was Kate running out after Agent Peahen.

Troy had worked with Peahen once before on an investigation out of Billings, and it hadn't been one of his favorite assignments. The agent had thought himself far above him, both intellectually and morally, and had made it clear. If he'd worn a general's uniform beneath the suit, Troy wouldn't have been surprised.

If he had added himself to the mix, there was no way Kate would have come out unscathed. Not with Agent Peahen on the warpath. There was no telling what he would do—he definitely didn't need any more artillery, and especially none in the form of an agent mixing business with pleasure.

Not that there was any real pleasure between him and Kate. Sure, they had flirted. They had even held hands and touched one another in ways that were definitely more than two friends…but that didn't mean they had gone beyond the point of no return, did it?

He looked over at the clock beside his bed—9:00 a.m. There wasn't anyone moving outside of his bedroom at the STEALTH headquarters, located on the Widow Maker Ranch. Everyone was probably already buzzing around their day, getting things done. He shouldn't have slept in so late. Zoey was supposed to call him in twenty minutes and he needed to be on his game when she did. No doubt, she would ring ten minutes early. She lived on the Anglo system of time—if a person was on time, they were ten minutes late.

It had been tough getting used to everyone's quirks when he had set foot back on American soil. Civilians, and even contractors who had never been in the military, were of an entirely different mindset than he was.

One of his friends, Jesse, had worked at his side and gone through training with him and finally into the same unit. Jesse went on to marry a woman and have four amazing kids, but even now when on the phone together, they would frequently admit that no one understood them better than they understood one another. They were brothers. No, deeper than brothers… Mike didn't even understand him as well as Jesse did.

Jesse had been with him when Tiff had been killed. That alone—that moment of horror—solidified a bond that was already stronger than diamonds or blood.

Maybe he should call him. At the very least, Jesse would tell him he was being a fool when it came to Kate, and maybe he could get his head straight. He hadn't been this screwed up when it came to a woman since, well…he would say Tiff, but even their relationship wasn't this unnavigable.

Then again, what was there to ask? He imagined exactly how the conversation would go down: "Hey, man, I think I'm falling for a woman who I'm helping to solve a shooting... Yeah, the dude was trying to take out Mike. Yeah... Her family owns the company I am investigating."

Jesse would tell him to tuck and roll, and get the hell out of the country as fast as humanly possible. It wasn't even worth the breath to ask him his opinion. Jesse was always of the rational frame of mind. The mind that rarely deferred to the heart.

Regardless of what he felt, wanted or yearned for, he needed to concentrate on the task at hand. And he needed to apologize for his sudden departure. Kate probably wasn't the kind of woman who was wondering about his welfare, but she did seem like the kind of woman who didn't appreciate anyone sneaking out of her place.

When he'd been helping her with the wine, there had been a picture on the wall beside the side bar. In it, Kate had been standing with her mother and father and what looked like her boyfriend...or past boyfriend. He'd dug around, but the internet was devoid of any sort of current information. She definitely wasn't a publicity junkie in either her public or her private life. It was great for her, but it made it more of a challenge for him when it came to investigations. Like most agents, she kept her social-media presence scant and locked tight.

His phone rang. Zoey. "Hello?" he answered.

"Are you happy?" Zoey wasn't much of one for hellos. Or goodbyes.

"Happy about what?" he asked, not sure based on

her tone if he should find a bomb shelter before she continued her rant or if he should purge his soul to her.

She sighed, now definitely annoyed. "Are you done watching over your girlfriend?"

Oh.

"What do you need from me?" he asked, taking the high road instead of getting hooked by her emotionally hijacking statement.

"Oh, so you are ready to get back to work. I'm glad to hear it." Zoey's tone dulled. "I need you to go back to the ConFlux building. You need to see if you can't hack into their system through their Wi-Fi—it's their weakest point. Then I will take care of the rest. After you are done with that, I need you to see if you can infiltrate the building without setting off any alarms. You have whatever resources you need to make this happen."

"Has there been any evidence that someone has been breaching their networks? Their building?"

"Not that they have divulged, but there is something going on. Solomon expressed concern that there may very well be someone trying to run a copy code on their servers, as there has been information in the past which has now gotten into the wrong hands. I asked him if anything new had been leaked, and he didn't believe so."

Troy made his way to the kitchen, took out a travel mug and poured himself a cup of coffee. "Which means that it isn't a hacker issue… At least, I wouldn't think so. If things are only going missing sporadically, this sounds like a personnel problem or someone from within their IT department—but you and I have talked about this before."

"Before the shooting, yes." Zoey paused. "Which is

part of the reason I thought I needed to call and talk to you. I just got a ping on our shooter. I don't have a confirmed identity, but I worked the known cell phone signals in the area against the buyers and sellers of that make and model of rifle and rounds. Then I went through the information I pulled, and there is a short list of possibilities—three potential suspects. Two are still in the area."

"Who is the third?"

"The third person on our list… Well, that's the tricky part. I don't think this person would have had anything to do with this. Not with their clearances." There was the sound of a pen clicking in the background as Zoey spoke, her nervous tic.

Whatever name she was about to give him—it was going to be good.

"I know we are probably at a dead end with this one, but it's a special agent named Aaron Peahen."

Troy spit out his coffee. "You have to be freaking kidding me. It really isn't funny."

"What?" Zoey asked. "I'm not messing with you. Why would you think I was? You know this guy?"

"Yeah, I saw him last night. You said he was the only one on your list who hasn't been using the Missoula cell towers, but I know for a fact that he was here at least within the last twelve hours."

There was the click of key strikes. "According to what I'm seeing here, he appears to be in Salt Lake City."

"When?"

There was more tapping. "He has been there ever since the shooting. At least according to his SIM card."

He shook his head. Peahen was a jerk, but he was

still an agent. He'd gone through nine months of background checks before he'd even been able to go to Quantico to train to be an agent. This was not their shooter. He wouldn't be a trigger puller, not in any sort of situation. He was closer to the kind of person who would be a computer jockey.

"That probably has something to do with whatever is going on at the FBI." His thoughts went straight to Kate. There were pieces missing in the puzzle, pieces that revolved around her, but he just couldn't imagine what exactly locked these things together. "There is no way that Peahen is our guy. He's an uptight dude who gets his jollies making people say 'how high' when he barks out 'jump.' Not the type to go haywire with a gun. Send me the info you have on the other two. I'll get to work."

"Will do." Zoey clicked away. "As for the other guys on my list, they are both current employees of ConFlux."

"And you didn't think that they were more likely to be our shooters than a verified *good guy*?" Troy scoffed.

"You and I both know that there is no such thing as good guys and bad guys. We are all human. We all screw up. We all hurt the people around us. We all occasionally make crappy decisions. It's part of the gig."

"Yeah, but two employees of the company we are investigating? These are our bad guys. One of them, at least."

"It's possible, thus why they are on my list. But these two, neither have any sort of record of violence or training with weapons."

"But you said that they had access to the right kind

of ammunition and rifle. But neither shoots?" Nothing about this rang quite right.

"One, Chris Michaels, is married to a woman who is a major in the army. She had bought a rifle similar to the one used. There was no serial number on the sniper's weapon. But we're having a team go over it to see if it was scratched out. Definitely could have been her gun. You look into it."

"On it. I'll send Mike over to their address. As long as they don't have an electronic lock gun safe, he should be able to make quick work of it and gain access to their guns and let us know if her new acquisition is missing—if it is, then it's possible she or her husband is our sniper." STEALTH operated without search warrants, and he knew his brother could get a look at that gun, if it was there, by staying just one millimeter over the right side of the law. He took a sip of his coffee as he tried to work through all their leads. "But we may be dealing with someone who had the armory skills to fabricate or build their own weapon. It would be what I would do if I was the one up there pulling the trigger, knowing I'd have to leave my weapon behind. I'd need to take a closer look at the weapon, though, and the FBI has it now."

He clicked on his email and scrolled until he found Zoey's latest. He opened it up. There were three images of the photos of each of their possible suspects and three PDF files with all applicable background information. First, he opened the photo of Peahen, likely the one that was from the Bureau, and his badge. The second, Chris Michaels, looked like a man who could hold his own in a bar, Jack Reacher style.

"And what about this third guy? Sal Baker?" The

man staring back at him from his cell phone was in his midthirties, fit, and professional looking with a black pin-striped suit.

"The possibility of him being involved in this is all low, but he is worth checking out." Zoey paused, probably pulling something up as she talked to him. "From what I have, his nose is clean. No history of anything remarkable. Just a typical nine-to-fiver."

"With a penchant for high-powered sniper rifles?" he asked.

His phone beeped with another call. Glancing down, he saw a restricted number pop up on his screen. "I got to go. I'll let you know what I find."

"Roger that," Zoey said, hanging up without another word.

He liked that about her; she definitely didn't waste a whole lot of time when it came to chitchat.

"Hello?" he asked, pressing on the other call.

"Come to your door." Kate sounded strange, rigid.

He walked out of his bedroom. The place was a mess, with clothes hanging over the back of a chair and work shoes pitched exactly where people had taken them off and flopped down in their chairs.

As he walked toward the door, the ranch dog, Chuck, bounded out from the back bedroom. "Oh hey, buddy." He gave the chocolate Lab a scratch behind the ear and was answered with a quick nibble of the fingers and a lick. "I see how it is, you snot. You don't care about getting up with me in the morning, but as soon as a hot woman shows up at the door, you're racing to go."

Chuck answered with a lolling tongue and a wag of the tail as he trotted to the door. There was a tap on the door and the dog started to prance from one foot to the other as he worked out excited circles.

"Yep, all you care about is the chicks." Troy laughed as he made the dog move back so he could open the door. "It's okay, bud. I feel exactly the same way."

Kate was standing on the front porch, her back to the door as if only moments before she hadn't knocked to remind him that she was still there. Was she as nervous to be here as he was to see her?

"I would ask how you found me, but I think I know," he said.

She turned around and he expected to see her smiling at him, or even maybe mad, but he didn't expect what he saw... Kate had been crying. Her eyes were red and bloodshot, and she looked like she hadn't slept since the last time he had seen her.

"What in the hell is going on? Are you okay?" His words came out in a rush.

She nodded. "I'm fine." Her voice was raspy and hoarse from what he assumed was a night spent crying. "I got some bad news a couple hours ago."

"Babe, what? What happened?"

"It's my father..." she said, the words sounding more like sobs than real words.

He walked over to her and wrapped his arms around her, holding her against his chest. Her body rattled with sobs as she let herself escape into his embrace.

"What happened?"

Her words were muffled, but he understood them just as well as if she had shouted them. "Someone... shot him. In his office. They murdered him."

Chapter Eleven

At her mother's house a little while later, Kate learned her mom had been calling every relative in her phone since she had found out about her husband's death. She told Kate she wanted to notify as many people as possible and to ask them not to speak to reporters or officials. But Kate knew the real reason for the busywork. It was so her mother could concentrate on a task instead of the pain that they were all feeling.

Her sister was flying in from Denver on the afternoon flight and would be touching down tonight. She hadn't taken the news well.

But then she couldn't blame her. She had gone to pieces when she learned about her father's death. She shouldn't have gone straight over to Troy's residence, but it was the only thing she could think to do after she had gotten over her initial shock.

She glanced over at Troy, who was busy making hot tea in the kitchen, complete with a tray of cream, sugar and lemon. She didn't even know her mother had lemons in the house and yet Troy had somehow found them.

Troy really was remarkable. He was unexpectedly chivalrous, kind and surprisingly open for a man who declared himself antisocial. If she hadn't known better or he hadn't told her, she would have actually thought he almost liked the general public. If she told him that, he would have some kind of snarky rebuttal.

He made his way out of the kitchen to them carrying the tray of tea and set it on her mother's marble end table. Her mother barely noticed.

In the past, her mother had been overly protective of the Carrara marble table specially imported from Italy. It was one of her most prized possessions, and the fact that she didn't seem to care now that someone put something on it that could potentially mar the gleaming white-and-gray surface was more shocking to Kate than her mother's sudden manic need to reach out to family.

"Troy, why don't you set that over here," she said, pointing toward the alabaster dining table in the adjoining room.

He picked up the tea set and followed her out of the living room, like an obedient member of her mother's household staff.

"Are you sure she's going to be okay?" Troy asked, motioning toward her mother.

In all honesty, she wasn't sure. Her mother had been through a lot with her breast cancer and forced retirement from the company, but she hadn't had to face that alone. Everyone in the family had surrounded her with love and understanding. Kate had even made a point of driving her mom to each and every one of her chemo appointments. Her mother had never really thanked her, but she hadn't expected her to.

Once her mother's cancer had gone into remission, Kate had assumed things would go back to normal and she would go back to work for the company, but she had become a woman who luncheoned.

It was as if her mother had decided after her illness that she was no longer going to devote herself and her life to the family business. She could only imagine how poorly that would have gone with her father had her mother made her intentions clear. Instead of telling him anything, so far as Kate knew, her parents had never addressed her mother's personality shift. It was as if her father had accepted it as part of the healing process.

Though he had seemed unaffected by it, when she and her sister had both declined his offer of going to work for ConFlux, he had blown up at both of them. So much so that her sister had stopped coming for Christmas and all major holidays for two years. It wasn't until she had gotten pregnant that she had finally come back to the family's fold.

No doubt, Julie was feeling terrible now, thinking about all the time she had lost with their father because their life plans didn't align.

And now who was going to take over the company? Her mother was the largest stockholder after her father's death. This would put her mother right back into the middle of the company's affairs.

"Here, have some tea. You need to focus on staying hydrated," Troy said.

It was quite the contradiction, this burly man handing her tea while he uttered the least manly thing he probably could have said.

The thought made her smile, the first real one all day. That he could bring her cheer, even in a moment like this, had to mean something, didn't it?

Her mother finally hung up the phone and walked into the dining room. She was wearing a white Dior suit with a blue Armani shirt beneath. It all complemented her platinum gray hair perfectly and Kate doubted it was by accident.

Perhaps her mother was already coming to accept that she was going to be a key player in ConFlux and had already started to dress the part.

"Your aunt Coraline is going to be flying in on Friday. Of course, she's going to bring her little dog, and if he pees on my floor again, she's going to have to attend another funeral service," her mother fumed.

"Oh my goodness, Mom, don't say things like that," Kate said, peering over at Troy to see if he had heard her mother's rant.

He was pretending to fuss with the teapot, lifting the lid and peering inside like he wasn't the one who had made the tea.

She appreciated his attempt to appear unobtrusive and spatially unaware.

"You know I was only kidding around. If we don't joke around about these things, then they tend to get so *emotional*. The last thing your father would have wanted would have been for us to shut down, get morose and stop working." Her mother's voice was high-pitched, almost frantic, as if she were fighting a battle for control, and she waved Kate off, as if she was nothing more than a nuisance. "Right now, the best thing we can do to honor Solomon and his legacy is to push through the heartache."

Troy poured her a cup of tea with sugar and lemon and handed it to her. "Here, that should make you feel better."

Her mother looked at Troy, seeming to notice his presence for the first time since they had arrived. "Who are you?"

"Mother, I already introduced you—"

"It's fine." Troy stiffened and stood up tall and straight as he extended his hand. "Mrs. Scot, I'm Troy Spade, a friend of your daughter's."

"A friend?" her mother asked, giving her a sidelong glance to gauge exactly the depth of her and Troy's *friendship* as she shook his proffered hand.

"Yes, Mom, my work colleague. He is helping me on a case and was there when I received the news." She couldn't help but fib slightly; if she didn't, her mother would press for answers she didn't want to give.

"I appreciate your helping Katherine during this difficult time." Her mother flashed her practiced corporate-wife smile. "I need to call the mortuary…and the medical examiner's office to see when they will release the body. If you'd excuse me," she said, looking to Troy and giving him an aloof nod before she made her way back to her cell phone in the living room.

"I'm so sorry about her. She can be insufferable at the best of times, and I swear, when she's stressed out, it gets a million times worse."

"Don't worry. She just lost her husband to violence. She has a right to be upset, even insufferable."

He took her hand and led her out of the dining room and into the kitchen, closing the door behind them. There was the ting of the doorbell and her mother's voice as more flowers were delivered. This was going to go on all day, this seesaw between incessant action and torturous malaise. Kate needed quiet. She needed to be alone. She needed to process all this. Instead, she was a slave to her mother's wishes.

"What happened to your dad?" Troy asked. "I want to help you get through this. I do. But I have to understand what exactly is going on before I can. What have you learned?"

Just the thought of what had happened to her father made a cold sweat rise on her skin. He didn't deserve to die the way he had, and though she knew she needed to tell Troy what had happened, she couldn't find the words. He'd let her remain silent on the ride here, not asking questions. She hadn't been able to manage a word or she would have sobbed uncontrollably. She barely had a grip.

"Take your time. I'm not going anywhere." Troy wrapped his arm around her shoulders, pulling her nearer to him.

She loved the feel of him against her, and the warmth that radiated from him. Just his touch helped her relax and feel ready to open up, not that talking about the attack was ever going to be easy. She was still coming to terms with what her mother had told her had happened. "We don't know everything yet, but according to Mom, he was found in his office this morning at 7:00 a.m. He had been shot once in the head and twice in the chest, and the initial responders noted stippling consistent with the shooter standing at a close range to the victim when they fired the gun." She swallowed and blinked fast, getting her emotions under control.

"So, then we know for sure that there was no sniper involved?" Troy asked. "It was up close and personal."

"The windows' glass was intact, so there is definitely nothing that came from outside his office. I got this from the officers on scene. The ones who called." Thinking about the logistics made some of the other things she was feeling dissipate. Maybe that was the best way to handle this. Keep emotions out of the way, be linear, be logical, and she would get through this. Better yet, they could find whoever it was who was responsible for her father's death. As for what would come of the killer after she found them, only time would tell.

"Do you know who is handling the investigation?" Troy asked.

"Due to the fact that he's my father, the FBI has offered to devote resources to the local law enforcement's investigation. So far, they haven't taken them up on the offer. I don't know why, but I'm sure the detectives will work their tails off to get to the bottom of this." She'd push on the FBI help if need be, but she didn't want to muddy the waters for the officers handling it right now. She knew local law could get their hackles raised if higher-ups got involved. It just slowed everything down.

Troy nodded. "Whatever you need from STEALTH, you got it. And Zoey can work on it from our tech angles. We can see what she can pull."

As she thought about Troy's offer, she realized all of the sacrifices he must've been making for her; sacrifices she hadn't totally thought about, until now. "I know you have a job to do, Troy. You don't have to stand beside me through all of this. If you need to go and do your job, that should come first." And his job had been investigating things at her father's company, so it might lead to his killer as well.

He squeezed her tighter, and, reaching up with his other hand, he caressed her cheek with his thumb. The simple action was unexpectedly sensual, and it made her weaken beneath him. Being touched like that by him made her realize how long it had been since someone had truly wanted to touch her.

"Babe, your father paid me to do a job. As far as I'm

concerned, this all falls under that umbrella. If anything, I feel like…" He paused and his arm dropped from her. "Well, this all could be my fault. Maybe I was so focused on keeping you safe, when I should have been thinking about the bigger picture. I should've sent Mike over to watch your family."

She shook her head, vehemently. "This isn't your fault. How could you possibly know that there was somebody out there who wanted to hurt my father?"

"I had a feeling that this thing with the sniper wasn't over. I should have listened to my gut. Well, I guess I did… I knew something was wrong. That was how I found myself at your doorstep. But I think my entire focus was *off.* I let my personal feelings for you—and, yes, I admit it, I have feelings where you are concerned—cloud my perspective, and it may well have ended up costing your father his life."

She could hear the pain and anger and rage in his words, all of which were too big for what had happened to him in the situation. He must have been thinking about his ex, Tiffany, the one who had been killed by the EFP.

He was hurting just as she was. And though time was supposed to heal, she held no doubts that in this case all time was doing was making his pain more acute.

"There's plenty of security at the ConFlux building. My father had a well-trained security team watching out for him. Again, this isn't on you. My dad must've gotten into something he shouldn't have." Her chest threatened to collapse in on itself as she heard the truth of her words. "If anyone is to blame here, it's me. I actually listened to my dad and slow-walked the sniper case. I mean, I wasn't pushing hard on it like I usually do. I allowed him to affect my work. I screwed up. He ended up dead."

Troy sighed. "None of our hands are clean. All we can do now is to stop this from happening again. Only the murderer—and the person, people or group behind them—has any idea who else they are going to kill."

Chapter Twelve

Troy made his way out to his car and got inside. As soon as the door clicked shut, he dialed Zoey.

It didn't even have time to ring. "I heard about Solomon." Zoey sounded breathless. "I haven't managed to pull a lot of details—they're not releasing much to the public yet—but I'm sure you're thinking the same thing I am."

Troy gripped the steering wheel and put his head down against the cool leather. He gazed toward the colonial-style home that belonged to Kate's family. She was still inside, talking to her mother, no doubt bickering about some sort of family matter. It was no wonder Kate had become the strong woman she was after having to grow up with a mother who, though well raised and well-heeled, had the tongue of a cobra. Even making allowances for her grief, the woman was singularly unpleasant. "And what exactly is that?"

"I think you walked into a snake pit."

He opened his mouth to speak, but stopped. There was no humanly way possible that Zoey could have known what he had been thinking, and yet the coincidence was unsettling. "More than you know."

"Did you have time to get anywhere with the list of

names I got you?" she asked, pushing forward without waiting for him to respond.

"Not yet."

"I can't blame you. Sounds like you have your hands full. Want me to pull some other members of your team in on this, give you some time to handle things with Kate?" Zoey asked, but he was aware that what she was really doing was trying to elicit a response that would tell her where his and Kate's relationship was currently standing.

"There's nothing beyond friendship between us."

"That's not what I said," Zoey countered.

"Yeah, but you and I both know what you meant. If you want to know if we've slept together, we haven't. We won't. We both have jobs to do."

Zoey laughed. "So, you have thought about it. Roger that."

He could feel the warmth rise in his cheeks. He didn't enjoy the sensation. "Why are you breaking my balls about this? About her? Right now, let's just focus on our next step. I don't need you stirring the pot."

Zoey laughed again, the sound full of mirth. "Got it. You're right," she said.

"I don't think I'll need any more team members. Mike is still working on this, right?"

"Yes, but I can call in your sister. She would be happy to come in and assist."

"Elle? Do you think bringing in K-9s would really be beneficial?"

"They are trained to track. Maybe they can pull something that the local LEOs are missing. A scent from the sniper, Solomon's shooter."

She had to have known she was grasping for straws on that one.

"No," Troy said, shaking his head though he was alone. He gripped the wheel tighter as he stared at the vehicle's make emblazoned on the steering wheel. "Why don't you see if you can get into the ConFlux security cameras and try to find who all came and went from the building in the last twenty-four hours before Solomon was found."

"You can't expect that I haven't already tried. Right now, I'm hitting brick walls," Zoey grumbled. "Well, figurative ones, at least. These guys, they had tight physical and cyber security. Which is good. The head of their IT department, Alexi Siegal, must have thought we were going to get attacked from all fronts."

That made it sound like his job in getting into the facility and finding weak spots was going to get a whole hell of a lot harder. If Zoey couldn't get in, he doubted he would be able to.

Maybe that was why there had been a sniper on the roof—as an even more extreme level of security. What if it had been part of Solomon's plan? Had he set them up to get shot at? No. He wouldn't do that. Not in front of the office where his own daughter worked. Right?

He wished he had a few answers instead of all these damn questions.

There was a tap on the passenger's-side window. "Got to go," he said to Zoey. He clicked the phone off in true Zoey Martin style.

Kate was standing there, so he unlocked the door and she got in. "I can't stand another minute in that house with my mother. It's hard enough dealing with Dad's death. Do you know she fired her maid and her gardener today? I'm not kidding—she is too much. This may actually have tipped her over the edge."

He wouldn't have blamed the woman if it had. "Does Deborah have someone she can talk to, a therapist or something?"

"I am sure she does, but if she doesn't, she definitely has access to just about anyone she would want to get." She rubbed her fingers together as she rolled her eyes.

"Do you hate your parents because they are affluent?" he asked, but as he spoke, he realized his mistake. "I'm sorry. I shouldn't ask something like that about your parents, at least not today."

"No, don't filter yourself. Ask me anything. I'll answer. Justice for my father comes first."

"I know this is a strange ask, but do you think you could get me and Zoey into ConFlux?"

"Probably. But why do you want in there—didn't my father give you access when he hired STEALTH?" She paused.

"They wanted to see if we could hack into the system, not for us to sign on." He chuckled.

She nodded. "Unfortunately, I don't think I'm gonna be able to get you into my father's office, not with the investigation in full swing."

He reached over and took her hand, giving it a squeeze. "We have a lead on the sniper's possible identity. Though the sniper might not be related to your father's death, if I can get into the building, then maybe I can look a little bit deeper. I just need to poke around a bit."

Kate lifted their entwined hands and pressed her lips to the back of his, giving him a light kiss. "Whatever you need, it's yours."

He was sure she didn't mean it to sound as torrid as it had, but he still found himself getting aroused. There were many things he would like to do to her, but none of those things were a good idea. And yet he couldn't stop his gaze from moving slightly lower than it should have. She did have a nice body. He would have loved to feel her nipple against his tongue. He felt himself grow stiffer.

He cleared his throat, in a feeble attempt to rid his body of the threatening sensation of lust. This wasn't the right time. Her father had just died, and he needed to focus on finding the man's killer and comforting his daughter. He started the car and began driving toward downtown Missoula.

When they arrived, they encountered an entire squadron of patrol cars. The vehicles were congregated around the ConFlux building, a black coroner's van among them. It was backed in to a spot out front, its back tires on the sidewalk, as if it just waited to be filled.

He made sure to park away from too many prying eyes, but close enough that they could make a quick exit if they needed.

Though he knew he had to let go of Kate's hand, he hated it. Out there on the street, with all the police officers running around, they couldn't risk being seen as anything other than work colleagues. When he moved his hand from hers, her face said it all. She was crestfallen. He mouthed *I'm sorry*, but as he did, she looked away.

As they made their way toward the front doors, they opened. Four men walked through them, carrying a black body bag. "Stop," he said, taking Kate's arm and turning her away from the sight.

Something like that, watching her father loaded into the coroner's van, was likely to haunt her for the rest of her life. She didn't need this kind of trauma, not today or ever. Her job would bring her enough; she didn't need it in her personal life as well.

"Troy," she said, looking into his eyes. "It's okay. I'm going to be okay. You have to remember, I'm not like others. I've been trained to handle situations like these, to dissociate and embrace the suck sometimes."

"Just because you have the ability doesn't mean that your body always listens." He knew.

"I know you are trying to protect me, babe. But this isn't something you are going to be able to keep from hurting me. This is all painful—it's going to be no matter what you do or don't do. All I need you to do is stand by my side, help me get through these days and work with me to find and bring down whoever pulled the trigger."

He wanted to hold her and tell her that whatever she asked of him, he would deliver. Instead, he merely nodded.

She led the way to the entrance, watching as the men latched the van's doors closed and the driver sat down behind the wheel. The driver was talking to an officer as Troy and Kate walked into the office building through the vast marble-laced lobby, complete with a Greco-style water fountain at its heart. People Troy assumed were staffers were intermingled with police officers, asking and answering questions. No one seemed to notice them as they walked by the gurgling fountain and toward the metal detectors that led to the interior of the building.

There was a large desk in the reception area, and behind it were a man and a woman who looked as though they were the receptionists. The man looked up from his computer screen as they approached. The phone started to ring, and the woman beside him answered.

"Good morning. How can I help you?" he asked, cutting them off from making their way over to the metal detectors and bypassing the checkpoint.

"Hi, I'm Kate Scot, Solomon's daughter."

The man blanched. "Oh, oh… Ms. Scot, I'm so very sorry to hear about your father. We've all been so upset after we learned what happened. They just…" He motioned after the van as it pulled away.

To think, her mother had already been pressing the issue about getting the medical examiner to release the body when they hadn't even gotten to see the man yet. Deborah was going to be in for a long emotionally rutted road.

"Do you mind if we go up?"

"It's… He's… You can, but…" The man stammered, clearly trying to come up with what he should or shouldn't do. But having no frame of reference, he finally sighed. "There are officers still doing their work in your father's office, but I'm sure there is probably someone up there you can speak to…someone who can help you."

"How about the ConFlux employees? Is everyone still on the clock, or did they all get sent home?"

"Um, they sent all nonessential personnel home today." He pressed a button. "You can step on through the detectors."

Kate shook her head. She reached down, took hold of her lanyard and pulled her badge from beneath her shirt, showing the man. "If you don't mind, we'll go around."

The man's face went impossibly paler. It was a wonder the man was still able to form words. The receptionist nodded, hitting another button that opened the gate to the left of the metal detector.

Or maybe he isn't able to form words after all.

He could hardly blame the man; there were times when Kate had exactly the same effect on him; though, for entirely different reasons.

Kate's loafers clicked on the floor as she led them around security and they made their way to the elevator. They rode it up to the top, neither speaking for the short trip. The doors opened with a ping.

Standing in the hallway of the fourth floor was a group of city police officers. One of the men, wearing a suit, looked over at them. He sent Kate an apologetic stare as he meandered his way over toward them.

"If you don't mind, I'm going to take a peek around while you talk to this guy. Cool?" Troy asked.

She nodded, and under her breath, she said, "The detective is a friend of mine, but he's a talker. Take your time. I'll get more details about the murder."

Troy hurried away, walking down the hall in the opposite direction of the pack of officers and the detective and moving toward the restroom sign. Behind him, Kate was greeting her friend. Troy would have preferred to have had Kate with him so she could tell him about the different offices and their purposes, but on the other hand, the freedom allowed him to poke around on his own.

He slipped into the first empty office he came to on

his right, checking over his shoulder and making sure that no one was paying him any mind. He closed the door behind himself.

The room was small, cramped and full of paperwork. It looked like the kind of office that belonged to an intern, some poor unpaid schlep who was at the bottom of the proverbial hill. When he'd started out in contracting, he had been the poor schlep…the guy who had to take the nighttime runs, when the chances of taking a bullet were even higher than they were during the day.

He had been forced to earn his place on every one of the teams he'd ever been a part of. But when it came to him and Kate, they were just an instant team fueled by a common goal and mutual anger.

He flipped through a few of the papers, but most looked like they were interoffice memos, and the only thing that struck him as odd was that a company like ConFlux would still use such an antiquated system for informing their employees about upcoming events. Maybe it was just that some old habits died hard…or, like in many branches of the federal government, the best kinds of security were the ones that couldn't be hacked. But, in situations like these, where security was stretched thin due to the unusual events, what couldn't be hacked could definitely be stolen.

He glanced around the room; there wasn't a camera in sight. Taking out his phone, he dialed Zoey. She answered even though he hadn't heard it ring. "Did you get in to ConFlux?"

"Yep, I'm in an intern's office now."

"Is there a computer available?" Zoey asked, a falsetto to her voice he didn't think he'd heard from her before.

He walked to the other side of the desk and sat down

in the cheap, squeaky rolling chair. He clicked on the screen. "I'm there."

"Great. Let's hope we have a Bob here."

"What in the hell is a Bob?"

"In every work environment, there is always that one employee, 'Bob,' who is a bit unaware when it comes to the importance of security, especially cybersecurity—maybe it's with their personal information or the company's. Doesn't matter. This person is the one who clicks on the phishing email and lets in the hackers. All we need is to find the Bob and we can crack the company."

He still wasn't sure he totally understood what she meant, but as he looked around the cluttered room, if there was a "Bob," Troy was probably in his office. Sometimes it paid to be lucky. Though, they didn't put CEOs' offices between a bathroom and an elevator.

The computer was typical, the usual PC that could be found in just about any office. There was a flashing cursor on the screen, waiting for him to input the key code in order to get to the home screen. "Zoey, I have a problem. Need a PIN. Any ideas?"

"Whose office are you in?"

He hadn't seen a name on the door and there were a variety of names all over the memos he had flipped through. Glancing at the walls, he saw there was a picture of a young family, a husband with a wife who was holding an infant. "Whoever this office belongs to, they likely just had a baby."

"Good," Zoey said. He could hear the click of keys in the background. "Anything else that can help pin this person down?"

Beside the computer screen was a mug. It read Daryl.

"I think his first name is Daryl." He chuckled. That was one name that was entirely too close to Bob.

There was a burst of keystrokes. "Got it," Zoey said. She paused for a few seconds. "Try 0127."

He typed in the pin number and he was met with the home screen. "Holy crap, Zoey. That worked. How in the hell did you know that?"

"I could lie and play it cool by telling you it was a lucky guess, or I'm that good, but that's hardly it… That is the birthday of his son."

She was damn good at her job. It was no wonder that she and her family had started their own contracting company, one with deep ties throughout the US and several foreign governments.

"Now, I want you to go into his email. Give me his address."

He clicked on a few keys, taking him to the man's inbox, and he read off the email address associated with the account.

"Good," Zoey said, typing. "In a few minutes, I'm going to send an email. It will have the subject line *Bagels for today's meeting*. Click on it. Download. And I will handle the rest." The phone line went dead.

That was one thing he was never going to get used to with Zoey, no matter how many times he was on the receiving end, and as unsettling as her hanging up was, he found he liked it. No fluff.

He filtered through some of the other emails on the man's computer, but most appeared to be as unimportant as the memos he had first seen. The only one that looked at all interesting was from a woman at the company. Mr. New Baby must have been unsatisfied at home.

His dislike for the intern grew, and the tiny ping of guilt for hijacking the man's computer he had felt deep—make that *very* deep—in his core disappeared. If anyone found out the company had been hacked, they might eventually find out whose computer and account had been the weak link and the man would be fired.

At least, here was hoping.

A new email pinged—bagels. He clicked on it and did as Zoey had instructed. He half expected the computer to flicker as he downloaded her file, but nothing happened aside from a pop-up that announced that his document had been successfully downloaded.

No wonder there was a Bob problem; it was entirely too easy for someone who wasn't aware of danger to download malicious code or malware. This, this right here was the reason banks and insurance companies were forced to pay billions in IT security each and every year.

There was a knock on the door and he flipped off the computer. Job done. This was in Zoey's hands now.

He cleared his throat. "Yeah?"

"You in there?" Kate asked. "Can I come in?"

He stood up and walked over to the door, opening it. She was standing with the detective, and from the look on her face, she was deeply uncomfortable. The man must have been asking questions.

"Thank you for letting me get into my office. I just needed to get a couple files sent out to clients today. You know, no rest for the weary," he said, careful to cover up any kind of tells that would give away his lie. "Besides, I know Mr. Scot wouldn't have wanted work to come to a halt—and deadlines missed—all because of him. He was a good man." He gave a respectful nod of the head, hoping that the detective would buy it.

He walked out of the office, carefully closing the door behind him as he looked up. The detective was giving him a once-over, analyzing his body language. Thankfully, the detective didn't know he was sizing up a man who had spent his entire life learning how to avoid detection, and when detected, learning how to get out of trouble.

"If our department was as dedicated as you, we would always stop crimes before they were even committed. Good friend you got there, Agent Scot." He gave Kate a pat to the shoulder, solidifying the physical bond as well as trying to reassure her. "I got to get back in there, but I hope you know...you need anything, got any more questions... I'll give you what I can."

Kate nodded and smiled at the detective, but Troy could sense the fire behind her smile. It made him wonder if the detective could as well.

"I'll walk you guys out," the detective said, making it clear that they were no longer welcome.

Chapter Thirteen

Fury flooded Kate as Troy drove her to her home. She hadn't been this angry since she had gotten a flat tire on the way to her final interview for the FBI.

She had thought the sacrifices had been worth it right up until now. How dare a detective think he could pull rank on her and force her out of an investigation that involved her family? Sure, she didn't have jurisdiction, but there was a damn thing called professional courtesy.

He should have thrown her a solid, just as she had done by not involving the FBI from the get-go. The last time they had worked together, she had broken a murder case for him, pulling strings in order to get him DNA samples in record time so that he could file official charges before the suspect disappeared. While he had thanked her, he had never repaid her.

That was the last time she helped him out.

She sighed.

That wasn't true. She allowed herself to be furious, but in her heart of hearts, she knew that if he came to her with another case that she could help in bringing down a bad guy, she wouldn't pass up the chance. She loved to make the guilty pay. It was what kept her going.

Troy parked his car in front of her house, not hiding. There was nothing wrong with her having a male colleague over during the day. And if someone wanted to judge, let them judge lest they be judged. She was over it.

"You know you don't have to talk to me. I can tell you are upset. I just hope you aren't upset with me. I was trying to make the best of a bad situation back there, and—"

She glanced over at him, shocked. "What? You think I'm mad at you?"

"I should have been in and out of that office before your detective friend even noticed. I compromised you. That wasn't my intention. I was just working on the fly." As he spoke, his words came faster and faster as his anxiety seemed to rise.

Kate softened as he tried to recover from his perceived misstep, one that she hadn't even noticed. He was so adorable flustered.

"I'm not mad about anything you did. Actually, the detective didn't even notice, and even when I went to get you, he didn't seem to think anything. You played that off perfectly. I was impressed."

He gave her a confused look. "So, why are you so upset?"

She rolled her neck, dispelling some of the stress at the admission she was going to have to make. "I was annoyed that we were dismissed. I didn't manage to pull anything about what happened to my father. They wouldn't let me into his office, or even close enough to catch a glimpse of the crime scene…" She paused. "Why?"

Troy shrugged. "I think there are a lot of odd things happening… Too many for them to be just random."

She was more than aware of that fact. "Who are the people on Zoey's list—the sniper suspects?"

"One's a guy named Sal Baker, then one Chris Michaels, and the other is...*stupid*. I told her that she couldn't have been right." He waved off his avoidance of telling her the other name like it was of no concern.

"You can't do that to me," Kate argued. "Either tell me the whole truth or nothing." Her voice was shriller than she had intended, but she didn't apologize. Not today, not with everything spiraling the drain. "Same team."

He frowned. "You... I—I'm sorry. I'm not trying to upset you. It's not like that. I'm all about us working efficiently together. I just don't think Agent Peahen would ever do anything as stupid as taking potshots off a building at private contractors or you. He's not the type."

"Are you kidding me?" She shook her head slightly, like the little motion would help her to make sense of what he had said. If only it would have worked.

"I told you..." Troy said, shrugging.

Peahen? Peahen a sniper? No.

There was no damn way. He was capable of many things. And he was definitely the kind of man who wouldn't have qualms about acting all tough, but he was not the kind who would pull the trigger when it wasn't in the line of duty.

"Yeah, you're right. He's not our guy." She chuckled at the craziness of the idea. "Besides, he said he's been in Salt Lake City."

"At the time of the shooting?"

"I don't know." She was suddenly exhausted. "When Peahen showed up on my doorstep the other night, he just said he had been passing through from SLC. I assumed he had been down there doing something with the regional headquarters. I doubt he would try to kill somebody and then turn around and head out to see me."

"You're preaching to the choir."

"And, plus… He has no motivation," she continued, trying to convince herself that she had to be right.

"Again…" Troy said, as he stepped out of the car and walked around, opening her door for her. He held out his hand for her to take as she stepped out. "I think we should look deeper into the Sal guy. See what kind of motivation he would have for taking out the surveillance team hired to look into the company. You don't know him, do you?"

"Sal?" she asked, grabbing her keys out of her purse as they walked up to the front door, and she let them in. "I only know the higher-ups from the company, the kinds my father would take out on golf trips around the country when they tried to work government officials in order to get new and greater manufacturing contracts."

"Sal wasn't one of them?"

She shrugged. "I don't think so. I am only invited to the holiday parties and a few of the bigger luncheons when he wants—wanted—to show me off like a prize pony to his cronies." The door clicked shut as they made their way inside.

She put her purse on the table next to the door, slipped off her suit jacket and hung it on the closet's doorknob. There was a little dribble of coffee just above her left breast that she hadn't noticed before. She would have to change before they went back out. "If Sal is in the upper crust, then he was new to the organization."

"Yes. Finally." Troy sounded excited as he walked and sat down in the chair in front of the television. He took out his phone and started pressing buttons.

"What are you so excited about?"

"He's new. He has a weapon like the one the sniper used. Maybe he got himself hired at the company just to do some damage or spying. The Russians love that approach." Troy smiled.

"Don't you think that is a little too Cold War style?" she asked.

"You can't tell me that it's not a valid possibility. These kinds of companies have information leaks all the time. It's why I have a job. And...more often than not, there is a foreign government behind the infiltration—be it in person or through technology. Thinking about technology..." He sent her a sly smile.

"You gonna tap Sal's phone lines? See if you can catch him speaking Russian?" she asked with a sarcastic laugh.

"Hey, don't judge. Your friends in the CIA used to do that kind of thing all the time... Though, admittedly, the tech has gotten a bit better since the 1980s. I don't think they try to tap as many landlines these days."

"Which makes them just about safer than any form of technology," she countered. "At least with phone lines only the person tapping in can hear what is being said. With cell phones...the possibilities of seeing, reading, hearing and looking into search histories are nearly endless."

He laughed. "If I look around, am I also going to find a telegraph? A dictionary for Morse code?"

"Don't judge," she echoed, feeling a little bit embarrassed. "There is nothing wrong with knowing an antiquated form of communication like Morse code. You never quite know when something like that can come in handy."

"Do you actually know Morse code?" He gave her a skeptical look.

"I do." She couldn't help the pride that flickered through her voice.

"Me too," he said, laughing. "I thought I was the only nerd out there who loved that kind of thing. In my free time, which I admit I haven't had a whole lot of lately, I also used to love to do origami. I did it with my mom before she died. It was kind of our thing. I haven't made anything since the day she died."

"Oh my goodness, that is so sweet. What was your favorite thing to make?"

"I always liked the cranes," he said, a nostalgic smile on his lips. "She would tell me a story about how they were the symbol for hope, happiness and healing. And if a person folded one thousand cranes, whatever he wished for most would come true."

"What would you wish for, right now?" For a split second, she hoped he would tell her that what he most wished for was her, but then she brushed away the naive hope.

There was a heavy silence as he pursed his lips. Finally, he stood up.

Is he going to walk over to me? she thought.

Her heart slammed against her ribs and her palms instantly started to sweat as he drew nearer. Yet, instead of stepping in front of her, he walked past her and toward the kitchen. The only things he left for her were the thin scent of his cologne and the cool breeze in his wake.

She was so stupid. Hope had a hell of a way of jabbing a person in the gut.

From the kitchen, she could make out the sounds of him opening a cupboard, then the running of the faucet. He came back bearing two glasses of water. "Here." He offered her a glass, and as she took it, she was careful to avoid his fingers.

If she touched him, she would lose what little control she had over her emotions—the least favorite of them being rejection. She was already on a razor's edge after her father's death, then being pushed out of the investigation.

She should have never let her guard down when it came to him. In her current state, she saw heartache around every corner, and she set herself up for it by being way too needy right now.

They were nowhere near a relationship. They'd been thrown together on this case, and one thing after another had led to heightened emotions.

Though she had promised him that he could trust her, she had never made him promise the same when it came to her.

Then again, she was being silly. They were just feeling each other out before becoming overly invested. If anything, it was good that he had rebuffed her coy advance now. In the end, it was going to save her heartache.

And who had time for a relationship anyway?

She certainly didn't. Not with her father's death. Not with the investigation. Not with her sister coming into town and all the things that would happen as soon as the medical examiner released her father's body to the family. Her mom could really use her help handling all the details, even if her mother acted like an unstoppable and unwavering freight train. All of that activity was going to catch up with her eventually, and when it did, she was going to come to the end of her tracks, teeter over the edge of exhaustion and fall into the canyon of grief.

Kate drained the glass of water in one long swig, careful not to catch Troy's gaze as he stood beside her. As she finished, he held out his hand, motioning to take her empty glass.

"Thanks," she said, handing it over.

"Do you need some more? Hungry?"

She hadn't eaten yet today, but food was the last thing on her mind. Even if there had been a full spread sitting in front of her, she wasn't sure she would have eaten a single bite. "Unless you have a bucket of Red Vines, I'm good." She tried to smile, but it felt stale and flat.

"I can whip you up some eggs at the very least, if you'd like." He motioned toward the kitchen.

"Nah. Really, I'm okay."

"You sure? All of a sudden, you seem *off.* Are you tired?"

She nodded. Yes, she was tired. And confused. And wanting something from him she wasn't sure he was offering. "So, what do you have on Chris and Sal? Anything?"

He took a drink of water and set the glasses down on the coffee table. "Is it okay if I put these here?" he asked, motioning toward them.

"I'm not my mother. My house is furnished by IKEA, not an interior decorator. My most expensive piece probably cost like twenty bucks," she said.

"Yeah, right. This place is great." Unexpectedly,

he walked over to her and took both of her hands. He looked her in the eyes. "I know what you are doing—I know you are trying to be cool. I know what you were hoping I would say about my wish. I didn't mean to hurt you."

Though she could hear his words and they were making their way into her logical brain, all they did was make the pain and embarrassment she was feeling worse. "I don't know what you mean," she said, scrunching her face in forced denial.

"You can lie to a lot of people and probably get away with it, but that will never be the way it is with me. I've been trained to read this kind of thing, remember?" He let go of her left hand as he reached up and cupped her face.

She nodded, but resisted the urge to lean into his touch even though he was being sweet and sensitive— exactly the kind of man she fantasized about.

"I have an idea of what you are going through right now. And though you are handling it all with a level of strength, grace and aplomb that even the royals would be envious of, you are hurting. I can see it on you."

Her chest tightened and tears started to well in her eyes. No. He couldn't bring her to her knees like this— she was stronger than this—he couldn't see her cry.

"It's okay to feel, Kate. You're home. You are safe with me. You can be your real self. You don't have to put on a front for me. I am not going to judge you for processing what you are going through—it's not healthy to push that crap down and not deal with it. I know." He ran his thumb over her cheek. "Let out your grief. Let's get through this together. I'm your friend. Whatever you say, whatever you need, I'm yours to open up to."

If only he had stopped at *I'm yours*.

A lump rose in her throat and she tried to swallow it back, but it was futile. He leaned in, pressing his forehead to hers as he put his other hand to her face. "Kate, it's okay to cry."

Though she hadn't given it permission, a single tear slipped down her cheek. Maybe it was his kindness, his sweetness or his strength in his candor, but whatever it was, it tore down the barrier of her heart.

Tears flooded her cheeks.

Her father was dead. Her mother was a mess. A fellow agent was possibly on the take. And they were no closer to solving any of it than they were when she had first received the news of the murder.

Murder. The word reverberated through her. Though she had heard it spoken and had spoken of it often, it was as if she was hearing it for the first time. This time the word was *hers*—it was like a pebble being thrown in the lake of her world. There would be ripples of what had happened today throughout every day for the rest of her life.

The only thing she could do to reduce their frequency was to do as Troy said…and to find justice.

At least she wasn't going through this completely alone or with her mother. In the state her family was currently in, she would have to be cool and collected. There was no room for real emotions, only actions.

Troy brushed the tears from her cheeks as others followed quickly behind. Letting go of her face, he wrapped her in his arms and pulled her close. Her sobs rattled against him, but instead of loosening his grip, he held her only tighter—like he was her anchor in this tempest.

She loved him.

As she cried, she thought of Neruda, Sonnet XVII:

I love you as certain dark things are to be loved,

in secret, between the shadow and the soul...

I love you without knowing how, or when, or from where.

I love you straightforwardly, without complexities or pride;

so I love you because I know no other way than this...

Though she was feeling as low as she ever had, the high of the possibility of someday loving him openly— even as only a dear friend—helped to calm the storm inside of her.

"You are going to get through this. We can do it together," he whispered into her hair.

She nodded, sniffing as she tried to keep from getting his shirt more wet than absolutely necessary from her tears. The man didn't deserve to become her tissue.

"Thank you, Troy." She laid her head against his chest and listened to the beat of his heart. The sound worked as a calming drum, stanching her tears.

She would grieve. But today, she wouldn't have to go through this pain alone; she had love.

Chapter Fourteen

The last woman he had held while crying had been Elle when they had lost their parents. Ever since then, even when breaking up with the few girlfriends he'd had, he had made it out of there before the tears had started to fall. Tears were his weakness, far too *feely*. At least they had been, until now.

He brushed her hair back from her face and rubbed her back. She didn't seem like the type of woman who cried easily, especially around other people, and yet here she was, sobbing her heart out to him. She could open up, be free to express herself, and he was actually glad to be the one holding her while she let go.

Did that mean this was love?

Was what he was feeling something more than it should be? Or was this feeling inside of him toward her exactly right?

He couldn't deny the fact that he wanted more. That he wanted all of her. To see her wake up in the morning. To sit with her while her hair was all messy and she sipped on her first cup of coffee. He would love to have her cold feet press against him in bed at night. And he wanted to know her favorite foods. Her favorite songs. He wanted to know everything about her.

Maybe he was sick or possibly losing his mind. He wasn't like this when it came to the opposite sex. Sure, he liked women. And he liked naked women. And he liked naked women who liked him. But he had always been careful to keep the naked women away from his naked feelings.

And now here she was, fully clothed and edging into the feelings he so carefully tried to conceal. Odd as it was, he felt more naked than if he had been standing there unclothed.

If he opened up to her right now, while they were both emotionally compromised, it would be the equivalent of a drunken late-night phone call. Things would be said that couldn't be taken back in the morning, things that were probably best left for a time when they were both working from a place of fully available and uncompromised emotional facilities—that was, if they were going to be said at all.

She leaned back, and reaching up, she wiped the last bit of wetness from her cheeks with the sleeve of her white button-down shirt. "I'm sorry. I don't know why I…"

"You don't have anything to apologize for," he said, meaning every syllable.

They stood there in silence for a long moment, and he thought about taking her face in his hands and kissing those perfect pink lips. They were the color of Starburst candies and they probably tasted just as sweet.

Late-night phone call.

The words rang in his mind.

Her stomach grumbled. She had told him that she wasn't hungry, unless he had Red Vines—he was more of a Twizzlers man himself.

"Babe, you need to eat something." He hurried into the kitchen and opened up her fridge before she had the chance to argue. She could say she wasn't hungry all she wanted, but her body told him the truth.

There was a small rectangle of cheese, a pint of milk, a carton of eggs, ketchup and mustard and a bunch of bananas. There was the scrape of a chair as she sat down at the bar.

"Seriously, who puts bananas in the fridge?" He laughed, breaking one off and handing it to her before turning back and grabbing the eggs, milk and cheese.

"You are lucky I have anything in there. I'm not much of a chef. But, if you look in the freezer, there are some frozen single-serving pizzas. We could throw a couple of them in the microwave."

He laughed. "I'm here. I'm going to take care of you. And, as luck has it, I'm actually a pretty good chef—not that you have much to work with here, but I bet I can whip us up a mean set of scrambled eggs and toast."

"No soufflés?" she teased, but there was still the rasp of post-cry pulling at her voice.

"Beggars can't be choosers, pumpkin."

She gave a little laugh. "Why do I get the feeling that you calling me *pumpkin* is just about as close to a declarative statement as I'm ever going to get from you?"

"What do you mean *declarative statement*?" he asked, grabbing a bowl and cracking an egg into it.

"You know… That you *like* me." She smiled.

Her eyes were red and puffy from her crying, but the softness from her voice mixed with her sweet grin made her seem even more beautiful than he had realized before. She was remarkably breathtaking in all of her imperfection.

"Do you want me to *like* you?" he asked, suddenly feeling entirely too much like a high schooler than an adult man.

She wrung her hands, playing the high school love interest almost perfectly. She shrugged, the motion weighted with so much meaning that he couldn't figure her out. "It's been a while since I've had a man around my house," she said, looking up at him like she was afraid that he would mind that she had a life before him. "My ex... He took my dog when he moved out. And seriously, I can't go through losing another dog. It broke my heart."

"You only miss the dog?" He smirked. "And you don't have a dog now, right? For me to steal?"

She sent him a look of surprise, then a guilty smile. "Why would I miss a man who treated me like crap? The dog loved me unconditionally. If anything, the only thing I felt guilty about was that I didn't fight harder to keep Max. My ex was good to him, but there's no way he could have loved Max as much as I did—the only thing he loved was himself."

"Ouch," Troy said, laughing. "I hate when you end a relationship and you don't stay friends. I know it's harder, but I always think that if you loved someone, you will love them forever—even if you find that they're not the right person for you. And, at the very least, they deserve your respect."

She cringed, her face pinching. "So, you're saying that you think less of me because I think my ex is a total jackass?"

He laughed. "I didn't say that I've remained friends with all my exes. I just said I don't like it when things turn sour. Sometimes there is just too much vitriol and hurt for two people to keep on liking each other. Though, even when I don't like someone, I *try*—and *try* is the key word—to be as close to respectful as I can be… But a man only has so much willpower."

She laughed. "So, you do have one or two who you can't stand?"

"I haven't dated a ton of women, and I would say that I would still help all of them if there was a subway train threatening to hit them…but there is a short list of exes whom I would wait until the last second to save."

"Ohhhh, ouch." She laughed, the sound from deep within her.

Just the sound made him lighten. Yes, he definitely loved this woman, but he couldn't face that. Not after Tiffany. Love led to pain.

He made quick work of the breakfast as she scrolled through her phone. "According to what I was able to pull, and from what my mother is saying, Sal Baker is one of my father's new hires. He came on as a new engineering director for our machining plant."

Before Solomon's murder, he'd chatted with Zoey, who had spent the night digging into the company's data. Though she hadn't found much yet, she had finally nailed down the man's identity.

"You didn't talk to your mother about someone we are investigating, did you?" he asked, stopping as he scooped the eggs onto her plate. The toast popped up, but he didn't move as he tried to make sense of what Kate had said.

"It's okay. My mom isn't the kind who would think anything of it. And besides, I asked her about all the people my father was working with." She waved him off, like he was making something out of nothing, but the misstep made his hackles rise.

Zoey would be irate if she thought he had compromised her investigation in any way.

"Kate," he said, taking the toast and slathering it with butter before handing it over to her. "I don't think you telling your mother anything, or even asking her any questions, is a good idea."

She popped a bit of egg into her mouth and slowly chewed, like she was carefully picking and choosing her answers before responding to him. "Troy, I appreciate your concern. You know I do. But just because I'm a woman doesn't mean that my training in the FBI has had no effect. I am a competent agent. I know how to get the information I need without anyone being the wiser."

"I wasn't questioning your training. I know you are amazing at what you do, but that doesn't mean that I am not going to worry about you—especially in a case like this. Sometimes, when things involve our family members, it is damn hard to remain objective. It's easy to be blind when it comes to those we love."

What was he blind about when it came to her?

He ate a piece of toast, watching her as she plowed through the plate of food that she had sworn she wasn't hungry for. With her plate empty, she sat back and yawned. He glanced outside, and for the first time, he noticed it had grown dark. Where had the day gone? It wasn't lost on him that when it came to spending time with Kate, time had a way of racing by—even when he had been outside and just standing guard.

"I know this is going to sound strange," Kate said, wiping her mouth, "but…would you mind staying here tonight? I have a spare bedroom." She pointed down toward the stairs. "It's not a king-sized bed or anything, it's only a twin, but it's comfy. I—I just don't want to be alone tonight."

He didn't want to be alone either, but he wasn't thinking about the kind of alone that meant sleeping in separate beds... Then again, he didn't mean that he wanted sex either. What he really wanted, more than anything else, was intimacy and to hold her while she fell asleep.

If only she felt the same way about him.

But no, she wanted him to sleep in a separate bed. If nothing else, at least he would get to see her again in the morning...and he could be the man she needed.

"Babe, even if you wanted to have me sleep on the moon in order to keep you safe, I would do it for you." He took her plate, afraid that if he looked at her, he would see his words register and her response would make the threadbare leash he had on his feelings for her give way and he would run straight into her arms.

"Lucky for you, the guest bedroom isn't quite so far away." She stood up with the squeak of the chair and made her way around the kitchen island. She stepped behind him and put her arms around his waist. "Thank you, Grim. Thank you for everything you do for me."

The air left his lungs in a gush, the string that held his feelings in check. "You're welcome, Scythe."

SHE HAD SET everything out that he needed for a shower, and when he got out of the bathroom between their bedrooms, her door was closed and her light was off. He stood quietly in the hall and he was sure he could hear the soft sounds of her sleeping.

Kate was his angel. He would take a bullet for her,

even if their friendship went nowhere beyond where they were.

After going to the guest bedroom, he lay there until a light, fitful sleep finally overtook him. It didn't feel like it had been very long when he was awakened by the creak of a door. He gripped the gun he had tucked under his pillow, but he was careful not to move and give his enemy any more of an advantage than they already had.

There was barely a sound, but he could pick up the rasp of footsteps on the carpet as someone approached the other side of the bed. He gripped the gun, readying to pull and shoot. No one was going to get the drop on him.

And then she sighed. The sound was soft and quiet, but it was as clear and filled with meaning as if Kate had shouted his name.

His grip loosened on his gun as he realized that, for now, they were safe from the outside world—from each other, well, that was an entirely different matter.

He had to pretend to be asleep; if she had wanted to wake him up, she would have. Perhaps what she needed right now was just the pacifying touch of someone who cared for her.

Whatever she needs...

She slipped between the sheets and, ever so gently, put her arm around him as she nestled into his body. Her breasts were pressed into his back, but he couldn't tell whether or not she was wearing any clothes, thanks to his shirt. No matter what, he didn't want to ruin the sensation by moving.

"I know you're awake," she whispered, as though the world would hear them.

He wasn't sure how to respond. He needed to say

something, to acknowledge her, but he wasn't about to ask her what she wanted or needed from him. Instead, he gave a sleepy, soft grumble.

"I'm sorry. Go back to sleep. I didn't mean to wake you," she said, her voice louder and quicker than it had been before, as if she suddenly was embarrassed for coming to him in the night.

"No," he said, turning his head toward her. "Don't be sorry." He reached down and took her hand. He lifted her fingers to his mouth and gave them a kiss. "I'm glad you are here."

Her body relaxed. "I was cold."

Oddly enough, she didn't feel cool. Instead, she felt warmer than he did, but he wasn't about to argue the point. "Here," he said. Letting go of her hand, he rolled over. "Why don't I hold you until you get warmed up. I don't want my little scythe to be chilled."

He expected her to roll over and scoot her body into his so he could spoon her, wrapping her in the warmth of his core. And yet she stayed still, facing him.

"That's not quite how I wanted you to warm me up." There was a sultry lilt to her voice he hadn't heard her use before.

His body instantly reacted and he pressed against his boxers.

Though his brain screamed at him that this wasn't a good idea, that he should try to talk her down from this ledge—one that once they stepped over there was no coming back from—his body took over. There was only one thought… He loved her.

Kate lifted her chin, beckoning him to kiss her. Who was he to deny her?

As his lips touched hers, every feel-good chemical

in his body swirled into his system, and he could sense himself grow high. He would have never thought just a kiss could be better than any sexual experience he'd ever had before.

Their kiss—it was like someone had opened up the floodgates after a spring thaw. Everything, every wintry pent-up emotion, laugh, cry and fear, came gushing out as her tongue caressed his bottom lip.

He reached up and pressed his hand into the center of her back, pulling her impossibly nearer to him. They couldn't be close enough. He wanted all of her.

Running his thumb over the subtle curve of her spine, he felt only the silky smoothness of her flesh. She had come to his bed naked.

Oh, for all that is good... I have to be dreaming.

If he was, he never wanted to wake up. This could be the moment that he could be stripped from the earth and he would die a happy and complete man.

She gently kissed him, loving him as he traced his fingers down her back, finding the thick round curves of her hips and her upper thigh. Nothing impeded his downward descent. He moved his fingers in small circles around the dimples of her ass, marking them in his mind as places his lips wished to travel.

Though Kate wasn't what media deemed perfect, she was better. She was imperfect, different in the way she viewed the world and people in it, and flawed in the sense that she was authentically herself.

And, truth be told, perfect was boring. Perfect was merely a mundane conglomeration of traits. Yes, perfection was striven for in most social circles, but it was also the prison that kept people from speaking from their hearts and finding the passion that came with being free.

Being with her was being free. Free to love. Free to explore. Free to experience everything he'd ever wanted to feel.

He stopped, letting his hand rest on her hip. As he stopped, she touched his chest right over his heart. She didn't say anything as their kisses paused and their lips brushed against each other.

She sighed, the cool air an odd sensation against the warmth where their kisses had heated.

He yearned to tell her that he loved her, but that was the one part of him that was still so scarred. That was one way he would never be free. That word only brought death and pain. He couldn't do that to either one of them.

But he could give her his body and receive hers— and love her in a way that she needed.

He moved to his elbow, kissing her lips and then kissing every millimeter until he was between her thighs. Sensing the motions of her body, the sounds of her sighs and the tightening of her grip on his hair, he worked her.

"Troy," she cried out, calling his name like it was the elixir of life. She uttered guttural sounds as she pulsed beneath him, riding the pleasure he reveled in bringing her.

Her body quaked as he brought her to the precipice. Smiling, he kissed the creamy skin of her inner thighs and rested his head on her leg.

And just when he had thought he couldn't be more turned on or more satisfied, she looked down at him. She looked sleepy, her eyes the hazy squint of the well sated. "I… You…"

Her inability to form words made his smile widen. "Having a hard time speaking?" he teased.

She nodded with a dazed smile. "You think you can handle more?"

"I could be down here for hours, babe."

She laughed. "Again, that's not quite what I was thinking."

"Then what exactly did you have in mind?"

Kate reached down and pulled him up toward her, kissing the wetness from his lips. "This time, it's going to be all about you."

Chapter Fifteen

There were a variety of kinds of sex. There was the first time, second time, the millionth time. Then there was the kind that came with partners who were only passing in the night—the kind full of passion and laughter, the type that both sought to please the other, but also themselves. Last night, it had been all of it, all wrapped into one.

And Kate had never had better.

She moved around the kitchen, humming as she put together a batch of pancakes and fried them up on the griddle. The bacon, the stuff from the package she'd found deep in the recesses of her freezer, was crackling in the microwave.

It felt good to be cooking for a man again. It was odd to think that the last time she had actually *cooked* was before the breakup. But it wasn't the same when a person lived alone.

Troy came walking into the kitchen, rubbing the sleep from his eyes. He smiled as he saw her. "Good morning, beautiful. Something smells awesome."

"There's coffee in the pot," she said, motioning toward the appliance.

He grabbed a mug. "You want a refill?" he asked, grabbing the carafe.

"I already had two. Thanks, though." She hummed, smiling as she flipped the next pancake.

He took a long drink of his coffee, then stepped behind her and wrapped his arms around her waist. "Babe, thank you for last night. You are effing fantastic."

"I don't know why you would think you would need to thank me. You did most of the heavy lifting." She giggled as she sent him a coy glance over her shoulder.

He kissed her lips as she looked back.

In this stolen moment, she was completely, blithely satisfied. For once, she was *happy*.

She scooped a stack of pancakes onto his plate and motioned toward the microwave. "Grab a couple of strips." She handed him his plate. "Here, you," she said, giving him a kiss on his cheek.

"Babe, you're the best."

"I could say the same of you." In that simple moment and exchange, she had a feeling that this—this could be their future.

She wanted nothing more.

Grabbing a plate from the cupboard, she heard a crack to the right of her ear. Fire erupted from the side of her head. Instinctively, she reached up and touched the place near her earlobe that burned. Bringing her fingers down, she saw they were covered in blood.

In what seemed like slow motion, she turned and spotted Troy lunging toward her as the flour she had set on the counter beside the griddle exploded. White powder filled the air. Troy's body connected with hers and his arms wrapped around her waist as they fell onto the floor together.

"Stay down!" he yelled, pulling a gun she hadn't realized he was carrying from the back of his pants as she lay there on the floor just watching.

Someone was shooting…*at her*. Why? From where? What in the hell was going on?

Troy moved behind the kitchen island in a squatting position facing the direction from where the bullet had come. Whoever was shooting must have been posted somewhere behind her house. There were several houses that were at the same or higher level than hers, so the shooter could have been anywhere.

She was going to need to invest in blackout blinds, something that no one could see through.

Be in the moment. She had to stay in the moment. She couldn't dissociate now.

She belly-crawled toward the living room, making sure that she stayed behind cover as she moved. Beside the doorway, by the pantry, was a Glock 43x she had bought and stashed for an occasion just like this one, one she'd never thought would actually happen.

Pulling it out, she made sure it was loaded. One hollow point in the chamber. It was a single-stack magazine; she had nine more hollow points, if need dictated. Hopefully, if she got her sights on the shooter, it would take only one.

But odds were good that whoever was shooting at her, they weren't doing it from right outside the window. This person, whoever it was, was probably perched somewhere high, waiting for the right moment to take another shot. This shooter was probably the same sniper who had left them high and dry, with only a few leads to use in order to discover their identity.

She had a sinking feeling that if they didn't get him

this time, she would be living the rest of her life constantly looking over her shoulder. That was, if she lived past today.

There was another whiz and crack as the next round struck the pantry door, not six inches from her head.

"They are shooting from up high." She could hear the terror in her voice, but she tried to temper it as she called to Troy. "They're probably coming at us from the old manor. It's about a hundred yards out, at your one o'clock position. You see anybody?"

Troy moved slightly to his left, peering up over the counter but then just as quickly ducking down again. They didn't need the sniper taking any more potshots, and they definitely didn't need him getting lucky and actually hitting either one of them.

"We need a distraction. Something that is going to pull our shooter's attention while I can get closer. Or else we need to pull him out of hiding and get him into the open."

"This person, whoever is shooting at us, clearly isn't the sharpest shooter, or they would have hit us by now." Troy looked over at her. "They're not a trained professional, but they obviously know enough about evasion to get away from a scene without getting caught."

"So? What are you trying to say?" She was utterly confused. "What do you want me to do? Stand up and flash the shooter?" she added, trying to make a joke in order to make the fear rising within her somewhat more manageable.

"Sure. I mean, if you took your shirt off and stood up, I think I could get out of this kitchen without him noticing. Then I could flank him, get the drop... We could get our man," he teased.

"What if it's a woman?"

Troy laughed. "Well, maybe I should take off my shirt... Do a little dance. She would love this rock-hard body."

"If it is a woman and you go up there without a shirt, it won't stop her from shooting—she'll just aim lower." Kate smirked. She reached into the drawer at the end of the counter and fished around until her fingers brushed against the cold metal of the flashlight. "Regardless, I think there are better options." She grabbed the flash-light as she pretended to lift her shirt.

"No. You keep covered," Troy ordered, no softness or questions in his tone. "There is absolutely no god-damned way I'm going to allow you to stand up and be shot at. There are a million better options."

"Don't worry. Not gonna get naked, but we gotta do something." She lifted the flashlight for him to see. "If we call in help, they'll just end up chasing him away. Like last time. You know we're on our own here." As much as she wanted to be wrong, she knew she was right.

Troy was silent.

"Cover my six, along with the rest of me. Get ready to run. I'm just going to do this one time." As it was, this one time was probably more than enough for her to end up dead. She clicked on the flashlight. "Go!"

She stood up and aimed the strobe in the direction of the shooter in hopes that the white flash would blind them. Looking to the left, up at the manor, she expected to see the muzzle flash, feel the pierce, then the burn of being struck with hot copper. The door outside clicked shut and she fell back down to the ground, clicking off the light and slipping it into her pocket.

Checking her body, she was surprised to find that the only real damage was still only to her ear. Lucky. This time, she had been right to act just a little bit crazy.

There was another crack and thump as the third round struck the microwave.

The jerk could ping her ear, shoot her flour, but the bastard couldn't screw with her bacon. Moving to the island, she leaned out just far enough to take aim at the building in the distance. She was a good shooter, but if she hit the window where she believed the shooter to be, it would be one hell of a shot.

She fired three quick, successive rounds.

Though it had to have been excruciatingly loud in the small space of the kitchen, she hadn't even heard the sounds. The only reason she was entirely sure she had stopped at three rounds were the three spent casings on the ground to her right.

She turned her back against the island, catching her breath as she waited for the next round of shots.

Her breath came in short, fast bursts as she held her Glock to her chest, readying herself to roll and fire again. This jerk had to be stopped—and if something happened to Troy, she would stop at nothing when it came to finding this shooter and making them pay.

Chapter Sixteen

Troy turned the corner and ran to the front of the manor. It looked as though it had once been a bed-and-breakfast, but it now sat empty—except for, possibly, their shooter. The door's windows were covered with decades-old newspaper, all except the window closest to the handle and locks. The glass had been broken out at some point, but there were no shards on the ground in front of the door; either the pieces had been pushed into the building or it had happened long ago.

It wouldn't have surprised him if the place had come to serve as a high school rave location or some homeless hangout. Though this didn't seem the right kind of area for either, not with neighbors just a few hundred feet in every direction.

There was the flutter of a curtain as the resident across the street peeked out at him. He was tempted to wave, but he just made a mental note as he opened the unlocked door. No doubt, it would be only a matter of time until the police showed up, thanks to both the neighbor seeing him and Kate's shooting.

In the meantime, he had to get his hands on the dude who was trying to take them out. Once he did, the only thing that would be up for debate would be whether or not he chose to kill him.

The place smelled of stale air, mold and old cigarette smoke, all mixed with the carb-loaded aroma of cheap beer. He liked beer, but he'd always hated that odor.

The place had once probably been a nice dwelling, with its floral wallpaper, now stained with orange spray paint declaring "Donny loves Becca" in sloppy, dripping script. The brass chandelier overhead was at a slant and hanging from wires where a kid must have, at one time or another, tried to swing. In the right hands, the place had potential. But when he was done here, the next owner would need to know how to remove bloodstains.

He held his SIG, quickly clearing the entryway and living room before hurrying up the stairs, carefully avoiding the center of each step in order to mask the sounds of his advance. They couldn't know he was coming; he needed every advantage, especially when he held the lower ground.

Ascending the top of the staircase, he turned in the direction of the rooms that faced the back of Kate's house and her kitchen window. There were two possibilities, but he chose the one with the clearest view. Pressing his back to the wall, he sidestepped toward the open door. Taking a deep breath, he readied himself as he pivoted partially around the corner, making sure to remain behind the thin protection of the wall.

A man was sitting with his back to him at a small folding table, an assault rifle on a tripod and sandbags positioning the weapon toward Kate's kitchen window. He was dressed all in black and had on a backward black baseball hat, and a black-and-gray shemagh was wrapped around his neck; the only bit of skin showing were his ears and a bit of his cheeks. The masked man must have been some sort of trained shooter based on his choice of rifle and gear, but Troy was glad he wasn't better at his job. Or had he not been trying to kill Kate, but rather, had he just been trying to warn her off?

If he'd been serious, and well trained, he could have easily killed them both without them even realizing what was happening until it was all too late.

"Put your goddamned hands up, or you will get one straight to the brain stem." Troy roll-stepped behind the man, stopping only inches behind the back of his head.

The man didn't move. He didn't even flinch.

The wind whipped through the open window, blowing toward him; with it, it carried the coppery scent of blood. With the scent came a strange sense of unexpected disappointment.

"I said *put your hands up*," Troy repeated.

Still, the man didn't move.

He nudged the man's shoulder with the tip of his gun. His limp body collapsed to the floor. As he fell, he rolled, exposing an entrance wound just at the base of his throat.

Kate's aim had been on point.

She had killed the man.

Just when he thought he couldn't love her more, she had made what must have been at least a hundred-yard shot with a handgun, into a darkened room, and took down the bastard trying to kill her. It was a kill shot for the books.

What a woman.

He knelt down and checked the man's pulse, even though the open, sightless eyes told him all he needed to know. There was no sign of life.

Screw this fellow. He'd had it coming. The only thing that disappointed Troy was the fact that he hadn't been the one to pull the trigger, but he liked that the woman he loved had done it instead. She was powerful, smart and courageous.

They would make one hell of a team if they ever got married.

He paused as he stood up. What kind of person was he that, while checking on a dead man, he was thinking about getting married? And not just that, but he'd never really considered getting married before. Nope, it wasn't the kind of relationship he'd even contemplated, let alone hoped for...and yet here he was.

He couldn't help the smile that overtook his features as he moved out of the room, clearing the rest of the house. From what he could make out, there had been only this man. There was nothing to indicate he'd acted with anyone else.

Outside, there were the careening wails of police cruisers as they descended on him and the place.

Crap. Here we go again.

He considered leaving, but he hadn't done anything to conceal his fingerprints or his identity when the neighbor had spotted him. It was going to be easier just to face this head-on. But that didn't mean his ass wasn't going to be facing a little bit of jail time while he waited to be cleared.

Hopefully the investigating officer would be friendly toward him, maybe even throw him a couple of bones and let him walk. But Troy would have to get damn lucky.

He wished he'd had time to check the shooter's ID, but he had an idea of who he was. He put down his gun and walked outside. He plopped down on the porch's top step and waited until the first police car screeched and skidded to a stop in the street in front of him. The city officer stepped out of his car, using his door for coverage as he pulled his weapon and aimed it at him. "Get on the ground!"

He rolled over, pressed his face against the wooden planks. The paint was chipping and peeling, and he stared at a bit that fluttered as he exhaled and put his hands above his head, his fingers interlaced.

The police officer rushed toward him as two more cars pulled up. The man patted him down, finding his holster. "Where is your weapon?"

Troy looked up at the man. "It's just inside the door. It's fully loaded. I just responded after the shooter shot at my girlfriend's place."

The police officer paused. "Where is your girlfriend?"

"Can I sit up?" Troy asked, being careful to not sound disrespectful.

"Keep your hands where I can see them and on your head. Got it?"

Troy nodded and the man pulled him up to sitting, using his interlaced hands. "My girlfriend is an FBI agent, and the man upstairs was trying to shoot and kill her. Her name is Kate Scot. She's with the Missoula field office."

The officer huffed and Troy wasn't sure if it was because the man was annoyed at Kate or annoyed at him. Hell, maybe he was annoyed that he had arrived two minutes too late.

"And what is your name? You FBI too?"

Troy laughed. "No. The name's Troy Spade. I'm a

private contractor working with the Scot family." He carefully skirted the truth as much as he dared. The officer didn't need all the answers, at least not right now.

"The man upstairs is dead. I checked his pulse, but that was the extent of my interaction with him. He was already deceased when I got here."

"So you say." The officer pulled at his hands, motioning that he could relax. "You know why the dude was shooting at you and Kate?"

"I think this is the sniper from the downtown shooting last week, but that's yet to be proved. That being said, you probably know more about the investigation than I do."

The man holstered his weapon as several other officers descended on the house and the block and began clearing the area.

"You have reason to believe there are any other active shooters in the area?" the officer asked.

Troy shook his head, but then shrugged. "I cleared the house, but that doesn't mean there aren't others in the area. Right now, you need to send medical aid to Kate's place. She took a round, but it wasn't life-threatening. But the shooter got off more rounds while I was making my way over here. She shot back. I think she may have struck him. All self-defense," he added, making sure to protect her. He rattled off her address as the man called it in on his handset.

Troy needed to get back to her house and make sure that she was okay. "Can I go over there?"

The officer scoffed. "Yeah, right. Think again, Mr. Spade."

The only people who ever called him *Mr. Spade* were those about to rain down some sort of punishment on him. Hopefully he wasn't about to get his ass kicked or find himself heading to the clink.

"You know Kate?" he asked.

The officer nodded. "Good agent, good woman."

"I love her." Troy was shocked as the words fell from his lips. "I mean… I haven't told her that yet, but *I love her*, man. And I have to know she is okay. Have you ever loved a woman like that?"

The officer chuckled.

"If you have, then you have to know that even the threat of handcuffs and jail time isn't going to stop me from going over there and making sure that she's going to be okay. She's been through a lot. And if she is lying there on the floor of her kitchen, shot and bleeding…and I didn't do everything in my power to get to her, I would never forgive myself." He put his palms up, pleading.

"I don't know." The officer sighed.

"Look, the last woman I fell in love with ended up dead. EFP and caught shrapnel. I watched the whole thing go down. I can't stand the thought of losing another person I love. Not like that. Not like this. I can't… She can't be hurt."

The officer's face softened. "Here's the deal, Troy. I don't think you are the one responsible for the dead dude, but…you know there are procedures in place that require me to handle this a certain way. But…let's say you think that there is something *I have to see*, something at Kate's place… Well, I'm sure I can make it work."

Troy jumped to his feet, a smile stretching over his face. "I owe you one."

"More than one," the officer said. "And let me just say, you got it *bad* for Kate."

"Patsy Cline couldn't have sung it better, man. I know exactly how crazy I am for loving her. I just hope she is just as crazy about loving me."

The officer laughed, the sound out of place in the manic motions that were taking place around them.

Troy started jogging in the direction of Kate's house. "We were cooking... Well...*she* was cooking breakfast when the shooting began. Did you call EMS? They en route to her?" Troy's words came out fast as the officer jogged along next to him.

"They are en route." The officer started talking into his handset, letting the other officers know where he was and what he was doing.

As they rounded the corner, there were already two police cruisers and a black BuCar he recognized as Agent Hunt's.

He slowed down his race toward the front door as he thought about the dead man. He should have taken a second to get a better look at the guy's face. He thought he'd recognized him from Zoey's info dump, but wasn't quite sure. What if that guy was only one of a selection of snipers?

Snipers typically acted alone, but that didn't mean that they weren't part of a team. For the right amount of money, a person could buy anything—or have anyone killed, not limited to a captain of industry like Solomon Scot or an FBI agent like his daughter.

But who would be trying to take out the members of this family and why?

Maybe that first shooting had been about him and his brother, and not about Kate, as he'd first suspected. This second shooting, though, had been about her.

Someone was working sloppy here. It was like whoever was at the wheel and driving these attacks wasn't used to doing this kind of work, but had one hell of a budget.

That left Peahen out. An agent made good money, but they didn't make that kind of money. And even if Peahen was getting paid by someone else, he was smart enough not to play sniper. Too many risks. It just didn't fit his MO.

The only people connected to the case, the ones with enough money to make a sniper happen—at least, the only ones he could think of—were those who were associated with ConFlux. Maybe there was someone on the board, someone who didn't want them to come under investigation for leaked secrets... That would explain why he and Mike had been shot at. And it definitely explained why someone would shoot and kill Solomon.

But why would they come after him and Kate?

Were they getting too close to the answers? Did someone need to stop Troy and Kate before being exposed?

Then again, the other two suspects both worked for ConFlux, and either could have been the sniper. And if one of them was the dead man in the manor, it was possible that he'd been working alone. Maybe he'd been the one selling secrets.

Kate had said Sal was one of her father's new hires. That moved him to the top of his personal suspects list. Damn—he wished he'd taken a picture of the dead shooter. He'd resembled Sal, but Zoey's photo of him had been of a younger man, probably something taken earlier. Maybe he was working for a foreign government—a spy of some sort. Hell, it made sense.

Zoey was probably having a tech field day with all of this.

His mind was working a million miles an hour as he ran around to the open back door and made his way into the kitchen. The officer with him had pulled his weapon, and Troy appreciated the effort as the officer pushed past him and took point so they would both be protected if they unexpectedly came under fire.

There were voices coming from the living room. Standing at the center was Kate. Agent Hunt had a bottle of hydrogen peroxide and was swabbing her ear with a rag. Troy pushed him aside.

"Kate," Troy said, taking her by the shoulders and looking her square in the eyes. "Are you okay? You didn't get hit anywhere else, did you? You're fine, right?" His words flooded from him as he looked her over, spinning her slightly as he looked for anywhere that could have been hurt.

The only thing that appeared injured was the tip of her ear, where only a small patch of skin was missing.

She smiled, relieved, and threw her arms around his neck. "Troy, I'm fine. Honey, it's okay. It's going to be okay."

He breathed in her scent, pulling the smell of pancakes and her shampoo deep into his lungs. But beneath the soft aromas of her was the heady scent of fear. No matter what she said, or what she swore to, Kate was still afraid.

Chapter Seventeen

Kate had killed a man. The locals had identified him as Sal Baker, an employee of ConFlux. Though they had a few answers, and the ballistics were all being handled by the FBI lab so they could get more, there were still too many questions, and only one real thought kept circulating through her mind... She had taken a person's life two days ago.

When she had taken on her role as a special agent with the Bureau, she had known that someday she would likely be faced with a situation in which she would have to possibly take a life. She had trained for hundreds of hours at the range over the years, to the point that calluses formed at the base of her thumb where her Glock's beavertail rubbed against her skin every time she pulled the trigger.

Yes, she was proficient with a handgun—more than capable, even—but she just couldn't get over the reality that she had taken aim at a nearly invisible target, pulled that trigger and made the kill shot on her enemy.

She didn't regret her actions. Not when the man was trying to kill them. Troy had made a point of saying that he was there to protect her, and she secretly loved the fact that when push had come to shove, she was the one who had protected him.

Maybe, in the future, if they were to really pursue a grown-up relationship, they could even face it together with some sort of pride.

She would never forget the look on his face when he had found her standing in the living room... He'd seemed absolutely at a loss. Relieved, yes, but at the same time like he had never been more terrified in his entire life.

In that moment, she had wanted to make him forget everything bad that had ever happened to him, and though she knew that not everything he had to have been feeling was tied to her, she wanted to take away all of his pain. If only she could. He had so many burdens, and they made all the seemingly terrible and heart-wrenching things that had ever happened to her pale in comparison. Really, what was a breakup in comparison to watching a loved one die?

Her father's murder came slamming back into her consciousness. For a split second, she had forgotten. How had she failed to recall the pain of losing him? Of seeing his body being wheeled out of his office building?

Did it make her a terrible person that all she had been really thinking about was what she and Troy had just gone through?

She stared at the far wall of her office. Though the SAC, Agent Raft, had told her to take the day off and stay home, focus on her family, it was the last thing she had wanted to do. Every time she peeked at her phone, there were messages from her mother, her sister and restricted numbers that she was more than sure belonged to the detectives and officers who were working on the task force and trying to solve all of these murders.

Agent Hunt walked up beside her desk and tossed down a bag of sunflower seeds. "Here, champ, have one on me."

She laughed as she picked up the bag. "Thanks, man."

"You doing okay?" he asked.

His question surprised her. He didn't usually pry or ask questions when it came to anything beyond work. They were friends, but they both respected the fact that neither delved too deep. Both knew exactly what they needed to know about each other, and beyond that, anything else was only a liability.

She nodded, opening the bag and stuffing a few seeds into the back of her cheek like they were some kind of pacifier. "Doing fine. One day at a time, am I right?"

Hunt nodded. He paused and an awkward silence moved between them.

"Something you wanted to tell me, Hunt?"

He sat half on the corner of her desk. If anyone else did that, she would have been annoyed, but she liked Hunt too much to give a damn. He took in a deep breath, as if he was trying to decide whether or not he wanted to divulge a secret.

"Just say it." She couldn't stand to think about what other shoe was about to drop.

"I know you and Troy are...well, getting *close*."

She clenched. Since when did everyone know about her personal relationship? As soon as she asked herself the question, she realized that everyone in the entire city probably knew by now. Their story, the shooting and the sniper's death had been the talk of every news outlet in the state for the last forty-eight hours, and she doubted that would stop anytime soon.

She and Troy hadn't seen each other since then. She had a lot to do in the aftermath of the shooting, and he'd texted her several times telling her he was happy to give her some space.

She'd been careful to avoid watching any of the news coverage, but from what she had managed to glean, most media sources hadn't seemed to say much about the nature of her and Troy's friendship. But anyone who knew her knew exactly what had transpired—especially Hunt, who had borne witness to *the look* Troy had given her when he'd first seen her after the shooting.

That look told her everything she needed to know about how Troy felt…and she felt it too. Though she hadn't seen her own features, she was absolutely certain that she had been his mirror.

"Are you jealous, Hunt?" she teased, though she was more than aware that Agent Hunt had a girlfriend.

"Hardly. You and I are many things. Romantically inclined toward one another, we are not. But don't think I wouldn't take a bullet for you," Hunt said, his voice unwavering and true.

"So, what, then?" she asked, giving him a playful half smile.

"Well, in an effort to take a bullet for you—I think I need to tell you something, before you get too hurt because of this thing with Troy."

Her stomach dropped and she was pretty sure every single drop of blood had just flooded into her feet. "Okay… What about him?"

Hunt sucked in a breath, letting it out in a slow, metered exhalation. "So, I have been looking into him ever since the shooting downtown. I know he's your friend, but has he told you anything about his past?"

She thought about his accident. "What about his past?"

"Well, you know he has been working private contracting?"

"Yes. He's currently with STEALTH. What about it?"

"Did he tell you which company he worked with before that?" Hunt's face pinched.

She shook her head.

"It was a company called Rockwood. You ever heard of it?"

"No. Why?" A sickening lump formed in her throat.

"Rockwood is a private contracting group. They work under the United Nations and are a big-time billion-dollar company that not many people in the public sector could name." Hunt crossed his arms over his chest, leaning back slightly. "Your boy worked for them for quite a few years, doing what—I couldn't find, but I'm sure with a few more phone calls I could at least get some basics."

She tried to swallow back the lump. "These guys, who work in the trade… There's a lot of lateral movements between outfits. What's your point?"

Hunt sucked on his teeth. "Well, that guy you put down, Sal Baker, he worked for that outfit as well. You don't think he was aiming at Troy all along, do you? Or—" Hunt paused "—you don't think that Troy and/ or his team are playing us all for fools, do you?"

She laughed at the outrageous conjecture. "That's crazy, Hunt. Seriously, that's a bit of a stretch, don't you think? That's like saying you're more loyal to your first boss than the Bureau."

He answered with the quirk of an eyebrow. "Is it? I've been thinking about it…and here is this guy who has admitted to trying to break into ConFlux. What if he and Sal were working together?"

The lump grew larger. "No…"

"Did he or did he not get you to walk him up to your father's office?"

She had. Kate had literally opened the door and gotten him waved past security. Who knew what he had done when he'd been alone in the intern's office?

"Okay, let's say they were working for the same team. Why would Sal bear down on us in my kitchen?"

"*Us?* Or you?"

There was some validity in what Hunt was saying, but she refused to admit the possibility that Troy would act in any way that would go against her. It wasn't possible. Not after what had happened between them—after how he had made her feel.

Or had he been using her heart against her? Had she been honeypotted by the man?

She ran her finger over the scab that had formed where she had been hit by the sniper's round. Troy had convinced her that Sal wasn't a great sniper, and she had gone along with it—what kind of sniper couldn't hit their target at around a hundred yards? It shouldn't have been a very difficult shot, and even an amateur shooter could have made it.

Though they had all discussed the logistics of the shooter's trajectory and path, the task force and investigating officer had agreed that it was likely a case of a poor-quality shooter. But what if that wasn't what had happened after all? What if she was only supposed to get a notch in the ear?

Had Troy treated her like a lamb and brought her to the slaughter?

Her entire body turned cold, but she wasn't sure if it was out of sheer terror or rage. "I need to go." She stood up, leaving her suit jacket on the back of her chair. "Oh, and call Peahen. I need to talk to him. I think I owe him an apology."

"Why? Wait—do you want me to come with you?" Hunt called after her.

"No." She didn't need a witness if she lost it on the one man outside the agency whom she had chosen to give her trust to.

This was what she got for opening up to a man. When would she learn her lesson and just get a dog and not try to go for the whole relationship package? This had all been too quick. She should have known better, been more cautious.

She took out her phone as she walked from the federal building and made her way to her car. Pushing the buttons, she dialed Troy. He had better answer his damn phone.

It rang, finally going to voice mail.

Her rage burned hotter, melting through what little self-restraint she still possessed. When she found him, he was going to not only get a piece of her mind, but he was probably going to get a swift throat punch right along with it.

But first, she had to find him.

How was it that when she didn't think she needed him, he was just around the corner, but now that she wanted to find him, he had gone completely dark?

As she made it to the car, she wasn't sure where she should start looking for Troy. Would he still be at STEALTH headquarters? For all she knew, like Hunt had implied, he had used her for what he needed and now he had already bugged out.

Then again, Zoey had vouched for him. Or he had said Zoey had vouched for him. Had that been a lie too? She hadn't *actually talked* to her or anyone else in STEALTH.

But her father had vouched for him and his brother... And was Mike his brother? Had anything he told her about himself been true? Had his girlfriend even been killed?

What if all he had been doing was manipulating her as he tried to get what he needed for his assignment or for whatever purpose he had in mind?

An icy chill ran down her spine.

No. She had to stop swirling the drain. Hunt had to be wrong.

But now that he had pointed out his suspicions, she couldn't help but follow her thoughts to the inky darkness of what Troy could have been doing. The farther she drove, the angrier she became.

By the time she was bumping down the dirt road that led to the Widow Maker Ranch, where STEALTH's headquarters was located, she was seething. She pulled the car to a skidding stop in the gravel parking lot and charged toward the ranch house's front door.

Using the mammoth cast-iron lion's head knocker, she banged on the door. The sound echoed out into the still morning. A cow bawled in the distance, the only one who dared to answer. There was an electronic whir as a camera moved overhead and the aperture moved to focus.

She knocked again.

"I'm coming," a woman called from the other side of the door. There were the sounds of footfalls and a metal slide. Zoey, her hair a dark purple, opened the door. "What are you doing here, Agent Scot? Is there something I can help you with this morning?"

She charged into the house. "Where is Troy?"

"Um, excuse me? What are you doing? What did *he* do?" Zoey slammed the door shut and chased after her, grabbing her by the arm and spinning her around so they were facing one another. "What happened?"

"Did you know that he used to work for Rockwood?" she spit.

Zoey frowned. "What about it? Several of our employees have worked for Rockwood in the past."

"I think they all may still be working for them. Are you in on this?" She nearly growled as she stared at the dark eyeliner that made Zoey's eyes appear catlike.

"What in the hell are you talking about?"

"Troy!" she yelled, pulling out of Zoey's grasp. "Troy! Where in the hell are you?"

Zoey jogged beside her as she charged down the hallway toward what looked like the bedrooms. "You have to tell me what is going on."

"Why don't you just tell me where Troy is? Then he can tell *both* of us what he is doing and why."

Zoey pointed toward a door at the end of the hall. Kate rushed in that direction, and not bothering to knock, she threw open the bedroom door.

Troy was just starting to sit up. He wasn't wearing

a shirt, and as he spotted her, he moved his hand away from the nightstand where his holster rested.

"Don't you dare lay a finger on that gun, or your friend Sal won't be the only one who I put a bullet into this week," Kate ordered.

Zoey grabbed her hand, flipping it behind her back and pinning it upward. "Look, I don't know what is going on here, but there is no way I'm going to let you charge into our headquarters and draw down on one of my employees. We have one rule here—no shooting in the house."

Troy put his hands up, shock registering on his features. "What is going on, Kate? What are you doing here?"

"Did you really think I wasn't going to find out about your past? What you are really up to?" She turned to Zoey. "Did you know that your boy here has ties to the sniper who *allegedly* tried to kill him and Mike? It's all an effing setup. And I was the fool who fell for it."

Zoey opened her mouth as she glanced over at Troy and then back to her, as though she was trying to make sense of all the things that Kate was saying. "Are you talking about Rockwood?" she asked, finally finding the words.

"Rockwood?" Troy asked, rubbing the sleep from his face. "Dude, I haven't worked for them in years."

"Don't lie. You may not be working for Rockwood, but you asked Sal to do what he did." There was the burn of tears as they started to collect in her eyes. "You never thought he would get hurt. You never thought I would take that shot. That I would make that shot. I killed a man. All because you and STEALTH wanted to get access to my family's company."

"What?" Troy frowned and his lips parted—he looked absolutely confused.

He was a gifted liar. He had to have known exactly what she was talking about. Or maybe she was wrong and she had flown off the deep end.

No. She was right. Everything pointed in this direction.

"If you're not in on this, then what in the hell is going on? If it walks like a duck, talks like a duck—it's a goddamned duck. You are a duck." She felt stupid as soon as she said it, but in her stressed state, she had a hard time coming up with anything eloquent. All she could focus on was her own pain in falling for the wrong man.

Why had she strayed from her Bureau training? The training that tried to impress upon them that everything anyone ever did was always selfishly motivated. Troy had done what he needed to do to get the answers that he needed. It was all about him, and she had forgotten about that, letting herself get swept away by the ill-advised belief that he cared about her.

As the tears threatened to leak through, she turned and charged out of the room. He couldn't see her cry again. She needed to get herself back into check, compartmentalize her feelings—especially any that were about him.

After arriving back at her car, she pressed her forehead against the steering wheel and counted to ten, pinching back the tears.

This was going to be okay.

She was going to be okay.

Sure, she had made a mistake in getting involved with Troy. But maybe there was some kind of positive outcome that she could draw from it… What had he taught her?

Her mind drew a blank. All she could think about was the ache within her.

At Quantico, they had taught her that there were two driving factors in everyone's psyche—love and fear. It was what motivated every single action a person took. Even hate could come back to love. Rage could come back to fear. And when a person mixed these two simple concepts, no weapon could be more deadly.

At the time during training, she had thought she had understood what her instructors had meant, but now… in this situation, the true visceral, terrifying truth of what they had said struck home.

She could never get in another relationship again. It was so much easier being alone, walls around her feelings and the sentinels of aloofness standing guard at her gates.

Chapter Eighteen

Kate's house was empty, the yellow tape still fluttering in the breeze like it was celebrating the desecration of their lives last night. He wasn't sure he had ever seen a more morose object, and it struck him how something so mundane could carry so much meaningful pain.

Troy had to find her. He had to set things right. To tell her everything about him and open up in as many ways as he could.

As good as he was at being a shadow, trying to find her this morning just proved to him that she was equally as qualified and adept at his kind of games—two shadows brought together could bring only darkness. And right now, he found himself restless in the inky black. Though he had vowed he would never let himself get to this point again, here he was. At least this time there was a slight glow of light at the edge of the darkness: hope. But with each passing second, the glimmer diminished.

Zoey's name popped up on his phone, and with it came a text message. She had spotted Kate's car downtown, near the federal building. She was parked in front of a bookstore called Fact & Fiction and was probably inside.

He knew the place and turned the car around, hitting the gas like he was bearing down on a fugitive—fighting for the love of his life was similar in a number of ways. Each was equally terrifying, and in both instances, lives depended on the outcome of his actions.

Kate's car was parked exactly where Zoey had pinpointed it, and not for the first time, he thanked his lucky stars. Parking on the street near the car, he got out and made his way to the bookstore. There was a note on the door: Closed.

About right. So much for things being easy.

It gnawed at him that he didn't know Kate well enough to figure out where she would go when she was upset. Did it mean that he didn't really love her? That what he was feeling was merely infatuation? Lust?

If that was all it was, then why hadn't her rushing into his bedroom and falsely accusing him of a crime put a stop to his feelings? And by rushing him, that had to mean she had feelings for him too, right? Otherwise, she wouldn't have tipped her hand and gone at him directly.

That had to mean something, didn't it? She had to have some sort of feelings, the kind that would make her bend rules and act against her better judgment.Which only meant one thing: love.

Though, it all could have been hopeful thinking.

Kate was probably just angry and not thinking straight. Then again, she was a better agent than that. He couldn't blame her for being upset or thinking what she did of him. He could understand the thought process that could have gotten her to where she was, but he had to talk her down. He had to bring her back to reality. She was fighting her biggest ally.

If only he had the answers to why her father had been

murdered and if it was truly Sal who was behind it. With Zoey's help, he'd followed some leads that had turned up only the obvious, that Sal had tried to steal info. If he knew more, he could prove that everything he had told her was true and that he was the man she needed in her life—not an enemy and certainly not someone who wanted to hurt her.

The street was quiet. The only other person was walking toward him, posting flyers on the light poles and traffic lights. The paper had a picture of a lost dog.

Turning left, he made his way down the block, peeking into the variety of sandwich shops, clothing stores and coffee shops as he looked for Kate. He walked to the end of the strip of downtown buildings and was going to turn and head back toward her car to wait for her to return, but as he neared an alleyway, he spotted a gray sedan parked in the shade of the building.

Inside the car were a man and woman. The man had his hand wrapped around the back of the woman's head, and even from where Troy stood, he could feel the intensity of their kiss. He felt oddly out of place for even noticing their embrace. As he watched, the man looked up at him and broke away from the woman, flattening his hair and stroking his goatee. There was a mole near his left temple, and it twitched as the man looked up at him, eyes widened with surprise and a thin sweat on his face. Guilt.

The woman turned around and, as she did, Troy recognized her brunette eyes and bobbed platinum gray hair. Deborah Scot looked much like an older version of her daughter. His gaze slipped back to the man—no wonder the man had looked shocked to see him.

He turned around, quickly moving out of their line

of sight before one of them recognized him. Not that they would have known who he was, even if they had actually taken note of him as more than anything other than a passing observer.

But what exactly had he just seen? They had definitely been kissing. No question. Which meant there was a relationship there. He didn't recognize the man, but it didn't matter. Troy had just found a motive for murder.

He hurried down the sidewalk, putting as much distance between him and his targets as possible. He didn't need to be the next one to end up dead.

Where was Kate? He had to find her. Taking out his phone, he ducked into the nearest door and walked into the busy coffee shop. It smelled of cinnamon and fresh-baked rolls mixed with the burnt caffeinated aroma of coffee.

He dialed Kate.

Answer. You need to answer.

It went to voice mail. It took three more attempts before she finally picked up. "What do you want?"

So, she is still pissed. Not a surprise.

"I need you to come meet me. I'm at The Break." He spoke fast. "It's important. Seriously."

Kate scoffed. "Are you kidding me? There is no way I'm going to meet—"

"I just spotted your mother in an alley kissing a man," he interrupted her, not waiting for her to come at him with more vinegar. "Now. Get your ass over here."

There was a long pause.

"I'll be there in a minute." The anger was stripped from her voice.

He stood awkwardly for a moment. A woman sitting

nearest the window was looking at him, so he walked to the counter and ordered a hot tea and a cup of coffee for Kate. He paid and they handed him his cups. He added cream and sugar to hers, making it just how she liked it, before moving to the back corner of the room and finding a table away from the rest of the patrons. He folded his napkin until the bell on the door jingled, and he slipped the crane away.

Kate walked in, and as she spotted him, a frown took over her face.

Yep, still mad.

He stood up as she approached the table, but her eyes darkened to the point of nearly black. One of these days he would really try to get things right with her.

"First," he said, motioning for her to sit. "I want to tell you that I understand where you are coming from. You're a good agent, and your father's case is still open. You are right to be suspicious of everybody. But I swear to all that is good in this world that I have absolutely nothing to do with any of what has happened to you."

"Then why were you so adamant about getting close to me, protecting me?" Her frown lessened, like she was truly trying to understand his motivation. "You know that's abnormal. Most people don't go out of their way for someone else. No one is selfless. That is a myth."

Unless they wholeheartedly love the other person.

Right now, it didn't seem like the right moment to point that out, so he tried stepping around the admission. "I know what you mean. And I know you are leery of trusting me or anyone right now, but if you give me a chance, I will prove to you that I'm worthy of your trust. I only want…" *To love you. To marry you. To have a future with you. To keep you safe.*

There were a million things he wanted with this woman, but he didn't know which thing he should say.

"You want to prove yourself?" she asked, skeptically.

"Exactly." He nodded, feeling like a castigated schoolboy. "It's why I called you. Why I had to talk to you about your mother. I couldn't just let you find out on your own. Regardless of how it made you feel, you have to know the truth. That, that ability to give another the truth even when it hurts, is *trust*. Isn't it?"

"Perhaps your candor helps, but it doesn't make any of this an easier pill to swallow."

"I know, Kate, and I'm so sorry I have to be the bearer of the bad news, but I promise I will stand by your side as long as you need me. We will get to the bottom of your father's murder—and the role your mother may or may not have played in it."

She gave a resigned sigh. "You said you saw her *kissing* someone?" She made a disgusted face as she sat down across from him at the table and took the cup of coffee he offered. "Thank you." She took a long sip like it was a salve for the wounds to her heart—if only he could be that for her too.

He yearned to reach out and take her hand, but he restrained himself. Right now, he needed to focus on proving himself. "Do you know a guy, gray hair, mole near the left temple?"

She looked up and to her right, trying to recall an image. "There is a guy. I think his name was Alex or Alexi or something. He worked for ConFlux. I think he was the head of the IT department."

Oh, holy... He'd struck pay dirt.

"Hold on," he said, motioning to Kate to keep that thought as he gestured for her to go with him.

He stood up from the table, taking out his phone and dialing Zoey. She answered before he'd even gotten to the front door of the place.

"What's the name of the guy who is the head of IT for ConFlux?" He walked outside, Kate close at his heels.

"Alexi Siegal. Why?"

"I want everything you can pull on the guy. See if he's dropped any out-of-place or nonrequired code on their servers." Troy's mind worked quickly as he thought about all the things he would do if he was Alexi. "Make sure to watch all major airlines. I have a feeling that if this guy catches wind of us being on his tail, he's going to disappear. Wouldn't even be a bad idea if you had our people put out a BOLO on this guy."

"What are you talking about?" Zoey asked. "What did Alexi do?"

"He and Deborah Scot are having an affair. That might explain how this whole bonfire was set ablaze." Even to his own ears, he sounded breathless.

"Oh, I'm on it." The phone went dead as Zoey hung up.

Ah, Zoey, that beautiful, beautiful soul.

Kate jogged so she was walking beside him as he strode back toward his car. "Where are you going?"

"I don't know." He stopped. He was sure that her mother and her lover were long gone by now, thanks to his spotting them. Luckily, neither of them would have known him—the ghost. "Who is the beneficiary of your father's will?"

"I'm sure it's my mother. Do you think she was behind his death?"

He scrunched his face as he spoke, not wanting Kate to face the pain of her mother being involved in her father's murder. "She might be guilty of something. She and this guy, this Alexi. But we are going to have to prove it. Do you think you could get me back into the ConFlux building?"

"I'm sure, but what do you think you are going to find? So far, none of the people the police interviewed have had any information. And there hasn't been a whisper of my mother...my mother having...you know...an *affair*." She said the word like it was filled with worm guts. "Are you sure you saw what you saw?"

"I'm sure." He hated that he had to push this thing in her face, especially so soon after her father's death, but there was no avoiding what he had seen. "Are you close with your mother?"

She swallowed what must have been a lump in her throat, and even he could tell she was struggling to get past it.

He reached out, hoping and praying that she would slip her hand into his. He needed to know that she would have faith in him, that she had put her suspicions about him aside. Especially with the new information.

She didn't move.

He dropped his hand by his side. "Maybe your mother and Alexi are still there." It was unlikely, but right now his word wasn't going to make her believe him. In a case like this, with so much at stake, the only thing she would trust was going to be what she saw with her own two eyes. He couldn't blame her. *Doveryáy, no proveryáy.*

Instead of waiting for her to take his hand, he slipped his fingers into hers. He couldn't make her feel anything, he couldn't make her trust him, but he could prove himself to her. As they made their way to the alley, he peeked around the corner. The car was gone. He stopped.

Crap.

He'd taken a chance not following them, but it had been a calculated risk to keep them from knowing he was on their tail. He had to find them, to stop them from getting out of the city and the state. Once they did, it would be a hell of a lot harder to pin them down and bring them to justice.

"This is where they were?" Kate asked, her voice flecked with annoyance.

"Yeah, but don't worry. They couldn't have gone far. And Zoey is working on putting out a BOLO." He reached over and took her hand, giving it a reassuring squeeze. "I know how hard this must be for you, but I've got you. We are in this together."

"Just as long as we find them. That's what matters now."

They stood there for a moment in tense silence as he dissected her words. He didn't want to tell her that there were many things that mattered more—namely, the way he felt about her and what he wanted for their future— but thankfully she hadn't let go of his hand. Maybe she was starting to forgive him for being the messenger.

He wished he could open up and tell her that he loved her, but right now…it wasn't right. When he finally let those words come out of his mouth, he wanted it to be perfect—if there was such a thing. She deserved to be told in a way that would create a memory she'd cherish. She was special and she deserved to be treated like the goddess that she was.

"Let's jump in and head toward the interstate," she

said, motioning toward his car. "Maybe we can catch them heading toward Idaho."

If he was trying to bug out, that would be his objective as well. More populous areas to get lost in, and no international border to cross. Though, he would never have been stupid enough to get onto the one interstate that ran nearly the entire length of the state. He would take the back roads, the logging roads that led to Idaho and would keep him far outside the sites of any law enforcement. The only thing a person would have to worry about on those roads would be a game warden. As luck had it, there were only two who worked in this county. The odds would ever be in his favor.

Then again, Deborah and Alexi, a desk-jockey tech geek, didn't seem like the types who would head out to the woods or anywhere that lacked high-end amenities. If anything, they seemed like the airport kind of people. They wouldn't want to merely leave the state—they had assets that most didn't, including a deep set of pockets.

And with deep pockets came endless resources. A person could get anything for the right amount of money. In fact, he had once had a boss at the UN who had requested he do something nearly impossible that required several NDAs and a threat of death. When Troy had tried to tell the man no and that it couldn't be done, the man had told him just to give him the number of zeros it would take on the check to make it happen.

It had taken some work, but his mission had been accomplished. And, as luck had it, the perfect number of zeros on the check was seven. Immense requests required immense bank accounts—luckily, that was something his contact at the UN had in spades.

Thinking back on it, he really didn't miss those days.

He opened the car door for Kate and she slipped into the passenger seat. And though she was safely tucked away with him, he hated having to stop touching her. As soon as he got in and was buckled, he put out his hand and waited until she slipped her fingers into his before he took to the road.

Turning off Broadway, he took to the interstate in the direction of the airport, soon pulling off on the exit.

"Where are we going?" she asked, surprised.

"I bet you twenty bucks that she is at the airport. That or they are renting a private jet at Minuteman. Let's start here."

Kate opened her mouth like she was thinking about arguing. She'd tried calling her mom but it had gone straight to voice mail. Either the woman didn't have her phone or wasn't picking up.

"Besides, we are not going to stop them even if they are on the interstate. MHP will have to catch up to them if they are going that way. At the very least, if they are trying to cross over to Idaho, there is only one point they can do that from the interstate. If I was an officer, I would be sitting ten miles before that state line, waiting. We're covered."

She gripped his hand tighter, and from her touch he could sense her frustration—he didn't blame her. With so much riding on them finding her mom, it was hard not to feel like they had her father's memory pressing down on them—not to mention the fate of her family's company. A company that for all intents and purposes would likely belong to her once her mother was found and faced justice if she'd been involved in her husband's murder.

Luckily the airport was only a few minutes away—

even less the way he drove. He pulled to a stop in front of the doors leading to the main terminal, not caring whether or not their car would be towed.

As he was about to put the car in Park, his phone pinged with a message.

Zoey's text was simple: Targets just entered airport.

"They're trying to catch a flight," Troy ordered, excited that his assumption had been spot-on. He would have liked to think he was just that good, but there was no doubt that half of this was luck.

Getting out of the car, they rushed into the main body of the airport. An airport police officer was standing beside the boarding pass kiosks, his hands over his chest and a stoic look on his face. Troy hurried over to him. "Hey, there is a BOLO out on a man and woman, late fifties, early sixties, gray haired. Have you seen them?"

The man dropped his arms from his chest and snorted a laugh. "You just described about half the people in this airport."

Kate flashed him her badge. "We need information on this couple as quickly as possible. They are involved in a murder investigation." She lifted up her phone, showing him a picture of her mother. "This is the woman. Man has a mole on the left side of his face, near the temple."

The man took a close look at the woman. Grabbing his handset and turning away from them, he called the other officers on duty. It took a couple of minutes while the officer talked in a truncated, coded conversation before he turned back to them. "From our video feed, they were in the airport about five minutes ago. Then went back out to the long-term parking lot. We don't have any record of them leaving the property."

They were still on the grounds. "Close down all the public exits. We need to make sure that they can't escape. And we need you to call in to the locals, let them know what we have here."

The officer nodded. "We're already on it. Unfortunately, there is only myself and another officer on duty, but we will work as efficiently as possible."

Kate gave him a tip of the head. "Great. We'll start in long-term."

Troy gave him a clipped description of the car and the license plate number, though they were already a part of the BOLO. "You guys work short-term and the toll booth areas. If you come in contact, let us know."

They jogged out of the terminal. Their car was still running in front and they got back in. Hurrying around the loop, they entered the long-term parking lot. It wasn't a huge area, but there were only a few open parking spaces. And, as they twisted through the lot, he noted three other sedans that matched the car he had seen in the alleyway, but not the license plate.

As they rounded the second-to-last row, he spotted the car. It was still running. He parked in front of the nose of the vehicle, blocking them in, stopping them from escaping.

Kate jumped out of the car, her gun at the ready, pointed in the direction of the driver's seat. The man with the gray hair sat there, gesticulating wildly, almost as if the two were having some sort of fight.They didn't even notice them bearing down.

Her mother was in the passenger seat, and though Troy couldn't hear what she was saying, he could tell she was yelling. As he and Kate approached the car, neither Deborah nor Alexi looked over. Whatever was going on was heated.

He unholstered his SIG Sauer, readying himself just in case all of this went south. Though he hoped the two would see the futility of their situation, desperation led to desperate and often dangerous choices; choices a person wouldn't normally make.

Kate carefully approached the driver's-side door and knocked on the window, pulling the man's attention away from her mother and directly to her. The man jerked like he hadn't noticed anything outside of the world that he had built with Deborah.

Troy watched the man's hands, his right moving toward his ankle as the left moved to roll down the window.

"Put your hands where I can see them!" Troy ordered, pointing his gun at Alexi, backing Kate.

The man jerked as the window rolled down. "Whoa. I just had an itch—don't worry. There's nothing going on here, at least nothing you need to worry about. Stand down." He sneered over at Troy, his voice dismissive.

"What are you doing here, Kate?" Deborah asked. Her hair was mussed, her lipstick smeared. Her makeup was streaked where tears had slipped down and disappeared.

"I'm wondering the same thing about you, Mom." Kate growled, nudging the barrel of her gun in the man's direction. "Alexi, you need to step out of the vehicle."

The man's hands moved to the steering wheel.

"Put your hands up!" Troy yelled, afraid that if the man took the wheel, he would do something stupid.

Kate stepped back, as if she too was worried that the man would punch the gas and ram their car.

Alexi chuckled, raising his hands. "I know how this probably looks to you guys, but your mother and I were just talking. She's been through a lot and—"

"Stop right there," Kate said, as she walked over and, leaning in through the car's window, turned off the engine, removing the keys. She stuffed the keys into her pocket. "You can lie to some people, but I'm not one of them. I know exactly what you two are up to, and don't think you can get away with it. Now, both of you need to step out of the damn car, or we will remove you from this vehicle."

Her mother reached down and touched the door handle, moving to get out.

"No," Alexi said. "Deborah, you stay exactly where you are. They have no right to tell us to do anything. And I don't know where they're getting off trying to order us around like we're some kind of fugitives."

Kate laughed, the sound dangerous and low. "Really? You think you can play that game with me? If you don't get out of this car right now, I'll make sure I have every police officer from here to Seattle on your ass."

Alexi laughed. "For what?"

There were a few moments in life that Troy hated. The worst was inarguably facing death. Then came moments like this... Moments in which two people who loved each other were forced to see the other for who they really were. Humans could be the ugliest, most despicable and cruel creatures in existence.

Though he had no doubt that her mother loved her, Deborah was quite possibly a murderer. Regardless of the love that she held for her mother, Kate would have to do what her job dictated no matter how much it hurt. And what made it all worse was the fact that Kate held the cuffs, ones that could place her mother behind bars possibly until her dying day.

Chapter Nineteen

Kate could've been sick.

Here she had been, completely convinced that Troy was her enemy. And now here she was, forced to face the fact that her enemy was the one person she thought she could trust. Sure, she and her mother had never been entirely close, but her mom had loved her. And she thought her mother and father had, for the most part, gotten along. Maybe they hadn't had the strongest marriage that she'd ever seen, but in the lineup of corporate men and corporate wives, they seemed stable.

She couldn't imagine what had pushed her mother to have an affair. Troy had made it clear that he thought her mother was behind her father's murder, but she wasn't entirely sure. Not yet. There were any number of possibilities. One thing was certain, however: her mother hadn't pulled the trigger. Though she hadn't gotten the fingerprint analysis and ballistics tests back, she was almost certain that her mother's prints wouldn't be on any of the shell casings.

"If you don't get out of the car right now, we will drag your asses out." She paused. "I just got my nails done and I really don't want to get physical, but if you make me, Alexi, I'll be more than happy to facilitate."

Alexi moved to say something, but her mother stopped him with a touch to his arm. "Just listen to her."

Alexi sighed.

Her mother and Alexi slowly stepped out of the vehicle, closing the doors behind them.

Troy visibly relaxed. Apparently, he had thought things were going to go haywire. Though she should've been focusing on her own emotional turmoil, finding her mother in such a compromising position, all she could feel was a little bit satisfied that she'd pegged her mother's reaction right.

Her mother wasn't perfect—she was an adult, and she was human, but she wasn't evil. Maybe she had just gotten herself in a situation that she couldn't get out of. Maybe she had been forced to make a choice between something crappy and something crappier. That was how most crimes happened. Not that she was making excuses for her mother. She was only trying to understand.

"I want you both to go and sit on the hood of this vehicle," Kate ordered, reminding herself that this was work and not merely some screwed-up family drama.

Alexi and her mother walked to the front of the car and sat down. Troy strode over toward them. "You want me to pat them down?"

She nodded. Though she knew she should go help him, there was something so very wrong about her going to look for weapons on her mother and her boyfriend. Instead, she took out her phone and set it on the top of the car, recording their conversation.

"Mrs. Scot, can you please turn around and spread your legs?" Troy motioned toward the front of the car. "I'm going to pat you down now. Do you have anything in your pockets that could potentially stab or cut me? Do you have any sort of weapon that I need to know about?"

Her mother shook her head.

"Mom, do you want to tell me how Sal was involved in all of this?" she asked, hoping that her mother would answer her honestly while she was in such a compromising position. "It's better for you if you do." She proceeded to give her mother and Alexi the Miranda warning. Whatever info the two gave up could be used in a courtroom later.

Her mother twitched and looked over at Alexi as Troy's hands moved over her and up between her legs. "Can you please turn around?" Troy asked.

She turned around, and as their gazes met, there were tears pooling in her mother's eyes. "Baby," her mother began, "I'm so sorry about everything that happened. I didn't want anything to go this far."

The little flicker of hope Kate had been holding, that her mother was innocent and Troy was wrong in assuming the worst, died.

Troy had been right.

"How was Sal involved?" She tried to sound confident, like she knew exactly what had happened and was simply waiting for an admission before arresting her mother.

"Your mother didn't do anything wrong," Alexi interrupted. "This was all my idea. Sal was on my payroll—he was working for me. But he was acting on his own in all of this. It wasn't our plan for him to shoot anyone. He went rogue."

That, right there, was enough of an admission to provide a valid reason to arrest and charge both Alexi and her mother with murder. And yet she hated the idea.

How had they gotten themselves into such a predicament? And how had she found herself holding the only sets of handcuffs?

"And what was he doing for you, exactly?" Kate asked.

"As you likely know, he was the engineering director at the company." Alexi sounded pathetic. "It started out as just a friendship, but he told me things… Things, about the projects we were working on, that others wanted to know."

Troy grimaced and motioned to Alexi's feet. "Spread them." He did a quick pat of Alexi and stepped back. "Which *others* wanted to know about your projects?"

"Well—" Alexi paused "—there were a couple of people. I don't know who they were with, but they were offering a hell of a lot of money. And…well… I make good change, but I could retire on what they promised. All they wanted were a few schematics. Nothing that could really compromise any sort of government project. It was just parts. You know? No big deal."

This was why the government had to use a variety of machining companies to do their work—small leaks like this.

"How much?" Troy asked.

"Fourteen million, all paid through Bitcoin," Alexi said, sounding a bit proud. "They started at five. Seriously, a little more time and I think I could have gotten them higher, but at what point do you just not need any more money, am I right?"

Kate's knees grew weaker as she listened to the terrible story unfold. There were so many things wrong that she couldn't find a silver lining. Her life was imploding around her.

And whether or not her mother and Alexi realized it, what they were doing was illegal. She'd let a lawyer sort out all the charges, but she could think of several, some with stiff penalties.

"You are not seriously gloating about how much money you made off Solomon's death." Troy's tone was nearly a growl, and she was grateful for it.

"Absolutely not. That's not what I meant." Alexi put his hands up in surrender. "There was nothing illegal about what I did. I was just trying to make some money. I wanted to start a new life, a life that your mother would love… In a way she had grown accustomed to." He looked over at her mother, and the gaze her mother gave him nearly made her sick.

There were many things illegal about what they had done, but she wasn't about to point it out to them—not when she had them both on the ropes and talking about their crimes. Right now, she needed them to feel safe so they would tell her everything. She needed to pretend to be their friend so she and the FBI could formulate a full case and prosecute them to the fullest extent of the law—mother or not.

"So, you were going to run away with this man?" She tried to check any emotions from seeping into her tone, but it was a struggle, thanks to all the hate and disgust she was feeling.

Her mother looked down at the hood of the car.

"Mom, I get that love happens. I get that you can't always make sense of the things that you feel, and you sure as hell can make some terrible decisions. But why?"

Tears ran down her mother's face. "Why what?" she choked out.

"Why did you have to have my father killed? Did he learn what you guys were up to? That Sal and Alexi were working together to sell governmental secrets?"

Her mother sobbed, sitting back down on the car and resting her chin on her chest. "We told you. His death wasn't planned."

"Then why, Mom, why?"

"It was never supposed to happen this way... When I told him I wanted to leave...he blew up at me. He threatened to take everything." She took out a handkerchief from her pocket and softly wiped at the tip of her nose. "I was fine with that. I was willing to accept losing it all. Your father was a good man. He helped me through the cancer, through everything. It would be a lie to say that I didn't still love him. I just was no longer *in love* with him."

Her mother looked to her as if she was asking for her forgiveness and understanding.

Though she didn't feel either, she gave her mother a nod, hoping she would keep talking. "Did you pull the trigger?"

"No," her mother said, violently shaking her head. "That was Sal. He'd found out what happened. About the divorce. That's when your father hired your friend there..." She motioned toward Troy. "When I didn't fight your father for a division of the assets, he started to look into things...wondering why. I think he had started to sniff out Alexi, but he wasn't entirely sure."

"Deborah, you need to stop talking." Alexi shook his head. "We are innocent in this. That's all they need to know."

Her mother shook her head. "No. Kate is my daughter. Agent or not, she deserves to know that I'm not a murderer. After this breaks in the news, who knows what the public or a jury will say. Right now is the only chance to give her my full side of the story."

Kate swallowed back the bile rising in her throat. Her mother was very likely going to go to a federal penitentiary for this, and yet all she wanted to do was keep her daughter's love…and keep her from thinking the worst of her.

The world was a screwed-up place. And what made it worse was the fact that she couldn't stop her mother from talking. It went against her oath as an agent. She was to serve and protect the innocent. And, in this case, she was going to protect her father's memory over her mother's future.

"So, why would Sal pull the trigger and kill Solomon?" Troy asked, taking the lead as though he could tell exactly how hurt Kate was and what kind of turmoil she was in.

"Sal knew you would uncover the truth, that we had been using code to divert secrets to our mystery contact. He knew all about STEALTH and the power you guys have to get into any place you need. He convinced us it was only a matter of time until we were going to get caught. Our plan was just to take the money we had been stashing away in the Cayman Islands and disappear. But then, one day, out of the blue, Solomon called Sal into his office." Her mother looked at the car. "Things went south."

"And what about me, Mom? Why did you have your guy try to take me out?"

Her mother's sobbing intensified, but Kate didn't feel sorry for her… Instead, oddly, she didn't feel anything.

"I told him not to. I told him he could have a bigger

share of the money. But he knew you were breathing down our necks. It was only a matter of time. After what happened… I wanted to turn ourselves in… It's why we were here today. But…"

"Your mother is taking blame where there is none. We didn't do anything illegal," Alexi countered.

He could believe whatever he wanted; his ass was going to jail.

"Why didn't you guys leave after the shooting?" she asked.

Her mother sobbed. "I couldn't. It hurt so bad. I had to honor your father's memory before I could make another move."

She shook her head, trying to make sense of everything. "I appreciate what you are saying, Mom. I do." She drew in a long breath, accepting what she was going to have to do. "And I know this isn't your fault—at least, not completely… But, unfortunately, I'm going to have to place you under arrest."

Slipping the cuffs on her mother's wrists would be one sensation she would never forget. And yet being true and dedicated to her job and the world that trusted her had to come before protecting a criminal—even one who was family.

Epilogue

Six months later, Troy held his hands over Kate's eyes as he led her up the stairs and to the front door of her house. "No peeking, okay?" he asked, taking out the keys she had given him for her home from his pocket. "Promise?"

She giggled, nodding. "What are you up to?"

"Birthday girl, don't you worry."

"Oh yeah, you telling me not to worry is definitely going to make me feel at ease," she teased.

"You know, if you are going to be snarky, I don't *have* to give you your birthday present. I could just give it to some poor, hapless bystander. At least they would appreciate it."

She did a little hop from foot to foot, revealing her excitement. "Come on. I know I'm going to love whatever you are doing, but you are killing me. Can you open the door any slower?"

He laughed. She looked so damn cute standing there in her down jacket, bundled up. She had always called him her iceman, but now, looking at her, she was the one who seemed to better fit the part.

"After everything that happened with your mom,

with Alexi's and her convictions, I wanted to do something special. I know you've been through a lot."

Her little happy dance stopped and he wished he hadn't started his speech out like he had, but there was no going back in time.

"Anyhow, I want you to know how I feel about you. And though we've kind of talked about things—we haven't *talked about things*." He could feel her eyelashes batting against his palm as he spoke.

Reaching up to the door knocker, he tapped out a rhythm of dashes and dots.

"Is that…?" she said, giggling. "Do it again."

"But I thought you knew Morse code," he teased, doing it again.

She laughed and she pulled his hand away from her face. "I do… And I knew what you were asking the first time. But… I wanted to hear you ask it again."

"Are you going to answer me?" he asked, smiling as he dropped to one knee.

"Yes." She clasped her hands to her mouth as he pulled the blue box out of his pocket. He opened it, and inside the box was a princess-cut diamond solitaire. "Oh my… Yes, Grim. Yes."

He took the ring out of the box, gently slipping it on her finger. "I love you, Ms. Scot. Or would you prefer *Mrs. Spade*?"

She lifted her hand, looking at the ring. "If I'm going to be your wife, I want to be *your* wife and you're going to be *my* husband. A name doesn't matter to me." She threw her arms around his neck. "I love you, Grim."

A single tear twisted down his cheek. "I love you too, Mrs. Spade."

She hugged him tighter, finally letting him go. "Hey,

why the big surprise entrance to my house?" she asked, tilting her head to the side.

"Oh yeah," he said with a laugh. He hadn't intended on asking her to marry him right there, right now...and he had nearly forgotten the rest of his plan. Everything was all screwed up, but at the same time, this proposal was just like them...imperfectly perfect, and he'd have it no other way. "Close your eyes."

She did as instructed, and he opened the door.

"You can look."

She gasped.

Inside, hanging from line after line, were a thousand white cranes—the first of which he had folded for her while waiting for her in the coffee shop. Here was hoping the one thing he wished for above all others, the wish he had wished with every fold of the paper, would come true...the wish that they would be each other's forever.

* * * * *

COLTON 911: UNLIKELY ALIBI

LISA CHILDS

With gratitude to Patience Bloom, whose hard work and dedication makes the Mills & Boon Heroes line so amazing! Thank you for including me in the series!

Chapter One

This is it! The thing that could catapult Colton Connections from a multimillion-dollar company to a multibillion-dollar company. Excitement coursed through Heath Colton's veins, so much so that his fingers shook as he punched in the code on the elevator panel so that it would bring him to his penthouse apartment.

He drummed his fingers against the mahogany wall as he waited for the trip to end. When the doors started sliding open, he was already pulling out his phone. Then he strode the short distance across the marble foyer to the big, hammered-steel door of his unit. With one hand, he shoved in the key and unlocked the heavy door as he told his smartphone to call Kylie.

Despite it being well after business hours, she picked up immediately. "Hey, I was just going to call you about an employee situation we might have…"

Like him, the vice president to his CEO position didn't work just during regular business hours; she worked all the time. She handled finance and human resources. Colton Connections had about fifty employees, but Kylie Givens rarely had problems with any of them, at least with any that had required his attention before.

"Serious?" he asked.

She sighed. "Right now more petty than serious, but I think it might become more."

"Then it can wait until it does," he said as he crossed the hardwood floor to the bar built into one of the Chicago brick walls of his living room. Tall windows in those walls looked out onto the city of Chicago with all its glittering lights. "I have news!"

She chuckled, a throaty deep chuckle that never ceased to surprise him because, at five foot four, she was so petite in stature. "You've heard about the patent? It came through?" she asked, her voice rising now with the excitement already coursing through him.

"Not yet," he said. "But I've been assured we're very, very close to having it approved." The concept was so unique that no one—but his dad and uncle—could have come up with it let alone try to claim credit for it. So there was no way that another inventor or company could file a pre-issuance submission to challenge it from being approved…unless they'd somehow gotten copies of the plans.

She chuckled again. "So is this a cause for celebration yet?"

"I think so," he said, casting aside any doubts he might have had. This was just too damn big. He put his phone on Speaker and set it in the bar cart. "I'm going to fix myself a drink."

"I will, too," she said. "And we'll toast."

He chuckled again. "You're going to toast with genmaicha, aren't you?" It was the green tea, roasted with rice, that she drank all the time either hot or over ice.

Ice tinkled from the phone speaker. "So who's going to do the honors?" she asked.

"Me," he said. However, he wanted to toast to more than the pending patent. She'd essentially been his partner the past five years she'd served as vice president, but he wanted to make it official. He wanted to bring her in as a full partner before the patent went public, before they became even richer, so that she benefited as much as the rest of the company had from all her work.

He grabbed a glass and poured a chilled white wine into his. He wasn't going to talk about the partnership yet. Not over the phone. That, he would offer her in person, maybe over a dinner at his cousin Tatum's restaurant downtown.

"So I'm waiting," she prodded him.

He chuckled, but before he could begin his toast, his doorbell rang. It was late for deliveries and visitors. Dread knotted his stomach as he considered that it might be Gina. He was too happy to deal with any more of that drama. Kylie probably wouldn't want to listen to any more of it either, but he left the phone on Speaker, saying, "I better see who's at the door. Hang on just a second."

The glass of wine still in his hand, he headed toward that heavy steel door. But when he peered through the peephole, it wasn't Gina standing in the foyer. Two uniformed Chicago PD officers stood outside his door. The security guard in the lobby must have given them the code for the elevator.

Whatever relief he'd felt over it not being Gina turned quickly back to even more intense dread. Instinctively he knew these men were not bringing him good news. Heath pulled open the door. "Hello, Officers…"

"Are you Heath Colton?"

"Yes."

"I'm Sergeant Brooks and this is Officer Chandler, sir," the older of the two men said.

"How can I help you, Sergeant?" Heath asked.

Was it Jones? Had Heath's younger brother gotten into trouble again? While he'd always been a bit of a rebel growing up, he'd been doing so well lately. He had finally seemed to get his act together. But better that the officers come to Heath than to Pop. Their dad would be furious.

While he was always so happy and fun-loving with everyone else, he had less patience with Jones for some reason.

"Mr. Colton, we need you to come with us," the sergeant replied.

"Why?" Heath asked.

Of course if Jones was in jail, he would have been given a phone call, not an escort to his brother's house. And Jones was not anywhere in sight. Heath was the one getting an escort. To jail?

"Am *I* in trouble?" Heath asked.

"No, sir, not at all," the younger officer replied which earned him a quick glance from his sergeant.

What was that look? A rebuke? Wasn't the younger man allowed to speak? Or had he misspoken because Heath was really in trouble?

"Someone needs to tell me what's going on," Heath said, his patience wearing thin. "Or I'm not going anywhere with you." At least not without a lawyer present.

Although he couldn't imagine why he would need one.

"Sir, we need you to come with us to the morgue," the sergeant replied. "We need your help identifying bodies."

Heath sucked in a breath. Oh, God…

It was worse than jail.

Jones had died. But not alone.

Tears stung his eyes, but he furiously held them back. "Of course," he said. "But I don't know who my brother would have been with…" Emotion choked him. "So I—I don't know who the other body might be."

"Brother?" The sergeant shook his head. "No, sir. We believe these bodies to be your father and uncle."

Heath gasped as all the air left his lungs. He felt like he'd been sucker punched and nearly doubled over from the force of the emotional blow. "No…" he murmured, shaking his head.

"Your mother and aunt are currently out of town and therefore not available, so your grandmother, Abigail Jones, told us that you would be able to make the identification for us," the sergeant continued.

"No, it can't be them," he said. Not Pop and Uncle Alfie. "There must be some mistake."

"When did you last see them, sir?"

"Just a couple hours ago. They were at the office, working late because Mom and Aunt Farrah are at that home show for their interior design business." The twin brothers had come up with another invention, probably one as brilliant as the one for which Heath was awaiting the patent. That was going to benefit the medical community so much. But not the pharmaceutical companies. The new breathing-treatment apparatus was going to eliminate the need for so many drugs.

"We are pretty certain that it's them," the younger officer said gently. "We just need the confirmation of a family member."

"I'll go," Heath said. "But you're going to see that there's been a mistake." A cruel mistake.

It couldn't be them.

Not Pop.

Not Uncle Alfie.

There was no way in hell either of them was gone let alone both. No way in hell.

SHOCK GRIPPED KYLIE so that she nearly dropped her glass of tea onto the kitchen floor. The voices emanating from the cell phone she'd left sitting on the butcher-block counter had to have been some kind of act, not reality.

Was Heath playing a sick joke on her?

No. He wouldn't joke about something like this. Even Ernie, famous for his bad jokes, wouldn't joke about this.

Ernie...

Or Pop as he always insisted she call him. But only his family called him that. Kylie wasn't his family. At least not his real family. She was part of his work family. His and Alfie's and Heath's and the rest of the employees. They were a family of sorts, one who reveled in the inventions the twins came up with although at least one of them might have too much interest.

"Heath!" she yelled his name, her voice ricocheting back from the speaker on her phone like an eerie echo. But Heath didn't answer her back. Had he left his penthouse without his cell phone?

Heath always carried his phone.

A strange fumbling sound emanated from the speaker of her phone, and Heath's voice rumbled out after it, "Kylie, I have to go now."

"Wait," she said. "I'll go with you." She didn't want to go, but she didn't want him going alone.

"No," he said. "I'm sure it's a mistake. I'll go with these officers and confirm that those bodies are not Pop and Uncle Alfie."

"No, don't go with them," she protested as an image popped into her head, of her mother being dragged through the doorway of their apartment, two officers grasping the arms they'd shackled behind her back. She was so tiny...even in Kylie's childhood memory, her long black hair tangled around her delicately featured face.

It's a mistake, Kylie. I'll be home soon...

But she hadn't returned. Ever.

"I'll be fine," Heath said. "I'll call you when I get back."

If he got back.

A click emanated from her phone, and the screen went black, the call disconnected. Even knowing that he was gone, she murmured, "Heath..."

She was worried about him—worried that he was wrong, that it wasn't all a mistake.

"No." She shook her head. She agreed with Heath; the police had to have made a mistake. And if they hadn't, what the hell could have happened? A traffic accident? It must have been, in order to have claimed both their lives.

But that wasn't possible. They couldn't be gone.

She glanced at the clock on her microwave, noting that the nightly news was just about to start. Hurrying into the living room of her small home, she scrounged around for the remote control she always misplaced. Maybe it had slipped between the couch cushions again. She picked up a sweater—one her grandmother had knitted her before her arthritis had gotten too bad for her to handle the big needles. While she uncovered some of the navy corduroy of the couch, she didn't find the remote…until she lifted a pile of papers from the trunk she used as a coffee table.

Her fingers fumbling with the buttons, she clicked on the TV she rarely watched. Whenever she had it on, it was mostly for white noise, so that she didn't feel quite so alone in the house now that Baba was gone. Baba was short for the Japanese word *obaasan* for grandmother. Her grandmother and mother had been Japanese. She didn't know what her father was.

Baba had loved her shows.

She hadn't liked the news. She hadn't wanted reality. But Kylie had been a realist since that night the police had taken her mother away. Heath hadn't been taken away like that. He wasn't being arrested; he was being devastated—if the police were right.

She should go and try to find him. But by the time she figured out which precinct and morgue, she would be too late. The police could not be right. But as she scrolled through the channels, she knew she'd found the news when flashing lights flickered across the screen. Crime-scene tape cordoned off a parking lot at the back of a big building with many businesses inside. Kylie recognized the building and the parking lot—where she worked, where she parked.

She fumbled with the remote again, trying to find the Volume button, so she could hear what the reporter was saying. She turned it up so loud that the words echoed throughout her living room. "Police have confirmed two casualties at the scene of a shooting earlier this evening. The victims have yet to be identified."

They were probably being identified right now. Alfie. And Ernie. Pop...

Heath's father and his uncle.

Her employers and her friends.

Shot.

It made no sense. But violence never made any sense. Not to Kylie. She hugged her grandmother's sweater against her chest, holding it close to her. But it offered no comfort. Not to her.

And what about Heath? Would anything comfort him for his loss?

HE WAS NUMB. Just earlier he'd been filled with such excitement. But now...

Now he could barely think. Barely feel.

He punched in the code in the elevator just as he had over an hour ago, and it brought him back where his nightmare had begun, where the police had come to his door. And it was a nightmare, one that would haunt him forever.

He would never forget standing in front of the viewing area of the morgue, waiting for the coroner, who stood on the other side of the interior window, to lift a sheet. Heath shuddered as he remembered what he'd seen—more than had been intended for him to see. It had been so terrible, so much worse than the scariest thing he'd witnessed before then—Kylie having an allergic reaction. Her face had gotten so red before turning pale, and he'd thought she was going to die. But she'd used some kind of injector and had saved herself.

There would have been no way to save Pop. Not from that.

The coroner had quickly adjusted the sheet and murmured, "Sorry."

But it was too late.

That image was forever burned in his mind, a nightmare that would never end. He'd had to clear his throat before turning to the sergeant who'd stood beside him. Then he'd answered the man's silent question. "That's my father."

The coroner had lifted the sheet on the second body then, and Heath had flinched. "That's my uncle."

"They look so much alike," the younger officer had murmured.

Almost exactly. Even in death.

They'd died the same way, at the same time.

Or maybe Alfie had gone first, just like he'd been first to come into the world and had never let his younger twin forget it. Heath's eyes burned with tears as he remembered the camaraderie and the love between the two men.

The men he'd idolized and tried to emulate from the day he'd been born. With his thick dark-blond hair and dark blue eyes, he looked the most like them. For a moment he imagined himself on those morgue slabs.

But why?

He wasn't in danger. He hadn't known that his dad and uncle were in any danger either. Everybody had always loved them—would always love them.

He blinked and focused on unlocking his door. When he pushed it open, light enveloped him. He must have left the lights on because it wasn't dawn yet; it wasn't even quite midnight, which would mark the end of the longest, most horrific day of his life.

He should go to the house, go to his mother and aunt. But he wasn't even sure they were home yet. They'd been out of town—at that decorating show. He would wait a bit, give himself a little while to try to get those images out of his head, the horrific images of what had been done to the men he'd loved.

Why would someone do that?

He could sooner imagine someone wanting him dead than either of them. But both...

He swallowed hard, choking on the emotion strangling him. He'd tried to be stoic in front of those policemen, and fortunately the shock had numbed him. It was wearing off now.

The pain was starting to grip him.

He shoved the door closed behind him and leaned back against it. He was just about to slide down it to the floor when a metallic clang broke the silence of his penthouse, like something clattering onto the hardwood. He couldn't see anything that had fallen in the living room, but the kitchen was around the corner, out of his line of sight.

Someone was in there, moving around…waiting for him, like the killer must have waited in the parking lot for his dad and his uncle to leave the building. Why the clatter? Was he looking for a weapon? A knife?

Hadn't he brought the gun he had used to kill Heath's heroes?

A gun.

For the first time in his life, Heath wished he had one. That he had more than his fists and his smart mouth to defend himself now. Because just as his dad and his uncle hadn't survived the bullets fired into them, Heath knew he wouldn't survive either.

He needed to open the door and run back into the hall, into the elevator, to try to escape…

But something stronger than fear gripped him now. Rage. If the person who'd killed his dad and uncle had come for him, Heath was going to give him a hell of fight.

Chapter Two

Soothing harp music emanated from her earbuds, drowning out all sound for Kylie but not all thought. No matter how loud she turned up the music, the reporter's words still rang louder inside her head. *Two casualties*...

Shooting...

Why?

Why would someone hurt the two kindest, most brilliant men Kylie had ever known? The casualties must have been them. Who else, besides she and Heath, would have been leaving the building at this late hour? The other businesses, on the other floors, worked more regular hours than Colton Connections did.

Tears rushed to her eyes, so she squeezed them closed, holding them back. She'd come to the penthouse to be supportive of Heath, not to bring him down even further than he was. Would he even come home, though?

No. He would go to be with his family. They were all so close. A pang of envy struck her heart over that closeness, over the very size of his family. After those police officers had dragged away her mother, all she'd had was Baba. Losing her a few years ago had been devastating, but at least she had died peacefully, of old age.

Ernie and Alfie hadn't been old. And they hadn't died peacefully.

Why had someone shot them?

It made no sense. Crime rarely did, though. Especially the crime perpetrated against her mother, who'd been wrongly accused of being a criminal. Her only real crime had been that she'd loved too easily and so unwisely.

Poor Mama...

Poor Alfie and Ernie...

And Heath.

Kylie had been a fool to come here, expecting him to return to his penthouse. She would have been smarter staying home. But in case he had come back to his place, she hadn't wanted him to be alone. She also hadn't wanted to be alone.

Seeing that yellow crime-scene tape fluttering around the parking lot that she walked through at least twice a day nearly every day had unnerved her. Scared her.

A strong hand gripped her shoulder, whirling her away from the counter where she'd been cutting up vegetables, and she screamed and raised the knife in instinctive self-defense.

Heath pulled his hand away and held it and his other one up, and his lips moved as if he was speaking. Remembering the earbuds, she pulled them out, and simultaneously they said, "You scared the hell out of me!"

"I'm sorry," she said. And not just about scaring him. She dropped the knife and wound her arms around his waist, offering him comfort, maybe seeking comfort, as well. Laying her head against his chest, she murmured, "I'm so sorry."

He must have sensed that she needed consoling as well because his hands touched her back, gently patting it. Even through her sweater and tank top, her skin tingled from that contact. She was probably just overly sensitive right now—with everything that had happened and with all the memories it had invoked for her. But this wasn't about her. It was about him.

She leaned back and looked up at his face—which was surprisingly stoic for him. Usually his handsome features played out every emotion he felt. "Are you all right?" she asked.

He nodded and now he pulled away from her, as if trying to shield his pain. She knew he had to be in pain. He'd been hoping so much that the police had been wrong.

But after seeing the news, she believed it must have been the twins leaving the office late as they so often did, as she and Heath so often did. "It was Alfie and Ernie?" she asked, just to confirm.

He nodded again, and a muscle twitched along his tightly clenched jaw.

"I'm so sorry," she said again as she moved back into his arms. "So sorry that they're gone and so very sorry that you had to identify them."

A shudder moved through his big body and into hers,

and he clasped her tightly now. "It was so…" His deep voice cracked with his grief as his body shook again.

She couldn't imagine how it must have been, what he must have seen. "Oh, Heath, that's why I didn't want you to be alone," she said. "I'm sorry that my letting myself in alarmed you, though." He'd given her a key some years ago in case she needed something he'd left at his penthouse while he was out of town.

"I heard you moving around in here, and my first thought was that maybe the killer came for me. Maybe I was the one he really wanted to take out. Because why would anyone want to hurt Uncle Alfie and Pop?"

She shook her head. "I don't know. It makes no sense."

He cursed. "No damn sense at all. Why? Why?"

"I don't know," she repeated. "I don't know. What did the police say?"

His broad shoulders moved in a big shrug. "Nothing really. They said a detective had been assigned the case and would talk to me when they were ready to question me."

She tensed with alarm and drew back in his embrace. "Question you about what?"

He shrugged again. "I don't know. I certainly have no idea why someone would have done this to them—of all people."

"How're your mom and your aunt?" she asked. "Are they holding up?"

"I—I talked to my mom on the phone," he said. "She's devastated. So is Aunt Farrah. And Grandma…" His voice cracked again. "I feel like a creep for not going over to Aunt Farrah's house, but I couldn't see them right now—not after what I just saw in the morgue." He shuddered again. "I can't get it out of my head."

Tears burned in her eyes, tears for him. She'd worried about that—when he'd said where he was going, what he was doing…

Identifying the bodies.

The bodies of his own father and uncle, of the men he'd grown up idolizing. She couldn't imagine his pain, but she wanted to help him through it. "That's why I came over here," she said, "I didn't want you coming home to an empty place."

He shook his head. "Sweet but unnecessary," he said. "I'm fine."

"Liar."

He chuckled. "Okay, I'm not fine. I probably won't ever be fine again."

"You will," she said. "It's just going to take time."

He narrowed his eyes. "You've been through something like this?"

"No." She shuddered. "Not like this…but…" She shook her head. "We're not talking about me. We're talking about you—about whatever you want to talk about."

She gestured at the granite island, where she'd cut up all those vegetables. "And you should eat. I'm sure you probably forgot to today." Like he usually did. Forgot to eat. To shave. To get his hair cut.

His dark golden hair was a little shaggy now and dark gold stubble clung to his strong jaw.

He looked at the food and shook his head. "I—I can't eat right now."

"Then how about some tea?" she asked. "Something to soothe your nerves."

He chuckled and pointed to the knife on the counter. "After finding you in here wielding that, yeah, I could use something to soothe my nerves, but not tea."

She pointed at the earbuds she'd dropped next to the knife. "I didn't hear you. I'm sorry."

"Stop apologizing," Heath said, as his hands gripped her shoulders slightly. "I appreciate that you're worried about me, but you don't need to take care of me."

She smiled. "Someone has to. You rarely take care of yourself."

"I took care of them," he said, his voice cracking. "That was my job, making sure they had everything they needed. I should have been there." He swallowed hard, as if choking on emotion. "I need a drink."

He headed back into the living room and straight to his mahogany bar cart. Kylie followed him. Just a couple hours earlier, they had been about to have a toast when his doorbell had rung. How everything had changed…

She shivered and pulled her grandmother's sweater tighter around herself. With it, she wore only the camisole and the leggings she'd been wearing when he'd called. She usually wore the camisole with boxer shorts to bed. She could have taken the time to change before driving over, but she'd wanted to make sure she got to the penthouse before him. Not that she'd offered him much in the way of comfort or support yet.

"You need food and rest," she told him as he splashed some whiskey into a glass.

He took a sip and shuddered again. Then he cursed. "I don't think I could get drunk enough to get those images out of my mind."

That was why she didn't drink very much or very often. She never wanted to use it as a crutch to make her feel better, like her mother had used the attention of men who'd only been using her.

"Let's put other images in your mind instead," she suggested. "Let's talk about happy memories."

He snorted. "What did you put in your tea earlier? You don't sound like yourself at all."

Heath did not know her nearly as well as he thought he did. But that was good. Kylie didn't like people knowing her too well. She didn't like being that vulnerable with anyone.

"You weren't like this when I talked about my breakup with Gina," he said. "You weren't looking for anything positive then."

"Because the positive was you breaking up with her," she said. "You two weren't right for each other."

He uttered a weary-sounding sigh. "She's beautiful and smart. How is that not right for me?"

"You weren't right for her," she said. "She wanted more than you could give her."

He chuckled. "Some time and attention?"

"You're busy running a business," she said. "And she couldn't understand that." Gina Hogan especially hadn't been able to understand the long hours Heath had worked with Kylie.

"She just wanted to know that I cared. She wanted a commitment from me," Heath said.

"Do you regret not giving her one?"

He shrugged. "I haven't really given it much thought. I've been too busy. And now…"

"When I said let's talk about happy things, I didn't mean Gina." She hadn't liked the clingy, possessive young woman at all. Gina had actually been jealous of *her*, as if there had ever been or would ever be anything between her and Heath but work and friendship.

"The patent?" he asked with a heavy sigh.

He'd been so excited about it earlier, but now he just sounded exhausted. Understandably so. What had happened must have taken such an emotional toll on him that it had physically affected him, as well.

"Come on," she said as she closed her hand over his forearm. "Let's go lie down." She glanced at the black leather couch, which was narrow and hard, and dismissed it as a comfortable option. "In your bedroom…"

"Maybe Gina was right about you," he said with a teasing grin. "Maybe you are after my body."

So he had been aware of his girlfriend's accusations. She glared at him but playfully. She couldn't be mad at him now—not over anything. She felt too bad for him, for his family, for herself…

She chuckled. "You wish…"

He managed a half-hearted grin. "I wish you weren't so worried about me. Go home, Kylie. I'll be fine. You don't need to babysit me. I'm a big kid."

A kid who'd lost his dad. He'd suffered such a loss tonight and had seen something so horrible that she didn't want to leave him all alone, like her mother had been in that jail cell.

She didn't want to lose him like she had Mama.

FALLON COLTON SLICED the knife through a carrot; the pendant light dangling over the island reflected off the blade—reflecting her own image back at her.

"It's after midnight," her sister Farrah said. "Why are you cooking?"

Her hand trembled and she grasped the knife handle tighter. "I won't be able to sleep. Will you?" she asked her twin who reflected her own image back at her, too.

Farrah shook her head, tumbling her short brown curls around her face. Fallon's hair was curly, too, but long. She'd pulled it up in a clip to keep it from falling into the food, though. Like their husbands, Fallon's husband Ernie and Farrah's husband Alfie, she and Farrah were identical twins.

Late husbands…

A sob bubbled up the back of Fallon's throat, but she struggled to choke it down and keep it there. If she started crying again, she wouldn't be able to stop. That was why she needed to cook. Maybe she should have gone home to do that, but she hadn't wanted to be alone in that big house without Ernie. The sob rose up again, but she swallowed harder, refusing to give in to the threatening tears.

"I can't eat either," Farrah remarked as she grabbed the bowl that had been full of cake batter and plunged it into a sink full of sudsy water.

Fallon glanced at her twin who was a little heavier

than she was because she usually enjoyed the food Fallon made more than Fallon did. Farrah's green eyes were swollen and as red as Fallon's probably were, as they would be if she kept crying. She closed her eyes for a moment and breathed deep, willing away another flood of tears.

"What are you two doing up yet?"

The voice startled Fallon so much that she dropped the knife, which clattered onto the counter. "Mom, you scared me," she said.

"I think we're all scared," Abigail Jones remarked in her usual no-nonsense manner.

"Is that why you aren't sleeping, Mom?" Farrah asked their mother. Abigail lived with Farrah in a mother-in-law apartment she'd moved into shortly after the stroke that had left her a bit wobbly.

She seemed even more fragile now, even older than her seventy-eight years as she stood in the arched doorway to the Tuscan-style kitchen. Her shoulders were bowed, her short silver hair a bit mussed, as if she'd tried sleeping but hadn't been able to get comfortable.

Fallon knew better than to even try. To even step foot in the bedroom she'd shared every night with her husband.

She started shaking, and Mom joined her at the counter, wrapping her slender arm around Fallon's waist. "I'm sorry, Mom," she said, knowing she should have been holding it together better, like her mother had when Daddy died.

Mom had been alone tonight—when the police officers had come to make the notification. She'd even been asked to identify the bodies.

"Shh…" Abigail replied. "You have nothing—"

"I do," Fallon said. "If I'd been home tonight instead of at that expo."

A sob escaped from Farrah, and she began to shake, too. "Oh, my God. That expo was my idea. I made you go."

Fallon shook her head. "You didn't make me do anything." She'd wanted to help her twin promote their decorating business. Big things had been happening for them.

"Shh…both of you," Abigail said. "What happened tonight was nobody's fault but the person who pulled that damn trigger. You're not to blame. Ernie and Alfie are not to blame."

Fallon thought of her oldest son, of the CEO of Colton Connections. "Heath—"

"It's certainly not his fault," his grandmother admonished her.

"No, it's not," Fallon said. "But I can't imagine that he isn't blaming himself, that he isn't hurting. And he had to go…" She swallowed the emotion that rushed up again. "…to the morgue. He had to identify them."

Abigail shuddered. "I'm sorry now. I could have gone. I had the police get Heath instead. I should have—"

"No," Fallon said. "I wouldn't have wanted you to go either."

"But Heath…" Abigail murmured.

"That's who I'm afraid for," Fallon admitted. "I'm

afraid that he's all alone and blaming himself." But when he'd talked to her on the phone, he'd told her that he would come over in the morning. She'd known then that he'd wanted to be alone with his thoughts—with his memories.

That was the last thing Fallon wanted—because she knew once she was alone, the grief and loss would over-whelm her—like it was probably overwhelming her old-est, proudest child right now.

A door opened somewhere in the house. Someone had come here, but she knew it wasn't Heath. He was too stubborn. Too proud to reach out…

It had to be one of her other children or one of her sister's children who were just like hers since they'd all grown up together—since she and Ernie and Farrah and Alfie had raised all their kids together on the property they shared, on which they'd built their two houses. The kids were grown now—self-reliant, even Jones, although Ernie hadn't acknowledged how much their youngest child had matured recently. Now he would never have the chance, never have with his youngest son what he'd had with his oldest son—a close bond of love and mutual respect.

Poor Heath…

Of all her children, he had probably lost the most to-night. His father and uncle and his best friends.

HEATH HAD WANTED to be alone tonight. He'd thought he'd needed to be alone to get so damn drunk that he couldn't think, that he couldn't feel…anything.

"Damn you," Heath murmured, and he rolled onto

his side to stare at Kylie who lay next to him in his king-size bed.

A slight smile curved her lips; she was as unrepentant as she was stubborn. "I'm not leaving," she said. "You shouldn't be alone right now."

It was as if she knew what he was going through. She had lost her parents somehow and had come to live with her grandmother. But she'd never talked about how she'd lost them, but Kylie didn't often talk about herself. She talked about business, like he did. He was the one who introduced the nonbusiness topics into their conversation, like his love life. Whenever he'd asked about hers, she'd claimed that she was too busy to have one.

He really was, too. That was why it hadn't worked with Gina or with anyone before Gina. He wasn't going to try to make it work with anyone else, especially now when so much of the business was going to be his responsibility.

While Kylie shared his bed, it was purely platonic, like it had always been between them no matter whatever else Gina might have thought was going on with them. But Heath couldn't help noticing how beautiful Kylie looked with her hair spread across his pillow like dark silk. She'd taken off that big sweater and wore only a thin camisole that clung to the soft curves of her body. Maybe she'd noticed his staring, or maybe she'd gotten chilled because she pulled up one of his blankets to her chin. But then she said, "Get comfortable. Because I'm not leaving. And you need to talk."

"I don't want to talk," he said.

"That's a first."

He chuckled at her teasing. Maybe having her here was better than being alone. He sighed and unbuttoned a few buttons of his dress shirt before shrugging it off. Then he reached for his belt.

"Hey!" she exclaimed. "Just how comfortable are you planning on getting?"

"I usually sleep in the buff," he lied—because it was his nature to tease her back.

She glared at him. "Then don't get that comfortable."

He just took off the belt and the shirt and lay under the covers in his dress pants and socks. It wasn't as if he was going to be able to sleep anyway.

"Tell me about them," she said.

"You know them." Heaviness settling on his heart, he corrected himself, "You knew them."

"Tell me what I don't know," she said. "Tell me about growing up with them. Was your dad always so fun? Your uncle always so shrewd?"

He lay back on his pillow and let the memories flow through his mind and then flow out of his mouth. He shared everything he remembered from his childhood. How his dad and Uncle Alfie had encouraged all his little inventions, how he'd gone to work with them so often that they'd given him his own little workspace on the ninth floor where all the creativity happened.

He shared everything with Kylie, so much so that he must have bored her into falling asleep because when he glanced over at her, her eyes were closed, her lips parted as she breathed softly.

And in watching her sleep, he grew so tired that

his eyes wouldn't stay open either. But moments—or maybe hours—later, a noise startled him awake.

Was she leaving?

He hadn't wanted her to stay, but now he didn't want her to leave him alone. "Don't go," he murmured. But when he opened his eyes, he found her lying beside him.

Still asleep.

So she wasn't making the noise he heard this time. Someone else was in the apartment. Before he could throw back the covers to confront the intruder, the person was there, standing in the bedroom doorway.

A curse slipped out of his lips.

If only he'd moved faster. If only he could have prevented the ugliness that was sure to come.

Chapter Three

Kylie had been dreaming of the perfect childhood Heath had described to her—of how he'd tagged along with his dad and uncle to work, of how they had stolen raw dough off the tray before his mother had a chance to bake the cookies, of how loved and happy he was.

Instead of feeling envy over what she'd wished she had, she'd felt only happiness for him, that he'd at least had that before it had all been taken away.

Like her mother had been taken from her.

Those officers dragging her through the apartment door.

Fingers grasped Kylie's arm, nails digging into her skin, as someone dragged Kylie from the bed. She opened her eyes as a cry of surprise and fear slipped through her lips.

"You bitch! You scheming, backstabbing bitch!" a woman screamed at her, the same woman who was pulling Kylie out of Heath's king-size bed.

Kylie fell onto the floor as the woman suddenly released her. Her elbow struck the hardwood, eliciting another cry—of pain—from her lips. Through eyes gritty yet with sleep, she looked up to find Heath with his arms around Gina Hogan, holding her back.

How the hell had she gotten inside? Heath must have given her the code, like he had Kylie.

The blonde woman thrashed against him as she strained toward Kylie, her arms flailing. "You bitch! You conniving bitch! I knew you were after him! I knew all your calls and those late nights at the office had nothing to do with work!"

"Gina!" Heath exclaimed. "You're wrong, and you're making a fool of yourself!"

The woman shook her head, swinging her long blond extensions toward Heath's face. "You made a fool of me. Both of you! Sneaking around behind my back, lying to me—"

"I never lied to you," Heath insisted. "There's nothing between me and Kylie. There never was."

She snorted. "You're lying right now. I just caught you in bed together!"

"Sleeping," Heath said. "That's all we were doing." She snorted again.

"It is," Kylie insisted, but she regretted falling asleep. Her intention had been to be there for Heath, to support and comfort him. She'd failed at that and now her presence here had caused an ugly scene he hadn't needed to deal with.

"Then you must be horribly disappointed," Gina said. "You're so in love with him that you can't stand him being with anyone else. That's why you sabotaged my relationship with him. You bitch—"

"Time to go," Heath said. "I don't have the patience

for this right now." With his arm around the blonde's waist, he guided her from the room.

Before Gina passed through the doorway, she turned back and glared venomously at Kylie. Moments later, her voice dripped sugary sweetness as she told Heath, "I came here for you. To comfort you. I'm so sorry about your father and uncle, Heath. Please, let me be the one to help you through this."

"I appreciate your sympathy," Heath said. "But I can't handle the histrionics right now."

"I didn't mean to get hysterical," she said. "It was just seeing you in bed with her and knowing that's what she's been scheming for all this time. She's taking advantage of your grief, Heath."

He sighed. "Nobody's taking advantage of me, Gina. Now you need to leave."

"But Heath—"

"Please, Gina, I don't want to fight with you, not anymore." He sounded so weary that he must not have slept much, unlike Kylie.

Heat flushed her face that she'd fallen asleep on him. She was also embarrassed about the wild accusations his ex-girlfriend was throwing around about her. He wouldn't actually put any credence in what she said, would he?

"I'm sorry, Heath," Gina said again. Apparently she realized she'd pushed him too far because, without any further remarks, the door opened and closed.

And Heath uttered another weary sigh. He must have run his hands through his hair because when he returned to his bedroom it was all mussed.

"I guess I shouldn't hold my breath waiting for my apology from her," Kylie said. Even when Gina had been dating Heath, she had barely managed to be civil to Kylie. And now...

His lips didn't even twitch into a slight smile, yet alone the grin she'd hoped to induce. "You better leave, too," he told her with less kindness than with which he'd handled the raving lunatic. But then he'd once admitted to Kylie that he wished he could fall in love with Gina; he had no such feelings beyond friendship with Kylie.

Or didn't he even consider them friends?

Or had he actually believed any of the outrageous accusations Gina had hurled at her? That she'd schemed to take him away from her?

Kylie tilted her head and studied his handsome face with its tightly clenched jaw and creased forehead. "What's wrong?"

"What the hell do you think is wrong?" he asked, his voice getting louder as anger bubbled out of him. "My dad and uncle were just murdered, and you won't leave me the hell alone! I just want to be alone!"

"Hea—"

"Go!" he shouted at her. "Get the hell out of here, Kylie!"

She flinched. For the second time in just minutes, a person was lashing out at her. While Gina had physically hurt her—her elbow and the scratches throbbed still—Heath's words hurt her worse. All she'd wanted was to help him. But she'd failed in every way. This wasn't about her, though.

So she drew in a deep breath and forced away her hurt feelings.

This was about him. And she wanted to do what was right for him—whether he knew what that was or not. Gina wasn't right for him or about anything she'd said about Kylie, either.

Had he actually paid any attention to what Gina had said? Was he thinking now that Kylie was in love with him and was using his grief to get her hooks in him?

If he suspected that it was true, it was no wonder he was trying to throw her out. He wanted a serious relationship about as much as Kylie did—which was not at all.

SHE HADN'T DESERVED THAT. Heath knew it even before the guilt weighed down his shoulders and settled heavily on his chest. For a second she looked like he'd attacked her as violently as Gina had.

But then Kylie, being Kylie, lifted her chin and forced a slight smile. "You really think you're irresistible, huh?"

"What?"

"You must believe that crap Gina was spewing about my being in love with you."

He nearly laughed, felt one actually bubbling up the back of his throat. But he didn't have the energy to let it out or to let Kylie stay. He was so damn tired. He needed to rest and while he had fallen asleep watching her sleep, his body wasn't nearly rested enough. Instead it was tense and strangely aware of her. That was why he wanted her gone—before he did something stupid, like actually believe Gina's accusations, not because Kylie had any designs on him but because he wanted her to...

She was beautiful with her long, dark hair tousled around her bare shoulders, with her delicately featured face and dark eyes. He wanted her.

That was crazy. She was a coworker he wanted to make a partner. A business partner only.

As Heath had told Gina many times, he didn't mix business and pleasure. And he would never risk a harassment lawsuit by going after an employee of Colton Connections, no matter how beautiful and smart that employee was.

"Why the hell won't you just go?" he asked, frustration eating away at his patience and his tact.

"Because you need me," she said.

Now he felt like she'd slapped him, as he drew his head back and gasped. Maybe she thought he had feelings for her—feelings beyond friendship and professional respect. "I—I don't need anyone."

"Yes, you do," she said. "You need me."

"Gina said you're in love with me," he said. "Not the other way around."

"Gina's crazy," she said.

It wasn't the first time Kylie had said it, but it was probably the first time she'd had a real good reason for saying it. Gina had lost it pretty badly when she'd found them in bed together. But he almost understood her reaction. Gina had loved him, only to have him break her heart because he hadn't been able to return her love.

"You and I are just friends, and you damn well know

that," Kylie continued. "And you need a friend now more than ever, Heath. So stop pushing me away."

"If you were really my friend, you would respect my wish for privacy right now, and you'd leave like I've asked you to over and over again," he pointed out, his patience wearing thin with her. And with his sudden awareness of her.

Maybe he was the crazy one.

She shook her head. "You think this is the worst of it?" she asked. "Last night? That's just the beginning. You have the funeral. The investigation…" Her voice trailed off with a little crack of fear.

What was she scared of?

"You don't think I know what's coming?" he asked. "I need to get to my family. I need to get the hell out of here myself, so I just want you to go."

She picked up her sweater from the foot of the bed and pulled it on over that thin camisole. Then she walked toward him, toward that doorway.

Was she finally leaving?

Instead of feeling the relief he expected, dread settled heavily into the pit of his stomach. Maybe he didn't really want her to go. He didn't want to actually be alone.

But he'd already shared more with Kylie—more of his pain and his memories—than he ever had with anyone else. But then he'd never experienced pain like this before.

What was his mother going through?

He needed to go see her. He should have gone to her last night. But when he saw her, he needed to be strong for her. And he hadn't been strong last night.

When Kylie walked past him in the bedroom doorway, he curled his hands into fists, so that he wouldn't reach for her. So that he wouldn't stop her from leaving. This was what he wanted—to be alone for just a little while before he joined his family.

They were probably all together now.

Everyone but him…

He needed to join the others.

But hell, Kylie was right. He also needed her. And he'd just treated her so damn badly. He'd had no right to lash out at her, no more right than Gina had had. All she'd wanted was to be there for him, as a friend.

And he'd proved to be a crappy one back to her. An unappreciative one.

He was going to need her now, more than ever, as a friend and as a business partner. But had he, in his grief, ruined that friendship?

He couldn't afford to lose any more right now. He couldn't handle losing anyone else that mattered to him. And Kylie mattered—damn her.

DETECTIVE JOE PARKER spread the crime-scene photos across his desk, studying every angle. The victims had been walking out of the building where their business, Colton Connections, took up two of the twenty floors. A lot of other businesses occupied the building, but these two men had been working the latest, were known to work the latest.

But for the CEO and VP…

Heath Colton and Kylie Givens…

Kylie was just an employee.

Heath was family. Ernest's son. Alfred's nephew.

Where had Heath been last night? Why hadn't he been working late like he was rumored to always do... with Kylie Givens? She hadn't been working late either.

Where the hell had they been?

Joe needed to know. He needed to know everything about the Colton family and the Colton business—because he'd discovered, after spending more than half of his forty-six years of life working for the Chicago Police Department, that rarely was it ever a good idea to do business with family. It usually brought out the worst in people.

Greed.

Ambition.

Resentment.

The people who'd told him that the CEO usually worked late were some of the other tenants in the building; they had described Heath Colton as a very ambitious, very hard-working businessman.

Joe had just gotten the case last night, but he'd already started working it looking for possible eyewitnesses then and this Friday morning. After canvasing the crime scene, he'd come into the precinct so that he could go over everything he'd already learned.

Not enough.

Not yet.

He ran his hand over his hair that he kept short—so it was easy to handle. Not like his son's longer, tight coils...

He glanced at the picture on his desk—of his giggling little boy, of his beautiful wife with her flawless dark skin and of him, a tall, proud husband and father. Joe was a lucky man because they were the happy Black family they appeared like in that picture.

What kind of family was the Coltons?

And what kind of man was Heath Colton? Just how ambitious was he?

Ambitious enough to kill his own father and uncle so that he had no one to challenge his completely taking over the company?

Chapter Four

"I thought you left," Heath said when he joined her in the kitchen of his penthouse.

Kylie clutched the cup of genmaicha tea in her hands, bracing herself for more of his anger. She could have gotten angry, too, with his attitude, with how harshly he'd spoken to her, but knowing him as well as she did, she understood why he'd lashed out. He was like an animal in pain, snarling and snapping at anyone who tried to help it. His heart was broken.

So was hers.

Alfie and Ernie had been wonderful men and she had loved them as if they were her own family. Hell, she wished she'd had a father like Ernie. She inwardly sighed. She'd wished she had any father at all.

"I didn't want to leave you with the mess in the kitchen," she said, indicating the clean granite countertop.

He chuckled. "Last night you reminded me of my mom. She always cooks to deal with stuff."

Maybe she had been acting like his mother—with how stubbornly she'd tried to take care of him. Maybe she hadn't been as respectful of his wishes as she should have been.

"And now you're acting like my aunt Farrah with the cleaning," he murmured.

She'd met and respected both women as much as she had their husbands. His family was so damn special. He probably didn't need her, like she'd told him. Maybe she just needed him to need her, especially now, when her heart ached for his loss and for her own. She couldn't imagine going back to the office today. But it was Friday.

She needed to work.

Especially because of that situation she'd wanted to address with Heath the night before.

But she didn't want to burden him with business now.

"I made you some toast," she said, pointing to the plate on the counter. The butter had melted into the golden bread which she'd slathered with the strawberry jam she'd found in his refrigerator. With all the big chunks of berries, it looked homemade, probably his mother's handiwork. He'd mentioned more than once that Gina didn't cook. "And I put together the vegetables for a salad if you want one later."

"Kylie…"

"I know," she said, and she raised her hands, palms up toward him. "You just want me to leave."

"And yet you keep refusing to go."

"I'm sorry."

He sighed. "No, I'm sorry. I shouldn't have spoken to you that way. I know you're only trying to help me through all this, and I appreciate your efforts."

She smiled. "I'm also being selfish," she said. "I didn't want to be alone either."

"I know you loved them, too," he said, acknowledging her feelings.

This was the Heath she knew and...

Respected.

He was a good man, like his father, like his uncle.

Tears choking her, she couldn't speak; she could only nod. He walked across the kitchen and wound his arms around her, like she had him the night before. Holding her close, he said, "Thank you."

"For what?" she asked. "For finally getting rid of Gina for you?"

He chuckled. "I don't know if you have."

She doubted it, as well. Gina knew she'd had a good thing, and Kylie didn't blame the woman for not wanting to lose it, to lose Heath. He was so smart and handsome and...

She pulled back from the hardness of his muscular body. "You think she might be coming back? That's why you're hugging me now?"

He chuckled again, just as she'd intended. "No, I'm hugging you to express my gratitude."

"For toast?" she asked. "It's not much." She intended to do more, to handle everything that she could at the office. "I am going to leave you now, though."

"You really don't have to go," he said. "I was being an ass earlier."

"Yes," she agreed with a little chuckle to indicate she was only teasing him. "But I do need to go into the office."

He groaned. "Oh, God, all the employees will have seen the news. They'll know…" He pushed a hand through his mussed hair. "I need to talk to them and assure—"

"You need to be with your family," she said. "I'll talk to the staff. I'll assure them that the company is in good hands. That you've got it all under control."

He shook his head. "But I don't…" His voice cracked. "If I had anything—anything at all—under my control, my dad and uncle wouldn't be dead. Murdered."

She pressed her fingers over his lips. "That was not your fault, Heath. That was some maniac out there who has nothing to do with you."

"Are you sure?" he asked, his lips moving against her fingers. "Are you sure it has nothing to do with me? With the business?"

A frisson of unease raced down her spine, chilling her despite the warmth of her grandmother's sweater. "I don't think we can be sure of anything until the killer is caught," she said. "And the police will catch him." She hoped, but she didn't have a lot of faith in them, not when they'd never caught the real criminal in her mother's case. But she wasn't going to express those doubts to Heath, not right now when he needed assurances.

Like their staff needed assurances.

"I better leave now," she said. "I need to go home and change before I head into the office." When she turned to leave, his hand caught her arm, holding her in place. She tilted her head back and smiled at him. "You've been trying to get rid of me since you found me here," she reminded him.

He shook his head. "I didn't mean that, and you know it."

She'd hoped he hadn't meant it. "But I really do have to go to the office now."

He nodded. "I know. I just…"

"What?" she asked.

"I just want you to be careful."

That was when it fully dawned on her that she wasn't just returning to the office. She was returning to the scene of a crime—a heinous crime.

The senseless murders of two wonderful men.

"Of course," she said. "I'll be perfectly fine."

But she doubted that even as she professed it. She wasn't going to be fine, not with Ernie and Alfie gone. But as hard as it was going to be on her, she could only imagine how hard it was going to be on the men's wives and children. "And please express my condolences to all your family," she told him.

He nodded. "They know how important you were to Pop and Uncle Alfie."

Tears rushed to her eyes again, and she turned to leave. But his hand closed around her arm again and he murmured, "And to me."

Her heart did a little flip in her chest, and her pulse quickened. But she reminded herself that he meant just as a friend, which was all she felt for him, as well.

Friendship and respect.

"You be careful, too," she said.

And finally his hand slipped from her arm, and she slipped away…slightly shaken. But that was from all the talk about the murders…

And danger…

Was anyone else in danger?

Or had Alfie and Ernie been the killer's only intended victims? There was no way of knowing until the killer was caught…or until he or she tried to kill again.

THE SOUND OF a door shutting startled Farrah, making her splash her hands in the water in the sink, sending droplets of water and suds into her face and hair. Had she fallen asleep standing up?

Maybe. They had been awake all night. She and Fallon. Mom had gone to sleep after they'd assured her they would get some rest. They'd lied to her. Both of them had known they wouldn't go to bed. That they couldn't go to their empty beds.

"Someone else has just arrived," Fallon said. "See, it's a good thing I cooked all this food last night. Everybody is showing up and will be hungry."

Farrah doubted that. She wasn't hungry, and usually her twin's culinary creations tempted her to eat more than she should, and she had the thicker waistline because of it. But she wasn't tempted to eat anything at all now.

Her empty stomach roiled at the thought of food and the smells that wafted from the Crock-Pots Fallon had lined up on the counter. Farrah didn't have the heart to tell her sister that even if an army showed up, they wouldn't be able to eat all of the food she had prepared.

Fallon wouldn't really care, though. She'd just needed to stay busy, just as Farrah needed to stay busy—so that she didn't think.

Didn't feel…

Didn't miss Alfie any more than she already did. He couldn't really be gone—not forever. There had to have been some mistake.

But then Heath walked into the kitchen, and she saw the grimness of his face, the pain in his eyes…and she knew. It was true. He had correctly identified the bodies.

Alfie and Ernie were really dead.

That look on his face, the devastation and pain.

That must have been what they'd felt. What he'd seen when he'd identified their bodies.

"Aunt Farrah…" he called out to her, but it sounded as if he was far away instead of just across the kitchen. Then he was at her side, but it was too late.

Her legs had already given out beneath her, and she dropped to the cold tile floor in front of the sink.

"Farrah!" Fallon called out to her. But even she— who was always so close—seemed far away. Nobody seemed as far away as Alfie. He was really gone.

Forever gone.

HE HATED THE way she'd looked at him—the way they all looked at him. It was almost as if by identifying them that he'd been the one who'd killed them. At least that was how Heath felt.

And how Aunt Farrah had reacted…that just the sight of him had had her fainting in horror. No. She hadn't fainted. She hadn't lost consciousness, and she'd tried to reassure him that her reaction had had nothing to do with him. But he knew better.

The rest of his family stared at him, too, as they milled around the kitchen, picking at the food Mom had piled on plates for them. She and Aunt Farrah were constantly in motion, Mom messing with the food, Farrah cleaning. It was as if they didn't dare to stop moving, as if they were somehow running from the truth even though they basically moved in slow motion.

"Good thing I didn't bring food from the restaurant," his cousin Tatum remarked as she looked down at the plate his mom had thrust in her hands. Her blue eyes were swollen and red, like she'd been crying all night, and her long blond hair was limp instead of in its usual waves. Tatum, a chef, had recently opened her own restaurant downtown, and it was doing so well that it was difficult to get a table—although she always made exceptions for family.

Gina had always wanted to eat at True. Maybe because it was so trendy that it was the place to be seen. He wasn't being fair, though. She could have just wanted to eat there because she wasn't a cook like Mom, like Kylie.

How was his vice president handling the office? He shouldn't have let her face all the employees' grief, questions and concerns without him. But she was better at dealing with the staff than he was.

She was better at dealing with *him* than anyone else was. Nobody but her would have stuck with him with as surly as he'd been last night and this morning.

"Heath!" Tatum called out with concern, like she'd been trying to get his attention for a while.

He hadn't noticed. "What?"

"Are you okay?"

"No," he admitted.

She slid an arm around his waist and leaned against him. "Me neither."

"None of us is," his sister Carly murmured as she joined them. With her pale blond hair and blue eyes, she looked more like Tatum's sister than his. She looked at him then quickly looked away, like everyone else had been doing. Even though Tatum had her arm around him, she was more focused on her plate of untouched food than his face.

Aunt Farrah couldn't even look at him now.

Did they all blame him for the deaths? Did they think as CEO, he should have had more security in that parking lot? Colton Connections didn't own the building, and he'd never been able to control his dad and uncle. They'd set their own erratic schedule based on whatever invention they were working on.

"When will the funeral be?" Carly asked, her voice cracking with dread.

"The police won't release the bodies until they've concluded the autopsies and evidence collection," he said, sharing what he'd been told.

Carly gasped in shock then rushed out of the kitchen. Tatum put down her plate of food and followed her cousin. And Heath groaned.

He wasn't helping his family; he was only making them feel worse. He would be of more use at the office. He set the plate he hadn't realized he'd been holding onto the counter next to Tatum's, then he slipped out of the crowded kitchen and headed toward the back door.

His hand closed around the knob, but before he could turn it, a small hand settled on his arm. He expected his mother to be the one trying to stop him, but he turned to see his grandmother standing behind him. Not remembering if he'd greeted her or not yet, he leaned down to kiss her cheek. "Hi, Grandma."

"Hi and bye, apparently," she said.

He nodded. "I really need to get to the office."

"You really need to get out of here," she said, as astute as ever.

He nodded again. "I feel like it's too hard on them to even look at me."

"It has nothing to do with you, dear. It's just hard for everyone right now."

"I know," he said, dread settling heavily into the pit of his stomach. "Especially Mom and Aunt Farrah."

"I'll take care of them," she promised with a strength that belied her seventy-eight years. She was a strong woman, though, and she loved fiercely and no one more than her twin daughters.

"I know," he repeated.

"Who will take care of you?" she asked.

An image of Kylie, her hair splayed across his pillow, popped into his head, but he shook it out. "I will take care of me and the company."

"You can't bury yourself deep enough in work to forget what happened," she said.

"I'll never forget," he agreed. "I don't want to forget. I want to figure out why and who…" His voice trailed off as rage joined his grief.

"Leave that for the police," she urged him. "That's their job, not yours."

"Then they damn well better get to it," he said. He hadn't even talked to a detective yet, just that sergeant and his sidekick last night.

"They will," she said. "But in the meantime, please be careful."

"Of course, Grandma," he assured her, and he leaned down to press another kiss against her smooth cheek before he left. Her words stayed with him, ringing inside his head.

Be careful...

Could he be in danger?

Had the killer gotten the wrong Colton last night? His dad and uncle weren't the only ones who worked late. He and Kylie often worked later than they had, much to the discomfort of a certain former girlfriend of his.

Heath jumped into his SUV and drove out the circular drive, past the other vehicles parked on it. Besides his siblings and cousins, neighbors and friends of his family had been in the house, offering support and sympathy.

He hadn't been able to provide either. Not like Kylie had provided him last night. He needed to talk to her... about work, about the murders.

Kylie was insightful, smart; she might have some ideas. Because he was clueless as to why anyone would want to harm his dad and uncle.

Like Grandma's words, a strange feeling stayed with him, too—that feeling he'd had in the house when everyone had been looking at him. But they'd looked away when he'd caught them staring.

Whoever was watching him now wasn't looking away because that sensation stayed with him all during his drive, so much so that he kept glancing into the rearview mirror of his SUV. And then when he arrived at that parking lot where the broken crime-scene tape fluttered in the breeze, the sensation intensified. Was someone watching him?

Why?

To make him the next target?

Or maybe he'd been the real target all along?

Or stress, grief and lack of sleep was making him paranoid. He really hoped it was the latter. Because if his dad and uncle had lost their lives because of him, he would never be able to forgive himself.

Chapter Five

Kylie swallowed a groan of frustration. This was the problem she'd wanted to address the night before with Heath. After what had happened last night, though, it had seemed inconsequential—until now. Until Tyler Morrison refused to leave Kylie's office.

"Tyler," she said, her voice getting sharp with exasperation. "I don't have time to discuss this with you now." Or ever.

He'd followed her back to her office after the meeting she'd held in the conference room. The meeting where she had been able to provide very few answers to all the employees' questions. Hopefully she'd at least been able to comfort them that Heath would continue to helm the company, and that it would survive and flourish. Their positions were safe. Their lives were safe.

Or so she hoped.

"Then let me help you out, so you'll have more time," he offered.

"You're a lawyer," she needlessly reminded him.

His constant arguing was a dead giveaway to that. He also looked the part, stereotypically, in the expensive, tailored suit with his dark hair slicked back and the ruthlessness in his dark eyes.

"You help us write up the patents and contracts—"

"I can do more," he persisted.

She suspected that he already had, but she didn't have the proof she needed. Yet.

Because of his help with the patents, he was one of the few who was privy to information on the new inventions awaiting patents. New inventions.

Her heart ached at the thought of how few of those there would be now. That bubble of excitement she'd always felt just working on these floors, with those brilliant inventors, had popped. Instead of excitement, she'd felt dread this morning, but she'd still forced herself to come in. She'd promised Heath she would take care of everything for him.

But he must not have believed she could handle it because she glanced up to find him standing in the doorway. Tyler whirled toward him. "Hey, Boss, I was just offering my services to Kylie to help out more, especially now, but she's refusing my offer."

"Not refusing," Kylie corrected him.

Heath glanced at the dark-haired man and narrowed his eyes, as if searching his memory for who the hell he was. "Excuse us," he told the lawyer, without adding his name. "But I need Kylie in my office now."

Tyler's slick smile slipped away. "I—"

"Need to get to your own office," Kylie finished for him. She stood up and followed Heath out as he took the few short steps down the hall to the office next to hers:

his. She didn't know if Tyler followed her order or not. And she didn't give a damn at the moment.

Heath waited until she stepped inside before closing the door. Dark circles rimmed his deep blue eyes, and his golden hair was mussed up, as if he'd been running his fingers through it.

"Are you okay?" she asked.

"I don't know." He shrugged. "I think I'm getting paranoid."

Maybe that was all she was, too, about Tyler, but she needed to be certain. "Why?" she asked.

He shook his head. "It's not worth talking about—not with everything going on. Fill me in."

She told him about the meeting and how she'd assigned the publicity department to handle the press.

"They've been calling?" he asked. Then his face flushed. "Of course they've been calling. It's been all over the news. Their deaths. Their murders."

Since he'd confirmed their identities and all family had been notified, their names had been used in the news coverage.

"What are the publicists telling the media?" he asked.

"Same thing I told the staff this morning," she said. "You're still CEO. The company is safe. They're safe."

His mouth curved into a slight grin. "So you're lying?"

"No," she said. "I believe that."

"I wish I did," he said, his voice gruff with cynicism.

"What's going on, Heath?" she asked.

Knuckles rapped against the office door behind her back. But she doubted he would have answered her even if they hadn't been interrupted. They didn't have a receptionist because they didn't need one. A company of inventions didn't have many unsolicited visitors. The staff used special ID badges to access their floors and offices, and if they had visitors, security called for them to go down to the lobby to escort them up. So Kylie opened the door expecting to see Tyler again, pushing his agenda.

If only she knew for sure what the hell that was.

Tyler stood there, but he wasn't alone now. He must have brought up the visitor from the lobby. A tall African American man stood next to him. Like Tyler, he wore a suit, but it wasn't as expensive or as expertly tailored. His broad shoulders tested the seams of his dark jacket.

"This is Detective Parker," Tyler introduced the man.

Kylie tensed as that image flashed through her mind from so long ago, of those officers dragging her mother through that doorway.

Heath stood up and greeted the man with a handshake. "Good, someone's been assigned to investigate the murders of my father and uncle."

"Yes, Mr. Colton, I am working the case," Parker confirmed as he stepped inside the office with them.

Heath's office was bigger than hers, but with those two tall, muscular men inside it, Kylie felt dwarfed and claustrophobic. The urge to run, to hide like she had when she was a child, came over her, but she suppressed it. She'd promised to be there for Heath through this nightmare.

"How can I help you, Detective?" Heath asked.

"I have some questions for you," Parker said with a glance at her and at Tyler.

"Tyler, you can go," she directed him. She had no intention of leaving, though.

"As legal counsel, I should stay," he insisted.

She shook her head. "You're a contracts lawyer, not a criminal lawyer." Not that Heath would need a criminal lawyer. Even the detective couldn't suspect that Heath Colton had anything to do with the murders of his own father and uncle.

But then she noticed the intensity in the man's eyes as he studied Heath. He definitely was looking at him like he was considering him a suspect.

"I don't need any kind of lawyer," Heath said. "Leave and close the door."

Tyler obeyed the CEO's command. Maybe it was only her authority he dared to test. That was why it was good she hadn't brought her concerns to Heath yet; it was better that she dealt with him.

Parker glanced at her. "And you are?"

"Kylie Givens," she said, but she didn't extend her hand to shake his, not with the disturbing image of those cuffs snapped tight around her mother's thin wrists still playing through her mind.

"The vice president," he said with a nod. Then he turned back to Heath. "And you're the CEO."

Heath nodded now. "Yes, I am. Between the two of us, Kylie and I should be able to answer any questions you might have about Colton Connections."

"So you'll continue to run the company?" Parker asked.

Heath nodded again. "Of course."

"Will you inherit it?"

Heath shrugged. "I have no idea. I don't know anything about my dad's or uncle's wills or if they even had them." His throat rippled as he swallowed hard, as if choking on emotion. "You'll have to ask my mother and aunt about that."

Parker nodded. "I have."

"Then you know."

"They will let me know when the will is read," he said.

"So they don't know?" Heath asked.

Or they'd been concerned with the direction the detective was leading his questions.

Like Kylie was concerned.

Straight to Heath.

"We were able to confirm your mother and aunt's whereabouts last night at the time of the murders," Parker said. "Now I need to confirm yours. Were you at the office?"

"No," Heath said, his broad shoulders drooping as if he carried a load of guilt over that.

"If you'd been here, if you'd walked out with them…" Kylie had to swallow hard now as emotion choked her. "You might have been killed, too." Her heart ached at the thought, at even more senseless loss, a loss which inexplicably felt even worse to her than theirs. But maybe that was only because she'd always worked more closely with Heath than she had the twins.

"You could have been here, as well," Heath pointed out. "Pop and Uncle Alfie walked you to your car so many times."

Tears stung her eyes. Yes, they had, out of concern over her leaving so late. Usually Alfie had offered some insightful observation about something while Ernie had been cracking lame jokes. They'd been such wonderful men.

She shook her head, trying to shake off her grief, and blinked back the tears.

"Where were you?" Parker asked Heath.

She knew he'd been home alone, but if he told the detective that, he wouldn't have an alibi that could be verified. And she was afraid that the detective would do the same thing to Heath that had been done to her mother, settle on him as a suspect and look no further.

"He was with me," she said. "We were at his penthouse."

Heath's brow furrowed with confusion. Fortunately the detective had turned his attention to her now.

"Really?" he skeptically asked. "If you were working late, why weren't you both here as I've been told you usually are."

She forced a smile. "Because we weren't working, Detective."

"Oh…" He glanced from one to the other of them, looking as dumbfounded as Heath looked.

"We're always together," she said with an even bigger smile. "Whether we're working or not."

"So you're a couple?" Parker asked.

"Because we work together, not many people know about our relationship," she said. "But, yes."

Heath's mouth opened, and she waited for him to call her on the lie. As she waited, she stared at him, silently pleading that he play along—for his sake. And for his dad's and uncle's sakes.

Not hers...

THE DETECTIVE STARED at him in speculation. Kylie stared at him in entreaty. What the hell was he supposed to do? Lie to the police or reveal that she had lied instead?

That image, of her hair across his pillow, flitted through his mind. She'd been there for him last night. He couldn't give her up to the police. But why the hell had she lied?

Did she actually think that he might need an alibi? That he had something to hide?

Fighting back the fury bubbling inside him, Heath nodded. "Yes, we were together." They had been...just not until after the murders.

"So you are a couple then?" the detective asked.

Heath swallowed hard, choking down the truth so that he could utter the lie, "Yes. Yes, we are." A couple of damn liars.

"And you were together last night?" the detective persisted. "The entire night?"

"Uh, we left the office separately," he said.

He'd had a meeting on the other side of the city, but by the time he'd found a parking space, the person—his contact in the patents department—had called to cancel. He'd given him some encouraging news, though, just hadn't wanted to chance meeting him in public because he wasn't supposed to divulge any information on pending patents. And if Heath had used him as an alibi, the guy probably would have lied and said they'd never had a meeting planned at all. When he'd left, Kylie had been heading out with a briefcase full of work she intended to do at home. Alone.

"Mr. Colton?" Detective Parker prodded him.

He cleared his throat and forced out the lie. "But yes, we were together the entire night."

"The police officers who picked you up to identify the body didn't see anyone else in your apartment," Parker said.

Damn. It was getting worse and worse…and if they checked phone records…

"I was in the bedroom," Kylie said, and her face flushed bright red. "We were being silly. He was mixing drinks for us in the living room, and we were actually on our phones at the time."

"And you didn't come out when the police officers arrived?" Parker asked.

Kylie's face flushed a deeper shade of red. "I—I wasn't dressed. And he left so quickly."

He had left quickly. That much was true. But not much else that came out of her mouth. How was it that she lied so damn easily?

He'd thought he'd known her so well, but now he couldn't help but wonder. And how little she must know him to think that he actually needed an alibi.

Detective Parker nodded, as if he believed them, but Heath wasn't certain that the lawman really believed anything he heard from suspects. And somehow, Heath was a suspect.

He shuddered at the thought, that anyone could think him capable of such a horrendous crime.

And for what?

Greed?

Power?

He had enough money, enough power. He wanted his dad and his uncle back. Hell, he wanted his life back because he knew it was never going to be the same. Not with them gone.

"Do you have any other questions?" Heath asked. "Is there any way that I can help the investigation?"

The detective studied his face for a long moment, his dark eyes speculative. "Just being truthful, that's the most important thing."

And yet, Heath had done the exact damn opposite because of Kylie. He'd lied during a police investigation. That was a crime; he knew enough from prior court battles over patents to know that much. But Kylie had lied first and he hadn't been willing to expose her.

He escorted the detective back down the hall with Kylie trailing behind as if she was worried that Heath would confess the truth to the man. He pushed a button to open the doors that led to the elevator. Leaning against those doors to hold them open, he said, "Goodbye, Detective Parker."

"I'm sure I'll be talking to you again," the lawman replied ominously.

Or at least it sounded ominous to Heath.

The minute the elevator doors closed on the detective, Heath turned on Kylie. After ushering her back down the hall and into his office, he slammed the door behind them. Then he asked, "Why the hell did you lie like that? Why the hell did you make me lie like that?"

But he wasn't sure he wanted her to answer, wasn't sure he wanted her to admit that she might have some doubts about his innocence. Enough doubts that she'd supplied him with a false alibi.

Could she actually think that he had something to hide? Or was she the one who'd needed the alibi? The one who had something to hide.

"THEY'RE LYING," JOE Parker murmured to himself as he stepped back into his PD vehicle. He had been a detective long enough to know when someone was lying to him. He was also a father, and his son Isaac, as young as he was, was a more convincing liar than they were.

No, Daddy, I didn't color on the wall.

No, Daddy, I didn't put the TV remote in the potty.

A smile curved his lips as he thought of his little boy. Heath Colton had once been Ernest Colton's little boy. Could that kind of love turn to such hatred and violence?

Unfortunately it could. That was why, for potential suspects, Joe always looked at the family first. So often the victims knew their killers and were even related to them by blood or marriage. The wives had alibis. That didn't mean they couldn't have hired someone to kill their husbands. But they'd been so devastated.

Like he would be if something ever happened to Kinsey.

God, he couldn't imagine his life without her in it... or their beautiful little boy. He'd been with them last night. Where had Heath Colton and Kylie Givens really been?

Because he sure as hell wasn't buying that fabricated alibi. They had both been lying.

Why?

Were they in on it together?

Had they planned to take over the company Heath's father and uncle had built?

Murder was one hell of a hostile takeover.

Chapter Six

Kylie flinched as Heath grasped the elbow that had been bruised that morning when Gina had jerked her out of his bed. She tugged free and turned toward where he leaned against the office door he'd slammed closed. She didn't know if she'd ever seen him look so furious—not even last night.

He hadn't been angry about the murders of his dad and uncle then; he'd just been devastated.

He was angry now. "What the hell was that about? Why did you do that? Why did you make me do that?"

"I didn't make you," she said defensively. He'd gone along with her lying about the alibi albeit apparently not willingly.

"If I hadn't backed up your lie, you might have been arrested," he said.

She flinched again as she considered getting dragged out of his office like her mother had been dragged out of their apartment. "I thought he was going to arrest you," she said. "That's why I told him that."

"Why would you think he would arrest me?" Heath asked. "Do you think I could have anything to do with the murder of my own father? Of Uncle Alfie? I love— loved…" His voice trailed off, thick with emotion.

"I know, Heath," she assured him. "I know how much you loved them and that you would never, ever hurt them."

"Then why did you feel the need to lie to the detective?" he asked. "I don't understand."

She sighed. "I know you don't, that you can't…unless you've lived through it."

"Lived through what? What are you talking about?" he asked, his brow creasing with a furrow of confusion like it had when she'd offered the false alibi for him.

She closed her eyes and saw again that image of her mother being arrested for something she hadn't done and how distraught she'd become.

"You know my grandmother raised me," she said. She'd talked to him about Baba; he'd even come to her grandmother's funeral with her.

"Yes, you were an orphan and your grandmother took you in," he said.

"I don't know if I'm really an orphan," she admitted. "I don't know who my father is. My mother would never tell me. I suspect he was married. She had a habit of falling for the wrong men and doing the wrong things for them."

Furrows formed in his brow again. "What are you saying? That you've fallen for me? That's why you lied for me?"

She chuckled. "Gina really did get to you this morning. I am not in love with you," she insisted. "But I do care about you, and I didn't want the police to drag you off like they did my mother."

He pushed a hand through his already rumpled golden hair. "What are you talking about?"

"My mom was a brilliant woman," she said. "A doctor, you know."

He shook his head. "I didn't know that. You never told me about her. Just about your grandmother."

"I don't like to talk about my mother," she admitted. "And I really don't remember all that much about her." But that image of the police dragging her away and then those few times she'd gone to visit her in prison before she…

"What did the police do to her?" he asked.

"They accused her of selling drugs," she said. "Of writing illegal prescriptions. She died in prison before she could prove her innocence."

He gasped. "I—I'm sorry, Kylie. I didn't know."

Heat flushed her face with embarrassment. "I don't like to talk about it."

He stepped away from the closed door then and approached her. His fingers touched her cheek, sliding softly over her skin. "I'm sorry you went through that."

She nodded. "I didn't want *you* to go through that. For you to be arrested for something you didn't do."

"But Kylie…" he said; she knew what he'd left unsaid.

"My mother didn't do it, Heath. One of her crappy boyfriends stole her prescription pad and forged her signature. She wouldn't sell drugs. She wouldn't…any more than you would have killed your father and uncle."

He nodded, but she could tell that he clearly didn't believe her. He made it even clearer when he said, "You were a child. I doubt she or your grandmother wanted you to know the truth."

"What? That innocent people go to prison? That's the truth, and if you've watched the news, you'd realize that it happens more often than you think."

He nodded, but she suspected he was only humoring her.

"I know," she insisted. "I know that she was innocent of those charges. She'd made some stupid mistakes, but that had been about the men she'd trusted and nothing else."

"What about you?" he asked.

"What about me?"

"Have you trusted the wrong men?" he asked.

She shook her head. "No. I'm very careful," she said. She'd only dated men she'd known very well, men that she hadn't been able to fall for. Because falling in love made a person stupid, like her mother.

Hell, even like his ex-girlfriend. Gina Hogan had probably been a nice, normal woman before she'd fallen so hard for Heath. She should have known better, like Kylie did, than to trust a man with her heart.

"What about me?" he asked.

She furrowed her brow now as she studied his handsome face. "What about you?"

"Why do you trust me?" he asked.

A chill chased over her skin despite how warmly she'd dressed—in a wool suit with a sweater beneath the oversize jacket. "I know you wouldn't kill your dad and uncle," she repeated.

She trusted that was the truth, but as a man...

She knew him much too well to ever fall for him. Even though he'd shared that he'd wanted to fall for Gina, he hadn't been able to give her the love and commitment she'd wanted, and that had broken the woman's heart.

No. There was no way Kylie would ever trust Heath Colton with her heart.

MAYBE HE SHOULD have been grateful for her loyalty and trust in him, but Heath couldn't shake the notion that Kylie's lie was going to come back to bite them both on the ass. Even after having the day to think about what she'd done, and how he'd blindly backed her up, he wasn't sure how to fix it, how to save her from getting in trouble.

And maybe it was for the best. This way the detective would rule him out as a suspect and focus on finding the real killer. He just had to make damn sure that Parker didn't find out that they'd lied because then he would assume the worst. And Heath might wind up like Kylie's mother, carted off to jail for a crime he hadn't committed.

Had Kylie's mother really been innocent, though? Or was it just a child's blind love and trust for her parent that had convinced Kylie of her innocence?

His heart ached for the childhood she'd endured—because of the poor choices her mother had made, or the mistakes the police had made. Either way Kylie had overcome a hell of a lot and was one hell of a strong woman.

Even now, she was soothing all the worries of his staff while he hid in his office, focusing on the pending patents for Pop and Uncle Alfie's latest inventions. They would live on in all the amazing things they'd created and in their family.

What would Heath leave behind if something happened to him? What had he created? Who had loved him?

Loneliness gripped him, pressing heavily on his chest, so that he struggled for a moment to draw a deep breath. He was alone by choice.

He could have proposed to Gina. She would have accepted; hell, she'd pressured him for months to propose. And the girl in college.

Melissa.

He could have married her. But he'd never felt for any woman like his father had felt for his mother or Uncle Alfie had Aunt Farrah.

Maybe there was something wrong with him. Maybe he just wasn't capable of that kind of deep love and commitment. He could be predestined to remain forever a bachelor. After all—unlike his parents who were from two sets of twins—he'd been born single.

Forever to remain single.

A knock at the door made him tense. Had Detective Parker returned? Had he already disproved Heath's fake alibi? It probably wouldn't take long to come up with evidence that they hadn't been together, that she'd been at her house and he'd been driving in his car until he'd arrived at his. Both alone. Not together like she'd claimed.

Before Heath could prepare himself, his door opened. Instead of Detective Parker, Kylie stood before him. Maybe she hadn't slept as long as he'd thought because dark circles rimmed her deep brown eyes, and her shoulders slumped beneath her jacket either with exhaustion or guilt.

She could have realized what a mistake she'd made in lying about his alibi, and she wanted to confess. But Heath was worried that it was already too late for that.

"Everyone else has left for the weekend," she said. "I think I will too unless you need something."

"I do," he said.

She stepped away from the door, closer to his desk. "What do you need?"

"You."

She tensed. "Wh-what are you talking about?"

"The only way we're not going to get in trouble about lying is to sell the hell out of this alibi," he said. "So we're going to have to make sure everyone thinks we really are in a relationship."

Her lips curved into a slight grin. "We could just have Detective Parker talk to Gina. He'd certainly believe us after talking to her."

He grimaced. His ex would definitely share how she'd found the two of them in bed together and how she'd always figured something was going on with them. "He's going to be talking to the rest of my family," Heath said—with dread. "He must have started with my mom and aunt." Because he'd already known where they'd been last night.

"Then he moved on to you as the next likely suspect," she finished for him.

He couldn't believe that anyone would think he could have actually killed the men he'd idolized. Even after identifying their bodies, he struggled to accept that they were really gone and not just working feverishly on some invention on the ninth floor. So many times today he'd been tempted to go up there, to look for them.

Tears threatened, but he blinked them back. He had to stay strong now. Stay focused.

For his family—so that the truth would come out, the real killer caught.

And for Kylie, so that she didn't get in trouble for lying for him.

"So how are we going to do this?" she asked. "How are we going to sell the hell out of your alibi?"

"We're going to do what you claimed we already do," he said. "We're going to spend all of our time together." He waited for the feeling of panic that had attacked him whenever Gina or Melissa had wanted to move in with him, whenever they'd wanted to spend all their time with him. But he didn't feel any anxiety at all.

That was probably just because he knew this was fake. He didn't have any feelings for Kylie and she had none but friendship for him.

"ANSWER YOUR DAMN PHONE…" Gina murmured.

But it went right to voice mail, Heath's deep baritone

emanating from her cell. *This is Heath Colton. I'm not currently available.*

He had never been.

But please leave a message and I will return your call at my earliest convenience.

She sighed, doubting his word. But yet she felt compelled to leave a message, to warn him. "Heath, it's Gina. I just want to say again that I'm sorry about your father and your uncle and about this morning."

She'd acted like such a fool. But seeing that opportunist in his bed...

"I just want to make sure that you're well and safe."

She was so worried about him, so damn worried about him.

"I'm really concerned about you," she said. "And I hope that you're being careful, especially now, about who you trust." And about who he shouldn't trust.

Kylie Givens...

Gina knew things about that woman that Heath didn't know, about her past, about her criminal mother.

"I'm just worried that you're so vulnerable right now that you're going to be taken advantage of..." And once Kylie got her hooks into him, she was never going to let him go—not like Gina had.

That was the biggest mistake she'd made. It had cost her her heart. If Heath trusted that woman he had working with him, he was going to lose more than his heart; he was probably going to lose his life.

Chapter Seven

January Colton leaned over and peered at the picture on the detective's desk. "Your little boy is adorable," she told him. Just his picture made her smile and that wasn't easy for her to do right now.

Not after what had happened Thursday night.

Even two days later, it still didn't seem real. Every time she dropped by the house to check on her mother and grandmother, she expected her father to walk out of his den and grab her up in a bear hug.

Joe Parker grinned. "Yeah, Isaac's a cutie for sure. He looks like his mother."

January hadn't met his wife, but she could see a resemblance between father and son although the little boy's hair was long enough to have some curl while the homicide detective kept his short. When she and Sean had children, they would probably resemble them both since they both had green eyes and her blond hair was just a couple of shades lighter than his light brown. Of course that was because of her highlights.

"How are you doing?" Parker asked her, and he seemed genuinely concerned.

She drew in a shaky breath and brushed away an errant tear. She'd been crying on and off for the past couple of days. Despite some of the horrors she'd witnessed as a social worker, nothing had prepared her for the murders of her own father and uncle. "I'll be okay."

"I'm glad that you have Sean," Parker said. "Stafford is a good man."

"Yes, he is," January agreed, her heart swelling with love for the detective she'd met when they'd both been protecting a little girl for whom January had been assigned as her caseworker and advocate.

"He says you were together Thursday night from early in the evening until you got the call from your grandmother," Parker remarked almost idly.

She suspected there was nothing idle about the remark or the man who made it. Heat flushed her face, but she nodded. "Yes, we were."

"Seems like you weren't the only one of your family who was with someone that night…" Parker murmured. "Like your cousin and that coworker of his…"

"What cousin?" she asked. She had three cousins although they were more like siblings than cousins since they'd all been raised together. "Jones?" Was he seeing someone? He hadn't mentioned her yet. But then that wasn't unusual for him; Jones wasn't as open as the rest of the family was.

"He's talking about Heath," Sean said as he joined them at Parker's desk which took up one of the cubicles in the detectives' bullpen.

"Heath," she said. Then realization dawned and she shuddered as she thought of the crime scene and how close her cousin must have been to it. "Of course. Were he and Kylie at the office when it happened?"

Parker shook his head. "No, that's the strange thing. He said they were together at his place."

"Guess they were probably working there instead," she mused, which might have saved their lives. "Sounds like a good thing."

"Or convenient," Parker remarked. "They admitted they weren't working."

"What?" she asked. "I don't understand."

"They told him that they're seeing each other, like all the time, as a couple," Sean explained. "I didn't know that. Did you?"

She shook her head. "No. I just thought they were coworkers and friends, like work spouses but nothing more." Sometimes work spouses were closer than real spouses, though. Heath was certainly closer to Kylie than he'd ever been with any of his former girlfriends.

Parker nodded. "That's what I'm hearing."

"I'm sure they weren't lying," January said in defense of her cousin. "They were probably just being discreet—not wanting their coworkers to get the wrong idea about their relationship."

He nodded. "And what would the wrong idea be? That she's sleeping with the boss to get ahead?"

January gasped. "That's sexist," she said. "Kylie is brilliant. She doesn't need to sleep with anyone to get anywhere. She can do that on her own merits." Her father had often spoken of how much the young vice president impressed him, and few people had impressed her father that much.

"So you don't think they're lying?"

"No," she said, offended now for her cousin and for herself. And Sean had told her what a good man Joe Parker was. "And neither am I if that's what you're going to imply next."

"Joe," Sean said, his deep voice holding a slightly threatening tone. "January came here voluntarily to answer your questions. You don't need to treat her like a suspect."

"I'm not the suspect," she said. "But you think my cousin Heath is." She shook her head. "That's not possible. He was so close to both my uncle and my father—probably closer than any of us. He worked with them every day."

"And he stands to gain a lot as the result of their deaths," Joe said.

She shuddered at the implication. "No. Heath's not like that."

"You're a social worker, January," Joe said. "You're well aware that sometimes the people who hurt us the most are those that are the closest to us."

She flinched, but she couldn't deny the truth of his statement. She could only say, "I know that's not true in this case." She knew her cousin too well, or at least she'd thought she had. She hadn't known about him and Kylie.

Joe shrugged. "Maybe not."

"You said Heath has an alibi," she reminded him.

"Maybe not," he murmured again.

January shook her head. "They wouldn't lie about that."

"No," the detective agreed. "Not if they had nothing to hide."

She bristled now. She'd always liked the detective, had always considered him to be one of the best investigators she'd ever met…until Sean. "My cousin has nothing to hide," she insisted.

Parker just shrugged again.

"Let's get some lunch," Sean told her. "Since you've come all the way downtown…"

For nothing. At least that was how she'd felt. She'd had nothing to do with the murder of her father and uncle, and she was certain she didn't know the person who did.

Parker stood up. "Lunch sounds like a good idea," he agreed.

"I didn't invite you," Sean said with a little grin, but that tone was still in his voice—that cautionary tone.

"I thought of a great place to go," Parker said as he headed toward the elevator.

January started after him, but Sean held her back. "Let him go."

"How in the world can he suspect anyone in my family of hurting Dad or Uncle Ernie?" she asked.

"You know why. Just like he said, you've seen it all, too, January," he reminded her—unnecessarily—of the sad realities of life.

And death.

"This is weird." Kylie murmured as she settled onto the chair Heath held out for her. While they'd often spent their Saturdays together, they'd been at the office, not dining in fancy downtown restaurants like True. Usually they ordered takeout that they ate at one of the conference tables. But she hadn't wanted to go back to the office, not so soon. Yesterday had been hard enough, being there without Ernie and Alfie.

And having that detective interrogate them…

Even now she felt as if everyone in the big dining room, with its high green ceiling, was watching them, and a strange chill raced down her spine. She should have kept her jacket instead of hanging it up. But her outfit, of sweater dress and tall boots, was warm, probably too warm for the dining room with sunshine pouring in through the tall windows in the walls of the old warehouse. Snowflakes shimmered within the sunlight as they fluttered to the ground and against the windows, leaving wet kisses on the glass as they melted. The long cold days of January were over, and February was starting to warm and brighten up.

The weather…

Not their lives.

Not their circumstances given the loss of such wonderful men.

"What's weird?" Heath asked as he settled into his chair across the table from her.

"You holding my chair," she said. "You acting like we're a couple."

"You're the one who started this," he reminded her.

Needlessly. She wasn't going to forget what she'd done, how she'd lied. "I did it to protect you," she said in her defense.

"And I'm playing along to protect you," Heath said. "I don't want you to get in trouble." He reached across the table and stroked the back of her hand.

And she shivered again even as her skin heated and

tingled. She tugged her hand from beneath his and put it under the table, on her lap with her other hand. The trouble she was worried about right now wasn't the police but him. He'd never turned his charm on her before. He had never acted like a boyfriend to her. She wasn't sure if she didn't like it or if she liked it too much.

He grinned and leaned across the table, so that his face—his handsome face—came very close to hers. "And you are going to play along with me, my darling, so that nobody suspects you lied during a police investigation."

No. She didn't like it. Not at all. But she would play along, so that neither of them got in trouble, so that the police would focus on finding the real suspect, not just the easy one. She smiled back at him and leaned closer, so that her mouth was just inches from his, and murmured, "You lied, too."

He reached out and slid his finger down the short length of her nose. "And we both know why."

So she wouldn't be arrested. She glared at him even as her lips stayed curved in that smile, even as her skin tingled again from his touch. "So the real killer will be caught."

Heath's wide grin slipped away as he grimly nodded. "I hope the detective will focus now on finding him or her instead of interrogating me and my family." But then he sat up straighter in his chair, his body tense as he stared over her head.

She turned and noticed the tall black man walking down the stairs that led to Heath's cousin's office. The detective must have been questioning Tatum, too.

"Do you think he saw us?" she murmured, tempted to slouch down in her chair.

Detective Parker answered her question before Heath as he headed toward their table. "Good afternoon, you two. I'm surprised to find you here, but you must not come that often—at least not together—because the proprietress had no idea you two are an item."

He knew.

The mad pounding of her heart confirmed it even more than the look in his dark eyes. The *knowing* look.

The *certain* look.

He knew they were lying. Her fake alibi had only made Heath look guiltier than he already had to the homicide detective. He stared at Heath now, his eyes full of all of his suspicions. Not only did he believe Heath had lied but also that he'd killed his dad and uncle.

A KNOT TIGHTENED in the pit of Heath's stomach as he stared up at the detective. He felt like a kid whose teacher was accusing him of cheating. Heath hadn't cheated in school; he hadn't needed to.

And while he could be ruthless in business, he had never cheated anyone. He just got very pushy and determined when he really cared about something, like he cared about Colton Connections and Pop's and Uncle Alfie's inventions.

But this time…he had lied.

For good reason.

He forced a smile for the detective. "As Kylie and I have already told you, not very many people know that we're more than friends."

"Why is that?" Parker asked. "Is dating coworkers against company policy?"

"No," Kylie answered, probably automatically since she was in charge of HR. "Not as long as both parties enter freely into the relationship, with no pressure."

Heath flinched—because he had been under pressure—under pressure to lie for her.

"Then why all the secrecy?" Parker asked.

"I've always been a very private person," Heath replied.

"Yet you brought your last girlfriend here often," Parker murmured as he cast a pitying glance at Kylie, as if he didn't think Heath treated her as well as he had Gina. Or that he was ashamed of her.

He was incredibly proud to be seen with her anywhere. But they had rarely gone out together for lunch or dinner, ordering takeout instead. A twinge of guilt struck Heath before he remembered that he and Kylie were only pretending. She wasn't really his girlfriend.

"Gina liked to come here," Heath said.

Parker turned toward Kylie. "And you don't?"

"I enjoy cooking," she said. "Heath and I enjoy cooking together."

"Your cousin said you're not much of a chef," Parker remarked.

That knot tightened even more now that the lies were being exposed, but was there enough evidence yet for Parker to press charges against Kylie—against him for aiding and abetting her fake alibi?

"What does my cooking prowess—or lack thereof—

have to do with the investigation into my father's and uncle's murders?" he asked.

Parker shrugged. "Maybe nothing."

Maybe. The detective clearly wasn't convinced yet that Heath had had nothing to do with it. How could he not see that Heath had really had nothing to gain but everything to lose? The men he'd admired most in the world.

As if seeing his discomfort, or maybe just wanting to sell their fake alibi, Kylie leaned across the table and grasped his hand with hers. "Don't worry, darling. Detective Parker will realize we have nothing to hide."

"Yet it seems you have been hiding your relationship," Parker remarked.

"Not hiding," Kylie said. "Just busy…"

"With what?" Parker asked.

"Business."

"With what?" he asked again. "Some big takeover?"

Kylie shook her head. "We're not that kind of business."

"We're? Are you part owner now? Do you have a stake in it?"

"No," she replied.

But she would have—had Heath asked her. He'd wanted to do it here, had wanted to surprise and reward her for all her hard work over the past five years. But he couldn't do it now…or Parker would consider it her payment for providing his alibi and they would both look guilty of a crime they hadn't committed. That neither of them could have with how much they'd loved those wonderful, creative, fun men.

A hollowness echoed inside his chest, his heart aching with a loss he wished he could have somehow prevented and never, ever would have initiated.

"You are way off base looking at my family as suspects," Heath told him. "My dad and uncle were so loving and so loved. There's no way any one of us would have hurt them."

Parker tilted his head, his stare still intense and speculative as he studied Heath's face. "What about your baby brother? I hear his relationship wasn't the greatest with your dad."

Heath flinched. "Jones loves—loved—my dad. He recently opened his own brewery—Lone Wolf Brewery. He was working hard to make our father proud of him."

Parker shrugged again, seemingly his favorite gesture to express his doubt. "Now I heard that wasn't as easy for Jones as it was for you. Sounds like you were the favorite, the golden son as it was."

"Heath and his dad and uncle were very close," Kylie agreed.

"Like the two of you..." Parker mused with a little chuckle, as if he found the idea of Kylie and Heath as a couple to be laughable.

Heath bristled even more. They could have been a real couple—if they didn't work together, if they didn't value their friendship over romance. At least he thought that was the reason Kylie had never seemed interested in anything more with him.

While he'd always found her attractive, he hadn't wanted to jeopardize the best working relationship he'd ever had. He and Kylie worked together like his dad and uncle had; they complemented each other. One's strengths were the other's weaknesses.

Heath turned his hand over and entwined his fingers with Kylie's slender ones, and a strange sensation trailed up his arm almost striking his heart.

"We are very close," Heath told the detective.

The man's brow creased and some of the suspicion faded from his gaze. Heath had spoken the truth this time, and Parker must have recognized it as such. Finally the man nodded. "There are all kinds of closeness, for all kinds of reasons."

So now he must have considered them both to be suspects in the murders. Frustration gnawed at Heath; he was never going to convince this man of his innocence, so maybe it was good that Kylie had lied for him.

"Well, Detective, we don't want to keep you from your investigation," Heath said, "and we haven't ordered yet." The waiter hadn't approached their table, probably not wanting to interrupt their conversation with the man standing next to them.

Parker nodded. "I'm sure I'll be seeing you both again," he said; his deep voice added a rumble of a threat when he continued, "soon."

Heath watched the man walk away before turning his attention back to the stairs leading up to his cousin's office. She hadn't come down. From his vantage point, he would have seen her, just as he'd seen Parker. It was lunchtime; usually the head chef and owner would be in the kitchen. "I need to go check on Tatum," he said.

Kylie nodded. "Of course."

Heath had to tug his hand free of hers to push his chair back and step away from the table.

Kylie's face flushed. "I forgot…"

"That we're just acting?" he teased.

Her face flushed deeper, but she glared at him. "I'm well aware we're just acting. I'm not your type at all."

He tilted his head and studied her face. "What do you think my type is?" he asked, curious since he hadn't even been aware that he had a type.

"Gina," she said. "Blond, clingy, hangs on your every word."

"You're not blond and clingy," he agreed. "But I thought you hung on my every word."

"What? Did you say something?" she said, amusement glinting in her dark eyes as she teased him.

He chuckled. "Order something for me for lunch, please, something that you'll want to eat later." Because he wasn't hungry. He hadn't been since that night he'd stared through the window of the morgue.

He turned to walk away but Kylie reached out and grasped his hand again, holding him back. "It's going to be okay," she said. "Eventually."

He wasn't sure if she was talking about their lie of an alibi or losing his dad and his uncle. The former might be okay, eventually, but not the latter. He would never be able to accept and understand that. He suspected he wasn't the only one.

He hurried up the steps to Tatum's office then. Even before he knocked, he heard her sobs emanating from behind the closed door. The sound stopped when he knocked, but when he opened the door, he found her sitting behind her desk, her shoulders slumped, her face wet and red with tears.

"Oh, Tatum…" he murmured. He crossed the small office and pulled her up from her chair and into his arms. She was as much a sister to him as Carly was, and her grief broke his heart. "What did the detective do? What did he say that has you so upset?"

She pulled back and shook her head. "It wasn't him. Well, not just him."

"You shouldn't be here," he said. "It's too soon for you to be working."

"You went to work yesterday," she said. "You have to stay busy, just like I do."

He nodded. "I know. I get that. But it doesn't matter. No matter how busy you try to stay you can't forget."

She uttered a ragged sigh. "I know. We'll never forget."

"No," he agreed. And he didn't want to—all he wanted was justice. "I don't understand why the detective is so focused on our family, though. I don't know why he's not looking at real suspects."

Another tear slipped down her cheek. "I know. He seems so damn certain that it's one of us." Her gaze slipped away from his face.

"Me," Heath said. "He thinks it's me."

Tatum still didn't look at him, making him worry that she was beginning to believe it, too. That all of his family would look at him as the detective did, as a killer.

Chapter Eight

The second Heath left her sitting alone at the table, Kylie felt as if everyone was staring at her, probably wondering if her date had ditched her. But Heath wasn't her date. Not really.

Just as she'd told him, she wasn't his type. He wasn't hers either. Not that she had a particular type beyond trustworthy. Whomever she dated she had to trust implicitly, and that came very hard for her. Sure, she trusted Heath as a friend and a colleague. Her boss.

But as a lover?

No.

He'd broken too many hearts for her to ever trust him with hers. She shivered as that chill raced down her spine again. Someone was staring at her. But when she glanced around, the other diners seemed intent on their lunch companions or their food. No one was overtly staring at her.

But...

That feeling persisted—so much so that she slid out of her chair and took Heath's—so that her back was not to the dining room or to the stairwell. He was already descending those stairs—behind Tatum.

His cousin's face was flushed, her smile obviously forced. She didn't stop at any of the tables and headed straight toward the kitchen. It was lunchtime, so she was probably needed there. Maybe that was why she and Heath hadn't spoken long, not long enough for Kylie to order more than drinks for them. And those had yet to come.

"Is she all right?" Kylie asked when Heath settled into her recently vacated chair.

He shrugged. "She's trying to be strong, trying to work through it all."

Like him.

"Are you all right?" she asked.

"No."

"What happened?" she asked because he was more upset than he'd been when he'd left the table just moments ago.

"He's questioning everybody like they're a suspect," he murmured, shaking his head.

She groaned. "If only he'd focus on finding the real killer." But the cops who'd arrested her mother hadn't been interested in finding the real suspect, just the easy one to convict.

"He thinks it's me," Heath said, and a grimace of pain crossed his handsome face.

"You already knew that," she said. "Something else happened that's upset you." She reached out and clasped his hand again, squeezing it for comfort. "What's wrong?"

"I think my family might be starting to think the same thing Parker is."

She shook her head. "No. They all know you. They know how much you loved your dad and Alfie. There is no way they would ever believe that."

He stared at her then. "Why are you so sure of me?" he asked. "We weren't really together that…" He trailed off and glanced around, as if he'd had that same sensation she had, that someone was watching them. Maybe Detective Parker hadn't really left.

But he didn't have to finish for Kylie to know what he meant. "I know you would never—ever—do anything like that because I know you. And your family does, too."

"They don't think they know me that well now," he said. "Because of us, of what we're claiming to be."

It had been a mistake to lie; she knew that now. The fake alibi hadn't removed suspicion from Heath but had seemed to increase it.

He said, "We shouldn't talk about that here."

There was more he wanted to say to her—obviously. But Kylie wasn't sure she wanted to hear it now, not when he looked so grim about it. Was he going to force her to come clean about the false alibi to the detective?

Then she would risk going to jail like her mother had, except in this instance she had actually committed the crime of lying, whereas her mother had done nothing wrong. The same panic and fear she'd felt that night so very long ago overwhelmed her now, making it hard for she breathe.

Heath had no such problem, though. He drew in a

deep breath and then grinned at her. Even though it was probably forced, the pressure in her chest eased somewhat…until he said, "So we're just going to have to work harder to convince everyone that we're really involved."

"What do you mean?" she asked, and she tried to lean back in her chair and pull her hand from his.

But he clasped it in his and leaned forward, brushing his lips across her knuckles.

Her heart did a strange little flip, or so it felt—which was ridiculous. She was probably just nervous about the detective. After what had happened to her mother, she was always nervous around the police.

She had never been nervous around Heath before, but for some reason she was now. Or maybe it was just that strange sensation that persisted all during their lunch that unsettled her—that feeling of being watched.

Of course Heath was putting on quite the show of flirting with her and touching her…so much so that her pulse was all fluttery and she felt a little breathless. Finally the bill came, easing some of the tension. They could stop their little show now and get back to business and friendship only. After he paid, he pulled back her chair and guided her through the dining room to the lobby.

He retrieved her jacket for her and helped her into it, pulling her hair from the collar as he did. He trailed his fingers through the strands, and he murmured something in appreciation.

Kylie turned to glance up at him, and he lowered his head and kissed her. His mouth slid over hers, his lips both firm and soft. Even though she knew he was only doing it to perpetuate the lie she'd told, something inside her reacted, making her pulse quicken, her lips tingle, and she kissed him back.

HER LIPS WERE as silky as her hair, which he found himself grasping as the kiss knocked him off-balance. Heath had just intended to brush his mouth across hers in a casual kiss—that would make it look like they were familiar with each other, like they kissed all the time.

But they didn't.

They hadn't.

Why the hell hadn't they?

Her mouth was so sweet, her lips so soft...

And his heart was beating so damn fast, pounding so heavily in his chest that he couldn't hear anything. But he reminded himself that they were not alone. They were in the restaurant lobby, so he pulled back. If they had been alone, he wasn't certain he would have been able to pull away—at least not without making the kiss more intimate, without touching more than her silky hair.

He slid his fingers free of it and reached around her to open the door to the street. His hand shook a little as that adrenaline continued to course through him.

That was all it was, a little rush from the dangerous game they were playing in lying to the homicide detective. A stupid game.

Heath had bigger things to worry about—like the murders and the business and his family. But at the moment Kylie filled his thoughts and his senses.

His head was full of that soft floral scent she wore. And his mind filled with images of how she'd looked in his bed. That night he'd just stared at her. But if she shared his bed again, he would be tempted to do more.

He was already tempted to kiss her again. And now he wondered if—in trying to fool everyone else—that he was beginning to fool himself into thinking that they were more than they were. Maybe that was why that kiss had affected him so much and was making him long for another.

He slid his arm around her and leaned toward her, but the sidewalk was crowded, bodies jostling them. She stared up at him, her dark eyes full of the same confusion gripping him. But it wasn't only confusion gripping him.

Desire did, too. Desire for her.

"Heath…" she murmured. If she said anything else, he couldn't hear it—not on the busy street.

"Let's go," he said as he guided her through the crowd toward the crosswalk. He had parked at a lot down the block, so they had to cross the street. He glanced at the light which was still lit up to walk. But as he stepped off the curb, a noise drew his attention— the sound of an engine revving.

Then tires squealed as the car rounded the corner, heading straight toward them. Using his arm around her, he lifted Kylie from her feet, but even as fast as he moved, the car was faster…

Such rage…

Blinding rage. So blinding that the driver couldn't be

certain that the couple had been struck. A glance in the rearview mirror confirmed they were on the ground, though.

Dead?

Wounded?

They had to be, at the very least, wounded. They couldn't have escaped unscathed. They had to be hurting, like the driver was hurting. It was only fair.

Chapter Nine

Kylie couldn't breathe—not with the weight of Heath's body pressing down on hers. Was it his body weight or fear that had stolen away her breath?

Was he all right?

What the hell had happened?

She shifted against the asphalt beneath her and asked, "Are you all right?"

He moved then, rolling off her before rising up from the ground. He extended his hand to her, but she stared hard at it—at him—before taking it.

"Is this your idea of sweeping a woman off her feet?" she asked.

He had literally swept her from her feet before running toward the opposite sidewalk. But they hadn't made it all the way there, to safety. Instead they'd been knocked down in the street.

He lifted her up and steadied her with his hands on her arms. "Didn't you see that car?" he asked. "It was almost as if it was heading directly at us."

"Almost or was?" she wondered aloud then repeated her earlier question, "Are you all right?"

He nodded. "Yeah, yeah, I'm fine. Are you? I didn't hurt you, did I?"

If that car had been heading right toward them, he had probably saved her life. But she couldn't be sure how much danger they had actually been in because she hadn't even seen the vehicle. Once he'd kissed her, she'd lost all sense of time and place and self.

Damn. Maybe she was more like her mother than she'd thought she was. First she'd lied to protect a man. Then she'd let his kiss affect her so badly that she hadn't even realized that she was potentially in danger. Which had been the real threat, though? The speeding car or the kiss?

Or the man?

He was clearly as shaken as she was. From the kiss? Or had that car really come that close?

"Are you sure you weren't struck?" she asked because he looked blindsided, his hair mussed, the sleeve of his jacket torn, his gaze unfocused.

He peered around them at the bystanders staring back at them.

"Are you okay?" a woman asked.

"Do you need an ambulance?" a man asked.

"Damn, that car was flying," another remarked.

It had been close, apparently closer than Kylie had realized. But she'd been in a daze thanks to Heath's kiss. At least he'd seen it; at least he'd saved them.

From what, though?

An accident?

That was all it had been, right? Or were they in mortal danger, too? Like Ernie and Alfie had been?

HEATH COULDN'T STOP SHAKING. Was that from the rush of the adrenaline, the anger over nearly being struck or that damn kiss? What had he been thinking to kiss her? To play along with the crazy fake alibi in the first place?

"Heath!" Kylie called out like it hadn't been the first time she'd tried getting his attention.

She had it. He'd been more focused on her than anything else. Where the hell had the car come from? And why had it been going so fast through a busy downtown intersection?

"Heath!" another woman called out his name, as Tatum rushed out the door of her restaurant. "Are you okay? Did that car purposely try to run you down? Should I call the police?"

He shuddered. He had no desire to deal with the police right now, not with the way Detective Parker had been treating him—like a suspect.

Tatum wasn't looking at him that way now, with suspicion or if not suspicion, at least doubt. Whatever doubts Parker might have planted in her mind were gone now. Only concern darkened her blue eyes. "Are you okay?" She turned toward Kylie. "Are you?"

Kylie nodded, but her hair was tangled around her face and one cheek was a little pink as if it had gotten chafed against the asphalt. Or maybe the cold had chafed it. The sunshine had gone now, leaving only dark clouds overhead and the snowflakes that a blustery wind whipped against them.

"Heath?" Tatum asked. "Do you want me to call 9-1-1?"

He shook his head. "No need. It was just an accident."

"Are you sure?"

He nodded. "Yeah, I was distracted." That was true; he had been distracted. Kissing Kylie had distracted the hell out of him.

But he was pretty damn certain the traffic signal had directed him that it was still safe to walk. Apparently it had been wrong.

"That car was speeding like crazy," someone remarked from the crowd that had gathered around them.

"Did anyone get a license plate number?" Tatum asked. "Or see the driver?"

The people shook their heads before finally dispersing, apparently assured that he and Kylie were not hurt. He wasn't so sure. She looked shaken, and she trembled, as if shivering in the cold.

"I still think we should call the police," Tatum insisted.

Heath shook his head. "Kylie is cold. I'm going to get her home."

"Come back inside," Tatum said. "It's warm in there."

"Is it?" he asked.

And his cousin's face flushed. "I'm sorry," she murmured. "I didn't really think for a moment that you could have anything to do with…"

He nodded. "It's okay."

"No," she said, shaking her head. "You could have been killed, too."

He forced a grin. "It wasn't that close. We're fine." But his arm throbbed a little where his jacket was torn.

The side mirror of the speeding car must have caught it. So it had been close. Too damn close.

Just like he was beginning to get to Kylie. And even a fake relationship wasn't a distraction he could afford right now. He needed to stay focused—for his family, for the business that was his dad and uncle's legacy.

And for justice.

If the detective wasn't going to try to find the real killer instead of just pitting Heath's family members against each other, Heath would find the person. Or had that person already found him?

God, he was getting paranoid since he couldn't help thinking that some random speeding driver had been trying to kill him.

"I'll see you soon," he promised his cousin. Then he clasped Kylie's hand in his as they carefully crossed the street and headed to where he'd parked his vehicle.

Even if his paranoia wasn't justified, he was going to be careful, for Kylie's sake more than his own. He didn't want to put her in danger—or any more danger than he already might have.

TATUM WAS AS shaken as if that vehicle had nearly run her down. That was what the hostess had rushed into the kitchen to tell her. "Your cousin was nearly killed!"

The young woman was known to be a bit overdramatic, but with the way the crowd had gathered around Kylie and Heath with such concern, she suspected the hostess was right.

And Heath had downplayed what had happened. Why?

Shivering, she rushed back into her restaurant to escape the cold wind and stinging snow. Instead of returning to the warmth of the kitchen, she headed up the steps to her office and to the cell phone she'd left sitting on her desk earlier. Her hand shook—with cold and with fear—as she pressed a button to make a call.

"Hey, Tatum," her sister answered immediately.

She hadn't called the police. It would have been too hard for her to file a report when she hadn't seen anything. But she could still talk to a lawman—her sister's boyfriend. "Hey, January," she replied.

"How are you doing?" her sister asked with concern. January was such a caring person, so caring that she'd made helping people her life's work.

"I—" her voice cracked as she struggled with all the emotions rushing over her. She hadn't realized just how much she'd been hurting until that detective had asked her all those questions and muddled her mind.

Or maybe he'd made it clearer for her.

Her dad and uncle had been murdered. Their deaths hadn't been an accident or an illness. Those would have been hard enough to accept. But murder?

It was unconscionable. January had seen a lot of unconscionable things as a social worker, though. Tatum, as a chef, had not.

"Do you want me to come over?" January asked. "Are you home?"

"No, I'm at True," she admitted.

"You are?"

"Yes, I need to stay busy," she explained. She didn't

want to think about anything but menus and meals and diners. But then that detective had arrived.

"Do you want me to come there?" January asked. "I would have earlier but Sean thought Detective Parker might have been heading to see you."

"He did. He was here," she replied.

"Did he question you like you were a suspect, too?" January asked.

"Yes. And he asked me about Heath."

"Me, too," January said. "And Kylie. Did you know they were seeing each other?"

"No, but they were here, too," Tatum said. "And I'm worried about him."

"You know he had nothing to do with their deaths," January insisted defensively. "No matter what Joe Parker thinks. And if Heath says he and Kylie are together, I believe him."

"I do, too," Tatum said.

As her hostess had said, one minute her cousin was kissing his girlfriend—the next they were nearly getting run down by a car in the street. Tatum shared that gossip with her sister, like she had shared everything with her since they were kids.

And she could hear the smile in her sister's voice when January said, "Good."

"That they were nearly run down?" she asked, but she was only teasing. She knew January was too caring to want that to happen—to anyone.

"That they're together. They're such a better match than Heath and that gold digger he was dating."

Tatum chuckled. She hadn't been a fan of Gina either.

Or of Melissa for that matter. Or of any other woman he'd casually dated. They hadn't matched him for work ethic or intelligence until now—until Kylie Givens.

"I'm worried, though," she shared.

"That he's going to get his heart broken?"

"It would be the first time he's put it on the line," Tatum said. But she couldn't talk. "I'm worried that that driver wasn't just going too fast."

"You think someone was actually trying to run them down?" January asked with alarm.

"Heath doesn't think so. But what if what happened to Dad and Uncle Ernie was because of the business?" she asked.

"Then you're thinking Heath and Kylie might be the killer's next targets," January surmised. "I'll talk to Sean."

"Good," Tatum said. "It's good having a lawman in the family."

January laughed, a sound Tatum had missed hearing the past couple of days with pain and loss consuming everyone instead. "He's not family yet," her sister said.

"But he will be soon," Tatum said. She had no doubt that her sister had met her match in Sean Stafford. They would definitely get married.

"Sean is worried about me," January admitted. "About all of us…"

"He doesn't share Detective Parker's opinion of Heath, does he?" she asked.

"No," January said. "But he did say that Parker's instincts are usually right on. He thinks Heath might be lying about something."

About what?

Him and Kylie? She hoped not; she really liked Kylie and while she hadn't witnessed the kiss, the hostess had described it as passionate as a soap-opera kiss.

Maybe Heath had lied about that car trying to run him down, but Detective Parker didn't even know about that yet. But he should. Then maybe he would stop suspecting Heath.

Maybe Heath was already aware that someone was trying to kill him, and he didn't want anyone to know about it because he didn't want to upset them any more than they already were.

Chapter Ten

Sean Stafford hadn't known Ernie and Alfie Colton very long, but what he'd known about them, he'd liked and admired. They were loving fathers, good husbands, honorable men. Brilliant men.

Now they were dead—far too soon and violently. The woman Sean loved was devastated over their deaths, and now she was worried that her cousin might become the next victim in her family.

Sean was worried, too.

Heath hadn't been at his penthouse. Or at Kylie's place either. But from what Sean had learned about Heath, he should have known to look here first, at the scene of the crime.

Of course Heath and Kylie weren't in the parking lot. But their vehicles were, along with a few other ones. Despite it being Saturday, they weren't the only people in the building. Just two of the twenty stories were Colton Connections. So there could have been people in those other offices.

They might have been there the night of the murders. They might have seen something, although Joe

Parker hadn't found any witnesses. That didn't mean they really hadn't seen anything. Maybe that they were too scared to admit it. So when Sean stepped into the elevator another man held for him, he studied his face.

"What floor?" the man asked.

"Eighth," he said.

The button was already pushed. "Fortunately for you that's where I'm going, too," he said. "Or you wouldn't be able to get in unless security called up for you. And security doesn't work weekends."

Was that why he was there? Because there was no security.

"Why are you going to eight?" Sean asked.

"I work at Colton Connections," the man replied. "And you?"

"I work for Chicago PD," Sean said, automatically flashing his badge.

"So you're here to interview Heath Colton and Kylie Givens again?" the dark-haired man asked, his voice nearly quivering with excitement.

"I'm here to talk to them," Sean admitted. But he wasn't working the case. The higher-ups had decided he was too involved to be objective, and they were right. He was as involved as if they were his own family.

"Good," the man replied. "I know that the other detective talked to them already, but I think he bought their alibi way too easily."

Sean narrowed his eyes. "You don't think they were really together? That they're really involved?"

The guy sighed. "Oh, I'm sure they're involved. It's

the only reason why she has the position she has. She's hardly qualified for it."

"I thought she graduated from some Ivy League school." He'd thought it was the same one Heath had attended—just at different times.

"I meant that she isn't qualified because of her criminal background," the man clarified.

"You're saying Kylie has a record?" Sean asked. Parker hadn't mentioned it, but then he didn't think Sean should be involved in the case either. So he wasn't sharing any details of it with him.

"Well," the man sputtered, "not her personally, but she comes from a family of criminals."

"Really? I hadn't heard this." And he suspected it might not be true.

"Her mother actually died in prison."

A twinge of sympathy struck Sean, and he wondered how old Kylie had been when that had happened. He'd recently grown really close to a little girl who'd thought her mother was gone, and he knew the pain it had caused her.

"Why was she in prison?" Sean asked.

"Some drug charge." He sniffed as if disgusted with Kylie just because of who her mother was.

Would people look at little Maya that way? Would they disrespect her just because of who her father was?

Suppressing the outrage that threatened to grip him, Sean held on to his temper and asked, "And who are you, by the way?"

"Tyler Morrison, I'm legal counsel for Colton Connections."

Sean nodded as if impressed. But nothing about this

man, from his expensive suit to his slicked back hair to his biased gossip, impressed him. "Were you here that night?" he asked. "When they died?"

The guy tensed. "No, of course not. I—I don't know why anyone would ask me that."

Maybe lawyers were naturally defensive or maybe this guy had something to hide. Sean suspected the latter. When the elevator stopped on eight, the man stepped out with him and swiped his badge through the security panel to open the doors to the offices. But he didn't walk through the doors with him. Instead he turned back to the elevator. "I just remembered I left what I needed in my car," he murmured as he closed the doors on Sean.

Sean stood there, in the doorway between the elevator area and the offices, and watched the lights above the elevator doors. It didn't go down; it headed up and stopped on the next floor. Sean highly doubted the lawyer had parked his car on the ninth floor.

No. This man definitely seemed to have something to hide. Sean intended to ask Heath about him, but when he walked into the CEO's office and both he and his vice president jumped as if he'd caught them doing something illegal, he suspected Tyler Morrison wasn't the only one hiding something. Heath and Kylie were, as well.

But what?

Had they really lied about their alibi like Joe Parker suspected? Usually the only people who lied about alibies were the people who knew they would need one— because they were guilty as hell.

SEAN STAFFORD DIDN'T seem to buy Heath and Kylie's story any more than his colleague had. But Heath wasn't sure which story he doubted, that he and Kylie were involved or that someone hadn't purposely tried to run them down.

"Tatum shouldn't have called you," Heath said as he walked the detective down the hall toward the elevator. He'd cut the lawman's impromptu visit short with the excuse that he was just too busy to talk right now. And his constantly ringing phone had supported his excuse. He'd left Kylie manning the phone while he walked Sean out the security doors, so that he could take the elevator down.

"Tatum didn't call me," Sean said. "She called January."

Heath chuckled. "And January called you."

"We were together, having lunch. Like you and Kylie. I didn't know the two of you were an item."

Neither had he—until Kylie had claimed to Detective Parker that they were. "Well, when you spend so much time with someone…"

Sean nodded in agreement. He had to agree since Heath knew that was how he and January had fallen for each other, when they'd spent so much time together protecting the child in one of the cases January had been assigned.

"But why have you kept it so secret from the rest of the family?" Sean asked.

Heath shrugged. "I wasn't trying to keep it secret. I've just been so busy with trying to secure the patent for Pop and Uncle Alfie's most recent invention." And now they wouldn't know when he got it. They would never be able to receive the accolades they deserved for inventing the life-changing medical device.

It wasn't fair.

"Do you think their murders could have anything to do with the business?" Sean asked.

Heath shook his head. "No. They're so well respected." Then he had to correct himself. "They were…"

Sean reached out and squeezed his shoulder. "I know. It's hard. January is struggling."

"I'm glad she has you," Heath said. "To help her through this."

"And I'm glad you have Kylie," Sean said, but he studied Heath's face as he said it, as if he was waiting for some indication that Heath had lied about their relationship.

But Heath wasn't lying when he said, "She's really been there for me." More than he had ever expected she would be.

"So you should keep her safe," Sean said, "make sure she's not in danger."

The only danger Heath thought she was really in was getting caught for lying during the course of a police investigation when she provided his false alibi. "I don't think that car was trying to hit us," he said. "I was just distracted and stepped off the curb without looking."

"So you didn't have the crosswalk sign?"

"I did but—"

"Then the vehicle shouldn't have turned when you were walking," Sean persisted.

"Like I said, we had just stepped off the curb," he

said. "They probably thought it was clear and the driver must have been in a hurry with as fast as they were driving." So fast that Heath hadn't even gotten a good look at the vehicle.

Sean narrowed his eyes, his skepticism clear now. "I don't know, Heath, if it was as accidental as you want to believe it was."

He did want to believe that. The murders were already too much to process. He couldn't accept that he might be in danger as well or worse yet that he was putting Kylie in danger. He shook his head. "I'm sure it was nothing."

"Just be careful," Sean advised him. Then the elevator arrived, saving Heath from more of the detective's questions.

"Thanks," Heath said as the doors closed on the other man's face. He would heed the detective's advice, more for Kylie's sake than his own. He didn't want to put her in harm's way more than she already was with the danger of being arrested over the fake alibi she'd given him.

When he stepped back into his office, he found her looking flustered as she spoke to someone on his phone. "That is kind, Mrs. Colton… Fallon, but I really…"

Her face lit up with relief when she noticed him standing in the doorway, and his heart did a strange little flippy thing in his chest.

"I really should have you speak to your son about that," she said, and she thrust the phone in his direction.

His fingers brushed hers as he took it from her hand, and a little zinging sensation arced between them. Or at least he thought it did. She must have felt that, too.

But she lowered her gaze, staring more at his chin than his eyes. Then she rushed around his desk toward the door.

Covering the receiver with one hand, he asked her, "Where are you going?"

"My office," she said as she whirled and headed out of his doorway.

What had his mother been telling her? It wasn't like Kylie to shy away from a conversation with anyone; she was much more of a people person than he was. He uncovered the phone and spoke into the receiver, "Mom?"

"Yes, dear, I was just talking to Kylie about coming to dinner tomorrow night, but she deferred to you before replying," she said. "She's such a sweet young woman. I've always liked her."

"Me, too," he said. And it was true. He'd clicked with Kylie from the moment he'd interviewed her. But then he'd only been considering her a colleague. Somehow she'd become so much more.

A friend.

And…

That kiss burned in his mind, on his lips. He could still taste her, feel her.

"Heath?" his mother called out to him.

"Yes?" he replied, wondering what he must have missed that she'd asked him.

"So you'll both come to dinner tomorrow night," his mother said as if it was fait accompli. "That's wonderful. We all need to be together now. It'll be especially good for Farrah. She's been so distraught."

He suspected her twin wasn't the only one who was

distraught. His mother needed to keep busy and didn't want to be alone. Unlike his aunt Farrah who lived with Grandmother, his mother had nobody living with her now. A pang of guilt struck his heart.

"Of course I'll be there, Mom," he promised her.

"And Kylie," she prodded him. "I want to get to know her better."

So did he. He didn't know his friend nearly as well as he'd thought he had. He hadn't had any idea what she'd gone through, with her mother being arrested, jailed, dying.

Another pang of guilt struck his heart. She'd always been there for him, listening to him go on and on about work, about Gina, about his family. He'd never been there for her like that, had never learned the most important things about a woman who had become very important to him. Maybe that was why he was single yet… because he was as selfish and self-centered as Gina had once accused him of being.

He glanced at his cell, seeing he'd missed more calls from Gina. And voice mails.

He wasn't going to play any more of them. The only one he'd played had been a warning about Kylie, about not trusting her. He was beginning to think Kylie was the only one he should trust right now.

But then he headed the short distance down the hall to her office and found it dark and empty. She had lied to him. She hadn't gone here; she'd left. And she must have sneaked down the stairs since he hadn't even heard the elevator ding. But then he hadn't even heard his mother ask him to dinner either.

He'd been so damn preoccupied with that kiss. Just like he'd been when they'd nearly gotten run down. That had been his fault, though, for being distracted.

Nobody could really be trying to kill him and Kylie.

Because if someone was, Kylie could be in danger. And all alone...

KYLIE NEEDED TO be alone, which was ironic given that she usually envied those with big families, like Heath. But when his mother had been interrogating her on the phone, Kylie had gotten flustered. She didn't want to lie to the woman who was very sweet and still so fragile over the recent loss of her husband. So Kylie had no intention of going to that dinner with Heath, no intention of going anywhere with him for a while—despite his insistence that they sell the fake alibi and relationship she'd told Detective Parker about.

Now another detective had come to question them. She had no doubt that was really why Sean Stafford had stopped into the office, not to check on them but to check *up* on them.

Panic pressed on Kylie's lungs, and it had nothing to do with the exertion of walking down eight flights to the first floor but everything to do with that feeling she'd had when her mother had been arrested.

Would that happen to her for lying during the course of a police investigation? She was less concerned about lying to the police, though, than she was about lying to Heath's sweet mother.

Kylie didn't want to fool his family. She respected them all too much and was too worried about them now, with the loss they were suffering. So she had done the right thing in providing him an alibi.

The last thing his mother needed now was her son getting arrested for murdering her husband and brother-in-law.

No. She'd done the right thing. But as she walked out of the building, a chill raced down her spine, and she shivered. That strange sensation rushed over her again, as if she was being watched.

Was Heath watching her walk to her car from his office window? No. His office was at the front of the building. But when she glanced up, she noticed a shadow at one of the windows on the ninth floor. Someone was up there, watching her.

Who?

She hadn't noticed anyone else at the office but her and Heath. And that window would have been in the creative space where Ernie and Alfie had worked with only a few other inventors and sometimes Heath.

Heath was just as creative as his dad and uncle, but he'd insisted he preferred running the business to creating business for himself to run. Had he gone to the lab, maybe to feel closer to his father and uncle?

She stopped and squinted up at that window, but the shadow disappeared.

Had she only imagined it?

She considered going back up to find out if anyone was there. But it had probably been just Heath, and she was uneasy being alone with him right now.

With no witnesses, he would have no reason to kiss her again or act like her boyfriend. But with no witnesses, she might be the one tempted to try to kiss him again, to see if it had really been as hot and heart pounding as she'd thought it had been.

But maybe she had just imagined all that, like she was probably just imagining someone was watching her—at the restaurant and here. When she opened her car door and slid behind the wheel, she glanced up at the building again. The shadow was still gone, but that feeling was back. And it was so persistent, so nagging, that Kylie was nearly certain: someone was watching her.

Why?

Chapter Eleven

Fallon spread the cream cheese frosting over the carrot cake which had cooled on the island in her sister's kitchen. She preferred to cook here and not just because Farrah cleaned up after her. She preferred being here now to being alone in her own house.

"The kids should be here soon," she told Farrah. "I'm so glad that all of them are coming. Heath is even bringing Kylie."

"That's good," Farrah said. "I'd like to get to know her better. Alfie was so impressed with her."

"So was Ernie…" A twinge of pain struck her heart as it did every time she thought of her husband because she immediately thought of his being gone. Forever now.

"The police need to release their bodies," Farrah said. "Everyone keeps asking when the funerals will be."

Fallon began to shake, and the cake knife dropped from her hands, clattering onto the countertop. Tears rushed to her eyes, but she tried to blink them back and focus on the cake again. Bodies.

Whenever she was alone, that was all she could think

about, the murders and of what her husband and brother-in-law had become.

"Bodies…" the word slipped out of her quivering lips.

"I'm sorry," Farrah said, and she wrapped an arm around Fallon's shaking shoulders. "I shouldn't have said that."

"Why not? It's what they are now, not the men we knew and loved—they're not here anymore." And the house felt so empty without them. She felt so empty without them.

"They're here," Farrah insisted. "They're with us always and with our children. They're not gone. Never."

Fallon hugged her, and then suddenly other arms wrapped around them both—slender arms. Their mother.

Despite her age and size, Abigail was strong. She'd been so strong for them. Fallon needed to be strong, like her mother, for her children and for her nieces and for her sister. She had to show them that she would fine.

And she would be. Maybe not now or anytime soon.

But eventually she would be fine, just like her mother had been, after Daddy's death. She'd survived. And so would Fallon and Farrah.

DREAD SETTLED HEAVILY into the pit of his stomach as Heath parked on the circular drive behind a row of other vehicles. "Everybody's here."

Would they treat him like they had the last time they'd all been together here? Would they be unable to even look at him? After how Parker had been questioning them, he'd rather they not look at him than look at him like the detective did: with suspicion.

"I shouldn't be here," Kylie said from the passenger's seat. "This is a bad idea."

"No," he said. "Lying to the police was a bad idea. This is damage control. Detective Parker has already questioned all of them about us. We need to assure them that we're not lying. Or else they'll be worried about me, and they all have enough to worry about right now." That was the argument he'd used to convince himself to come—that he needed to assure his family that he was being honest about everything, even the lies.

Kylie's face flushed. "I'm sorry."

"You were doing what you thought was right," Heath said.

She smiled as if she was amused that he'd defended her—to her. "Why didn't you let me do what I think is right now and let me stay home?" she asked.

"I told my mom I would bring you to dinner," he said. "She really wants to get to know you better."

"Which is why I didn't want to come," Kylie said. "I can lie to Detective Parker no problem but not your mother."

"You never lied to yours?" he asked with genuine curiosity. Though it was clearly a difficult subject for her, he wanted to know more about Kylie, especially the difficult subjects.

She released a shaky sigh. "I did…when I visited her in prison. I lied and told her that I was fine, that I wasn't getting teased at school, that living with Grandma was just as good as living with her." Her voice cracked with emotion. "Then she killed herself."

Heath gasped. "Oh, my God, Kylie… I am so sorry." He was most sorry about not knowing everything she'd endured and survived in her life.

"Not your fault," she murmured.

"Not yours either," he said. "I hope you know that."

She nodded. "I do. I know."

But he wasn't so certain she'd really absolved herself of guilt or if she was only trying to reassure him that she had no lingering effects from her traumatic upbringing.

"Why haven't you ever told me about your past?" he asked, as he felt a little twinge of regret and concern that she might not have trusted him to know about it, about her.

She shrugged. "Because it's the past. I can't change it. I can't undo it, and I certainly don't want anyone to pity me over it."

She was so strong, so brave, so determined. And he was so damn impressed. He'd never had any challenges in his life like she had in hers—until now—until the murders of his father and uncle.

He reached across the console and slid his arm around her shoulders, pulling her in for slight hug.

"I said I don't want anyone's pity," she said, her voice muffled against his shoulder. "Especially not yours."

"Why *especially* not me?" he asked, as that little twinge of hurt struck his heart again.

"Because I work for you," she said with a little snort of derision, as if the reason was obvious.

It hadn't been obvious to him.

"Is that the only way you think of me, as your boss?" he asked. He wished so much that he'd already made her a partner in the business like he'd intended before those police officers had showed up at his penthouse door asking him to identify bodies.

"You are my boss," she said, her slim body tense against his.

"I thought we were more than that," he said.

"That's just an act," she replied. "Just to support your alibi."

His false alibi. "I meant that I thought we're friends," he explained. "And I need your friendship right now more than I ever have."

"Oh, Heath," she murmured and slid her arms around him. "Of course we're friends. That's why I did what I did."

"And it's why you're going to go inside that house with me," he said. "Because you're my friend."

She pulled back and lightly smacked his shoulder. "You manipulator."

He grinned at her accusation. "I don't want to disappoint my mother," he said.

But he was disappointed—disappointed that she wasn't as affected as he'd been by that kiss and by the hug he'd given her, that had his body tense with the desire that had gripped him when he'd kissed her. He wanted to kiss her again…so damn badly.

So he leaned down and brushed his mouth across hers. Her lips were so silky and so damn sweet. He nibbled at her bottom one, deepening the kiss. His heart pounded against his ribs as desire rushed through him.

She slid her fingers into his hair, but instead of tugging him away, she pulled him closer, and she kissed him back for a moment. But just a moment before she pulled away with a little pant for breath.

Then she murmured, "Somebody's watching us."

He nodded. But he had no idea. He had only kissed her because he'd wanted to, because he'd needed to kiss her again. It had done what he had wanted it to do. It had confirmed that he hadn't imagined the passion that burned between them when their lips touched.

"We should get in the house then," she murmured, and when she reached for the handle on the passenger's door, her hand was visibly shaking.

Was she nervous about lying to his family and trying to fool them? Or was she nervous, like he was, that maybe the only people they were fooling were themselves?

KYLIE HAD HOPPED out of his vehicle because she had thought it would be safer inside the house—with Heath's family—than to be alone any longer with him in the close confines of his car.

That kiss...

She wasn't certain for whose benefit he'd kissed her, but she suspected more than one of his family members had witnessed it—because they had pounced the minute they'd walked in the door—like they'd been watching for them.

Or watching them.

But their attention hadn't given her that creepy sensation she'd had the night before, when she'd walked out of the building where Colton Connections was located and she'd noticed that shadow at the window on the ninth floor.

Whoever had watched her then had unnerved her.

She was a little unnerved by the Colton family, as well, though. From some of the smiles directed at them, it was obvious that they had witnessed the kiss. Or maybe they were just smiling over Heath's over-the-top, affectionate behavior with her. He'd never acted that way with anyone else she had known he dated, and some of his family confirmed Heath had never acted that way with anyone he had dated before Kylie had met him either.

"This is a new side of you, Heath," his sister Carly remarked. She was so pretty with her pale blond hair and bright blue eyes. "Usually you would leave a date to fend for herself amongst us while you talked business with…" Her voice trailed off as she must have been about to state that he would have talked business with Ernie and Alfie.

Her brother Jones came to Carly's rescue with a remark. "You don't even seem to want to leave Kylie's side. Don't trust us alone with her?"

"You?" Heath asked with an arched brow at his younger brother. "Not at all…" But then he flashed a wicked grin at her before turning back to his brother to finish, "But don't take it personally. I don't want to leave her alone with anyone or no one at all."

Kylie's heart skipped a beat over his words and the wicked grin that accompanied them. Was he teasing? Or flirting?

With her?

"I thought you two always spent an awful lot of time together," Jones remarked. "But I didn't figure you would ever mix business with pleasure, Heath."

"He considers business to be pleasure," Kylie answered for him.

"I can see why with you working at his side," his brother said with a wink. Jones was good-looking with dark brown hair and bright blue eyes.

But he wasn't nearly as handsome as his older brother, at least not in Kylie's opinion. Some women might have preferred his darker, shorter hair and leaner build to Heath's shaggy blond hair and more muscular build—but not her.

Heath tightened his arm around her. "Stop hitting on my lady," he warned his younger brother. While he smiled, there was no hint of humor in his voice. He was acting like he was serious, like she was his lady.

Kylie suppressed a shiver of apprehension over how good an actor he was. He nearly had her believing him, believing that he was jealous and possessive of her. A giggle bubbled out of her at the ludicrous thought. "Stop acting like a Neanderthal," she teased him.

"That's why you two work," Carly said. "You're honest with each other and comfortable." Tears suddenly shimmered in her eyes, but she blinked them away. She had probably been thinking about her parents who'd had such a loving relationship.

Kylie had admired the happy marriages Ernie and Alfie had had, but she'd never even considered she might someday be in a relationship like that for herself and especially not with Heath. She was well aware of how hard it was for him to commit to anyone.

He was sure as hell committed to his act, though. He kept his arm around her as his mother called them into the dining room for dinner. Playing into the part of loving girlfriend, Kylie rose up on tiptoe, clinging to his side, and whispered in his ear. "Don't you think you're overselling this?"

He shivered and chuckled. "Oh, darling…not at all."

"Jeez, get a room," Jones teased.

Heat rushed up Kylie's face, probably turning it dark red. "I told him to dial it down," she admitted.

Jones laughed. "Yeah, Heath, I think you're finally dating someone who can handle a relationship with you with no problem."

Heath glanced down at her then, but the flirty grin had slid away from his sexy mouth. And the look in his dark blue eyes had gone speculative.

As if he was considering the truth of his brother's words.

Kylie doubted that she really could handle a relationship with him…or anyone else. While she dated, it wasn't often or for long. Even the most trustworthy of men had raised doubts in her. Heath's track record with women wasn't going to inspire any confidence in her. The only thing she was confident of was that he had not harmed his dad and uncle.

His mother approached them then, her face flushed from the heat of the kitchen. Her long dark hair was bound up on top of her head in a style that made her look younger than she was but for the dark circles beneath her eyes. She obviously hadn't been sleeping.

Sympathy gripped Kylie over the woman's devastating loss.

Then Mrs. Colton pulled her into a hug. "I'm so glad you came," she said. She reached for Sean's hand, too, as he and January stood beside them. "It's so great that the family is expanding."

Kylie swallowed hard, choking on her lies now. His mother thought she and Heath were serious, that Kylie was going to become family. Along with the lies, she choked on a rush of emotion over the possibility of finally having the big family she'd always longed for.

But she and Heath were not a possibility at all—no matter what his family thought.

"Thank you for inviting me," Kylie said. "I hope I'm not intruding, though."

"Not at all," Fallon Colton assured her. "You're part of the family now, too. Like Sean here." She glanced at the other Coltons present. "Now the rest of you need to start settling down, too."

"Mom…" Carly murmured.

Fallon patted her cheek. "I'm sorry, baby. I know you…" Her voice trailed off.

Seeing the discomfort of both women, Kylie jumped in to change the subject. "I would have helped you in the kitchen, but Heath insisted you like cooking alone."

"You cook?" Fallon asked, and the sadness was gone from her beautiful face, replaced with a look of delight. "That's wonderful. I would have welcomed your help, as my son knows. He just didn't want you to leave his side."

"Guilty," Heath said as his tightened his arm around her once again.

Sean Stafford chuckled.

Kylie thought he'd dropped by the office the day before because he suspected Heath was guilty of something, like lying about their relationship and his alibi. But the detective didn't seem too concerned about it now.

"You will definitely cook with me another time," Fallon said. "You and Tatum."

Kylie flushed with the certainty that cooking with Tatum would embarrass her. "I'm no professional chef."

"Me neither," Fallon said.

"It smells wonderful," Kylie praised her.

"Yes, Mom, can we eat now?" Jones asked.

She clapped her hands together and said, "Of course. Everybody, sit down. Let's eat." But as she walked around the table, she glanced at the empty chairs at both ends—the chairs that Alfie and Ernie must have taken. Almost reluctantly she settled into a chair to the right of an empty one, and her sister did the same at the other end.

And another twinge of sympathy gripped Kylie's heart for the pain on their beautiful faces. They were too young to be widows, too young to have lost the men with whom they'd intended to spend the rest of their lives. It wasn't fair.

Tears rushed to Kylie's eyes, but she blinked them back. She was not going to fall apart, not when all of

the Coltons were being so strong. As she settled into
the chair Heath held out for her, he gripped her shoulders briefly and squeezed. He must have seen her reaction, or he was just acting again. But when he sat down
next to her, she noticed that he was blinking hard, too,
fighting against his own rush of emotion.

As she glanced around the table, she noticed similar reactions from everyone else. But for Jones, whose
jaw was clenched nearly as tightly as he clenched a beer
bottle in his hand.

This wasn't easy for any of them—being here—without the men whose larger-than-life personalities had always dominated a room. They'd been such vibrant men,
such brilliant men, such loving family men.

Kylie reached under the table and touched Heath's
thigh, murmuring, "Sorry."

He glanced at her, and if he'd been fighting back any
tears, they were gone, replaced with a glint of desire as
his pupils dilated. "You might be if you do that again."

She jerked her hand away.

He chuckled, which brought a smile to his mother's
face again.

"I don't know if I've ever seen you like this, Heath,"
she said. "I like it."

"It's sickening," Jones remarked.

"It's sweet," January defended them. "They've gone
from being friends to being…" Her face flushed, and
Sean chuckled now and leaned over to kiss the blush
on her cheek.

"I always knew they were perfect for each other,"
his grandmother remarked.

Kylie glanced in surprise at the older woman, who sat across from her daughter Farrah. "Really?" She hadn't seen Abigail Jones as often as she had the rest of the family. The older woman had only occasionally stopped by Colton Connections with one of her daughters.

"It was the way that Heath talked about you," Mrs. Jones explained. "With admiration."

Heath uttered a wistful sounding sigh. "I do admire her. Even more so now."

Now that he knew about her past. She hadn't told him her sad story because she'd been worried that he would pity her. She hadn't realized it might have the opposite effect on him. Not that he was falling for her or anything. And she would be wise to remember that so she didn't do something stupider than providing him a false alibi, so that she didn't fall for him.

"Yes, they are perfect for each other," Simone remarked. She was the cousin closest to Heath's age. In fact they'd been born just days apart. With her brown hair, she looked more like Jones than she did her sisters January and Tatum. The psychology professor was very like her father Alfie, very astute, so much so that her comment unsettled Kylie.

Could Simone be right?

Kylie cast a surreptitious glance at the handsome man sitting next to her. She had always admired him, as a CEO, but she'd never considered him as any more than a colleague and a friend. A hot friend.

But just a friend...until that kiss. That kiss had sparked something between them, a chemistry Kylie had never felt before with Heath or with any other man.

Could there ever be something more between them than friendship? Since their fake relationship was built on nothing but lies and deception, she doubted it. It reminded Kylie too much of the relationships that had led to her mother's greatest humiliation and downfall.

To her arrest. And losing her medical license, her freedom, and then ultimately her life.

She shivered.

"Are you okay?" Heath asked with concern. "Do you need a sweater? Or I can get your jacket for you?"

She shook her head. "I'm fine. I'm not cold. I just felt…" What was the saying? Like someone had walked across her grave. It was more like she had walked across her mother's, though. Like she was walking in her shoes.

But that was silly. She had always been so careful not to make the mistakes her mother had, not to want so badly to be loved that she chose untrustworthy men.

"What the hell is he doing here?" It was Mrs. Jones who spoke up, her voice sharp with disapproval, so sharp that she startled everyone else at the table.

"Who, Grandma?" Simone asked from her seat next to the older woman.

"That detective." she pointed toward the window behind Kylie and Heath.

Kylie turned and saw Joe Parker stepping out of his unmarked police car. And nerves tightened in her stomach.

He must have figured out that they'd lied. That she'd lied.

It probably wouldn't have been hard to verify that she hadn't been where she said she'd been—with Heath—at the time of the murders. He could have looked at phone records or talked to her neighbors or his.

She should have known better than to try to provide Heath with a false alibi. But she'd been worried that he would be dragged off to jail like her mother had been.

Unjustly…

But now she was worried that she was about to be arrested for interfering in a police investigation. She was more like her mother than she had ever wanted to admit. She was probably about to go to jail over something she'd done for a man, too.

Chapter Twelve

Joe Parker would have rather been home having Sunday dinner with his family than interrupting the Colton family dinner. But he had news he knew the widows had been waiting to hear. He also wasn't that big a fan of his mother-in-law who was sitting at his table right now, spoiling his son and criticizing everything that wasn't up to her exacting standards.

He couldn't imagine living with her, like Alfred Colton had lived with his mother-in-law. Abigail Jones was the one who'd opened the door for him. He had a feeling the spry seventysomething year old had beaten everyone else to the foyer.

"This is not a good time, Detective," she told him, her green eyes as cold as her icy-silver hair. "We have just sat down to a family dinner."

He'd seen them all through the tall dining room windows. Everyone had been staring back at him with different expressions of dread and fear and curiosity.

Sean had looked curious, like he wondered what lead Parker might be following up on. The Givens woman had looked scared, and the man next to her, Heath

Colton, had put his arm around her as if to reassure or comfort her.

Joe still had doubts about that all-too-convenient alibi of Heath Colton's, especially after talking to so many of his family members who hadn't had a clue Heath was even dating his vice president. Some of those other family members had admitted to having no alibis, but Parker felt better about them because they clearly hadn't felt they needed one.

Why had Heath felt like he needed one?

The brothers' wills were to be read after their funerals. Well, now they could have the funerals, and Joe could find out exactly how much Heath gained from the deaths of his business partners.

"Why are you here?" Heath was the one who asked the question, with obvious dread, as he and the rest of the family joined Joe and the family matriarch in the foyer. All except for Kylie Givens.

She had remained in the dining room. Maybe because she wasn't family—though Sean was here, his arm around January Colton's shoulders. He wasn't family yet, but it was clear that he would be one day, probably soon.

No. The other son was missing as well as Ms. Givens. Parker had noticed his vehicle parked on the driveway, though, so he was here. Or he'd been here. The sudden rumble of an engine indicated that someone was leaving. It could have been Ms. Givens.

"Detective Parker," Heath Colton prodded him. "Why are you here?"

The twin widows, their hands clasped, stood near

the oldest son. From their grim expressions, it was clear that the women knew…before he even said it. "We're ready to release the bodies."

The one with the longer hair, Heath's mother, Fallon Colton, gasped while the one with the shorter hair, Farrah Colton, nodded in acceptance. "Thanks for letting us know. We'll contact the funeral home."

Fallon's gasp turned into a sob, and she ran from the foyer. Farrah turned and headed after her.

"You should leave," Mrs. Jones said. But she didn't take the time to shove him out the door, instead she rushed after her daughters.

The others all left, too, but for Heath who stood in front of him, staring hard at him. Parker didn't mind being alone with the businessman, with getting another shot at breaking that alibi of his, with breaking him like he had broken other suspects. If everything he'd heard about the man was true, though, Joe probably would have had more luck getting Ms. Givens to crack…unless she was the one who'd driven off.

Despite the hardness of Heath's stare, there was emotion in his eyes, making them glisten. Hearing about the bodies, about the upcoming funerals, had affected him. Maybe that was grief glistening there.

Maybe Heath Colton wasn't as ruthless as his business acquaintances claimed he was. Or maybe that was guilt in his gaze, and he was even more ruthless, ruthless enough to kill his own dad and uncle.

HEATH PUSHED ASIDE the pain that had gripped him from the detective bringing up their bodies, which had elicited for Heath that horrific memory of identifying those bodies. Along with the pain, he felt a twinge of guilt for not going after his mom and aunt to console them. His pain didn't compare to what they were feeling.

To what the detective's callousness had compounded.

Heath couldn't do anything to ease their suffering but lash out at the man who'd increased it. "You didn't need to come here to tell them that," he said. "You could have had someone call." That would have been less painful for them, less disruptive.

The detective offered a slight smile. "Coming here to notify them in person was a courtesy."

Heath snorted in derision of the man's idea of courtesy. "Yeah, right. Why did you really come here? Why are you harassing my family? Haven't we been through enough?"

"I'm trying to get justice for your father and uncle," Parker replied. "I'm trying to find their killer. Isn't that what you want, as well?"

That fury inside Heath turned now—to the rightful target—to the monster who'd murdered his loved ones. "I want nothing more than to find their killer, but you're not going to find the real suspect by interrogating my family. We all loved my dad and uncle too much to ever want to harm them."

"Money is often a motive for murder," Parker replied. "And it looks like with you as CEO of the company, you control most of that money now."

Kylie handled most of the financial stuff. But Heath wasn't going to involve her in the detective's investigation any more than she had already involved herself when she'd provided him with a false alibi.

And ultimately, the big decisions were his to make anyway. So he replied with total honesty, "I would spend every damn dime in the Colton Connections' account to bring my dad and uncle back."

But money couldn't bring them back. But it could help them find their killer.

"And I will. I'll offer a reward. I'll hire independent investigators," he said. "I will do whatever necessary to do your job since you don't seem to want to."

Parker tensed and stood up straighter, so that he seemed to stare down at Heath. "I am here on a Sunday," he said. "I am working this case nearly every waking hour. I want this killer caught, too."

Heath believed him—even before Sean stepped forward and gripped his shoulder. "Joe is the best homicide detective with the department, Heath. He'll find the son of a bitch responsible for the murders."

"Thanks," Parker told his coworker. "Unfortunately, we all know that sometimes that can take a while to sort through all the suspects before we find the real perpetrator."

Heath bristled again. "There are not any suspects in this case," he said. "Nobody inside my family or outside my family, who knew them, would hurt them. You're wasting your time."

"Or he's avoiding his mother-in-law," Sean remarked with a chuckle. "But thank you for the courtesy of stopping by with the news. It'll be good for the family to have the funerals, to get some closure."

"The funerals aren't going to bring closure," Heath said with total certainty that burying his dad and uncle wouldn't make them feel any better. "The killer being caught might." But he didn't hold out much hope that anything would make this better, would lessen the pain of the loss of two such amazing men.

Tears burned his eyes—like they had when everyone had silently noted those empty chairs at the dining table. He wasn't sure he would be able to blink them away this time, so he left the two lawmen standing in the foyer and rushed into the dining room. Blinded with emotion, he wasn't sure who wrapped slender arms around him…until his pulse quickened in reaction.

Kylie held him, like she had that first horrible night after he'd identified the bodies. She held him and offered him comfort and friendship.

He found himself wanting more from her, though—so much more than friendship. So much more than the false alibi that was risking her freedom.

But what he wanted from her would risk his, and he'd always been so careful to protect it, to stay single.

"LET'S GET OUT of here," Kylie implored Heath. She felt bad for his mom and aunt, who were clearly distraught. But she felt the worst for him, with how the detective persisted in treating him like the only suspect in the murders of his own father as well as his uncle.

Why and how couldn't Parker see how badly Heath was hurting? His pain was so palpable to Kylie that she felt as hollow and empty inside as she knew that he did.

The two lawmen continued to talk in the foyer. So

Kylie tugged Heath in the other direction. Everyone had gathered in the kitchen except for Jones. When the detective had rung the doorbell, Heath's younger brother had headed for the back door while everyone else had headed to the front. But for her...

She hadn't wanted to see the detective again. And she didn't want to see him now either. She didn't want to see any of the other Coltons right now. She didn't want to intrude on what was a very intimate family moment. Because no matter how much she longed to have a big family of her own—this wasn't it. She and Heath were lying to these people, and anything based on a lie would never last.

Heath must not have wanted to see his family either because he murmured, "There's another door through here." Closing his hand around hers, he led her into a dark-paneled library, out of the French doors and through a small courtyard to the front driveway.

Once they were outside, he still held her hand, his fingers entwined with hers. Her skin tingled from the contact. They'd left their coats in the foyer closet— where the lawmen were—but she didn't actually feel cold.

Heat suffused her instead from Heath's touch, from the way he looked at her, like she really mattered to him. Like he needed her.

He did need her now, as he reeled from his devastating losses. And being a potential suspect in those murders had to have compounded his pain.

Her heart aching for him, she rose up on tiptoe and pressed her lips to his. His mouth was warm, so he must not have been feeling the cold either. Then he parted his lips and the kiss got hotter yet, as his tongue teased hers.

His fingers slid into her hair, combing through the long tresses before clasping the back of her head. He kissed her passionately, his lips nibbling gently at hers.

Her pulse quickened, and her heart pounded as desire overwhelmed her. She wanted more than his kiss. She wanted Heath.

Maybe she'd let all those comments from his family get to her, get her thinking that maybe they were as perfect for each other as they all thought. Or maybe she'd let him get to her—with his good looks and his charm.

But it was all an act.

Just like this kiss.

She pulled back, and a sudden chill rushed over her, making her shudder.

"What's wrong?" Heath asked, as he panted for breath. "Was kissing me that disgusting?"

She shook her head. "No…" In fact it had been exactly the opposite. Something else had inspired that chill—or someone else.

"You must be cold then," he said. "We did forget our coats."

She shook her head again. "It's not that." She still didn't feel physically cold. It was more like her soul had been chilled.

Heath's brow creased as he stared down at her. "Then what it is?"

"I've just been getting this odd sensation the past couple days," she admitted, "like someone's watching me."

"I know," he said. "That's why you kissed me—

because the detective's probably watching us and you wanted to sell our fake alibi and relationship."

The alibi was fake. She was beginning to wonder about the relationship. Was it really just work and friendship? Or had she always had other feelings for him, feelings she hadn't wanted to acknowledge? Maybe that was why she had impulsively provided that alibi—for the same reason her mother hadn't turned in the man who'd stolen her prescription pad and forged her signature on it.

Kylie didn't even glance at the house where she was sure there were people watching them. She didn't believe any of them had inspired that sudden chill. "It's not the detective…"

At least she didn't think it was him, unless he'd been following her or maybe he had assigned someone to follow her. "Or your family. It feels like someone else has been watching me."

Someone who wanted to hurt her…or worse.

Chapter Thirteen

Already shaken from her kiss, Heath reeled from Kylie's other admission—that she'd been having that same sensation he'd been having, of being watched. He glanced back at his aunt and uncle's house, where shadows darkened the glass of some of the windows.

"Who else would be watching you?" he asked.

"I don't know…" she murmured.

Who watched them from inside? One of his family? All of his family? Or Parker who had yet to leave? How the hell could the detective think that any of them were capable of murdering the men they'd loved so much? There wasn't enough money in the world worth their lives. His eyes suddenly stinging, he blinked hard.

"But it's like I get this sudden chill," she said. "And it just feels like someone's staring at me so coldly."

"Maybe it's just the cold," he murmured. But he didn't want to go back inside for their jackets. He didn't want to see the detective again or even any of his family.

Not now…

Heath knew that he was the reason the detective kept coming around, kept questioning them all. Because he'd been in business with his dad and uncle, the detective had fixated on him as the prime suspect. Like he'd staged some kind of extremely hostile takeover.

Would Parker convince Heath's family that his suspicion was true? That Heath had the capacity, the greed, to kill? Could his family have those kinds of doubts about him?

He'd already wondered if they had. Kylie had no such doubts, though, or she wouldn't have provided him that alibi. She'd respected his dad and uncle too much to help out someone she suspected of killing them. No. She'd offered him the alibi to save him and to save the detective from following a false lead.

Heath...

Her effort had backfired though, making Parker more determined to hound Heath. He uttered a weary sigh.

"Let's go," he said, as he opened the passenger door of his silver SUV for Kylie.

She stepped closer to him, but before getting into the vehicle, she peered up at his face. "Are you okay?" she asked, her dark eyes full of concern.

He shook his head. He didn't know if he would ever be okay again—not with such a massive hole in his life and in his heart. The only time he didn't hurt was when he was kissing Kylie.

Was his family right? Was she perfect for him? Had he always had feelings for her beyond friendship? Maybe she really was the reason—as Gina had accused—that he hadn't been able to commit to her.

He'd assured his ex that he wasn't attracted to his

colleague, though. And at the time he'd believed what he'd told her. Sure, he'd always been aware that Kylie was beautiful, but as a woman with whom he'd worked, she'd been off-limits to him. He'd respected her too much to hit on her and risk her suing the company or, worse yet, leaving it.

"Are you really okay with all of this?" he asked. "With my kissing you."

Her lips curved into a slight smile. "I kissed you."

"This time," he acknowledged. "But I was the one who insisted we play the part of lovers—"

"Because I told the detective that we are," she finished for him. "I'm fine. Worried that I'm going to sue you or Colton Connections?"

If she did, she'd be suing herself—eventually. He fully intended to make her a partner, but now he needed to wait until the wills were read, until he knew if he still had the power in the company to make her a partner.

A business partner.

That was all she could ever be to him, though. Because he couldn't risk losing her for Colton Connections. The company needed her, especially after losing the creative genius that had made it the multimillion-dollar business that it was.

While he needed her now, he still wasn't convinced that he was even capable of the kind of love and commitment his parents had had for each other or that his aunt and uncle had shared, as well.

After the upbringing Kylie had survived, she deserved more security than he could offer her. Hell, he couldn't even offer himself any security now especially if she was right and someone else was watching them. Was it his father and uncle's killer?

"SEE?" FALLON SAID to Detective Parker. After taking several long moments to pull herself together, she'd rejoined him and Sean in the foyer. She'd intended to invite him to join them for dinner—even as her children were disappearing. Heath and Kylie had slipped out through the library while Jones had stormed off through the kitchen.

As she'd approached the two detectives, she'd overheard Parker questioning her niece's boyfriend about Heath's alibi—Kylie. And she'd bristled with protectiveness of her firstborn child. Not that Heath had ever needed her protection; he'd always been strong, as a kid and even more so as a man.

"See how they look at each other?" she told the detective, as she peered through the sidelights of the front door to where the couple stood close together next to Heath's SUV. "They can't take their eyes off each other. They are more than friends and coworkers." She was so grateful that Heath had someone special. Someone who so obviously cared about him and could help him through this terrible time.

"I'm not doubting that they're involved," the detective conceded.

"You're doubting his alibi," Fallon said. That was what she'd overheard him asking Sean about, if he really believed that Heath and Kylie had been together that night—that horrible, devastating night. "He doesn't need one. Heath is a good man."

"What about Jones?" Detective Parker asked. "What about your other son?"

She gasped with shock that another of her sons was considered a suspect. But then she and Farrah had probably been considered the prime suspects because they were the spouses. If they hadn't been out of town at that home show...

Would it have even happened? Or would Ernie and Alfie have headed home earlier. Her heart ached that she would never know what might have saved them... or if anything could have.

"Jones went racing out of here the minute I showed up," Parker remarked. "Didn't give me the chance to ask him any questions."

"I didn't think that's why you came," she said. "I thought it was just to notify us..." Her voice cracked. She would not give in to the tears again—not yet. Next time she cried, she would wait until she was alone. She needed to be strong—for her children, her sister, her mom and mostly for Ernie. He would have wanted her to be strong for their family and for herself.

She drew in a deep breath and lifted her chin. "What did you want to ask Jones?" she asked. She had a few questions for her youngest child, too. Like how he was doing.

He seemed so broken, even more so than the others. The only time the grim expression had left his face was when he'd been teasing Heath about Kylie. That young woman was good for her entire family—not just Heath.

"Do you doubt his alibi, too?" she asked.

"I doubt everything, Mrs. Colton," Detective Parker admitted with a slight smile and a heavy sigh.

"It must be sad to be so cynical," Fallon mused with genuine sympathy. While she hated how he was looking at her family, like suspects, she respected that he was just doing his job and seeking justice was admirable—just sometimes hard to come by.

He shook his head. "I'm not cynical. I'm realistic. And despite some of the horrible things I've seen on the job, I'm very happy."

Fallon wondered then if she would ever be happy again—truly happy. Ernie would definitely want her to be, but she knew that there was only one thing that would bring her true happiness now. If her kids—all of her kids—were happy, then she would be, too.

KYLIE SHIVERED AGAIN and slid into the car. Maybe she was just cold. Maybe there wasn't anyone watching them…besides that detective and Heath's family.

Heath's family…

Guilt twisted her stomach over having to deceive them. But if she and Heath admitted now to lying about the alibi, they would be in so much trouble. Even with the alibi, Heath was still apparently Parker's number-one suspect. If having an alibi hadn't convinced him of Heath's innocence, what would?

Finding the real killer.

Like Heath, she didn't believe it was anyone within his family. The patriarchs had been too beloved for any of their family to harm them.

But who else could have wanted them dead?

Someone from Colton Connections?

While all of the employees had loved them, too, there were a couple that Kylie didn't quite trust. One in particular…

Of course, trust had never come easily for her, though, so she'd wanted proof before bringing her concerns to the company CEO.

To Heath…

He passed in front of the vehicle before jumping into the driver's side. "Good thing I left the keys in here instead of my coat pocket," he murmured as he started up the SUV.

She waited until he eased down the driveway, away from that house, before she asked, "When did you feel like you were being watched?"

He chuckled. "Besides now?"

"Yes," she said, although she had had the sensation that someone besides his family had been watching them. But how? From the street? The driveway was pretty long. But if they'd had a telescope…

God, she sounded paranoid even to herself now.

Once around the curve of the circular drive, he stopped the vehicle and turned toward her. "When did you feel like you were being watched?"

"Yesterday," she said. "But maybe I'm just paranoid."

"That's what I thought, too," he said, and he glanced across the console at her. "I had the feeling for the first time that night I found you in my kitchen."

She nodded. "You did immediately assume I was an intruder when I could have been any of your family or…"

Gina. But his ex-girlfriend hadn't shown up until the next morning—when she'd caught them in bed together. They hadn't done anything but talk before they'd fallen asleep, though. She suspected that if they shared a bed now, they would be tempted to do more than talk.

At least she would be.

"But I'd just been to the morgue." He shuddered.

She couldn't even imagine what he'd seen, the evidence of how violently his dad and uncle had been murdered. "And you knew that had happened in the parking lot where you and I are every day." She nodded. "I felt someone watching me when I left the building yesterday. Was it you?"

He shook his head. "I didn't know you left until I found your office empty."

"You weren't on the ninth floor?" she asked.

He shook his head again. "I haven't been up there since their deaths."

Ernie and Alfie had had their offices on the ninth floor—just off the open area where they'd designed and invented so many amazing things. They were the only ones with offices up there, but several other employees used the space.

"It must have been someone else," she mused. "I thought I saw someone at a window."

He shrugged. "Some of the other inventors work odd hours."

She nodded in agreement. But she wasn't thinking of other inventors. "There is a certain lawyer who is always hanging around."

"Tyler," Heath said. "He's ambitious."

She wasn't sure that was all the man was, though. "I wonder if there's more to it than that with him."

"Are you thinking he would try to kill you to get your job?" he asked.

Apparently Heath was more aware of the situation between her and Tyler than she'd realized. "Maybe. But maybe it's not just *my* job he wants. He could be after yours, too."

Heath chuckled. "He is ambitious."

Kylie sighed. "Ambitious, yes, but a killer? I don't know." She didn't want to believe that of a man with whom she'd worked for so many years.

"Maybe he was just watching you because you're hot," Heath said.

She chuckled, thinking he was joking, but when she glanced at him, he returned her look with a certain glint in his blue eyes.

And her pulse quickened in reaction.

"Then he wouldn't be the same person watching you," Kylie remarked.

"You don't think I'm hot, too?" he asked.

Now she knew he was teasing, or so she hoped—because she was not about to admit just how incredibly hot and sexy she thought Heath was.

"I don't know what to think," she said.

"About my hotness?" he teased.

"I don't know if someone really is watching both of us," she said.

"We were also almost hit by that car," Heath mused, and his voice was all serious now.

"You said it was an accident," she reminded him. "That we weren't paying attention."

"I wasn't," he said. "I also don't want to think that someone could have purposely tried to run us down, though. So I don't know what I was wrong about— being watched or someone trying to run us down."

"What if it's both?" she wondered aloud. "What if someone is watching us and did try to run us down?"

"You think someone's trying to kill us?" he asked, and he glanced at her again, his blue eyes wide with shock.

She didn't want to think it either. "I don't know." And there was only one way they would know for certain… if someone tried again to kill them.

But she didn't dare express that opinion aloud. She didn't want to tempt fate any more than they already had with their fake alibi.

Heath must have felt the same because he lifted his foot from the brake and pressed on the accelerator. He said nothing as he drove out of his aunt's drive, past his mother's French provincial house and down the street.

Oak Park reminded Kylie of the *Home Alone* movie she'd watched over and over with Baba. It was such a quaint neighborhood full of nice homes as well as a mix of shops and businesses and parks.

They had just approached the corner near one of those small parks when a loud noise shattered the silence that had fallen between them.

"Get down!" Heath yelled. "Someone's shooting at us!"

They had their answer: they weren't being paranoid. Someone was trying to kill them.

Chapter Fourteen

The windshield hadn't broken. Only one small hole pierced it, but from that one hole, a spiderweb of cracks spread out. Heath couldn't see through it. He had no damn idea what was on the road ahead of them.

But for a gunman.

More shots rang out, the gunfire sounding like claps of thunder. That first bullet, that had struck the windshield, hadn't been fired in error. It wasn't like some hunter with lousy aim had struck them instead.

No. It seemed more like open season on them. Someone was definitely trying to kill them. And coming too damn close this time.

"Get down!" he shouted again at Kylie.

That first hole had pierced the windshield more on her side than his. But it couldn't have hit her. Could it?

He glanced over the console at her, but she was leaning over, her head near the dash. He couldn't see her face, couldn't see if she was conscious.

Had she been hit?

Panic pressed hard on his chest, stealing his breath

away. "Kylie?" he called out to her, fear for her filling him. That hole was so close to where her head had been.

Needing to make certain she was okay, he took one hand from the wheel and reached for her, but as he did, another bullet struck the SUV. One of the tires blew, the rubber squealing against the asphalt of the street. The steering wheel shuddered within his one-handed grasp as the SUV started spinning out of his control.

He pulled his other hand back to the wheel, gripping it tightly, grappling to bring the vehicle back under control. Where the hell could he go? How could he get out of the line of fire?

Yet another bullet struck, scraping across the metal of the roof. Then another tire was struck, and the vehicle started to careen across the street.

He lost all control of the SUV...as the firing of those gunshots continued. There was no way to avoid them now, no way to avoid getting hit.

HIS HEART HEAVY with sympathy and with regret for upsetting the Colton widows even more, Detective Joe Parker headed toward his vehicle. He was only doing his job, but sometimes the job sucked. The worst part of it was the suffering—of the victims and of survivors—and that sometimes in the course of his investigation, Joe had to add to their suffering.

Hopefully, he was as wrong as Mrs. Colton and Heath Colton had told him he was, and that nobody within the family was responsible for the murders of the patriarchs. But he wasn't certain yet.

Money was so often a motive for murder that he

couldn't rule out the heirs. And as far as he could tell, Heath Colton stood to gain the most and along with him, his next in command at Colton Connections—Kylie Givens. Along with the show of affection, which he suspected might have been for his benefit, they'd also been talking for a long while in the vehicle parked just down the driveway.

They were gone now, as he climbed into the driver's side of his. But they couldn't be far ahead of him. Maybe he could catch up and see where they were heading.

But as he pulled the door closed, a noise caught his attention. A familiar noise…

The sound of gunshots. He cursed and reached for the police radio. "Shots fired…" He gave his location.

What the hell was going on?

And why did he suspect it had to do with Heath Colton and Kylie Givens? Were they firing the shots or were they being shot at?

THAT FIRST SHOT and the shock of someone shooting at them had struck Kylie hard, making her freeze in silence. But when the SUV careened off the road, she found her voice again. A scream tore from her throat as the SUV skidded off the road into the ditch.

Airbags exploded out of the dash and the side of the vehicle, hitting her in the face like a soft slap. Like someone might have struck her to stop her hysteria.

She stopped screaming and gasped for air for a moment, coughing and sputtering at the slight powder that emanated from the inflated bags. Tears stung her eyes, and she blinked, furiously trying to see…anything. But the airbags enveloped her. As quickly as they'd inflated, they began to deflate. She turned her head toward Heath who was slumped over the airbag that had sprung out of the steering wheel.

A shaggy lock of blond hair had fallen across his eyes, so she couldn't see if he was conscious or not. But his big body was so still, so frighteningly still that it was almost lifeless.

"Heath?" she called out to him. "Heath?"

Had a bullet struck him?

She couldn't even remember how many had been fired. Did the shooter have any bullets left in the gun?

She peered around the deflating airbags into the shattered but intact glass of the windshield. Was the shooter out there yet?

Coming for them?

"Heath!" she called out. She reached across the console and grabbed his arm. "Heath!"

With her other hand she reached for the door handle, tugging at it to open her door. But it wasn't budging. Had the SUV stopped against something?

Was the door too crumpled to open?

They had to get out of the SUV. They had to run to some cover. Now, trapped inside the SUV, they were easy targets for the shooter.

Realizing why her door wouldn't budge, she pushed at the lock until it clicked. When she grabbed the handle now, the door creaked open.

But she had no intention of getting out alone and leaving Heath behind and at the mercy of the merciless shooter. Worried that he was seriously hurt, she didn't dare shake him, though. So she just squeezed his arm and implored him, "Heath, please wake up!"

He murmured something, and her heart thudded with a surge of relief. He was alive.

"Heath," she breathed his name with a sigh of that relief. But then she heard movement outside. Because of the shattered windshield and all the dangling curtain airbags, she couldn't see who was coming toward them.

Innocent bystanders or the shooter making sure that they were dead?

"Heath, if you can move, we have to get out of here," she urged him. "We have to find some cover."

He murmured something and finally his body moved, shifting against the steering wheel. And he turned his head toward her. "Are you okay?" he asked her, all his concern for her.

She nodded. But she really wasn't sure. Between all the gunshots and the crash.

So much adrenaline coursed through her now that she couldn't feel anything but the quick pace of her pulse and her madly pounding heart.

"But we have to get out of here," she said. "I don't know if the shooter is still out there or..."

His hands still gripped the steering wheel, so when he straightened his arms, he pushed back against the seat. "Yeah, yeah, we have to get out of here."

He reached for the shifter, but it wasn't in Park.

"We crashed," she said. "We have to get out of here on foot."

They had to run, but it was clear that he could barely

move. Then it was too late as a shadow fell across that shattered windshield.

Someone had found them.

To help them?

Or to finish them off?

Chapter Fifteen

Heath flinched as he drew in another breath. The airbag or the steering wheel behind it had struck him like a fist to the chest and the chin. He ran his hand over his face, which was stinging a bit from the blow.

"You should have let Detective Parker call an ambulance," his mother said as she fussed around him where he sat at the island in the kitchen of Aunt Farrah's house. Tears dampened her face.

The last thing he wanted was to be the cause of any more crying for her. She already had enough reasons to weep.

All of his family did, and all of them were in the kitchen except for Jones, who'd left earlier. His sister and cousins looked as if they'd been crying. He doubted it was over him, though; it had been because of the news the detective had brought them earlier.

About the bodies...

"I'm fine," he assured his mother. "Just had the wind knocked out of me for a moment when the airbags went off."

Kylie made some little noise in her throat, and when

he glanced at her, he could see, from the concern on her beautiful face, that he'd been out for more than a moment. He remembered then that desperation in her voice as she'd called his name. She'd been worried that they were trapped with the shooter still out there.

He was still out there. Nobody had seen anything. Not even Detective Parker who'd arrived on the scene shortly after the SUV, with the two blown tires, had careened into the ditch. "It seems so surreal."

But then everything did—the murders of Pop and Uncle Alfie, the detective suspecting him of those murders, Kylie providing him an alibi and more.

"Could it have been a hunter?" his mother asked. "Someone accidentally firing toward the road?"

"I wish it was, Mom," he said. He understood her wanting to believe that—just as he'd wanted to believe that nobody was really following him, that nobody had really tried to run down him and Kylie. "There were just too many shots fired directly at us for it to have been an accident."

She gasped, and he stood up. But before he could comfort her, Aunt Farrah was there—with her arm around her shoulders. He was so glad that they had each other and their unbreakable twin bond right now.

"But who would want to harm you?" his sister Carly asked. "It makes no sense."

"No more sense than anyone wanting to harm Pop and Uncle Alfie," he said. Had he been the real intended target? Had the killer been waiting for him instead of them?

"Kylie and I both have had a feeling that we're being watched," he admitted.

Kylie nodded and shivered. "Yes, I have."

"Was it you?" Heath asked Detective Parker. "Did you have someone following us?"

"I wish I had had a detail on you," Parker replied. "Then we'd have seen who shot at you. Did either of you see anything? Anything at all?"

Heath cursed. "No, damn it."

Kylie shook her head, tangling her long hair around her face. He automatically reached out and pushed a dark brown lock across her cheek. And his fingertips tingled from that brief contact with her silky skin and hair. Damn she was beautiful.

So beautiful.

And she'd nearly been killed. They'd both nearly been killed.

"Then it wasn't an accident when someone almost ran you over outside True," Tatum remarked.

"Someone tried running you down?" Parker asked. "Why the hell didn't it get reported?" The last question had probably been addressed more to Sean than Heath, as the detectives exchanged a glance.

But Heath answered, "I didn't think it was intentional. Just someone driving too fast." That was what he'd wanted to think—not that he was being targeted next by the person who'd killed Pop and Uncle Alfie. Or worse yet, that maybe they had been killed instead of him.

Parker groaned. "You should have reported it and that you felt as if you were being watched."

Heath stared hard at the man. "I didn't think you would believe me. Or that you would think I'd made it up." Like Kylie had made up his alibi.

Parker didn't argue with him, prompting Heath to ask, "Do you believe me now? Or do you think Kylie and I staged the shooting?"

Parker looked from him to Kylie and back, as if considering it. "There were an awful lot of bullets fired without either of you being struck."

"Thank God," his mother murmured.

Heath bristled at the detective's comment. "What's it going to take for you to believe I'm innocent? My own murder?"

Because it was clear to Heath that someone wanted him dead and maybe Kylie, as well.

THE RAGE WAS all consuming. Too consuming.

How many bullets had been fired? Even the shooter didn't know—not now—as the rush of adrenaline faded to just a slight buzzing in their ears and veins.

Who had been hit?

Anyone?

The SUV had crashed, so someone could have been injured then. But the shooter hadn't dared to stick around, hadn't wanted to risk getting seen or, worse yet, caught.

But even if no one had died—yet—the message

should have been clear. The warning sent—loudly and succinctly—with every fired shot.

Someone was going to die…

ANGER BUBBLED UP inside Kylie now, and she jumped off the stool at the island in Farrah Colton's kitchen. "Detective Parker, there is no way that you can think either Heath or I fired those bullets into his own vehicle! That's crazy." She hadn't been able to stop shaking since that first fired gunshot. Her whole body trembled as she stood before him, staring up into his stern face.

Frustration overwhelmed her. "Someone tried to kill us, and you're treating us like the suspects!"

Heath wrapped his arm around her and pulled her close to his side. "It's okay, Kylie. You're okay now. We're fine."

She shook her head. "No, it's not fine."

"She's right," Fallon Colton agreed. "It isn't fine. You two could have been killed." A sob slipped out of her trembling lips.

A twinge of guilt struck Kylie's heart. She hadn't meant to upset the woman any more than she'd already, rightfully, been. "I'm sorry…" she murmured as she closed her eyes and willed away the tears that threatened to slip free.

Heath tipped up her chin, and she opened her eyes to stare up into his face.

"It's okay," he assured her. "You have every reason to be upset. So am I."

But he didn't look shaken up. He looked mad. And madly handsome.

His golden hair was mussed, his stubble almost as thick as a beard on his strong jaw. He looked so rumpled and sexy, like he'd just crawled out of bed—a bed he'd shared with a woman, and not just slept in like he had that night they'd shared his.

Then she felt it, the slight tremor, in the hand he'd cupped under her chin. He really was unnerved, too. Then he dropped his hand from her face and turned toward the detective. "Are you going to do anything constructive besides hurl accusations at us?"

"I haven't accused you of anything," Detective Parker pointed out. "All I've done is ask questions."

But he clearly hadn't liked or trusted the answers they'd given him. Some with just cause. Maybe she shouldn't have lied about Heath's alibi. But if she hadn't...

She worried that the detective would have already arrested him. But then he might have been safer in jail than he was with someone trying to shoot him.

"You're asking the wrong questions," Heath said. "Of the wrong people."

Sean Stafford finally stepped forward then. "Joe, I'm worried that they're in danger. All of them."

Parker didn't argue with his coworker; he just nodded. "It's possible that someone might have a grudge against the whole family. You could all be potential targets."

Gasps emanated from some of the other family members. But not Heath.

Of course he knew that he was definitely a target. Why? Because he was CEO?

"No, we're not," Mrs. Jones denied. "We can't be."

"No, you're not, Grandma," Heath assured her before turning back to Parker. "Detective, you should really go. You've upset this family enough for one day."

The detective didn't argue with Heath now either. He just nodded. But instead of turning to leave, he warned them, "You need to stick together."

"We do," Mrs. Jones said.

"Even when you try to turn us against each other," Heath remarked.

The detective shook his head. "I wasn't trying to do any such thing. I'm just looking for answers, Mr. Colton. Answers that you should want now more than ever."

Because Heath could become a victim the way his dad and his uncle had.

"I've always wanted the answers," Heath corrected the detective.

"Let me find those," Parker advised. "You all just need to stick close to each other—keep each other safe." He exchanged a nod with Sean Stafford before he walked out of the kitchen toward the foyer.

He'd already taken their statements at the scene of where the shot-up SUV had crashed into the ditch. After writing up their report and calling the technicians to collect the vehicle and the evidence, he had driven them back to Farrah Colton's house. Although riding in the police car had made Kylie uneasy, she had been in too much shock to protest then.

But now she tugged Heath aside to murmur, "I should leave, too."

She'd already felt that she was intruding. Now she felt even more so that she didn't belong. But then she'd never belonged in a family. She'd never really had one.

Just her and her mother and her grandmother and then just her and her grandmother.

"Yes, we should leave," he said. "I'll see if I can borrow a vehicle from Mom or Aunt Farrah." He glanced toward the twins.

With the tips of her fingers along his jaw, she turned his face back toward her. "No, *I* should leave. Alone."

His blue eyes widened in surprise. "Alone?" He shook his head. "You're not going anywhere alone."

She reached for his arm and tugged him out of the kitchen and into the hall, but she still pitched her voice to a low whisper when she said, "You can stop overacting now. Despite what Detective Parker said, he can't consider you a suspect any longer...not when someone's trying to kill you, too."

"Me? Or us?" he asked.

A chill chased down her spine again. "Uh, you, of course. I'm not a Colton."

"I don't think the whole family is in danger. Just me and maybe you."

"Me? Why?"

"Because you're the VP of Colton Connections," he said.

She shrugged. "So, an employee."

He flinched. "I—I..." He sighed. "I will talk to you about that after the funeral. At any rate you said you felt like you were being watched even when I wasn't with you."

She shivered again. "So you're thinking maybe I was the target?"

The thought filled her with horror—that someone

could have been trying to kill her and had nearly killed Heath, too. Twice.

With the car. And then with the gunshots.

But why the twins and then her? It made no sense. Unless...

Had Ernie and Alfie had the same suspicions she had about Tyler Morrison? Had they already found the evidence she'd been looking for?

"If I am the target," she said, "then you'll be safer if I'm not with you."

"I'm not saying you are the target," he said. "I'm just saying that we don't know for certain who is. And although I never thought I would say this, I agree with Detective Parker. We all need to stick together."

She shook her head. "I can't stay here with your family. It's too much of an imposition, especially now..." With everything they were going through. "They don't need a stranger staying with them."

"They don't need me staying here either," Heath agreed. "I think they're safe. I am the intended target and maybe you, too, so neither of us is staying here."

She expelled a little sigh of relief. "Good."

But then he added, "You're staying with me. We're going to get your stuff and move you into the penthouse."

She shook her head. "No."

This wasn't a good idea for so many reasons. Living with him would put Kylie in more danger, not less. Because not only would she be in danger from whoever had tried to kill them, but she was also in danger of falling for Heath.

Chapter Sixteen

This isn't a good idea...

Moving Kylie into his penthouse was dangerous—for both of them. But it would have been more dangerous for her to live alone in her little house.

"I've been doing it for years," she'd told him as she'd packed up some things and he'd carried them to the little SUV he'd borrowed from his mother. "I'm safe here. The neighbors all watch out for each other."

"Do you want to put those neighbors in danger then?" That question had compelled her to finish packing and climb back into the passenger's seat.

She was unpacking now in his guest room and not his room.

She wasn't moving in permanently, just until whoever had tried to kill them was caught. Though given Parker's penchant for interrogating the wrong people, Heath wasn't confident that would be any time soon.

Needing to stay away from the guest room, where he could hear drawers and doors opening, Heath focused on the view out his living room windows. The last remnants of sunlight had slipped away, leaving only a black sky. There was no glimpse of the moon. No stars.

The only lights shone from buildings and the street. Someone was out there. Someone who wanted them dead.

That was why Kylie was here.

The only reason.

She wasn't moving in because she wanted to be here—like Gina. Gina Hogan had wanted to live with him. Hell, she'd wanted to marry him. But even after dating her for months, he hadn't been ready to live with her.

Or with anyone.

His phone vibrated, and he pulled it from his pocket to glance at the screen. It was as if she'd realized he was thinking about her.

Gina was calling again. He slid his thumb across the Ignore option. He'd been doing that the past couple of days, ignoring her calls.

He knew he'd broken her heart when he'd resisted her ultimatums and chosen breaking up with her over being forced into an engagement. But with his own heart broken over the loss of his father, he couldn't deal with her right now—especially after how angry she'd been when she'd let herself in the other morning and found him in bed with Kylie.

All those months ago, when they'd been in a relationship, he'd thought giving her a key to his penthouse would placate her over his refusal to let her move in, but she'd still kept pushing for more.

More of a commitment…

Was *more* something he was even capable of? He'd never felt about anyone the way his parents had felt about each other or how his aunt and uncle had. The only thing that made him as happy as his mom and pop had made each other was work.

Maybe that was all he was capable of caring about.

What would happen after the wills were read? Would he be removed as CEO? Would the company be sold?

He had no idea what provisions, if any, his dad and uncle had made regarding Colton Connections in the event of their deaths. Since they'd been so young and healthy, they might not have made any, and they certainly probably hadn't counted on their dying together.

Although they'd done everything together, so in some sick way, it was fitting. And, at least, they hadn't died alone.

Would he?

If he didn't find some way to open up his heart, would he die alone? He hadn't thought about that possibility—until now—until he could have been killed by any of those bullets that had been fired into the SUV.

But he wouldn't have died alone then. Kylie had been with him. Kylie might have died, too.

Maybe her moving in wasn't a good idea—for her. Maybe he was just putting her in more danger.

Because he couldn't imagine anyone wanting her dead. But then he couldn't imagine anyone wanting Pop and Uncle Alfie dead either. And they were gone.

He realized that an eerie silence had fallen in the apartment. There were no more sounds of drawers and doors opening and closing.

Had Kylie sneaked out of the penthouse like she had the office the other day?

WITH THE CLOTHES, shoes and other personal items she'd brought with her already unpacked, Kylie had no reason to remain in the guest room though it was quite comfortable. With a walk-in closet and en suite bathroom, it was also larger and nicer than her master bedroom in the small house she'd inherited from her grandmother.

The king-size bed was also so much larger and more comfortable than her lumpy full-size mattress. While she'd checked it out, she hadn't remained in bed. It was too early to go to sleep even though she'd already changed into boxer-type shorts and a tank top. But she felt awkward walking out into the penthouse, acting like she lived there.

Because she didn't…

This was only temporary. Maybe she'd packed too much stuff.

But Heath had insisted that she should—because who knew how long it might take Detective Parker to catch the person who'd tried to kill them? He might never.

Her mother's boyfriend had never been arrested for his crime, for stealing her prescription pad and ruining her life. Her mother's.

And Kylie's.

Her mother never should have trusted that man or Kylie's father or any of the other men who'd let her down. That was why Kylie shouldn't trust so easily either.

Could she trust Heath?

She'd known him—worked with him—for five years. Of course she could trust Heath…as a friend. Not as a lover.

Not that they were going to become lovers. They were just acting the part for Detective Parker's benefit and hers because she'd lied to the lawman. Heath was only protecting her from getting arrested and from whoever had tried shooting at them.

So why was she so reluctant to leave the guest room? To be in his home?

She hadn't felt awkward the other night. But she'd been so focused on Heath then, on making sure that he was okay after identifying the bodies. She hadn't considered how the situation looked until Gina had dragged her out of his bed the next morning.

Not that she would ever be back in his bed. That wasn't why she was here. She was here because she was in danger.

She shivered now as that chill raced down her spine. And she turned toward the guest-room doorway. It was open but for the man who leaned against the jamb, blocking the passage.

Kylie's escape. And suddenly she did want to run. From him. And from the sudden awareness coursing through her.

Maybe it was the kisses they'd shared, or all the things his family had said about how perfect they were for each other, but she couldn't see him just as a colleague and a friend any longer.

He was more.

So much more…

They'd always had chemistry between them in that they'd effortlessly understood each other. About work...

But how would that chemistry translate to a physical relationship? Would they effortlessly know how to please each other in the bedroom like they had in the office?

They could have died today...in that shower of gunfire.

If they had, Kylie wouldn't have had the chance to see if everyone was right about them. If they were perfect for each other.

She wasn't thinking of the long run, of permanence. She doubted she was any more capable of that than Heath was. She knew him even better than she knew herself.

But what about one night...?

Dare she risk it?

SHE WAS SO damn hot. So sensual...

Her hands skimmed over his bare chest, caressing his muscles, as she passionately kissed him.

How the hell had he gotten so lucky?

But then the hands on his chest pushed him back. He lifted his head from hers. "What? What's wrong?" Sean asked January.

She gazed up at him, her green eyes full of fear and concern. "I'm scared..."

"I'm here," he said. "I'm not going to let anything happen to you."

"I'm not worried about me," she said.

Of course she wasn't.

She never worried about herself—just about everyone else.

"Who are you worried about?" he asked. "Maya?"

"No." A slight smile curved her lips as she thought of the little girl with whom they'd both fallen in love while they'd been falling for each other. "She's safe. She's happy."

"Then you're worried about your family," he said. And she had every reason to be worried. He was, too.

She nodded. "Of course I am. I can't believe that we all might be in danger."

He pulled her gently back into his embrace. "I'll make sure nothing happens to you," he promised. "I'll be your police protection."

She pushed him back again and smiled up at him. "I told you I'm not worried about me. I don't think I'm in danger."

"You're worried about your mom?" She had been spending as much time as she could with Farrah Colton since her father and uncle had been murdered.

"I'm worried about everyone but especially Heath and Kylie. They could have been killed today." She shuddered at the horrific thought.

And it was horrific. The Coltons had already had too much tragedy with the murders of Ernie and Alfie.

"Yes, but I'm not sure that means everybody else in the family is in danger, too," he said. He hadn't been happy with Joe for suggesting that, either, but he understood the older detective's desire to make sure everyone was cautious and vigilant until the killer was caught.

January stared at him, her brow slightly creased.

"Do you think that Heath and Kylie might have been the intended targets instead of Dad and Uncle Ernie?"

He shook his head. "I doubt, even as late as it was, that the twins could have been mistaken for Kylie Givens and your cousin. But it's curious that the murders and attempted murders have been only of the people involved with the company."

January gasped. "You think it's related to Colton Connections?"

He nodded. "It must have something to do with their work."

"You were there the other day, after the car nearly ran Heath and Kylie over," January remembered. "Did you notice anything?"

The guy from the elevator flitted into his mind. "There was a guy who told me about Kylie having some kind of criminal background."

January chuckled and shook her head. "No way."

"Not her but her family," he said. "He didn't seem to be a fan of Heath's, either, but I figured he was just some disgruntled employee."

But often disgruntled employees were the ones who came into the workplace to kill their bosses.

The same thought must have occurred to January because she said, "You better warn Heath."

Sean nodded in agreement. But Heath wasn't the only one he needed to warn. He had to talk to Joe, too.

He hadn't wanted to share with him what the Colton Connections employee had said, though, because he knew Joe was already suspicious of Heath and Kylie.

And he hadn't wanted to tell Heath then because he hadn't wanted to worry him until he was more sure.

Until those gunshots had been fired.

It was clear now that either Heath or Kylie or both of them were the next intended target of the killer.

Chapter Seventeen

She was so damn beautiful.

And she was so close. Living with him.

Heath hadn't been able to resist the urge to seek her out, to invade what was now her space in his penthouse. He hadn't been willing to do that for anyone, to let them bring more than a toothbrush to his place.

But here Kylie was...

She had that big sweater draped over the back of a chair. An afghan thrown across the foot of the bed. Books scattered throughout the room. Her laptop.

Her phone.

Her briefcase.

There was now more of her in this room than there had ever been him. Of course it was the guest room. And she was a guest. That was all she was.

Until the killer was caught. Until she was safe.

But in the meantime, he was in danger. In danger of crossing a line with her, a line that once crossed could never be uncrossed.

He pushed his hand through his hair, messing it up even more than it had already been. "I see you've settled in," he remarked when she turned and caught him staring.

He had been staring, too. His gaze hungrily devouring the sight of her bare legs, her soft curves, her long hair.

"Are you really okay with my staying here?" she asked.

He'd told her all about never wanting to live with anyone before. So she knew; she knew him so damn well.

He nodded and reminded her, "It was my idea."

A bad one. One that would probably come back to bite him on the ass.

"I know, but you've never let anyone live with you before," she said.

She knew him too well.

Better even than his family knew him. And his family knew that, knew he and Kylie were close. Thanks to his acting, they thought they were even closer than they were—that they were romantically involved.

And no one had been all that surprised.

In fact they had seemed damn well pleased about his fake relationship with his vice president.

"Not that I'm really *living* with you," Kylie quickly added. "In fact, if you're uncomfortable with this, I can leave."

"You can't stay alone at your house," he said.

"I could check into a hotel," she offered. "One with good security."

"This building has good security," he said. A doorman. Special codes to access elevators and floors. "And if you left, I would be much more uncomfortable worrying about you."

"You're not worried now?" she asked.

He shook his head because he couldn't utter the lie. He was worried about her, but he was more worried about her getting to him.

"I am," she said.

"You're safe here," he assured her. "There's security, and I'm here."

Her lips curved into a slight smile. "That's why I'm worried."

He raised his hands, palm up, toward her. "I would never hurt you." Not purposely.

But he had hurt women before—because he hadn't been able to give them what they'd wanted from him. Love.

He sighed. "But you're right to be cautious," he admitted. "My track record isn't the greatest."

"With house guests?" she asked, a teasing glint in her dark eyes.

He chuckled. "You know what I'm talking about. What my family was talking about. About the two of us."

"They think we're perfect for each other," she mused aloud, as if she was considering it.

Like he had considered it. While Kylie was perfect—beautiful and smart and funny—he doubted he would feel any more for her than he had any of his previous girlfriends. And he didn't want to hurt her like he had them.

He shook his head, trying to dislodge that traitorous thought. "But that would be crazy."

"Definitely," she agreed—wholeheartedly. Maybe too wholeheartedly.

He winced, his pride stinging at how quickly she'd agreed with him. That pride and his male ego prodded him away from the jamb, so that he walked into the room and stood close to her, to where she stood so close to the bed.

If she gave him any encouragement, he would have pushed her back onto the mattress and followed her down, covering her body with his, her mouth with his. He was so damn tempted to reach for her that he had to curl his fingers into his palms and hold them tightly at his sides. A muscle even twitched along his jaw as he clenched it, too.

She arched a dark brow and asked, "You're mad that I agree with you?"

He nearly chuckled over how ridiculous she made his reaction sound, but he held back the smile that twitched at his lips and admitted, "I'm mad over how quickly you agreed with me."

Kylie didn't hold back her smile though it didn't stay for long before slipping away as she tilted her head and studied his face. "Why would that make you mad? Do you want me to want a relationship with you?"

Now he did laugh. "I don't know what I want." But that was a lie. He wanted her.

"That's a first," she mused. "You usually always know what you want."

He groaned. "God, they were right, weren't they? You know me so damn well."

She shrugged. "I don't know. Some of them claimed they knew we were together already."

"Grandmother..." He chuckled. "She likes to think that she knows everything about everyone." But she hadn't known that Pop and Uncle Alfie would be murdered. Nobody could have known that but for their killer.

Kylie continued, "She and others commented on the chemistry that's always been between us."

He wanted to snort in derision, but she seemed almost serious now, pensive, as if she was contemplating that chemistry. They'd had it working together in how easy it was for them to understand each other, to finish each other's sentences, to instinctively know what the other one wanted.

Would sex with her be the same way? That easy? That instinctive?

He wanted to find out. To test that chemistry, he leaned down, so that his head was close to hers, his mouth close to her lips. And he knew, without even kissing her, that the chemistry was there in how his pulse quickened and his heart pounded.

He wanted her so damn badly. But he had no excuse to kiss her now; there were no witnesses, no one he needed to convince of their fake relationship.

So he forced himself to step back.

She opened her eyes, that he'd not even realized she'd closed, and stared at him in shock. "What's wrong?"

"Everything," he murmured. "I didn't ask you to stay

here for this…" He gestured toward the bed. "I don't want you to think that, and I don't want to jeopardize our real relationship by believing our fake one."

Then he forced himself to turn and walk away from her, from that bed, from that temptation.

But before he could slip through the doorway and into the hall, she called out to him.

"Heath…"

He froze, his body tense with all the desire for her coursing through him. But he still wouldn't turn back. He couldn't look at her—not without wanting her.

As much as he desired her, he wouldn't risk ruining their friendship and their working relationship. He'd never been as close to anyone as he was to her, and he didn't want to lose that closeness when he disappointed her. Eventually, he would disappoint her as he had every other woman he'd dated.

So he drew in a deep, unsteady breath and kept walking away from her.

HE WAS WALKING AWAY—without stopping, without kissing her.

The anticipation of his kiss, that had had her pulse humming, turned to indignation now. She'd called to him—twice—and he hadn't turned around, he hadn't come back to her. So she pursued him now, down the hall and through the living room where he didn't stop before heading through the double doors to his master suite on the other side of the penthouse from the guest room.

Clearly he wanted to get away from her.

But Kylie didn't want him to go.

Not without her…

Once he walked through those double doors, he turned back toward her as he began to close those doors on her. She pushed her hand against the wood and pushed her way inside with him. "What the hell is wrong with you?" she asked. "Why won't you talk to me?"

"Because I won't be able to just talk to you," he said. "All the acting got to me." He pushed both hands through his hair now and shook his head. "And I'm going to cross that damn line."

"What line?" she asked.

"The line no coworkers should cross with each other," he said.

"You're my boss," she reminded him—because he always seemed to forget that she worked for him.

"That makes it even more important that I don't cross that line with you," he said. "I don't want to do anything to ruin our working relationship."

A little smile tugged at her lips as she was compelled to tease him. "Are you worried that I'll sue you for harassment?" she asked.

His face paled somewhat even though he shook his head.

"You don't need to worry about that," she said. "I know we're only faking the romantic relationship, but you just mentioned our real relationship."

He nodded. "Yeah, a working one."

"Is that all we have?" she asked, her heart heavy that might be all he considered them to be—colleagues.

"Of course not," he said. "We're friends, too. And I don't want to jeopardize that."

"Have you never been friends with anyone you've slept with?" she wondered aloud. The only men she'd been intimate with had been friends first, or she wouldn't have trusted them enough to be intimate with them.

He shrugged. "I don't know. Not like you and I are friends anyway."

"Because we are friends," she said. "I won't sue you. And because we are friends, I know you're not looking for that relationship we've been faking for Detective Parker and your family. I won't expect more of you than you can give."

Some of the tension that had had him clenching his jaw and hands eased from his body. But his brow creased as he asked her, "What do you want, Kylie?"

"You." She wanted to see if their chemistry carried over from the boardroom to the bedroom.

He released a shaky breath. "Are you sure?"

"We could have died today when those gunshots were fired at us," she said. "Or yesterday when that car nearly ran us over, and then we'd never know." If that chemistry was more than work, more than friendship.

"Know what?" he asked, already reaching for her, his hand encircling her wrist to tug her farther inside his bedroom.

"If the passion we feel when we kiss is real or just part of our fake relationship."

He leaned down then and finally gave her the kiss she'd anticipated. And it was clear from how hungrily his mouth moved over hers that he'd been anticipating it, too.

Wanting it.

Wanting her.

But he pulled back, panting for breath, and asked, "Are you sure?"

"I'm not going to sue you," she promised with a smile.

"Are you sure you want me?" he asked, his voice gruff with his vulnerability.

She knew that even as handsome as he was, as smart and sexy, he had the same insecurities she had. They both knew they weren't relationship material. Maybe that was why this made sense, why *they* made sense.

Desire overwhelming her, she couldn't speak; she could only vehemently nod as she reached for him. She tugged at his shirt, pulling it up over his washboard abs, over his muscular chest and then over his head. He was so damn good looking that her heart pounded even faster, her hands shaking with desire as she ran them over his skin that was smooth but for a dusting of golden hair across his chest.

The twitch was back in his cheek as he tightly clenched his jaw. Then he was sliding up her tank top to pull it over her head. Because of its built-in bra, she didn't wear anything else with it, and her breasts sprang free.

He cupped them in his big, slightly unsteady hands, and he stroked them.

She shuddered in reaction, overwhelmed by the feelings coursing through her. She was so close to an orgasm from just the touch of his hands. Then he lowered his head and closed his mouth over one taut point, and she moaned as pleasure flooded her. "Heath…"

Her knees might have given out had he not slid his arm beneath them and lifted her from her feet. He didn't carry her far, just to his bed—the bed they'd already shared once.

Kylie knew she wasn't going to just sleep with him this time, though—not with both their bodies so damn tense with the need for release. After lowering her to the mattress, though, he stepped back.

She reached out for him, wanting to pull him down with her, on top of her. She ached for him.

With those slightly unsteady hands, he fumbled with the button on his jeans. Then he pushed the denim down his long legs along with the boxers he wore.

Kylie reached for her boxers, too, skimming them over her hips and off her legs until she lay naked before him. His gaze ran over her like a caress and he shook his head.

Scared he'd changed his mind, her heart slammed against her ribs. "What? What's wrong?" she asked.

He shook his head. "Nothing. You're perfect. So damn perfect."

Well aware that she lacked the curves of his other girlfriends, she chuckled. "Are you drunk?"

"Not on alcohol," he said. "Just on you…"

Then, in all his naked deliciousness, he joined her on the bed. And he sipped at her lips like he was drinking her, kissing her deeply before moving down her body.

He acted as though he worshiped it, caressing every curve with first his hands and then his lips.

She quivered with pleasure. When he moved lower, kissed her intimately, slid his tongue inside her, she screamed his name as an orgasm shuddered through her. She tried to roll him onto his back, tried to repay him the pleasure he'd given her. But he was too big, too tense.

"I need to be inside you," he said. And he reached into his nightstand and pulled out a condom packet.

She jerked it out of his hand and ripped it open, then she rolled the latex over his engorged flesh. He was so long, so hard, pulsating within her grasp.

"You're killing me, Kylie," he said with a groan.

So she guided him inside her, and with a gentle thrust he joined their bodies.

"You're so hot, so tight..." he said with another groan.

So full. He filled her and ignited her passion again. Need clawed at her, making her buck and writhe beneath him. He moved, sliding in and out of her.

She locked her legs around his lean waist, clutching him close with her inner muscles as she came again, screaming his name. Then his body tensed and he joined her in release.

He dropped back onto the bed next to her, panting for breath. "Damn it..."

Hearing the regret in his voice, she tensed. "What? What's wrong?"

If he said it was a mistake, she would die of embarrassment and regret.

"I went too fast," he said. "Now we're going to have to do it all over again."

She chuckled as he reached for her. And they did it all over again and again and again.

HIS PHONE VIBRATED on the nightstand, drawing a murmur of irritation from Kinsey who lay against his side. Joe brushed a kiss across her forehead before reaching for his phone. Had there been another attempt on the lives of Heath Colton and his vice president at Colton Connections?

He'd told Dispatch to call him if there was. He'd also told the crime-scene techs to call him, too, and that was the number that showed up on his caller ID.

"Parker," he answered the cell, his voice gruff with sleep.

"I'm sorry to call at this hour, Detective," the tech replied. "But you said—"

"I know," Joe said. "If you discovered anything interesting to give me a call. What did you find interesting? Do the ballistics match?"

"Not even close," the tech said. "Different caliber. Different weapon from the murder scene."

He sighed.

"Killer could have dumped the previous weapon and be using another one," the tech speculated.

"Could be," Joe agreed. But that would make it harder for him to catch the killer.

Or there was a whole other possibility…

That someone else was trying to kill Heath Colton

and Kylie Givens. Which meant Joe had two killers to find. Or one killer and one would-be killer.

He had to find that second one before he or she actually became a killer. Before Heath and Kylie wound up as dead as Heath's father and uncle.

"Thanks," Joe told the tech before disconnecting the call. He kept the cell close, though, waiting for it to ring again, waiting for Dispatch to call.

Because he had no doubt, there would be another attempt on the lives of Heath and Kylie.

Chapter Eighteen

Heath squinted at the computer monitor on his desk at Colton Connections. Despite the size of the screen, he could barely see the words on it. Maybe he needed glasses.

His eyes felt gritty and raw, and he blinked, trying to clear his vision. More likely lack of sleep was causing his inability to focus on the screen, on anything but last night and how amazing sex with Kylie had been.

Her passion had overwhelmed Heath but it hadn't really surprised him. She had always been passionate about work. It was one of the things they had in common. That and, apparently, an insatiable appetite for sex.

She'd reached for him last night as many times as he'd reached for her, his body aching with the need for another mind-blowing release. He'd gotten greedy.

Or maybe it was like she'd said—that their near brushes with death had inspired him to take what he wanted with no thought of the consequences of his actions.

And there would be consequences, like his inability to focus, and the hardness of his body every time she popped into his office. Even in clothes—dark slacks and a gray sweater—she looked beautiful, sexy, desirable.

Dark circles rimmed her eyes, though, attesting to her lack of sleep. It wasn't just because of the sex, though. Even when they'd been lying together in the dark, neither of them had slept.

"Someone tried to kill us," she'd murmured, as stunned as he'd been when those shots had rung out.

That was when they'd decided to get up early and come into the office before everyone else.

Pop and Uncle Alfie had been killed. There had been attempts on his and Kylie's lives. Colton Connections was what connected all of them.

"The answer has to be here," he said as he focused again on his lists of pending patents and recently acquired ones.

Oftentimes he had beaten some other company to filing because he was fast and had connections but mostly because Pop and Uncle Alfie had been so brilliant that they'd always been ahead of everyone else when it came to inventions and ingenuity. When he was a little kid, he'd wanted to be an inventor like them. He'd even had some good ideas, he'd thought, and while they'd encouraged him, he'd known that he would never come close to their brilliance. What he'd excelled at was helping them ensure they got the credit for that brilliance and that they reaped the rewards.

Now they were gone—even before he'd secured that last patent. Not that anyone was going to challenge it with a pre-issuance submission. It was going to come through, and they would never know. He had to blink again, to clear emotion, not sleep, from his vision.

"You need to take a break," Kylie said, her voice soft with concern.

He glanced from the monitor to her, and as usual now, desire gripped his body. He shook his head, trying to fight off his feelings for her so that he could focus. "We need to look at everything we've received, any kind of threats or opposition or challenges to our patents," he said, "any reason why someone might have shot at us after killing Uncle Alfie and Pop."

She blinked now as her eyes glistened with tears. She'd loved his dad and uncle, too. "I know there's a lot of money involved in these inventions, but it's hard to believe that someone would kill over a patent."

"There are a lot of ruthless businessmen out there," Heath said.

Her lips curved into a slight smile, the one that got his pulse quickening because it usually meant she was about to tease or challenge him. "You've been called one of them."

Instead of smiling or chuckling, he flinched.

She hadn't missed his reaction because she hastened to apologize. "I'm sorry. I didn't mean it as an insult and I don't think the people who've said it about you did either."

"Detective Parker thought I was ruthless enough to kill my own father," Heath reminded her. He would never forget being a suspect for those murders. Hell, he probably still was one because the detective seemed to think it was possible that either he or Kylie had fired those shots at his vehicle.

"He doesn't know you," Kylie said.

"No, he doesn't," Heath agreed. "And he doesn't know anything about this company. You were right that we need to investigate on our own."

Hadn't she been the one who'd suggested it in the first place? He couldn't remember now. So much had happened over the past few days.

Them…

They'd happened over and over again.

"The police aren't going to find out who's responsible," she agreed. "That's why we need to look at everything to do with the company from the patents and competitors to our own employees."

He gasped. "You think an employee might have killed them? Might have tried to kill us?"

She knew them better than he did. As well as the finances, she handled human resources and all of the fifty employees.

"I don't want to think that," she said. "Especially that one of them could hurt your dad and uncle. Everybody loved them so much."

He nodded. The employees had all loved Pop and Uncle Alfie. He wasn't so sure about him and Kylie, though. They had to do what was best for the company on the whole and sometimes that made an individual feel slighted. Like Tyler Morrison.

"But it's a possibility," he agreed, albeit reluctantly. "First Dad and Uncle Alfie are killed right in the parking lot." Since his office was at the front of the building, he couldn't see the lot where the murders had happened, where Kylie had been when she'd noticed someone watching her from a window on the ninth floor. "And now someone is trying to kill us."

"What do we all have in common?" she finished for him as she gestured around the office.

He knew she wasn't talking about just his space but the whole damn company. He'd give it all up, just as he'd told Parker, if he could bring back Pop and Uncle Alfie. Nothing was going to bring them back, though, but at least he could bring them justice.

And he could keep Kylie safe from the shooter. He wasn't sure if he could keep her safe from him, though. He wanted her again.

Still…

His body ached with desire. He was just about to tell her to shut and lock his door when her cell phone rang.

She pulled it from her pocket and answered it, "Kylie Givens…" She hadn't put it on Speaker, so he couldn't hear what was being said to her but he could see the alarm cross her lovely face as her skin paled and her bottom lip quivered a bit. "I'll be right there," she murmured before clicking off the cell.

"What's wrong?" he asked. "Where are you going?"

"My house was broken into," she said. "I need to go."

He jumped up from his chair. "Not alone."

"The police are already there," she said. "That's who called after a neighbor called them. They want me to see if anything's missing and file an official report."

"I'm going with you," he insisted. Because he knew the break-in hadn't been random.

It had to have had something to do with last night and the attempt on their lives. Was this another attempt?

Had the police really called or was someone just trying to lure her out by herself? Not that she was any safer with him. Hell, he might have been the reason she was in danger in the first place.

KYLIE CLOSED THE door behind the uniformed officer and leaned back against it, her knees shaking. She shut her eyes, unable to look at the destruction of her property, of her grandmother's property.

But even with her eyes closed, she could see the damage. Holes had been knocked into the plaster. Mirrors and pictures had been broken. Cushions had been torn apart.

"Was someone looking for something?" she wondered aloud. "What would they think I had?"

After her mother had gone to jail, there had been a couple of break-ins at her old apartment. Even as young as she'd been, she remembered the police telling her grandmother that they'd probably been looking for her mother's drugs. Like her mother had been a drug dealer.

She'd just been a fool for love.

And the break-in had probably been her mother's old boyfriend looking for more of her prescription pads to steal.

Kylie had always been so careful to never fall as hard or as fast as her mother had for men. Except for now.

Not that she was falling for Heath. No. She was just falling apart right now. With fear…

She shuddered and opened her eyes and found Heath staring at her with concern.

Or suspicion?

"I don't have anything valuable here," she said. "Nothing of the company's, except for whatever is on my laptop, and I brought that back to your place." She'd learned not to leave it at the office in case someone was compelled to snoop. "But maybe they didn't know that. Maybe that's what they were looking for."

Heath picked up a broken picture of her and her grandmother at her high school graduation. "In a frame or a pillow?" He shook his head. "This wasn't about someone looking for something. It was about them looking for someone. You."

She forced her lips to curve up in a slight smile. "In a frame or a pillow?"

He shook his head. "Here. And when you weren't here, they left you a message."

She shook her head. "It doesn't make any sense. Why go after me?"

Heath lifted his broad shoulders in a slight shrug. "I don't know. But we're going to make sure they don't get you. You're staying with me until we find out who the hell is after you."

"But that'll put you in danger if this person is only after me and not you."

"I think they broke in here because there's no security. If they could have gotten past it at the penthouse, they probably would have broken in there, too," he said. "That's why we need to be so careful, why we need to stick together, to keep each other safe."

But he looked grim about spending all that time with her, as grim as she probably felt. Because she wondered what the greater danger was. Being at the mercy of whoever was trying to kill her. Or spending so much time with Heath that she wound up falling for him.

Not that that would happen. She wouldn't let that happen, just as she'd assured him the night before. She knew him better than anyone else. She knew he wasn't looking for a commitment to her or to anyone.

And she wasn't one of those women who believed, like her mother had, that she could change a man, that her love could bring out the love in him.

Kylie didn't want to fall for Heath Colton. But she didn't want to fall into the hands of the killer either. So she would stay with Heath. But she was sure as hell going to step up their investigation so that she wouldn't have to stay much longer with him.

She wasn't going to wait for Detective Parker to find the killer because that might never happen. In order to get her life back and stay alive, she had to find the killer herself.

ALMOST GETTING RUN down and being shot at hadn't gotten through to that little bitch that she was out of her league. The break-in at her sad little house probably wouldn't affect Kylie Givens either.

No. It was time to send a message that she would never forget—because it would be her last.

That message was: death.

Chapter Nineteen

Sean always kept his promises. So as he'd promised January, he'd called to warn her cousin. He'd worried that he was too late though when Heath's phone had gone straight to voice mail. The businessman had called him back just a short time ago, though.

With that conversation over, Sean figured it was time for another, and he dropped into the chair next to Joe Parker's messy desk. "Hey…"

The detective glanced up and narrowed his dark eyes at his colleague. "You know you can't get involved in this case," Parker warned him. "You're too close to it."

"That's why I have to be involved," he said. "January's heart is broken."

And that broke his, as well. She was grieving her father's and uncle's deaths. She didn't need to grieve anyone else, like a cousin who was as close to her as a brother.

Joe exhaled a ragged breath. "I know, and I'm sorry. From all accounts, it sounds like her father was a great man. Her uncle, too."

"What about her cousin?" Sean asked.

"Heath?"

Sean nodded.

Joe shrugged. "I don't know. I can't get a handle on him. I still think he hasn't been totally forthcoming with me."

"Do you know about the break-in?" He only knew because he'd talked to Heath. Officers from another department had responded to the neighbor's call since Kylie's house was in the burbs.

Joe tensed. "No. Was it at the company?"

Sean shook his head.

"His penthouse?"

"No. Kylie Givens's house."

Joe cursed. "I told all of them to stick together—"

"She was with Heath last night," Sean said. "She wasn't home when the intruder got inside. A neighbor saw lights on this morning and knew Kylie wouldn't have been home then, that she would have been at work. So she called the police."

Joe jumped up. "So the intruder was caught?"

Sean shook his head again. "No. By the time a patrol unit got there, the intruder was gone, and the damage was done."

"Damage?"

He nodded this time. "I talked to the unit that took the report. Lot of petty destructive stuff." Which had reminded him of the petty comments a certain disgruntled employee had shared about Kylie Givens. He shared those now with Joe, whose eyes narrowed.

"I told you not to get involved," Parker reminded him.

"I know."

"But that doesn't mean you don't share with me whatever you learn, the minute you learn it," Parker said.

Sean nodded. "I know. I just didn't think…"

"You know how cases like this are—you have to look at everyone as a suspect."

"Even Kylie and Heath?" Sean asked, wondering if his colleague had finally ruled them out as suspects.

Joe nodded. "Especially them—because they haven't been forthcoming about anything except that damn alibi."

"Is that why you suspected they'd made it up?"

He nodded. "I just felt like there was more going on with them than they were admitting."

"That's what the rest of the family said when we found out they've been seeing each other," Sean said. "You could always tell that there was more than a working relationship between them."

"Yeah, and I've been trying to figure out what kind," Joe admitted. "Romantic or coconspirator?"

"And while you've been working on that, someone's been trying to kill them," Sean remarked.

Parker sighed. "I know."

But it was clear he wasn't ready yet to let go of his suspicions about the couple. So Sean was glad that he'd talked to Heath, that he'd warned him, just like he'd promised January he would.

But was a warning going to be enough to keep her cousin alive?

HEATH STARED AT the picture he'd taken from Kylie's house—the one of her and her grandmother, arms around each other, faces full of pride and happiness as well as a faint wistfulness.

"I didn't see you take that," she remarked as she peered across his desk at the picture.

"I grabbed it when I was checking my messages." And had found the one from Sean Stafford. While she'd spoken with her neighbor on the front porch, Heath had called Sean back.

Anger surged through him now as he recalled what Sean had shared with him. "Why didn't you tell me about Morrison?" he asked.

She arched a brow. "What about him?"

"How badly he has it out for you."

She shrugged. "I thought you knew. You said that you figured he wants my job, maybe yours."

"How badly though?" Heath wondered. "He talked to Sean the other day, trying to cast suspicion on us."

She groaned. "Like we need to give Parker any excuse to look at us as suspects."

Their false alibi had done that, had piqued Parker's suspicions. The guy must have been a human lie detector.

"Why would he want to implicate us?" Heath asked. "Just because he wants our jobs?"

She sucked in a breath, as if bracing herself. "Or maybe to cast suspicion away from himself."

"You suspect him?"

"Of murder or attempted murder?" She shrugged. "I don't know. But I have a feeling he's been up to something else..."

"What?" Heath asked. "Embezzlement?"

"Espionage," she admitted.

"He's spying for someone?" he asked. "For whom? And what has he given them?"

"He's been really interested in the patent that's pending now."

"The one with the medical equipment?"

She nodded.

And Heath cursed. "That's huge. Why the hell didn't you tell me?"

"I wanted proof," she said. "But I started telling you the other night."

And he remembered he hadn't been interested enough to even let her finish. He'd wanted to talk about the patent instead and leave human resources to her.

"I'm sorry," he said.

She shrugged. "It doesn't change anything. I still don't have any proof."

"Let's talk to him," Heath said. Maybe he could play Parker's role of human lie detector well enough that he could get the traitor to crack. He was furious enough to beat the truth out of the man.

"Just talk?" Kylie asked. "Because he's a lawyer."

He grinned. "Worried that he'll sue me if I use a rubber hose on him?"

"Worried that he knows the law too well to tell us anything that we could use against him," Kylie said. "I don't care if you beat him, especially if he had anything to do with the murders." Her eyes darkened with emotion, but it wasn't just grief over his dad and uncle. She was furious, too.

That was why she knew him so well. They were very alike in so many ways.

"Maybe I'll have to hold you back," he mused.

But when Tyler Morrison joined them in Heath's office at her request, she said nothing to the man—almost as if she didn't trust herself to speak.

Heath had no such problem. "What the hell are you up to, Morrison?"

The man's eyes widened in feigned innocence. "I don't know what you're talking about. I've just been trying to help out now more than ever given the situation."

"Let me clarify that the situation you're talking about is the cold-blooded murders of my dad and uncle," Heath said.

The guy's head bobbed in a quick nod, but none of his slicked-back hair moved. "Of course. I just didn't want to dredge up bad memories."

"It just happened," Heath said. Not that he was ever going to forget the men or what had been done to them.

"Of course, I know that," he said. "Do you even have plans for the funerals yet?"

"My mom and aunt are working on those." He'd missed another voice mail from his mother, probably providing him with the details. The thought filled him with dread.

"Well, I would like to attend, of course," Tyler continued.

Heath snorted and shook his head. The guy was too damn slick—even for a lawyer. "I am curious about what you'd like, Tyler. Kylie's job? My job?"

The guy's face flushed and he stammered, "I—I don't know what you're accusing me of."

"Not murder." Not yet. "Which is what you basically accused the two of us of having done when you spoke with Detective Stafford the other day."

Tyler shook his head. "I—I don't know what you're talking about."

"The man's dating my cousin," Heath said. "In fact I'm pretty sure they're going to get married, so he's almost family. He told me what you said about Kylie, about us."

The man's face flushed a deeper shade of red now. "I'm sorry that I don't trust you." He glanced at Kylie now. "Either of you, especially after what happened to your dad and uncle. My allegiance was to them. They were the heart and soul of this company."

Heath's eyes burned again, and it wasn't just because he was tired. He was touched that at least about Pop and Uncle Alfie the man spoke the truth. "They were the heart and soul," Heath agreed.

"And the brains," Tyler added. "You and Ms. Givens are in over your heads."

Heath snorted. "I've been CEO for a while, Morrison. Kylie my VP. What do you think we can't handle that we haven't been handling successfully for years?"

"Arvock Pharmaceuticals."

"What about Arvock?" Kylie said, finally joining in the conversation. Her gaze was intent on Morrison's face. "What do you know about them?"

The lawyer shrugged. "Just that they're going to

do everything they can to stop the latest patent from going through."

"How the hell do they know about it?" Kylie asked. "You told them, didn't you? You sold them information."

Heath cursed. "You son of a bitch! You're terminated right now."

"On what grounds?" Tyler asked. "You have no proof."

"You pretty much just admitted it," Heath reminded him. "Very few people knew about that invention. You looked over the paperwork for the patent for me, so you were one of the few."

Tyler shook his head again. "You still won't be able to prove it."

"I'll ask them," Heath said.

The man's face blanched now. "You—you should stay the hell away from them."

"Why? What else are they going to tell me about you?" Heath wondered. "That you killed my dad and uncle?"

"I'm no killer," Tyler insisted. "I—I had nothing to do with their murders." He glanced at Kylie again and then at him. He really did have suspicions about them.

Which meant he was so mercenary that he understood people killing to get ahead.

"We would never do anything to hurt Ernie or Alfie," Kylie spoke in their defense. "And now there have been attempts on our lives."

Tyler nodded. "Of course there have. I told you Arvock is not going to let that patent go through. You're messing with the wrong people."

Heath sucked in a breath. Just how dangerous was this company? He intended to find out if they were dangerous enough to actually kill off their competition.

"Get the hell out of here," he told Tyler. "And take all your stuff with you. You're not going to be allowed back in the building." He would make sure the man's ID badge was deactivated and that security and all the other employees knew he was barred from the offices.

"We'll see about that," Tyler said. "The wills haven't even been read yet. You might be the one leaving soon, Heath, and taking your little plaything with you."

Heath jumped up from his desk then, ready to reach for and throttle the slimeball. But Tyler left then—in one hell of a hurry.

"What a little creep," he remarked as he unclenched his fists. He'd never wanted to hit anyone more than he had Morrison.

"He is a creep," Kylie agreed wholeheartedly. "But is he a killer?"

"I almost want it to be him," Heath admitted. Just so that he would have the opportunity to beat the hell out of the man. Then he would turn him over to Detective Parker with a ribbon tied around his scrawny neck.

"Me, too," Kylie admitted. "But I never knew him to have a problem with Ernie or Alfie."

"No," Heath agreed. "But that doesn't mean he wouldn't have killed them if he thought he'd profit off it."

"He's not the one who will profit the most if that patent doesn't go through," Kylie pointed out.

"Arvock Pharmaceuticals," he murmured. "But why

would they break into your place and how the hell would they know where you live?"

"You don't think that drug company has the resources to find out where I live?" she asked.

Arvock was a billion-dollar corporation. They had resources, resources to find out where she lived and break in looking for information on that patent. They also had resources to hire an assassin to kill his father and uncle and now him and Kylie.

His hand shaking, he reached for his phone.

"Are you calling Parker?" she asked.

He shook his head. "No, I'm calling Arvock Pharmaceuticals."

She gasped. "What? Why?"

"Because I want an appointment with the CEO. I want to find out if they're the ones who killed Pop and Uncle Alfie and if they're trying to kill us."

She snorted now—derisively. "And you think they're going to agree to meet with you where they'll just confess everything to you?"

He shook his head. "No. But I'll know, just the same way that Parker knew we were lying about that alibi— I'll know."

"The only way you'll know for sure is if they try to kill you while you're talking to them."

"That's a chance I'm willing to take."

KYLIE HADN'T PACKED a ball gown for her stay at the penthouse, so she had nothing to wear but a black dress that might, in a pinch, pass for a cocktail dress for a night on the town. Hopefully that was all this black-tie event was that they were crashing.

"You should have stayed at the penthouse," Heath admonished her from the driver's seat of the vehicle he'd borrowed from his mother.

He, of course, owned his own tuxedo, and in the crisp black bow tie and pleated shirt, he looked like a movie star. So damn handsome.

Kylie hadn't wanted to leave the penthouse. She hadn't wanted to leave his bedroom. But he'd been too focused on confronting the monsters he suspected had murdered his dad and uncle.

"I wasn't going to let you do this alone," Kylie said.

"For my sake or theirs?" he asked. He was that angry, the rage glinting in his blue eyes.

"Yours." She wasn't just worried about what might happen to him, though. She was worried about what he might do. She reached across the console and squeezed his leg. The muscles in his thigh tensed beneath her hand.

He emitted a little groan. "Kylie..."

She smiled. "Let's go back to the penthouse," she suggested.

"And leave the investigating to Parker?" he asked with a sniff of disdain. "He'd never check up on this. Arvock isn't related to any of the Coltons, and he seems determined to pin this on a Colton."

She shook her head. "Just on you." She released a weary sigh. "I know you're right." She'd already determined that Parker wasn't going to find the killer. *She* had to. "We need to do the investigating ourselves."

"Myself," he said. "You don't need to get involved in this."

"I'm already involved," she said. "I was with you when someone tried running us down and when those shots were fired at your vehicle—"

"That's why you shouldn't be with me now," he said. "It puts you in danger."

"And my place was broken into," she continued as if he hadn't spoken. "My stuff damaged. I am part of this, and I am going with you." Because she wouldn't be able to return to her place until the threat to her life was gone and the longer she stayed with him the more danger she was in.

Of losing her heart.

"You've gone," he muttered as he parked the vehicle in one of the last available spaces in a corner lot that was open to the elements. "We're here. Well, we're as close as one of us is going to get to the hotel."

Since they weren't staying at it, they hadn't been allowed to park in that garage. So he'd been circling the downtown area for a while, looking for any open spaces.

"What are you saying?" she asked, narrowing her eyes at him.

He didn't shut off the vehicle, just turned toward her. "You're going to stay in the vehicle."

"Alone?" she asked. "Vulnerable?"

It was the argument she'd used to get him to let her go with him. Of course he'd countered that she would have been safe in the penthouse, but she'd let him know that if he wasn't there, she might be compelled to leave.

The twinge of guilt she felt for manipulating him

was only a little one. Sticking together was the safest for both of them because they were both in danger no matter where they were.

Even his penthouse.

Because if they'd stayed there, they would have had sex again. And again…

And every time they had, she'd felt closer to him and closer to falling for him. What had started out as curiosity about their chemistry had become something so much more powerful and compelling.

But once the killer was caught, she would have to move out. Heath didn't live with women. He didn't commit to them.

Because she knew him so well, she'd thought she was safe from getting attached to him. But she was afraid that she might have thought wrong.

About herself…

About him…

About everything…

Because once he walked around and opened her door and she stepped out of the car, she felt that strange sensation again. Someone was watching them.

Chapter Twenty

The bar was busy, which was good. Jones needed to keep busy, to keep his mind off…

Everything. His dad. Uncle Alfie. Heath.

He couldn't believe what had happened after he'd left Aunt Farrah's yesterday. Someone had shot at Heath. Carly had come into the bar in tears, distraught that they could have lost another loved one.

And despite how much they razzed each other, Jones did love his big brother. He would never be like Heath, who was totally like Pop, but he loved him. Just as he'd loved Pop.

If only…

He blinked and turned back toward the patrons. He was tending the bar tonight, working behind the twenty-foot-long structure of reclaimed wood and metal. God, he loved the Lone Wolf, the brewery he'd started in the West Loop, but the rush of pride he usually felt during a busy night didn't lift his spirits.

Nothing could right now.

But he forced a welcoming expression, if not quite

a smile, for the guy who slid onto a just vacated stool. "What can I get you?"

"Jones?" the man asked.

In a tailored suit, with his dark hair slicked back, the guy didn't look like the usual patron, but then quite a mixture of people patronized the microbrewery. So Jones wouldn't have been unsettled if not for how Detective Parker had showed up a couple of nights ago just like this.

In a suit, with the same question.

He thought about shaking his head, about denying who he was. But someone called out a good night to him and he automatically waved at the departing guest.

"Yeah," he replied to the man. "What can I get you?"

"Uh…" The guy glanced at the large beer tanks behind the bar, his beady eyes widening slightly at the sight of the system that created all Jones's microbrews. "Do you only have beer? No wine?"

"We have wine," Jones said. "White and red."

"Uh, white? Chardonnay? Sauvignon blanc?"

A smile twitched at Jones's lips, but he suppressed it. "White and red."

The female bartender working with Jones emitted a soft chuckle and stepped in to ask, "Which would you like? Chardonnay or sauvignon blanc?"

"The sauvignon," the man replied with a disdainful sniff.

No. This guy didn't belong here, but Jones doubted he was a detective. Parker had asked Jones as many questions about his beers as he had about his alibi for that night and about Heath and Kylie.

Who knew?

The two of them?

They made sense, though—about the only thing that actually made sense lately. When Becky handed the stemless wineglass to the slick guy, Jones started to step back, but the man reached out—not for the glass—but for his arm.

"Don't go," he said. "I need to tell you what I can do for you."

"Oh..." He nodded with sudden understanding that the guy was a sales rep. "You sell restaurant supplies?"

The guy's forehead creased with confusion, and he shook his head. "No. I work for you."

Jones snorted at the guy's weak sales spiel. "No, you don't."

The man's face flushed somewhat. "Well, I work for your family company. I'm the lawyer for Colton Connections."

Jones's stomach dropped, as dread settled heavily in the pit of it. He shrugged, trying to shrug off that horrible feeling. "Well, I don't have anything to do with that business."

"You should," the man replied. "You're clearly a good businessman. You should be running the company instead of your brother."

Jones snorted again. "Yeah, right. My brother lives and breathes Colton Connections." He'd been going to work with Pop and Uncle Alfie since he was a little kid. "Nobody knows it better or cares more about it."

Now that Pop and Uncle Alfie were gone...

"Kylie Givens thinks she does," the man remarked with a sneer. "She's changed your brother."

"For the better," Jones acknowledged. And she was there for him now, when Heath needed someone most. Jones, on the other hand, was so alone.

But then he was used to that. He'd always been the odd man out in his family. The Lone Wolf.

He shrugged again, trying to cast off his self-pity this time. "I don't get why you're here." Though it was clear the guy had an agenda.

His face flushed again, and it wasn't from alcohol. He had yet to take a sip of his white wine. "I want to help you claim what's rightfully yours."

Jones snorted again. "The wills haven't been read yet, but no matter what they say, that company is rightfully my mom and aunt's with my brother running it."

"Why?" the man asked. "Why should Heath run it and not you?"

Jones gestured at his busy bar. "Because I have my own place to run."

"Proving that you can handle a business," the man pursued. "You can handle Colton Connections."

"I don't know anything about it," Jones said—because he'd never been interested.

"I do," the man replied. "I can bring you up to speed. I can be your right hand."

Jones chuckled now. "Like Kylie is Heath's. You after her job or my brother's?"

"I'm trying to do what's right for Colton Connections," the man replied. "I figured you would, too."

"And I told you what's right for it—my brother running it like he always has." With Kylie at his side. Sure, Jones had flirted with her to needle Heath, but he could see they belonged together.

The man shook his head, his face twisting into a grimace of either disgust or pity. "I thought you would want to make it up to your father."

Jones tensed. "What?"

"That you would finally want to honor him instead of just disappointing him over and over again."

Jones curled his fingers into his palms, tempted to throw a fist across the bar. But he locked his arms at his sides. "Get the hell out of here," he said through teeth gritted in fury.

The man pointed at his glass. "I haven't touched my drink yet."

"Don't. Just leave. Now."

"But I—"

"I reserve the right to refuse service, and I'm refusing service to you," Jones said. "Get the hell out!"

A few other patrons glanced at him, their eyes widening in alarm. He forced a slight smile for their benefit. But it slipped away when he focused on the sleazy lawyer again. "Just get out of here."

"I will," the man finally agreed as he slid off the stool. "I'll let you think about it. And I'm sure you'll realize that you should get involved—for your sake but most especially for your dad's sake."

Jones shook his head. If the guy really did work for Colton Connections, he'd had even less of a relationship with his father than Jones had had.

Or he would have known that Heath was the chosen one, his father's golden boy. Not that Jones was jealous. Anymore...

He was just resigned. Because now Pop was gone, and Jones would never have the chance to prove himself. Even if he did what this guy wanted and forced his way into Colton Connections, his father wouldn't know.

He was gone.

And Heath, like he had always followed Pop, had nearly followed him to the grave. His brother was in danger, and it was clear he had few—if any people—he could trust.

DESPITE NOT HAVING an invitation, Heath got him and Kylie into the event in the ballroom of the swanky downtown hotel that Arvock Pharmaceuticals had rented to celebrate something.

What?

Pop and Uncle Alfie's murders?

He hadn't asked that yet, but he would—once he found the CEO. Or the CEO found him.

He'd used his Colton name at the door, something he rarely did unless he was trying to get into True without a reservation. He hadn't realized how many other doors Colton might open, or more specifically Colton Connections.

"This was a bad idea," Kylie murmured as she glanced around the crowded ballroom.

From the din of voices and the movement of waiters through the crowd, the conversation and the alcohol were flowing. "This was a great idea," Heath insisted.

"A great place to talk to them where their guards will be down."

"You don't even know who we're supposed to talk to."

"The CEO," Heath said. He'd looked up the guy. Randall George. With his white hair and lined face, he looked nearly twice Heath's age and experience. "And the VP."

The VP wasn't female, like Kylie, but another older male who was white. In the profile of the company that Heath had found, the entire board looked the same, so clearly Arvock struggled with inclusivity and diversity. While pretty women walked around the ballroom, they were probably either pharmaceutical reps or trophy wives of those older men.

Kylie glanced at those women and then at herself. "I knew it was a mistake for me to come here without a ball gown," she said.

He wished she was wearing one, too, not so that she fit in but because he selfishly wanted to see her looking all glamorous and gorgeous. But hell, she looked the best in nothing at all. He couldn't wait to get her back to the penthouse and undo all the buttons down the front of her black dress. "You're the most beautiful woman here," he assured her.

She snorted. "You're a liar."

Having been called that before, he flinched and defended himself. "To me you are," he insisted.

Her lips parted on a slight gasp of surprise at his sincerity. He wanted to lean down and kiss her—deeply, passionately.

"Mr. Colton."

Startled, he spun toward the intruder. And the man had intruded on what could have been a moment.

Randall George held out his hand. "I'm surprised but nevertheless pleased that you joined us this evening."

The man wasn't alone. His VP and another younger, broader man stood behind him. Did he have a bodyguard? Or was that his hired muscle? The person who did his dirty work.

Like murder...

Heath tensed and slid his arm protectively around Kylie's small waist. Even these guys probably weren't ruthless enough to try anything in a room full of witnesses, but Heath wasn't taking any chances.

At least any *more* chances with Kylie's safety.

He should have tied her to the bed and locked her in the penthouse. But if he'd tied her to the bed, he wouldn't have been able to leave her.

She extended her hand toward the white-haired CEO. "I'm Kylie Givens," she introduced herself.

The man nodded. "Yes, the vice president of Colton Connections." He introduced his VP then but not the other man, the man who had a curious bulge beneath his ill-fitting tuxedo. A gun?

"You seem much more aware of Colton Connections than we've been of you," Heath observed.

"Unfortunately you've been in the news recently," George reminded him. "My condolences on your loss. Your father and uncle were brilliant men."

Heath nodded. "Yes, they were. And they were taken far too soon."

"Is that what brings you here, Mr. Colton? Are you

looking to sell your business?" The man all but rubbed his hands together in glee.

Heath shook his head. "But if I was, would you be interested?"

"Of course."

"Why?" he asked with genuine curiosity. "We're not a drug company."

"No. But you hold several patents for medical equipment. One, currently pending, is of particular interest to us."

"I bet it is," Heath said. "How did you learn about it? Do we have our former legal counsel, Mr. Morrison, to thank for that?"

George chuckled. "Former?" He glanced at the man he hadn't introduced. "Did you hear that?"

The man nodded. "Noted."

"So Tyler Morrison has been spying for you?" Kylie asked.

George shrugged. "I am not sure how he came about the information he gave us."

"Gave?" Kylie asked, her soft voice full of doubt.

George chuckled. "You must know Tyler well then."

"So you paid him?"

"He asked for money, of course," George replied.

"Of course," Heath said, wondering what else their former employee might have done for money.

Murder?

He glanced again at the man in the suit. Arvock wouldn't have needed Morrison to do their dirty work; they clearly had their own resources for that.

"Did he offer you anything else?" Kylie asked.

"Like what?" George asked, as if he expected Kylie to sell out Colton Connections right in front of Heath.

Heath chuckled. The man did not know Kylie and the depths of her loyalty.

"Like an address…" She glanced toward the man in the suit, probably surmising the same thing Heath had. That if dirty work had been done, this man had done it. Had he trashed her place?

He was hardly going to admit it, and he didn't betray, with so much as a flicker of an eyelid, any reaction to her comment. Neither did the CEO or VP.

Randall George shook his head and turned back toward Heath. "So if you're not selling Colton Connections, what are you doing here?" he asked.

"Just trying to find out how far a company might go to protect their profits."

George tensed. "Are you accusing Arvock of illegal practices? If you are, you need to be careful. Our legal counsel is much better than your former one."

Pride stinging, Heath pointed out, "Morrison was just one of a few lawyers we have on staff."

"Let's hope the other ones are better then," George replied. "Because you may run into some difficulties with procuring that patent as well as other difficulties…"

Heath tightened his arm around Kylie's waist. "Are you threatening us?"

"Not at all," George replied with a little smirk. "I don't need to threaten you. I may not even need to deal with you once those wills are read."

Heath narrowed his eyes, wondering what the guy knew or thought he knew. "If I were you, I wouldn't put much stake in the accuracy of any of the information you bought from Morrison," he advised the man.

The guy's face paled to nearly the same color of his white hair.

Kylie must have noticed, too, because she chuckled. "He's our former employee for a reason."

George glanced at the unidentified man again, sending him some kind of silent message. To get rid of Tyler Morrison? Or to get rid of them?

"Well," George said. "This has been an enlightening conversation, but I need to return to my duties as host. And you two really shouldn't stay. Wouldn't want you to overhear anything proprietary." After dismissing them, he and his VP turned and walked away.

But the other man remained. "I will see you out," he told them, his deep voice brooking no argument.

"So where were you Thursday night?" Heath asked him for his alibi for the murders.

Once again the guy betrayed nothing, his expression as grim and unreadable as it had been from the moment he'd walked up with his employers. But his hand moved, closer to that bulge beneath his jacket.

Kylie tugged at Heath's arm. "We really should leave," she told him.

"Listen to the lady," the man advised him. "She's as smart as she is beautiful…"

Heath nearly chuckled at how quickly the guy had gone from stoic to charming—for her. "She is," Heath agreed.

"So it would be a damn shame if she got hurt," the guy continued. "Because of you…"

Heath flinched. The guy obviously knew more than he was willing to admit. "Are you threatening us?"

He shook his head. "Just offering you some badly needed advice." But he was focused on Kylie now. "Be careful."

She shivered.

Knowing that he wasn't going to get any kind of confession from the man, Heath guided Kylie away from him and toward the door to the hotel lobby. The guy followed them, though, very closely, so closely that Heath felt a prickling between his shoulder blades.

Kylie had been right. He shouldn't have come here, and he damn well shouldn't have let her come with him. Because he had no doubt that he'd put them both in danger.

KYLIE SHIVERED AGAIN when they exited out of the hotel lobby onto the street. While the day had been almost unseasonably warm for February, night had fallen and brought back the chill of late winter.

Or maybe it was just that meeting that had chilled her. Had the man been giving her unsolicited advice or had he been threatening her?

"I'm sorry," Heath said. "I should have listened to you."

"You should always listen to me," she replied with a smile.

He chuckled—just as she'd wanted him to. "You're a smart-ass."

"I like how he said it better," she admonished Heath. "That I'm as smart as I am beautiful."

His grin slipped away as he stared down at her. "You are…"

"Liar," she teased.

But he flinched again, as he had last time.

"Sorry," she said. "I'm just joking, like you." Because he couldn't possibly be serious.

But he certainly looked serious. He slid his fingertips along her jaw. "I know you felt self-conscious in there, without a formal gown, but you were every bit as glamorous as those other women."

Something gripped her heart, squeezing it, and she gasped. She could not be falling for him. She couldn't. If she did, she was just going to wind up getting hurt, like the man had warned her. She needed to be careful. She drew in a breath of cold air and forced a smile.

"You don't have to sweet-talk me into going home with you," she said. "I already am."

"And I am suddenly in a very big hurry to get back there," Heath told her. His arm still around her waist, he guided her down the street toward the lot where he'd parked his mother's vehicle.

Was he in a hurry because of the thinly veiled threat they'd just received? Or because he wanted to make love with her again?

Or because he felt the same sensation she did, that they were being watched?

She would have thought it was the man who'd just threatened them, but she'd had the feeling even before meeting him. Not that he couldn't have followed them there.

Arvock might have hired him to tail them and threaten them and…

Kill them?

Was he the one who'd shot at them the day before?

The one who'd tried running them down?

She hastened her step to keep up with Heath and because she was suddenly anxious. Anxious to get back to the safety of the penthouse.

The lot was just ahead on the other side of a busy intersection. They stopped at the corner, waiting for the Don't Walk to change to Walk. But even after it changed, Heath held her back from starting across the street. He looked both ways twice before stepping out.

But even then, he'd missed the vehicle. Of course it must have had its lights off. Until now, until they flashed on with the high beams blinding them. Along with the lights, the engine revved. Then the tires squealed as it pulled away from the curb and headed straight toward them.

This was clearly not someone going too fast. The driver had been waiting for them and seemed intent on not missing this time.

Chapter Twenty-One

Anger coursed through Joe, but he wasn't sure to whom it was directed. Heath Colton and Kylie Givens. Or himself for wasting his time being suspicious of them.

"You two have to stop playing Hardy Boys and Nancy Drew," he advised them. "You're going to get yourselves killed."

"Then that would lower your number of suspects," Colton quipped back at him as the three of them rode the elevator to the man's penthouse apartment.

"No. It would just increase them," he corrected the guy. "Clearly you two make enemies much easier than your dad and uncle ever did."

Colton flinched then. "You're right. Everybody loved Pop and Uncle Alfie."

Especially him. The guy didn't need to say it; it was written in the anguish on his face. Parker sighed in resignation.

"I know you loved them," he acknowledged.

"Too much to have ever been involved in their murders," Kylie Givens added.

Joe nodded. "I realize that now—just as I hope the two of you realize how much danger you're in."

They'd nearly been run down in the street—would have been had Heath Colton not managed to pull Kylie back onto the sidewalk and out of harm's way. The vehicle had jumped the curb, though, and nearly struck them anyway.

Joe had watched it all on the security footage of a nearby business. Unfortunately, the footage hadn't caught a license plate number, but that had been because the vehicle hadn't had one. Someone had removed the plate before trying to run them down. So clearly it had been no accident but a premeditated attempt on their lives.

"You can't believe that was just a car going too fast tonight," he said.

Heath shook his head while a muscle twitched above his tightly clenched jaw.

The elevator doors opened, drawing Joe's attention to that small foyer on the top floor. One hand holding open the doors, the other on his weapon, Joe scanned the area for any threats before letting the couple step off the elevator. He gestured at the steel door. "Unlock it and then step back," he advised them.

"We're safe here," Heath said, but he kept one arm protectively wrapped around Kylie Givens and his body between hers and the door to the penthouse and to the elevator. Once he turned the key in the lock, he stepped back as Joe had requested.

Joe checked out the apartment, inspecting every

room before joining them in the living room. They looked nervous, and he knew a couple of reasons why. Someone had tried to kill them and he'd just noticed Kylie's things in the guest room.

"I don't want you to admit it because then I'd have to do something about it," he said. "But I know you lied about the alibi." He focused on Kylie. "After checking out your background and your mother's case, I think I understand why."

Once again Heath Colton stepped between her and a threat—in between her and Joe. Joe smiled. Her stuff might have been in the guest room, but he doubted she'd actually been sleeping there.

"You didn't want to lose someone else you love," Joe finished. "Because of that, you both need to be careful. No more investigating on your own."

"Will you?" Heath asked. "Will you check out Arvock Pharmaceuticals and Tyler Morrison?"

Joe nodded. "Of course. I already have people working on those leads. So you don't need to do anything but lock yourself inside this penthouse and stay put and stay safe."

Heath shook his head. "We can't."

The anger ignited again, but then the man added, "The funeral is tomorrow."

And Joe felt only sympathy now. That was probably going to be as tough on Heath as nearly getting run down and shot at.

He nodded. "I'll request a police detail at the church,"

he said. "But you both still need to be careful." With a sigh, he turned and headed toward the door.

Heath stopped him, his hand on his shoulder, before he could walk out. "Thank you, Detective," he said.

Joe figured the man's gratitude was more over ignoring their fake alibi than for seeing them safely back to his place. "I really do want this killer caught," he assured him. "Almost as much as you do."

Almost…because while Joe was going to pursue all suspects, he wasn't going to willingly put himself in danger like Colton and Givens had.

"Be careful," he said again before he walked out and left the two of them alone for the night.

CAREFUL…

Heath had thought he'd been, that he'd been vigilant, that he'd been on guard for vehicles and gunshots. But that car had come out of nowhere; the lights suddenly flashing on had nearly blinded him. Thankfully he'd been able to pull Kylie back and hurled them to safety before it had struck them.

It had been too close.

"Are you okay?" he asked her like he had after the car had nearly run them down.

As she had on the sidewalk, she nodded. But she'd spoken so little—so very little—since they'd nearly died. Again.

"I'm sorry," he said.

"Why?" she asked.

"I keep putting you in danger."

"I was the one who insisted on going with you," she reminded him.

"You should have stayed here," he said. "And stayed safe."

She shook her head. "I don't know if we're going to be safe anywhere until this killer is caught."

"Parker checked out this place," he reminded her. "You're safe here. Maybe you should skip the funeral tomorrow and stay here."

She shook her head again, this time vehemently. "No way. I'm going."

He couldn't deny her right to go and pay her respects. He couldn't deny her feelings. She'd loved Pop and Uncle Alfie, too.

And maybe, selfishly, he wanted her there for him, to support him. He had his entire family, but he didn't feel as close to any of them as he did to Kylie. She understood his relationship with Pop and his uncle best. She'd been there with all of them.

Tears rushed to his eyes, and he blinked hard, admitting, "I don't want to go."

Her hand touched his, her fingers entwining with his. "I'll be there," she said. "I'll be with you."

He could have lost her, too, tonight. Could have lost her the night before and the day before and that time she'd had the allergic reaction.

He shuddered at the realization. She was so much a part of his life. Not just as a coworker but as a friend.

And more...

A lover and...

He couldn't think beyond lover now, not when desire

gripped him suddenly and powerfully. "I need you," he admitted, and he swung her up in his arms, carrying her toward the bedroom.

She wound her arm around his neck, holding her body close to his. She was trembling, so much that when he lowered her to her feet, her legs nearly gave beneath her. "You're not okay," he said.

She shook her head. "No."

He moved to lift her again, to carry her. "I'll bring you to the guest room then."

But she gripped his shoulders. "No. I want to stay here. I want to be with you."

He could understand her not wanting to be alone; he didn't want to be alone either. "I'll just hold you then," he said, not wanting to pressure her. Not when she was so vulnerable.

Her lips curved into a slight smile and she teased, "I sure hope that's not all you do." Her hands were steady now as she attacked the studs on his shirt, pulling them loose to bare his chest. She pushed the silk from his shoulders along with the tie that dangled from the collar.

He chuckled at her impatience. He was impatient to get her naked, too. But there were more buttons on her dress, from neck to hem. He only managed to undo a couple of them before she pushed his hands away.

He expected her to pull the dress over her head and get rid of it. But instead she teased him, with a twinkle in her eyes, as she slowly undid those buttons herself. One at a painstaking time…

He groaned with impatience, with need. But even as desperate for a release as he was, he enjoyed the anticipation. His pulse quickened. His heart pounded. And somehow he found himself holding his breath until finally she parted the dress and slipped it slowly from her body, leaving her clothed in only a black lace bra and a black lace thong.

Then his breath shuddered out in a ragged sigh. "You are so beautiful," he murmured in appreciation.

Her smile widened slightly before she tugged it back down.

"I'm not lying," he said, before she could utter the accusation again. "You really are beautiful. Why can't you accept that?"

"Because you never told me before," she said.

"I didn't want to harass you," he admitted. "I didn't want you to quit the company." He needed her in the office too much. But he was finding that he needed her even more in the bedroom.

"I'm not going to leave," she told him.

And he didn't know if she was talking about Colton Connections or him. He would make sure she couldn't leave the company because he wanted her to have a stake in it, as well. Once the will was read and he knew if he had the authority, he was going to make her partner.

"Good," he said. "Because I would tie you to the bed this time."

She chuckled. "Promises, promises."

He scooped her up then and gently tossed her onto the bed. She giggled as she bounced on the mattress.

And something shifted in his chest, his heart clenching. She really was so damn beautiful.

"What?" she asked. "What's wrong?"

He shook his head. "Nothing."

She sighed. "Everything."

"Not now," he said. "Right now everything is right. Here. In this bed. With just you and me."

Even as he said it, his cell phone vibrated in his pants pocket. He pulled it out and tossed it down on its screen but not before he noticed who was calling. Gina. Again.

"Is it important?" Kylie asked, pointing toward his phone.

"No," he said. "What's important is finding something to tie you to this bed."

She giggled again. "You don't need to. I'm not going anywhere." She reached out, grabbed his hand and tugged him toward her. "And neither are you."

"I don't want to," he promised her. And he didn't want anyone but her. He wasn't ready yet to admit that to himself, though, let alone her. So he showed her instead.

He joined her on the bed, pressing his lips to her cheek and her chin and the side of her neck.

She giggled and wriggled. Then she was touching and kissing him, too. And his skin heated and flushed as desire consumed him, as she consumed him.

She pushed him onto his back and unzipped his pants and she tortured him with her soft hands and her silky lips…

He could have come, needed to come. But he wanted to be inside her, part of her. So he pushed her onto her back, and he unclasped her bra and pulled down her panties. And he made sure she was as hot and desperate for release as he was. When he shifted away from her to kick off his pants and boxers, she tugged at him.

"Heath, I need you."

He needed her, too.

His hand shook as he reached for a condom. He had to tear open the packet with his teeth like she had. Then, sitting on the edge of the bed, he rolled it on.

Before he could turn back toward her, she straddled his lap and guided him inside her. Her hands gripping his shoulders, her legs wrapped around his waist, she rode him.

He lowered his head and kissed her, deeply, intimately, as he slid in and out of her body. Then her inner muscles gripped him, convulsing around him, as she screamed his name.

Then he came, too, his body shuddering with the power of the release, with the amount of pleasure he found with her, inside her. "Kylie…"

He'd never felt like this before—never so much—with anyone else. And for the first time he wondered if his problem with commitment had less to do with him than it had with his significant other.

Or was he only caught up in the adrenaline again like she'd been the other night? Once again they'd escaped death. Was that why everything felt so much more significant than it ever had before?

He didn't know. But he had to be sure before he shared any of his thoughts or feelings with her. He didn't want to hurt her like he had the other women he dated. And he didn't want anyone else hurting her either.

ONE MINUTE HEATH had been buried deep inside her. The next he was gone. First he'd slipped into the bathroom to clean up, but then instead of returning to bed with her, he'd said he was going to bring them some food from the kitchen.

So he would be back.

He had to be back. He'd promised Detective Parker that he was going to stay here until the funeral. Not that they hadn't lied to the lawman before.

Fortunately, for their sake, even though the man realized that, he wasn't going to press charges against them. Someone trying to kill them yet again must have removed the last of his suspicions about them, about Heath.

If only Kylie could feel the same.

She wasn't suspicious of Heath regarding his dad's and uncle's murders. She knew he would never have harmed them or the company. But it was the way he talked to her, looked at her, made love to her.

She wasn't sure she could trust it. She knew him too well, knew that he had never fallen really deeply for anyone before. Not that she wanted him to fall for her.

But...

Oh, hell, she was beginning to fall for him. And she knew better. She knew him better than to make that mistake. But she must have gotten caught up in how heroic he'd been, in how he'd protected her the past few days.

But yet...

That suspicion still lingered, and she reached for

the phone he'd put facedown on the bedside table. The screen lit up with a missed call.

Gina.

He hadn't locked his phone, so the screen opened, revealing more than just that one missed call and several voice mails, as well.

Gina was still in his life, which left no room for Kylie. She wasn't going to be the other woman Gina had accused her of being.

Not even for Heath.

Chapter Twenty-Two

Heath's eyes burned with the tears he'd fought back and with the ones that had slipped out. The funeral was even harder than he had imagined it would be.

But it was worse for his mom and Aunt Farrah. Every sob that slipped from their lips struck him like a blow to the gut, making him want to double over with pain. With their pain.

They had loved their husbands so much. It wasn't fair that they'd lost them so soon. Too soon. It wasn't fair for any of them to have lost Pop and Uncle Alfie.

No. They hadn't lost them. The men had been stolen from them, robbed of their lives by some vicious killer. That killer had to pay.

Was it a single disgruntled greedy worker like Tyler Morrison? Or was it a heartless corporation like Arvock Pharmaceuticals?

More tears slipped through Heath's defenses as the caskets were lowered into the graves that had been dug side by side. Pop and Uncle Alfie would spend eternity like they had their lives—together. He'd once envied them that—envied them and his mom and aunt having a twin. He'd figured, because he'd been born alone, he was destined to always be alone.

Single.

Was that why he'd always considered himself incapable of making a commitment? Because he hadn't believed he would know how to be a couple?

He blinked and cleared his gaze, so that he could focus on the woman standing at his side. Tears trailed down Kylie's beautiful face. She had one hand holding a tissue pressed against her cheek and the other on his arm. But it was almost as if she'd forgotten it was there, that he was there.

Ever since last night she'd been distant. She'd claimed she was just exhausted when he'd come back to his bedroom from the kitchen. She'd been too tired to eat, or even drink the tea he'd brewed for her, she'd said before she'd slipped off alone to the guest room.

Leaving him alone. Like he felt now.

But then her grasp on his arm tightened as she gently squeezed and he discovered her staring up at him, the pain in her dark eyes echoing the pain he was feeling. That tight, achy sensation in his chest eased slightly with the sympathetic smile she offered him.

Then the service concluded, and her smile slipped away and so did she, as the other mourners started to exit the cemetery. Where had she gone?

Panic caused an even tighter feeling in his chest, stealing his breath away until he found her with Carly. "Go with your mom," she told him when he joined the women. She gestured at the limousine that the widows were going to ride in back to Aunt Farrah's house from the cemetery. "Fallon needs you."

He shook his head. Even though Detective Parker had kept his word about having police protection at the funeral, Heath wasn't sure it was safe for him to be too close to his mom. "She has Aunt Farrah and Grandmother." He was the one who had no one…now…that she was growing distant from him.

Why?

What had happened?

Had she realized that being with him was putting her in danger? Was she angry with him? Scared to be with him?

He peered closer at her face, and he discerned something in her eyes that looked almost like fear. Was she afraid *of* him?

He wanted to ask her—wanted to talk to her—alone. But Carly looped her arm through his and leaned against his side. "Can I ride back with you two?" she asked.

"Of course," he said, and he lowered his head to kiss her forehead. Today had to be especially hard on his sister. Hell, it was hard on all of them. Kylie, too.

He reached for her with his other arm, linking his through hers and pulling her close. She tensed, but she didn't fight him. She also didn't lean against him like Carly did. Something was definitely going on with her. With them…

They would talk later—when they went back to the penthouse. Right now he had to be present for his family. Kylie felt like family to him, though. She had since the day he'd hired her, and they'd just clicked.

And it suddenly clicked with him.

Maybe Gina had been right. Maybe Kylie had been the reason he hadn't been able to commit to her—because even then he'd been falling for the dark-haired beauty. Did she know?

Was that why she looked scared of him? Maybe she didn't want him to confess his feelings and ruin their friendship and working relationship.

Kylie hadn't ever been any more eager than he was to make a commitment. He'd just thought it was because, like him, she cared more about work than her personal life. But now he was beginning to care more about her. Much more.

But he had a horrible feeling—from the way she was distancing herself from him—that he was about to get his heart broken. Maybe that was only fair. Some kind of karma for all the hearts he'd broken.

DESPITE HOW DISTRAUGHT they all were, Heath's family was still welcoming to Kylie, still treating her like one of them. And she felt like a fraud.

She hadn't just lied to Detective Parker; she'd lied to them, too. She wanted to come clean to them, but she knew now was not the time. Hell, she just wanted to cook or clean or do something to help out. But she found the kitchen in pristine condition.

Farrah Colton stood in her domain, gazing around with the same lost expression on her face. "There's nothing to do," she murmured. "Tatum's restaurant catered everything and cleaned up."

"That's good," Kylie assured her.

The older woman nodded. "Yes, and the food was good."

"Excellent," Kylie said, though she hadn't had much more than a bite of anything. She'd felt too sick to eat.

"There you are," Abigail Jones said as she joined them in the kitchen.

Kylie assumed the older woman was talking to her daughter until her slender arms wrapped around Kylie, pulling her into a hug. "You must be so lost, dear, with Ernie and Alfie gone. I can't imagine what the office must be like."

Tears stung Kylie's eyes, at the woman's kindness and understanding, over her loss.

"At least you and Heath have each other," Mrs. Jones said. "I'm so grateful for that."

No. Kylie couldn't come clean—not yet—not when she was able to give at least some of the Colton family some comfort.

Abigail turned toward her daughter now. "Guests are looking for you, Farrah. They want to say goodbye before they leave." And she led her daughter from the kitchen then, leaving Kylie alone.

But she was only alone for a moment before Carly joined her. "I'm sorry," Heath's sister told her.

Kylie turned to in confusion. "For what?"

"For third wheeling on the way back here," she said. "I just didn't want to be alone."

"Of course," Kylie said. "You weren't third wheeling at all. I understand how difficult this day must be for you."

"Of course, Heath must have told you about Micha…" Her voice cracked as it trailed off.

Kylie nodded. "I'd already been working at Colton Connections for a few years when it happened." When Heath's sister's fiancé had died in combat. "I'm so sorry."

Carly drew in a shaky breath and nodded. "It's been two years, but his was the last funeral I attended, so…"

"It's hard."

She nodded.

"And I thought I was doing so much better," Carly said. "I actually just started dating someone."

Kylie smiled in encouragement. "That's great. Who?"

"A friend of Sean's, Harry Cartwright. He's a really nice man," Carly said, as if she was trying to convince herself of that. "I don't know if we'll ever have the kind of relationship…"

"That you had with Micha?" Kylie asked when the blonde trailed off again.

Carly smiled, "Or that you have with Heath."

Kylie flinched, hating that she'd lied to all of them.

"I'm sorry," Carly said again. "I could sense that something was wrong earlier between the two of you. Do you want to talk about it?"

Kylie shook her head. "I really shouldn't. Not now."

"What did Heath do?" Carly asked with a sister's exasperation for her older brother.

Kylie smiled. "I don't know if he did anything," she admitted. "But I saw a bunch of calls and voice mails from Gina on his phone." Heat suffused her face. "Not that I was looking or anything, but he has been ignoring some calls and acting strange about them."

Carly smiled. "So naturally you were curious. I understand." Her smile slipped away. "There seemed to be a lot that Micha never shared with me."

"I'm sure he would have if he'd been allowed," Kylie assured her. "But with his being in the military, a lot of what he did must have been classified."

Carly shrugged. "I don't really know."

Kylie expelled a shaky sigh. "I understand that feeling."

"But you can ask Heath," Carly said. "I don't have that option anymore."

A twinge of guilt struck Kylie. "I feel silly talking to you about this."

Carly chuckled. "I'm glad that you did. I want us to be close."

That twinge of guilt struck her again, harder this time. She didn't deserve Heath's sister's kindness. "I'm not sure that'll be possible now," Kylie murmured.

"You need to talk to Heath. I'm sure he has an explanation about those calls and voice mails," Carly said.

He probably did, but Kylie was afraid to hear it, to hear that he'd started up with Gina again.

Carly must have seen that fear because she reached out and grasped her hand. "You're imagining the worst," she said. "And you don't need to. I've never seen Heath as in love with anyone as he is with you. He certainly never cared that much about Gina."

In love with her? He cared about her, as a friend, but

he was hardly in love with her. But the sudden yearning in her heart confirmed that she wanted his love.

She wanted Heath. Not just for his family, that she'd always wished she was a part of, but only for him. For his intelligence and his integrity and creativity and sexiness...

Carly smiled. "And you're so in love with him that it's scaring you," she said.

With a sudden rush of fear, Kylie realized Heath's sister was right. She had fallen in love with him.

"You know Heath better than anyone else does," Carly continued. "You know you can trust him."

She did know Heath better than anyone else, but that was why she wasn't certain she could trust him. He'd never been able to commit to a real girlfriend. Why would he suddenly be willing to commit to a fake one?

JONES'S HEAD POUNDED and he flinched against the sudden light as Heath opened the blinds in Uncle Alfie's den.

"This is where you've been hiding?" his older brother asked.

"Not hiding," Jones said defensively. He had nobody to hide from—nobody sought him out like they did his mom and aunt and his siblings and cousins. "I just wanted to rest a minute."

"You look like hell," Heath said. "I can't believe you're hungover on the day of Pop and Uncle Alfie's funeral."

Jones couldn't believe he was either. Usually the amount of alcohol he'd had wouldn't have affected him, but he hadn't been eating or sleeping the past few days. "I can't believe you're lecturing me right now," Jones remarked—since there were dark circles beneath Heath's eyes too and he looked thinner, as well.

He probably wasn't hungover, but he clearly hadn't been sleeping or eating well either.

"I have to," Heath said. "Pop's not here to do it anymore."

Pain clenched Jones's heart, squeezing it tightly. That was mostly what his father had done with Jones, lecture him, while praising Heath.

"You're not Pop," Jones said. "Even though you've been trying your damnedest to be him all these years."

Heath's brow creased. "What are you talking about?"

Jones lurched out of the chair where he'd been sitting and stalked over to his self-righteous brother. "You're not beloved like Pop and Uncle Alfie. Your employees hate your guts."

Heath shook his head. "I have no idea what you're talking about, and I don't think you do either."

"Some lawyer stopped by the brewery last night," Jones said. "He's so disgusted with you that he wants to back me to take over the company, to be CEO."

Heath laughed in his face, enraging Jones. He was just like Pop—thinking Jones was an idiot, inept, incompetent—not as smart or successful as the rest of them. He shoved his brother back against the bookshelves behind him. A couple volumes tumbled from the shelves.

"What the hell is wrong with you?" Heath asked.

"Stop laughing at me," Jones said. "Stop lecturing me! You have no damn right!"

"I'm laughing at Morrison," Heath said. "I fired him yesterday, and he just refuses to accept it."

Heat suffused Jones's face. Clearly the lawyer thought he was an idiot, too, and had tried to play him for a fool. But yet Jones wasn't entirely certain his brother hadn't been laughing at him, too. "So you think that I could take over Colton Connections?"

And Heath laughed again.

Jones reached for him, but Heath's arms were just a little longer. He pushed at Jones this time, knocking him back. He stumbled and fell over a chair, sprawling across the floor. The wind knocked out of him, he gasped for a breath. Then he lurched up from the floor. Before he could swing at his brother, strong arms pulled him back.

"What the hell are you two doing?" Sean Stafford asked as he held tightly to Jones despite his wriggling in his grasp. "Your family is all upset enough. They don't need to deal with you two fighting."

That heat suffused Jones again, burning his face with shame and embarrassment. His shoulders sagged, and he stopped fighting. Sean held him for a moment longer before propelling him back into the chair he'd been in when Heath had walked in to lecture him.

Heath's face was also flushed and probably not from that brief shove he'd given Jones. "I'm sorry," he said. To Sean...

Jones flinched.

"And I'm sorry I bothered you," Heath said. "I should

have just left you alone in here, but I didn't want to do that—today of all days."

"You wanted to lecture and belittle me instead?" Jones asked.

Heath chuckled. "I'm sorry, okay? I didn't mean to. The words just came out."

"Like you were channeling Pop," Jones said, then admitted, "I shouldn't be hung over. It's just so damn hard."

"I know," Heath said. "I also know that you've made a hell of a success of your brewery."

Jones's lips curved into a slight grin. "You just don't think I could take over Colton Connections like Morrison suggested?"

"You want to deal with patents all day long?" Heath asked.

Jones chuckled. "God, no. I'll leave Colton Connections to you."

Heath sighed. "I guess we'll see—after the wills are read."

"So you two are good?" Sean asked. "All made up?"

Heath nodded. "Yeah, Morrison was causing some more trouble, though. The guy just won't go away even after I fired him."

Sean's eyes narrowed. "The lawyer? Parker pulled him in today for questioning."

"Questioning in what?" Jones asked.

"The attempts on Heath and Kylie's lives and in the murders."

Jones gasped at the thought of being so close to his

father's killer. "God, I should have beaten the hell out of him."

"I wanted to, too, but Kylie stopped me," Heath admitted.

"You guys have no proof that Morrison is guilty of anything," Sean said.

"Company espionage," Heath said. "I know he was selling information to that drug company."

Jones's head pounded hard as he tried to follow their conversation. He rubbed his gritty eyes. "God, you're right—I don't want anything to do with Colton Connections."

"Good thing," Heath said with a heavy sigh. "It puts you in danger."

Fear gripped Jones as he finally processed everything that had been happening since the murders. Someone was trying to kill his brother, too. The big brother he'd always loved and admired and wished he was closer to.

Now he might not have the chance if this killer was successful. "You mean that Morrison guy might be trying to take you out next and not just out of your chair but out of the world?"

Heath shrugged. "I don't know."

"Parker's looking at him as a serious suspect," Sean said. "When did you talk to him?"

"I don't know exact time." Jones searched his memory. "I think he showed up at the bar around nine or so."

"Would he have had time to get from the West Loop to that hotel downtown when Kylie and I were nearly run down?" Heath asked.

A surge of fear overwhelmed Jones. He had nearly lost his brother the night before his dad and uncle's funeral. He gasped.

"Parker will check," Sean assured him as he pulled out his cell. "But you gotta be extra careful. You and Kylie. You don't know who the hell is coming after you."

Heath nodded.

Sean tapped his phone. "I'm going to call Joe, fill him in." He stepped through the French doors to the little courtyard between the den and the driveway.

Jones jumped up from his chair and reached for Heath who stepped back as if suspecting his brother might be going after him again. But Jones hugged him. "I'm sorry," he murmured as emotion overwhelmed him.

Heath clutched him close and murmured, "Me, too." When Jones pulled back, his brother's eyes were damp. "I'm so sorry," Heath said. "And I hope you know that Pop was very proud of you. He told everybody about Lone Wolf."

Tears flooded Jones's eyes now. "I—I didn't know that. He didn't tell me."

"He would have," Heath assured him. "If he hadn't been denied the chance."

Jones wasn't so sure but he nodded at the sentiment his brother had expressed.

"And though it might not mean much from me, I am proud of you, too," Heath said.

"Damn you," Jones said as the tears flooded his eyes again.

Despite the tears in his eyes, Heath chuckled. "It's the day to express feelings. When it's over, we'll go back to ignoring them and just grunting at each other."

"Promise?" Jones asked.

Heath nodded and started to pull out of their brotherly embrace. But Jones gripped his shoulders.

"Promise me," he began.

"I promise to stop talking—"

"No, promise me you'll be careful," Jones said. "Promise me that I won't lose my big brother, too."

Heath nodded, but they both knew that wasn't a promise he could make. He had no way of knowing if there would be more attempts on his life.

But Jones suspected there would be, that the killer would keep trying until Heath was dead.

Chapter Twenty-Three

Heath and Kylie had driven back to the penthouse in silence, but it hadn't been silent inside Heath's head where his words to his brother echoed. Today was the day to express feelings. But his fight with Jones had drained him.

Hell, the whole day had drained him. So he remained silent, and so did Kylie, while he parked the SUV and they rode the elevator up to the penthouse. But when Kylie started toward the hallway leading to the guest room, he reached out and caught her hand in his.

"Please…" he said.

She turned toward him. "What? What do you want, Heath?" She was tense. Maybe she expected him to drag her to his bedroom for sex.

"I just want you to talk to me," he said, imploring her. "I want you to tell me what's going on with you… with us."

"What do you mean?" she asked.

"You've been different since last night," he said. "Something's wrong. You're upset about it, and I don't know what I've done."

She expelled a shaky sigh. "Okay…"

So he had done something, something that had upset her—just as he'd upset his brother. Regret gripped him, but maybe he could make it right with her like he had with Jones, if she would give him the chance. "You'll talk to me?"

She nodded. "Yes. Let me make some tea and we'll talk."

He expelled a shaky sigh of his own as he followed her to the kitchen. "I don't know if I should be relieved or worried."

"Why?" she asked.

"My talk with Jones today didn't go well." At first.

"I heard," she said.

Everybody apparently had because the hallway outside the den had been crowded when he and Jones had walked out of it. Without getting into details, they'd assured everybody that they were fine.

"What were you fighting about?" she asked as she filled the kettle before putting it on his stove. Then she reached for her canister of teabags on the counter.

Just as she'd spread her things about the guest room, Kylie had spread them about the kitchen. But he liked seeing her things here almost as much as he liked seeing her here—in his home. With her here, it was finally beginning to feel like a home and not just the place where he crashed after working all day.

She waved a teabag in front of his face. "Want some?"

He shook his head.

"Can't you tell me about the fight?" she asked. "Is it between you and Jones?"

He snorted. "Even if it was, I would tell you. I tell you everything." Which Gina had hated.

Kylie's eyes narrowed in a faint glare, though, as if she didn't believe him. "Really?" She sounded doubtful, as well.

"Yes," he said and hastened to do just that. "Morrison stopped by the brewery last night and wound Jones up with a lot of crap about disappointing our dad."

"What a jerk," she said. "What was he trying to do?"

"Get Jones to take over the company, so I couldn't fire him."

"Jerk," she repeated.

"Yeah, but maybe a jerk with an alibi." Which was a pity. He really wanted Morrison to be guilty of something—something more than company espionage.

"He might have been with Jones when someone tried running us down?" she asked.

He nodded. "But I don't want to talk about my fight with Jones," he said. "I want to talk about my fight with you."

She shook her head. "We're not fighting."

"But we're not talking either," he said. "What happened last night? One minute we were so good and the next…"

The kettle whistled then, and Kylie turned either eagerly or gratefully toward the stove. When she turned away, his cell phone began to vibrate.

Frustrated with the interruption, he pulled it from

his pocket and dropped it on the counter. Gina's name illuminated the screen, and he cursed.

"That," Kylie said. "Her."

"She called when I was in the kitchen last night?" he asked. What the hell had the woman said to her? After how Gina had reacted to finding them in bed together, he could only imagine how ugly it must have been. Feeling like he might need to sit down, he settled onto a stool at the counter.

Kylie's face flushed, and she shook her head. "No, she didn't call then."

"So what happened?"

"I—I might have peeked at your phone when you went to the kitchen," she said.

His brow creased. "Might have?"

"I did," she said. "I don't mean to sound like her, like some crazy, possessive girlfriend, but I saw you ignore calls a few times and I wanted to see what was going on."

And he hadn't told her about the calls, like he usually told her everything. Realization dawning, he nodded. "I understand."

She groaned and covered her flushed face with her hands. "I don't..." she murmured. "I don't understand why I'm acting like this, like her."

He chuckled. "You would never act like her," he assured Kylie.

She drew in a deep breath and pulled her hands from her face. "I know. I have no right. She really was your girlfriend and I'm just..."

"What?" he asked, curious what she saw herself as

now that he saw her as *everything*. She'd started out as his best friend; now she was his soul mate.

"I'm your fake alibi," she replied. "That's all I am to you."

He shook his head. "You're so much more," he assured her. And he wanted to tell her what she was, what she meant to him. Today was the day to express his feelings, but unlike his promise to Jones, he would keep expressing them to her—if she stuck around once he confessed to falling for her.

But when he opened his mouth to speak, she jumped in with a question. "What is she?" Kylie asked. "Is she your ex-girlfriend or your girlfriend?"

He tensed. "What? You think I would be sleeping with you if I was still seeing her?" He felt like he had when his mom and aunt had sobbed at the funeral, like he could double over with the pain racking him. He jumped up from the stool and started out of the room. "I thought you knew me better than that. Hell, I thought you knew me better than anyone."

Good thing he hadn't expressed his feelings to her because she obviously didn't share them. And he'd thought his heart had broken when he'd identified the bodies of his dad and uncle.

If it had, she must have healed it the past few days... only to break it again.

HEATH HADN'T ANSWERED her question. With another man that might have roused Kylie's suspicions even more. It might have made her think he was gaslighting her like so many men had gaslighted her mother.

But this was Heath, and she did know him better than anyone. Before he could leave the kitchen, she stepped in front of him and blocked his escape.

"I'm sorry," she told him as she wound her arms around his lean waist and hugged him. "I'm so sorry."

His heart pounded hard beneath her cheek as she laid her head on his chest. He put his hands on her shoulders, but instead of pulling her closer, he gently eased her away from him. He still looked like he had when she'd asked that stupid question, like she'd slapped him.

"I'm sorry," she repeated. "You're right. I do know you. And I know you're not seeing Gina anymore."

He drew in a shaky breath and nodded. "Good."

His phone vibrated again against the counter where he'd left it. She pointed toward it. "Apparently she doesn't know that, though. Why does she keep calling you?"

He shrugged. "I don't know. I haven't picked it up, and after playing her first ridiculous message, I haven't played any more of them."

"Why not?" she asked.

He sighed. "I can't deal with her histrionics right now. Not with everything else." He rubbed his hand over his face. "I should have told you about her calls, but I didn't want to talk about her—not with everything else going on, everything that's so much more important."

Like the murders.

And the attempts on their lives.

She'd been a fool to let those missed calls play on her insecurities. "I understand," she assured him. "But I don't think ignoring her is going to make Gina go away. You're going to have to talk to her."

He reached for his phone then. But she stopped him, just as she'd stopped him from leaving the room.

"Maybe play her messages first, though," she suggested. "Better to have an idea of what she wants before you talk to her."

She also needed to have an idea of what Heath wanted—from her. Was he looking for more than sex? Did he want a real relationship with her? And when he called Gina back, what would he tell her? Would he tell his ex that he'd moved on...with Kylie?

She needed to ask all those questions. And she would, but she wanted to stall for a little time before she did, because asking them would leave her vulnerable in a way she'd never let herself be vulnerable before. It would expose her feelings to him.

Her love...

Her mouth dry, she reached for the pot of tea she'd left steeping on the counter. She quickly poured a cup and took a quick sip. It was hot.

"Careful," Heath said as he pointed at the steam rolling off the top of the small cup. "You're going to burn yourself."

That was what she was worried about, that if she confessed her feelings she would get burned. "Don't you want to play the messages?" she asked.

He glanced down at his phone as if he'd forgotten all about it. Then he shrugged. "I really don't care, but since you do..." He pressed the voice mail icon, scrolled back through and pressed Play.

Despite the heat, Kylie took another sip of her tea—to brace herself as the other woman's voice emanated from Heath's phone. As she'd expected, Gina maligned her character and her intentions.

I can't believe you've fallen for her tricks, the woman said. *She has always been after you. That's why she broke us up.*

Kylie wasn't surprised about that message. But they got steadily worse.

She wants to take over Colton Connections, she said. *That's why she wants you. She's probably the one who killed your dad and uncle.*

Kylie gasped and nearly choked on the sip of tea she'd just taken. How could anyone believe that of her? Would Heath...

He was shaking his head in horror but clearly more over the messages than the woman herself. Gina ranted and raved and sounded totally unhinged.

"Oh, my God," Heath murmured, his eyes widening with alarm.

That alarm shot through Kylie as well because her throat started feeling odd. Not just burnt but as if it was closing...

She gasped again, but she couldn't draw a breath. She couldn't speak. She couldn't tell Heath what she'd just realized.

Nobody had been trying to kill *them.* He had never been the target.

Just her...

Gina had been trying to kill her and she might have just succeeded.

ANGER COURSED THROUGH GINA. She should have been at his side during the funerals—not that little bitch. She should have been the one holding his hand, offering him comfort.

Kylie had barely been able to stop her own crocodile tears long enough to pay him any attention. But Gina had been paying attention.

She'd always paid attention to everything Heath had said and done and needed. He needed her. Not Kylie...

So instead of openly attending the funeral, she'd slipped away from the cemetery unseen and she'd come back to the penthouse while she knew they'd be out.

And she'd used one of the many things Heath had told her about Kylie.

She'd always hated how incessantly he had chattered on about his vice president—until he'd shared something useful about her. Like how she'd nearly died once when they were having lunch, because of her severe allergy to iodine.

Just a small amount of it could kill her.

Gina had even fantasized then about killing her. About slipping it into that damn tea she always drank.

But she'd refrained from acting on that inclination then. After all, Heath had assured her over and over again that he had no interest in Little Miss Kylie Givens.

Then Gina had caught them in bed together...

And that white-hot rage had consumed her so much that she'd almost killed Heath with Kylie. She'd been stupid to try to run them down or shoot them.

She didn't want Heath dead. She just wanted Kylie gone forever.

It would happen soon. She was sure of it, and unlike with the car and the gunfire, Heath wouldn't be able to protect her and save her.

Kylie Givens was finally going to get what she deserved: death.

Chapter Twenty-Four

Heath was in shock from realizing that Gina was the one. She'd tried to run them down, had shot at them.

How had he dated such a lunatic?

"Oh, my God," he said. But at least he could speak.

Kylie could only make some strangled sound. He turned his full attention to her, and an even greater alarm gripped him. She was clawing at her throat, and her skin was bright red. Her bottom lip, tinged with blue, quivered. Fear had darkened her brown eyes even more, and that fear overwhelmed Heath.

"Oh, my God…" he murmured again even as he rushed to her side.

He was too late, though. She dropped to the floor before he could reach for her, her body lying limp and lifeless. Her throat must have closed up. He'd seen her have a reaction like this before, to iodine.

Remembering what she'd done for it, he grabbed her purse off the counter. She always carried an EpiPen. Instead of rummaging through the bag, he upended it on the floor next to her.

Every second that she wasn't breathing…

It would make it harder for her to come back to him.

A small prescription bag lay among her wallet and phone and crumpled receipts. He ripped it open and pulled out the auto-injector. The needle would pop out of it once he pressed it against her thigh.

She had stuck her thigh that day. Today she hadn't even had the chance to reach for her purse. How the hell much iodine had she ingested?

Would the EpiPen be enough to save her?

He pushed up the hem of her dress and pressed the end she had used, the orange end, against her skin. He flinched at the thought of hurting her. But he had to… to save her.

He tried to press the top of the injector but it didn't go down. What the hell was wrong with it?

He grabbed the directions from the pharmacy bag. "Okay…" There was another cap, the safety cap. He popped it off and pushed the orange end back against her skin. A soft click signaled the release of the needle.

One.

Two.

Three…

The injector looked empty. Had it been full? Was there enough in it? He leaned toward Kylie's face, pressing his ear nearly against her blue-tinged lips. Was she breathing? His heart pounded so fast and hard with fear that he couldn't hear anything but it, but the rushing of his blood through his veins along with his fear.

He reached up to the counter and felt around for his cell phone. He had a call to make—9-1-1.

"What's your emergency?" a dispatcher asked as she answered.

"My—my girlfriend has had an allergic reaction. She stopped breathing—"

"Does she have an EpiPen?" the woman asked.

"Yes, but I don't know if I did it right. I don't know if she's breathing again."

Or if she was already dead. Her face was no longer red but so deathly pale.

HE'D TOLD THEM to stay close to each other, to stick together, to be careful. But yet here Joe was, responding to an emergency call at the penthouse.

He parked behind an ambulance that sat at the curb outside the front doors of the apartment complex, lights flashing. Before he opened his door to step out, the back doors of the ambulance opened as an EMT lifted the head of a stretcher into it. His breath caught when he noticed the slight body lying limply on that stretcher.

Kylie Givens.

Parker jumped out and rushed up. "Is she okay?" he asked.

An oxygen mask covered her mouth and nose— hell, most of her delicately featured face. She looked so small, so vulnerable, like Isaac when he was sleeping…

But she might not have been just sleeping.

"No, she's not okay," Heath Colton answered, his voice gruff with concern and fear. "My crazy ex-girlfriend might have killed her."

"You let her into your place?" Parker asked. "Where is she?"

"I don't know where she is," Heath said. "She had the code to the elevator and a key to the penthouse. I know I should have changed the locks, but I didn't think she would do something like this. She poisoned Kylie."

"We have to go, sir," one of the EMTs said.

And Parker knew the situation was grave yet. Kylie might not make it.

"Go," Parker urged them.

Heath had one foot inside the ambulance when he cursed and jumped down. "There she is!" He pointed across the street, and Joe whirled around to find a blonde watching them.

Before Heath could start toward her, Parker shoved him back toward the ambulance. "Go with Kylie!"

If this was who'd been trying to kill them, the woman had a gun since she'd fired the shots into his SUV and maybe into his dad and uncle.

Joe drew his weapon before he started after her.

"Be careful," Heath called after him, just as the ambulance doors began to close. "She's crazy!"

Crazy scared Joe. It made a suspect too damn unpredictable and dangerous.

He hadn't answered his phone…

So Gina had had to come back to check on him. To check on that bitch, too. To find out if her plan had finally worked. If the bitch was finally dead…

The sight of the ambulance, lights flashing, had filled her heart with hope. She'd breathed a deep sigh of relief and a smile had spread across her face.

Until she'd seen that stretcher.

Kylie was on it. Dead or alive?

Wouldn't they shut off the lights if she was dead?

Or maybe they were just going through the motions to comfort Heath. He looked distraught. Like he'd really cared about that manipulator. How could he be so stupid?

He hadn't deserved Gina at all. He hadn't deserved her love. She reached into the purse dangling from her shoulder and found the gun she'd fired at him before, the gun she would fire again now that she knew.

He didn't deserve her. He deserved the same thing his little girlfriend had gotten. Then he looked up and met her gaze, almost as if he'd felt her watching him. She snorted.

She'd been watching him ever since she'd heard the news about his dad and uncle. She'd been watching them both, and they'd never noticed. They'd had no idea that she'd tracked their every damn movement.

He started across the street, toward her, but the tall black man caught his arm and held him back.

Detective Parker.

She knew who he was, and she knew that when he reached beneath his jacket, he was pulling out his weapon. She could have fired at him.

But she didn't want him dead. She wanted Heath dead. Like Kylie…

But the doors of the ambulance closed and it pulled away from the curb with a squeal of tires, the siren wailing and the lights flashing.

Maybe Kylie wasn't dead.

Gina would have to try again.

Parker was attempting to cross the street, holding up his badge against the vehicles that kept driving. She laughed as she turned and ran. She would get away from him. Her car wasn't parked far from the penthouse.

She would get away from him and she'd get to the hospital before he could. She would finish what she'd started.

No one was going to stop her.

Chapter Twenty-Five

A strong hand gripped hers, gently squeezing her fingers. Kylie didn't have the strength to squeeze back. Hell, she didn't even have the strength to open her eyes. Her lids felt so damn heavy, too heavy to lift.

And her throat. Was it still closed? Was she dead?

"I'm so sorry," a deep voice said.

Heath.

He was blaming himself. Hadn't he realized what she had? That Gina Hogan was responsible?

Gina had a key to the penthouse door. She'd used it that morning she'd found them in bed. And she must have let herself in some time over the past few days when they were gone. And she'd poisoned Kylie's tea.

"I'm so sorry," Heath said again. "I should have been a man…"

He was definitely a man. All man. And he'd given her more pleasure than any other man ever had. She tried again to open her eyes, but she just wasn't strong enough.

"I shouldn't have been such a coward," he continued. "I should have told you how I felt about you, how I must have always felt about you."

How?

She tried to ask the question, but her tongue was too thick. It wouldn't move. No sound emanated from her throat.

But she had to know. How did he feel about her?

"I love you," he said. Almost as if he'd heard her.

The two of them had always seemed to instinctively know what the other needed. And that chemistry hadn't been just because of their working relationship or their friendship.

It had been because she loved him, too. Because they were perfect for each other. Just as everyone had believed but the two of them. Why had it taken them so damn long to realize it?

"I was scared," he continued, his voice gruff with emotion. "I was scared that you didn't feel the same way. That you would leave the business and I'd never see you again." His grasp on her hand tightened. "Now I might never see you again, and I hate that you won't know how I feel about you...how much I love you."

Was she dead? Was that why her dreams were finally coming true? Was that why Heath didn't think she would be able to return his feelings?

She didn't want to be dead—not now. Not when everything she'd ever desired could be hers. Heath...

She fought against that damn lethargy, finally drawing a deep breath that filled her lungs as his love filled her heart. And her love for him overflowed it...along with the tears that streaked down her face.

She returned his grasp, entwining her fingers with his as she squeezed. And she opened her eyes.

He'd been crying like he had at the funeral. He'd been crying over her. His pain filled her now, along with his love. "I'm sorry…" she said, her achy throat making her voice raspy.

He blinked, as if he didn't believe his eyes. "You're sorry? For what?"

"I'm not dead yet," she said, in a raspy whisper.

He shook his head. "What? Why are you sorry about that?"

"Because I heard your confession," she said. "I know that you love me."

He leaned over the side of her bed and pressed his lips to hers. "Good, because you better get used to me saying it," he said.

He kissed her again, and her lips curved beneath his. "I guess I can," she said, as if it was going to be a burden. But it was a gift. One she wanted to return with all her heart. "I love you."

He pulled back, and he looked like he had at the penthouse, when she'd doubted him, as if she'd slapped him.

"I'm sorry," she said. She'd thought he would want her to return his feelings. But maybe she'd just been dreaming this whole time…

Or maybe she was dead and this was some cruel kind of hell.

HEATH WAS STUNNED. He'd known he loved her. He'd known it long before he'd been brave enough to acknowledge his feelings. But he hadn't dared to hope.

"You love me?" he asked.

Her voice was so soft, her throat probably so raw from swelling closed, that he couldn't be sure he'd heard her correctly. Maybe he'd only imagined it or projected what he wanted to hear coming from her lips, her sweet lips.

She didn't speak now, only stared up at him. Then finally, her chin bobbed as she moved her head up and down.

"Save your strength," he advised, as he noticed how the small motion seemed to take such effort.

She pointed toward the carafe of water on the tray next to her bed. A glass with a straw sat next to the carafe, so he poured some water into it and brought the glass to her lips.

She coughed and sputtered as if the water was choking her. But when he moved the glass away, she pulled it back. She was getting stronger, strong enough to take a long draught from the straw, before pushing it back.

He put it onto the tray again. "I should get the nurse, let her know you're awake now," he said.

"How am I alive?" she asked, as if she wasn't certain that she was.

"I found your EpiPen," he said. "It took me too long to figure out how to use it."

"But she wouldn't be alive if you hadn't," the nurse said as she joined them in the bay of the ER where the paramedics had brought her. "How are you feeling?"

"Like I got hit by a bus," Kylie admitted.

He wasn't sure if that was because of the poisoning,

or because of his confession. She must have realized that because she winked at him.

"You're lucky you survived," the nurse said.

"I am lucky," Kylie agreed, and she was looking at him.

He was the lucky one.

The nurse inspected her throat with a flashlight and nodded in approval. "The swelling is gone now. It's just red and irritated, but you'll be able to go home tonight."

"Thank you," Kylie said.

The nurse nodded. "I will have the doctor get the paperwork ready for your release."

"You can't go home," Heath said.

Kylie's eyes widened. "I can't?"

"She hasn't been caught yet," Heath said. "Gina is still out there somewhere." And she was so deranged that she would definitely try again. "You'll have to come back to the penthouse with me. We'll throw out everything in it, everything that Gina might have poisoned with iodine, and get the lock changed for the door. Something I should have done long ago. I'm sorry, Kylie. I'm sorry I put you in so much danger."

She reached out and grabbed his hand. "You saved my life—over and over again."

"But I wouldn't have had to if not for putting it at risk in the first place."

She squeezed his hand, her grasp strong now. She was definitely recovering quickly. "You didn't do anything wrong. She did."

"You always knew she was crazy, didn't you?"

She shook her head. "Jealous and possessive. But I

didn't realize until you were playing those messages how unhinged she truly was."

He nodded. "Me neither." If he hadn't put off playing those messages, they would have known sooner who was after them. If he'd told Kylie his feelings earlier, he wouldn't have had to worry that she might die without ever knowing. "I'm not putting off anything ever again," he said with sudden resolve.

She nodded. "Good plan."

"So marry me," he said. "Right now. Right away."

"What?"

"I love you," he said. "You said you love me. Just as my whole family has been saying, we're perfect for each other. So marry me. Become my partner in every way."

Her brow creased. "What are you talking about?"

"I'm proposing," he said. And apparently doing a very poor job of it.

Maybe if he matched actions to his words she would understand. He slid out of the chair he'd taken beside her bed and knelt beside her. "Kylie Givens, will you do me the incredible honor of becoming my wife? Of sharing my life in every way?"

Her lips parted, but he couldn't hear her answer. He could hear nothing but the quick report of a gunshot. Gina had followed them to the hospital.

She was here, apparently hell-bent on finishing what she'd started. On killing Kylie...

"Shots fired," Sean told the dispatcher as he pressed his cell phone to his ear. He stood guard at the waiting room door, his gun drawn.

He wanted to go out, to investigate where those shots had come from, but he didn't want to leave everyone alone and unprotected in that waiting room.

The entire Colton family but for Heath was in that room, waiting on news about Kylie. If Parker had been right and they were all targets…

His heart pounded hard in his chest.

"Two units are already at the hospital," the dispatcher told Sean. "Detective Parker called them to aid in the pursuit of a suspect."

Sean cursed.

Heath had called him on his way to the hospital. He'd told him how his ex-girlfriend had tried to kill Kylie. Apparently she'd showed up at the hospital to finish the job.

"You can go," January told him. "Go—try to stop her."

Obviously she'd figured out who was firing those shots, too.

He shook his head. If the woman wanted to hurt Heath, she might go after the rest of his family. And here they all were.

Footsteps echoed in the hallway outside the waiting room, and Sean gestured for the others to get back, to get away from the door.

As the knob of it began to turn, he raised the barrel of his gun. He had yet to officially join the family, but it didn't matter. To him the Coltons were already family, and he would willingly die protecting them.

Chapter Twenty-Six

Kylie's heart pounded with fear. First Heath's declaration, then his proposal and now this.

The sound of gunshots.

"She's here," she whispered.

Gina was determined. She would give her that. Too bad what she was so determined to do was kill Kylie. What irony that it might happen just as she was about to get everything she'd ever wanted.

The love of a man she could trust with her heart as well as the big family she'd always longed to be part of.

Tears stung her eyes, but she blinked them back. Then she swung her legs over the side of the bed. She wasn't going to just lie here while that crazy woman came for her. Heath's hand clutched hers yet, so she tugged at it. "Let's get out of here!" she urged him.

But just as she turned toward the curtain drawn across their area of the ER, it was jerked back. Gina stood there, her eyes wild with desperation. She gripped her gun in two hands, the barrel directed straight at Kylie.

But Heath stood up, blocking Kylie with his bigger,

broader body. He was bigger and broader, but even he wouldn't be able to stop a bullet.

Kylie gripped the edge of the bed with the hand that Heath didn't hold. But then his other hand covered hers, and the same thought must have entered his head...because at the same time, they pushed that bed toward Gina as they dropped to the floor.

Another shot rang out, but the bullet struck the ceiling, raining fragments of drywall onto them. Then Gina screamed as Joe Parker snapped the gun from her grasp and handcuffs around her wrists. He expelled a ragged breath. "I thought I was too late," he admitted. "But you two, you work well together."

"Yes, we do," Heath agreed, as he helped up Kylie from the floor.

She was shaking with reaction and with fury.

So was Gina as she bucked against the detective's grip on her. "You should be dead! You should be dead! That's what you deserve!"

Kylie shook her head. "No. I deserve Heath—because I really love him. You don't even know what love is." Disgusted, she shook her head.

Maybe Gina realized she was right because she stopped fighting. She let the uniformed officers who suddenly joined them take her away.

Kylie shuddered in revulsion. "She's so messed up."

Parker nodded. "I'll get a psychiatrist to help me question her."

"Do you think she killed my dad and uncle?" Heath asked.

Parker shrugged. "I don't know. I don't see what her motive would be."

"Maybe she thought Heath would turn to her for comfort," Kylie suggested. "That he would take her back if he needed her."

"I never needed her," Heath said. "I only need you." And he wound his arms around her.

Kylie leaned against him and not just because her legs were shaking like the rest of her. She leaned against him because she needed him, too. "Yes," she said.

"What?" Parker asked.

She shook her head. "I'm answering a question Heath asked me just as she started firing those shots..." She peered up at the man who was grinning down at her.

Parker chuckled. "I think I know what that question was. Let me be the first to offer congratulations."

Somehow it was fitting.

If they hadn't lied to him about their relationship, they might never have taken the chance to have a real one.

HEATH TURNED THE new key in the lock and pushed open the door to the penthouse. Then he swung her up in his arms and carried her over the threshold.

She giggled and clutched at his shoulders. "What are you doing? We're not married yet."

"We will be soon," he said. "I'm not sure I can wait much longer."

She giggled again. "You just proposed last week."

"And again tonight."

Tonight he'd done it right. At True, over candlelight,

with a ring that encircled her finger now, and his entire family present.

A happy smile curved her lips. "On Valentine's Day," she said. "It was perfect."

She wore a silky red dress and heels, looking more beautiful than his madly pounding heart could handle.

"It was a mistake," he said as he pushed open the double doors to the master bedroom.

The smile slid away from her face as she slid down his body. "It was?"

"It was a mistake to do it in public," he said. "And with so many people there. It took too long to get away from them and get you back here where I can make love to you."

Her smile was back, even bigger than it was. "They're your family," she said.

He shook his head. "Yours, too. They all love you so much."

Tears shimmered in her eyes. Happy tears. "I love them, too."

"But I love you most of all," he assured her. "Forever and always."

"I love you, Heath." She linked her arms around his neck and pulled his head down for her kiss.

He tasted the champagne they'd had to celebrate and the passion. Desire coursed through him, too. He'd had to wait so long to get her alone. He needed to be patient, to take his time. But he wanted her too badly.

She must have wanted him just as much because her fingers frantically fumbled with the buttons on his shirt, tugging them free. Then she shoved his shirt from his shoulders and nipped at one of them with her teeth.

He chuckled then groaned when her tongue flicked out to soothe where she'd bitten him. She trailed her mouth over his chest, to lap her tongue across one of his nipples. She knew what he liked because she liked the same things.

He pulled back and reached for her dress. Instead of worrying about zippers or buttons, he just lifted the red silk over her head. Then he saw that she wore red silk beneath—bra and G-string—and he groaned. "You are so damn beautiful."

She smiled. "You say that like it's a bad thing."

"It is," he said. "For me—because I will never be able to deny you anything."

"Do you want to?" she asked.

He shook his head. "No." Because denying her desires was denying his own.

He lifted her again and carried her the short distance to his king-size bed. Once he dropped her lightly on the mattress, he shucked off his pants and boxers and rummaged in the drawer of his bedside table for a condom packet. "Running low," he murmured.

Because of her...

Knowing that, she giggled again. But he shut off her giggle with his mouth, kissing her deeply before he moved down her body. He kissed her everywhere until she was moaning and writhing.

Then he rolled on the condom and joined their bodies—like their hearts and souls were already joined.

They moved together like longtime dance partners, matching each other's rhythm, anticipating each other's next step. Even as tension wound tightly inside him, he was conscious of her—making sure she reached her orgasm first. Her body shuddered, her inner muscles clutching at him. He came, too, shouting her name.

Long moments later, when they'd stopped panting and could speak, she murmured, "Is it real?"

"The ring?" he teased, and he held up her hand, making the diamond twinkle under the can lights. "Can you tell it's cubic zirconia?"

She laughed. "I wouldn't care if it was."

He believed her. She didn't care about status or money. She cared only about honesty and love and family.

"It's real," he said.

"I'm not talking about the ring," she said. "Is…everything?"

"You know I love you," he said.

She nodded. "I will never be insecure enough to doubt you again," she assured him. "I meant…everything else?"

He grinned as he realized what she was referring to, what he hadn't been able to ask her until the will was read and he knew what his authority was. "I told you—that day at the ER—that I wanted you to be my partner in every way," he reminded her.

She nodded. "But I thought we were already partners in the business."

"We were," he said. "That's why it was necessary

for it to become official. You work harder than I do at Colton Connections."

She shook her head. "I don't—"

"You will for a while," he said.

She laid her head on his chest and hugged him tightly. "I know it's going to take you a while to feel the same about work. I will handle whatever you need me to handle."

He trailed his fingers down her bare back. Her skin was as silky as her dress had been. "I wasn't talking about that. I don't want to work the same as I used to."

"You don't want to be CEO anymore?"

"I want to be co-CEO," he said. "With you. And with you taking up my slack, I want to work on some ideas I've had."

She propped her chin on his chest and peered up at him, excitement in her dark eyes. "What kind of ideas?"

He chuckled. "I have plenty of those kinds of ideas," he assured her. "But I also have an idea for an invention."

"Oh, Heath…"

"I know I'm never going to be as good as Pop and Uncle Alfie but—"

She pressed her fingers over his lips. "You will. They both had regretted not encouraging you more when you were younger. They'd hoped you would come back to the creative side someday."

Tears rushed to his eyes, but he blinked them back. "I hadn't needed to." But with them gone, there was a void to fill. He wouldn't be able to fill it completely, but to honor the men he'd loved and admired so much, he would try.

"They'll be so happy," she murmured, tears pooling in her eyes.

"They will," he agreed. "They loved you, too. They will be thrilled that the company will be more in your hands than mine now."

She laughed. "You are the company now, Heath."

He shook his head. "We are." They had to be. Pop and Uncle Alfie were gone. "Do you think she did it?" he wondered.

"Gina?"

He nodded. "Do you think she killed them?"

"I don't know," Kylie admitted. "But Detective Parker has plenty of time to find out while she's in jail with bail denied."

"On one hand, I want it to be her," he admitted. "So that it's over. On the other, I will feel so damn guilty if my ex-girlfriend is the one who killed them."

"Don't," Kylie said. "You had no way of knowing how disturbed she is. Nobody knew."

"You were never a fan," he reminded her.

She smiled. "I think I was as jealous of her as she was of me."

"But you never tried to kill her," he said. Kylie would never hurt anyone. She was too good and honest a person. His heart was safe with her, and he hoped she knew hers was safe with him.

He'd committed to her, and he knew they shared the kind of love that his parents and his aunt and uncle had shared. Lasting…no matter what obstacles they encountered. Even death.

JOE WASN'T A fan of psychiatrists, especially ones like Dr. Reeth who'd kept him from interrogating his prime murder suspect. He'd had to wait a week for Gina Hogan to be treated and medicated before he was allowed to speak to her. But maybe that was a good thing; apparently she was considered sane enough now that she could refuse a lawyer and he could still question her.

He settled onto the chair across from her. One of her wrists was handcuffed to the metal tabletop. He considered uncuffing her, but then he remembered how she'd eluded him outside the penthouse.

She was fast and maybe not nearly as crazy as he'd thought. Better to be safe than sorry.

"How are you, Ms. Hogan?" he asked.

She smiled at him. "Much better now thanks to Dr. Reeth. I should be able to go home soon."

He hoped the doctor hadn't told her that—because there was no damn way he wanted to release her. Ever.

"You're not going anywhere but back to that jail cell," he said. "And then you'll be going to prison."

She shook her head. "No, that's not what Dr. Reeth told me."

"Maybe he isn't aware of the charges you're facing."

"Charges?" she asked. "For what?" She blinked at him, acting all innocent.

Was it an act, though, or was it possible she didn't remember what she'd done?

He was going to remind her. "You shot the security

guard at the hospital—in front of several witnesses and cameras." The guy was going to be fine, but she didn't know that.

Or did she? She just blinked again, but she betrayed no other reaction. No guilt.

How the hell medicated was she?

He wanted a reaction out of her, so he persisted. "You're already going down for his murder. You might as well confess to the other ones."

He got a reaction.

She smiled and leaned eagerly across the table. "Kylie Givens is dead?" she asked hopefully. "The iodine killed her after all?"

Parker shook his head. "Not Ms. Givens. She's fine. In fact she's better than fine." Thanks to her and Heath's quick reaction. Joe had been too slow in getting to the ER; he'd stopped to check in the waiting room first and had nearly taken a bullet from Stafford.

Her smile turned into a sneer of disgust. "That's not fair. It's not fair."

"What's not fair is the other lives you took too soon," he said. "They were only fifty-seven. Young men still."

Her forehead creased with confusion, and she stared at him as if he needed medication. "What are you talking about?"

"The other murders you committed," he said. "You killed Ernest and Alfred Colton. You shot them dead in the parking lot of the building that Colton Connections is in."

She shook her head. "No, I didn't."

"Yes, you did," he insisted. "It's okay to admit it. One

murder, three murders, attempted murders…it doesn't make a difference. You're going to plead insanity anyway, so it doesn't matter. Just tell the truth."

She leaned across the table then and stared directly into his eyes. "I. Did. Not. Kill. *Anyone*." Her mouth curved up slightly at the corners.

She knew the security guard had survived—probably thanks to damn Dr. Reeth. Her smile widened. "Like you said, I'll plead insanity, so it doesn't really matter. I'll tell you the truth."

His stomach sank as he realized she was being honest. She hadn't killed anyone.

"The only person I actually tried to kill was Kylie Givens."

At least he was getting a confession from her. "Why?"

"Because she was the reason Heath could not love me," she said.

"Because he loves her," he said.

Tears shimmered in her eyes.

"That wasn't her fault," he said. "And even if you killed her, he wouldn't have come to love you. It doesn't work that way."

"But he should have been mine."

He shook his head. "No. You deserve someone who loves you. Truly loves you."

She tilted her head and studied his face. "You're right. I do."

He nodded. "So you have no reason to want her dead any longer?" He was checking—just in case her damn doctor did get her out on a technicality.

She sighed. "No. I guess they deserve each other."

"Yes, they do," Joe said. "I've never met two people more perfect for each other." But for him and Kinsey...

He stood up then, eager to get home to his wife and son. He wasn't going to get any more confessions out of Gina Hogan. She'd admitted to what she'd done. Attempted murder.

She wasn't a killer.

The twins' killer was still out there.

But Joe would find him or her. He just hoped that he did before the person killed again.

* * * * *

COMING SOON!

We really hope you enjoyed reading this book.
If you're looking for more romance, be sure to
head to the shops when new books are
available on

Thursday 4th
February

LET'S TALK
Romance

For exclusive extracts, competitions and special offers, find us online:

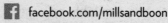 facebook.com/millsandboon

@MillsandBoon

@MillsandBoonUK

Get in touch on 01413 063232

For all the latest titles coming soon, visit
millsandboon.co.uk/nextmonth

MILLS & BOON

THE HEART OF ROMANCE

A ROMANCE FOR EVERY KIND OF READER

MODERN
Prepare to be swept off your feet by sophisticated, sexy and seductive heroes, in some of the world's most glamourous and romantic locations, where power and passion collide.
8 stories per month.

HISTORICAL
Escape with historical heroes from time gone by. Whether your passion is for wicked Regency Rakes, muscled Vikings or rugged Highlanders, awaken the romance of the past.
6 stories per month.

MEDICAL
Set your pulse racing with dedicated, delectable doctors in the high-pressure world of medicine, where emotions run high and passion, comfort and love are the best medicine.
6 stories per month.

True Love
Celebrate true love with tender stories of heartfelt romance, from the rush of falling in love to the joy a new baby can bring, and a focus on the emotional heart of a relationship.
8 stories per month.

Desire
Indulge in secrets and scandal, intense drama and plenty of sizzling hot action with powerful and passionate heroes who have it all: wealth, status, good looks...everything but the right woman.
6 stories per month.

HEROES
Experience all the excitement of a gripping thriller, with an intense romance at its heart. Resourceful, true-to-life women and strong, fearless men face danger and desire - a killer combination!
8 stories per month.

DARE
Sensual love stories featuring smart, sassy heroines you'd want as a best friend, and compelling intense heroes who are worthy of them.
4 stories per month.

To see which titles are coming soon, please visit

millsandboon.co.uk/nextmonth

JOIN US ON SOCIAL MEDIA!

Stay up to date with our latest releases, author news and gossip, special offers and discounts, and all the behind-the-scenes action from Mills & Boon...

 millsandboon

 millsandboonuk

 millsandboon

It might just be true love...

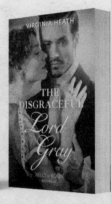

MILLS & BOON

MODERN

Power and Passion

Prepare to be swept off your feet by sophisticated, sexy and seductive heroes, in some of the world's most glamourous and romantic locations, where power and passion collide.

MILLS & BOON
MEDICAL
Pulse-Racing Passion

Set your pulse racing with dedicated, delectable doctors in the high-pressure world of medicine, where emotions run high and passion, comfort and love are the best medicine.